Pole Position

Julia started unpacking the plastic shopping bags
Stevie had dumped onto the kitchen table. 'Just think
of all the things you can do now you're single again.'

'Like wanting to swat every couple you see snogging on the bus with a baseball bat, you mean.'

'No, I mean like you can wear tights instead of
stockings – and you don't have to have sex if you
don't want –'

'I always want to.'

'– and you can do all the things he hated, like
Immac-ing your legs in the sitting-room in front of
EastEnders –'

'At least I'll never have to spend all night arguing
with you about why I'm still going out with him,'
Stevie said.

'And you'll lose weight.'

Stevie perked up. 'Why?'

Julia shrugged. 'I don't know. But you always lose
weight when you break up, it's in *Cosmo*.'

'Oh, that would be typical,' Stevie said, her gloom
returning.

'I mean, now I haven't got a man to lose weight for I'll
be a size eight by this time next month.'

Tess Stimson was born and brought up in Sussex, where much
of *Pole Position* is set. After graduating from Oxford University,
she worked for four years as a producer with ITN before
emigrating to Cyprus to write her first novel. She is married to
CNN correspondent Brent Sadler and lives with her husband and
eighteen-month-old son Henry in Rome. She is currently
working on her fourth novel, a sequel to *Pole Position*.

TESS STIMSON

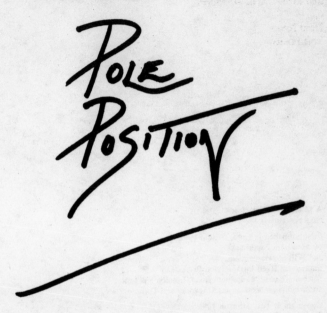

Mandarin

A Mandarin Paperback
POLE POSITION

First published in Great Britain 1996
by Mandarin Paperbacks
and William Heinemann
imprints of Reed International Books Ltd
Michelin House, 81 Fulham Road, London SW3 6RB
and Auckland, Melbourne, Singapore and Toronto

A CIP catalogue record for this title
is available from the British Library
ISBN 0 7493 1816 3

Printed and bound in Great Britain
by Cox & Wyman Ltd, Reading, Berks.

For my parents,
Michael and Jane,
With love.

ἕξι ἡ ὥρα has a lot to answer for.

Acknowledgements

I suppose my editor, Louise Moore, was quite useful once or twice, and on the odd occasion that my agent, Mark Lucas, bothered to return my calls he wasn't completely useless. I can't fault Ami Smythson's brilliant cover either, much as I want to. I'd also like to say that my PR, Fiona McIntosh, was always there when I needed her, but –

Robert Hardman, of *Daily Telegraph* notoriety, was very free with his expert opinions on the subject of motor racing, and my stay at his house in Cannes was one I shall never forget. Gordon Cruikshank at *Motor Sport*, on the other hand, gave me much helpful information and I hereby absolve him from any inaccuracies in this book, which are entirely due to other friends' appalling advice.

Chantal and François Guillot provided the inspiration for the title, so I suppose the French can't be all bad. And Kelly Evans test-drove as many Italians as she could find in the cause of my research, which proves even the Welsh have their uses.

My father, Michael, explained complex technical procedures to me in words even a moron could understand (he's had a lot of practice). My mother, Jane, corrected my grammar fearlessly. Thanks, Mother. Words fail me when it comes to my brother Charles, and his excellent computer advice. I suspect a lot of people's do.

My son, Henry, was invaluable in assisting me. My qqqkeybo!ard@ will never be the same again.

And as for my husband, Brent – what can I say? There just aren't the words.

Rome, February 1996

Dramatis Personae

Patrick Alexander. Senior racing driver for Quisling Mild/Terroni. Dishy in an older-man sort of way.

Annabel Alexander. Patrick's wife, beautiful, cool, should have been a career diplomat's wife really.

Lily & Jamie Alexander. Five-year-old fiends of hell.

Harry Alexander. Only a baby, but has fiend potential.

Peter Appleby. Gay golden-haired gardener for the Alexanders.

Mr & Mrs Arcor. Couple who 'do' for the Alexanders, only most of the time they don't.

George Cobbit. Publican, *The Gilt Edge*, flashy nouveau yob who's a dab hand in the kitchen.

Sharon Cobbit. His gold-plated wife.

Stevie Colvin. Our heroine, pot-belly, bitten fingernails, lousy choice in men and all.

Oliver Colvin. Her brother, a trainee lawner and bit of a cocksman but all right really.

Damien. Stevie's bright pink Fiat Panda.

Rafe Dussi. Junior racing driver for Terroni. Smooth, charming, gorgeous, but Italian.

Robin Halford. Stevie's first employer. An ageing roué with a heart and soul of jelly.

Bronwyn Halford. His diminutive Welsh firebrand wife.

Jack Halford. Stevie's first charge.

'Mace'. A mysterious drug dealer.

Candida Mornay. Annabel's younger sister, superbitch but, unfairly, also beautiful.

Humphrey Prince. Patrick and Rafe's agent. Weak, obsequious and a total wimp.

Susan Prince. His wife. Boobs, WI and famines in Africa.

Edmund Prince. Their son. Bit of an Adrian Mole, but then with a mother like his, it could've been a lot worse.

Rosie Knighton. A writer, and Annabel Alexander's best friend. Terminally adulterous.

Laurie Knighton. A doctor. Her long-suffering husband.

Portia Knighton. Daughter of her mother.

Charles Lytton, 7th Earl of Cusack. Team manager. Brilliant, tragic and bad-tempered.

Nigel Purvis. Marketing executive for Quisling Mild. Oily and ruthless, but a sucker for a title.

Lillian Purvis. His intelligent, poetic wife.

Will Purvis. Their son, got the world taped.

Martin Romaine. Test driver. Likes cars, not glory.

Emmanuele Terroni. The Mafioso who owns Terroni cars.

Cinzia Capone Terroni. His shy daughter-in-law.

Julia West. An estate agent, Stevie's best friend and pulling partner. They've known each other since playgroup.

Paul Whittington. Stevie's (married, bastard) lover.

Amy Whittington. A significant bump.

Hugo Yeates. Last and least, Julia's sometime boyfriend.

WALK-ON PARTS (in order of appearance)

Two florists. Admirers of Stevie's chassis.

A shelf stacker. An unfortunate victim of Stevie's wrath.

Mr & Mrs Mitchell. Prospective employers, beige train-spotters.

Carrie. One of Oliver Colvin's girlfriends, a girl who can tie knots in cherry stalks with her tongue.

Tammy Baynard. Terroni race manager, one of the lads.

Canulf. A surprisingly civil hound.

Christie Bradley. Sickeningly glam reporter with INN.

Mickey. Her very unglam cameraman.

Andy. Her positively rustic soundman.

Ollie. The news tyrant who drives them all.

Jake. A teenage drug pusher.

Clinton & Saddam. Two ill-fated gerbils.

A check-in girl. All foundation and attitude.

Renato. Rafe Dussi's Italian driver.

Leonora. His devoted housekeeper.

A young PC. A giver of sound advice on tea.

YEAR PLANNER

STEVIE'S

	January	February	March	April	May	June
Mon					1	
Tues					2 Mum's b-day	
Wed	1	1			3	
Thu		2 Paul pm	2		4	1
Fri		♥ Dad's b-day	3 ~~Boat pm~~ canx		5	2
Sat		4	4 bastard!	1	6 to Mums	3
Sun	1	5	5	2	7	4 to Mums
Mon	2	6	6	3 pm Jules	8	5
Tues	3	7	7	4	9	6
Wed	4	8	8 Interviews Mitchells 1pm	5	10 pm Jules	7
Thu	5	9	9	6	11	8
Fri	6 Paul p.m.	10 ~~Boat pm~~ canx	10	7	12	9 pm Jules
Sat	7	11	11	8	13	10
Sun	8	12	12	9 ARGIE GP	14 SPAIN GP	11 CANADA GP
Mon	9	13	13	10	15	12
Tues	10	14 ♥ Valentines Day!!	14	11 Patrick INN Interviews	16 Annabel dinner party	13
Wed	11	15	15 Interviews Alexanders 3pm	12	17	14
Thu	12	16	16	13	18	15 Jules Oliver Gilt Edge
Fri	13 ~~Boat pm~~ canx	17 Paul pm	17	14	19	16
Sat	14	18	18	15	20	17 to Mums
Sun	15	19	19	16	21	18
Mon	16	20 3pm gym J	20	17 pm Jules	22	19
Tues	17	21	21 Interviews Evans 4pm	18	23	20
Wed	18	22	22 Happy's b-day	19	24	21 Gilt Edge 2 6pm
Thu	19	23	23	20	25	22
Fri	20 ~~Boat pm~~ canx	24 Paul pm	24	21	26	23
Sat	21	25	25 11pm rave	22	27 To Monaco	24
Sun	22	26	26 BRAZIL GP	23 S MARINO GP	28 MONACO GP	25
Mon	23	27	27 Start work	24	29	26
Tues	24	28 Got the job!!	28	25	30	27 Gilt Edge 4.30
Wed	25		29	26	31	28
Thu	26		30	27		29
Fri	27 Paul pm		31	28 Jules 3pm San Lorenzo		30
Sat	28			29		
Sun	29			30		
Mon	30					
Tues	31					
Wed						

DIARY

Day	July	August	September	October	November	December
Mon						
Tues		1				
Wed		2			1	
Thu		3			2	
Fri		4	1		3	1
Sat	1	5 To Mums	2 Jules party		4 Jules cinema	2
Sun	2 FRANCE GP	6	3	1 EUROPE GP	5	3
Mon	3	7 2:00 Jamie check-up	4	2	6	4
Tues	4	8	5	3 Kevin meeting	7	5
Wed	5	9	6	4	8	6
Thu	6	10	7	5	9	7
Fri	7	11 To Oxford my b-day!	8	6	10	8
Sat	8 to Mums	12	9	7 Oliver's b-day	11 Jules b-day	9
Sun	9	13 HUNGARY GP	10 ITALY GP	8	12 AUSTRALIA GP	10
Mon	10	14 6:30 Jamie check-up	11 to Rome	9	13	11
Tues	11 Gilt Edge 3:30	15	12	10 pm Jules	14 YES!!!	12
Wed	12	16	13	11	15	13
Thu	13	17	14	12	16	14
Fri	14 festival J.	18 pm Jules	15 Rome - Heathrow	13	17	15
Sat	15	19	16	14	18	16
Sun	16 UK GP	20	17 Mums	15	19	17
Mon	17	21 Jules cinema	18	16 Patrick's b-day	20	18
Tues	18	22	19	17	21	19
Wed	19	23	20	18	22	20
Thu	20	24	21	19	23	21
Fri	21	25	22	20 Mums pm	24	22
Sat	22	26 to Mums	23 to Jules	21	25	23
Sun	23	27 BELGIAN GP	24 PORTUGAL GP	22 PACIFIC GP	26	24 Annabel's b-day
Mon	24 2:30 Jamie check-up	28 12:00 Jamie final check-up	25	23	27	25 XMAS
Tues	25	29 check-up	26	24	28	26
Wed	26	30	27	25	29	27
Thu	27	31	28	26	30	28
Fri	28		29 Alvin's b-day	27 pm Jules		29
Sat	29		30	28		30
Sun	30 GERMANY GP 11:30			29 JAPAN GP		31
Mon	31 Jamie check-up			30		
Tues				31		
Wed						

One

Bald men have sex. Stevie was willing to bet her next three free weekends that bald women didn't.

She glared at the follicly challenged Porsche driver on her left as he revved his engine, ready to carve her up the minute the lights changed. It was a common phallacy – she chose the word advisedly – that baldness in men was due to an excess of that virile male hormone, testosterone. But no one went round claiming bald women were sexy little nymphets underneath their wigs, did they? Men and women spoke a different language. In Stevie's experience, men of a certain age and income who were fat, old, or ugly were invariably described as substantial, distinguished or rugged. Women who were fat, old or ugly were invariably described as fat, old or ugly.

The Porsche driver leered and blew her a kiss. Stevie upped her glare to full beam. Typical. How come she never got stuck in a traffic jam next to Tom Cruise? It was her own fault for ending up next to a Porsche. She was currently working on the theory that a man's fuckability was inversely proportional to the value of the car he was driving. Extensive research on her part suggested that the most favoured habitat of Homo Fanciable was a beaten-up, two-tone Volkswagen Beetle with its wing-mirrors missing. In these days of 1990s austerity, they were hardly ever found anywhere near the wheel of a fully insured, kosher-MOTed, M-reg sports car.

Stevie couldn't help feeling cheated. In 1987, the year she'd finally turned sixteen and been able to take advantage of all the gorgeous, rich young men cluttering up wine bars everywhere she'd looked, the entire country had been plunged into world-wide recession. Overnight the wine bars had been turned back into Co-ops and the Filofaxes repossessed. In 1995 the only men left propping up the bars were maudlin drunks weeping into their Frascati over their negative equity and alimony payments.

The lights changed to green. The only vehicle able to move was the paperboy's BMX. Stevie glanced at her watch. If she'd known they were going to dismantle the A264 again she'd have stayed in bed an extra twenty minutes and avoided the rush hour. She might even have had time to put her make-up on after she'd put her contact lenses in, rather than before. She flipped the sun visor down to check herself in the mirror. She couldn't in all honour give herself more than four out of ten this morning, not after last night. 'House white' were not words she wanted to hear ever again. At least she hadn't out-lined her eyes with scarlet lip-pencil by mistake, like she'd done last Friday. She'd looked like a rabbit with myxomatosis all day, and no one had said a word. It was only when she'd collected Jack from nursery school that afternoon and seen his painfully accurate painting of his nanny that she'd realised what she'd done. No wonder his teacher had looked at her so strangely.

She jumped as a car beeped impatiently behind her. Before she had a chance to coax Damien into first gear, the Porsche driver on her left had pulled sharply across her lane of traffic and shot past her, gesturing rudely in her direction. Stevie stuck her tongue out at him. May your clutch forever dis-engage. She remembered his leer and swiftly amended that to crutch.

Her thoughts were still occupied with boiling wax and sharpened knives when she swung Damien into Bronwyn and

Robin's gravel drive ten minutes later. She braked suddenly as she came bumper to bumper with the local florist's van. Bronwyn and Robin must have made it up, then. She wondered how much it had cost him this time.

The florist gestured for Stevie to move backwards, unaware of the information which Stevie and four nervous driving examiners shared regarding her ability to perform certain mandatory reversing manoeuvres. Stevie studiously examined her bitten nails. The two vehicles faced each other for several minutes before the florist bowed to the inevitable and reversed sulkily back up the drive. Stevie squeezed Damien past the van and parked, opening the door and extending her legs gracefully before her the way the model did in the Pretty Polly ads, for the benefit of the rather gorgeous florist driving the van. It was only when she tried to stand up that she realised you had to be six foot four to complete the manoeuvre successfully. She glanced up and saw that she now had the full attention not only of the florist and his mate but the postman and milkman as well. It was difficult to be inconspicuous in a bright pink Fiat Panda. The salesman had made a selling point of the colour, told her it would be a bonus, she'd never lose it in the car park. He'd been right, she never had, no matter how hard she'd tried.

Stevie straightened her short denim skirt and casually stretched her arms and rotated her wrists as if the Pretty-Polly bit had just been part of her morning exercise routine.

The two florists grinned at each other.

'Mmm, nice chassis.'

The dishy one nodded. 'Well upholstered, good suspension. I wonder how she takes a corner?'

The two florists fell about. Stevie decided to cut her losses and show them what they were missing. She walked slowly up the garden path in what she hoped was a seductive fashion, rolling her hips from side to side and wishing she'd worn her black stilettos instead of the dog-eared trainers that had been

3

first out of the wardrobe. By the time she reached the rhodo-dendron by Bronwyn's gazebo she was no longer Stevie of the Generous Hips, size twelve and five-foot seven if she really stretched and wore two pairs of her brother's thick rugby socks. Now she was the unapproachable Stephanie Colvin, international jet-setting supermodel, a waif-like size eight and six feet tall in her Fogal-stockinged feet.

'Stevie? Are you all right?'

The catwalk disappeared in a puff of reality. 'Oh – er – hi, Robin. Sorry I'm late.'

Robin eyed her doubtfully. 'Are you sure you're OK? Only you were walking a bit strangely, you haven't pulled a muscle, have you?'

'No, no, I'm fine.' Stevie was keen to change the subject. 'Where's Bronwyn?'

'I wouldn't go in just yet if I were you. Bronwyn's – um – a little bit upset.'

Stevie peered over his shoulder at the roses strewn around the entrance hall. 'I thought you two had made it up?'

Robin twitched. 'Well, we did, but then there was a bit of a mix-up with the flowers. It really wasn't my fault, they muddled up my order –'

'Oh, Robin, you nob-end.'

Robin shifted uncomfortably, but didn't argue. Stevie pushed past him and started to pick up the pieces of broken crockery before three-year-old Jack toddled down the stairs and cut himself. Bronwyn had surpassed herself this time, but Stevie didn't blame her. Robin's fortieth birthday was fast approaching, and he was mounting a last, desperate bid to recapture his lost youth by means of mounting every last, desperate woman he could find. In the past few months, he'd grown his hair long and taken to wearing Ray-Bans instead of his usual bi-focals, but the result was less the Mel Gibson he hoped for than Lovejoy meets Victor Meldrew.

Stevie glanced up as Bronwyn appeared in the doorway, still

undressed in her faded blue candlewick dressing-gown, her fiery red hair unbrushed and crackling around her thin shoulders.

'I'm taking Jack to stay with my mother this week,' she hissed. 'I'm not having him upset any more. You can go back home, Stevie, have a holiday. I don't want any witnesses to what I'm going to do to this bastard.'

'Look, Bron, there's no need to drag Stevie into all this –'

Bronwyn ignored Robin, hovering in the background. 'Do you know what that stupid shit's done? He only sent me some flowers addressed to that British Airways slut he's been screwing. "Darling Libby, thank you for a wonderful night, I'll make it up to you later, love Robby-boy." Jesus, it's bad enough being stuck with an unfaithful, lying, cheating son-of-a-bitch. I didn't realise I'd married a complete moron as well.'

Stevie stared at the floor and tried not to laugh. Robby-boy. Oh *please*.

'Bronwyn, I told you, the florists made a mistake. They muddled up my order. It's over with her, I promise –'

'Damn right it is. By the time I've finished, even Lorena Bobbitt's going to feel sorry for you.'

Robin backed away as Bronwyn advanced towards him. 'Bronny, please –'

Bronwyn scanned the open-plan kitchen-cum-living room for something else to throw. Her eyes lit on the stack of blue Le Creuset saucepans in the corner and, as one, Stevie and Robin dived for cover behind the squashy white leather sofa.

'She's never going to chuck those?' Robin whispered. 'They weigh a ton. I can't even strain spaghetti with them without dislocating my shoulder.'

'You should've seen her after she found out about you and that blonde from The Packhorse,' Stevie whispered back. 'Took us two days to pick up all the pieces. It was like pine needles from the Christmas tree. Little bits of china turned up in my knickers for months.'

The milk saucepan smashed into the wall ten feet to their left, gouging out a large chunk of plaster before ricocheting across the parquet. Stevie gave thanks that Bronwyn was a rotten shot.

By the time Robin had made a hasty exit through the french windows and Bronwyn had stormed off to her mother's with Jack, Stevie was too exhausted to go back home to the flat she shared with her best friend, Julia. She poured herself a medicinal gin and tonic and sank back into the leather sofa with the TV remote control in one hand and, in the other, a box of Belgian chocolates Robin had belatedly bought Bronwyn for Valentine's Day last week, completely forgetting his wife was on a diet. She switched on *Good Morning with Anne and Nick* but changed channels when she realised they were doing a feature on swimwear. It was only the twentieth of February; there was plenty of time to get back into shape before she exposed herself to ridicule on the beach.

She promised herself she'd do an extra ten sit-ups at her aerobics class this afternoon to make up. It wasn't fair, men never got cellulite. God just might be a man.

She leafed idly through a stack of Bronwyn's magazines as she tried to decide what to do with herself. She wasn't used to all this spare time. Normally by eleven o'clock in the morning she was covered from head to toe in Play-Doh, Rice Krispies and spilt Ribena, wistfully eyeing the gin bottle and wondering how the hell she was going to survive the rest of the day.

Being a nanny was not all it was cracked up to be. Her friends fondly imagined she spent the day sipping margaritas by Bronwyn and Robin's swimming pool, rocking a cherubic, ad-clean baby cooing softly in his pram with one hand while she rubbed suntan lotion into her shoulders with the other. The wisecracks were not deflected by the twin facts that she lived in Sussex where it was February for nine months of the year, and that Jack was a three-year-old with more energy than the

National Grid. And she loathed that swimming pool with a passion that would have done credit to D. H. Lawrence. She was the one who had to net the leaves and twigs that blew into it, vacuuming the bottom with something inexplicably called a barracuda and checking its pH balance, whatever the hell that was. Robin needed a nuclear physicist, not a bloody nanny.

She toyed with the idea of getting him under the Trades Description Act. Life was hardly the halcyon paradise she'd envisaged when she'd answered their ad for a nanny three years ago. They'd offered her a salary that had been half as much again as she'd been earning at the local nursery, and the idea of looking after one harmless little baby plus a few 'light household duties' instead of seventeen four-year-old psychopaths had been irresistible.

Stevie had assumed that since Bronwyn didn't work, her hours – 'eight-thirty until six, five days a week, oh, and three weeks' holiday a year' – wouldn't be that exhausting. She hadn't known then that for Bronwyn, keeping track of her husband Robin was a full-time job, involving daily searches through his trouser pockets, careful analyses of his credit card statements and secret readings of his milometer to make sure he hadn't travelled any unexplained distances. Stevie wished Robin's cock had a milometer as well. It would save them all a lot of trouble.

Bronwyn had had neither time nor energy to spare for little Jack, who had been the result of a misguided attempt to inject some romance into their marriage. Bronwyn had taken it as read that Stevie's signature on her contract of employment meant she was responsible for Jack whenever he was awake, which in the first six months of his life was every two hours, day and night. Technically, Stevie had been 'living out'. In practice, she and the sofa had become intimately acquainted, and on the days when Bronwyn and Robin weren't speaking, she'd had to fight Robin for possession of it. They'd also neglected to explain at her interview that 'light household duties' included repainting the spare bedroom after the water tank burst, lacing Bronwyn into a corset from Rigby & Peller in a desperate attempt to derail Robin's roving eye, and shinning up the drainpipe and crawling over the roof to run the baby's intercom wires round the house because Robin got vertigo and Bronwyn's life insurance had run out.

By the time she realised she'd been had, Jack had started sleeping through the night, and Stevie had been so grateful to go home every night to six blissful, uninterrupted hours of sleep in her own soft bed that she'd been prepared to put up with anything. And of course, there'd been Jack himself. He'd been worth everything, even the diabolical spring in the middle of the end cushion that got her in places her lovers had to wait six dates to reach.

She replaced the magazines on the bookshelf and bent to pick up Jack's favourite battered teddy, half-stuffed beneath the sofa in question. He'd only just stopped taking it everywhere with him. Stevie straightened the chewed green ribbon round its neck, inhaling the sweet baby smell of talc still lingering on its fur. Her heart ached every time she thought about it, but her days with Jack were numbered. In a couple of months, he'd start at nursery school full-time instead of one morning a week, and Bronwyn certainly didn't want any more children. She clearly expected Stevie to spend the time she'd have spare looking after the house. But Stevie hadn't become a nanny to end up dusting ornaments and drowning her brain in gin and daytime TV. Perhaps she should've stuck to teaching the tiny terrors at nursery. At least that way she'd have had a new batch every year to keep her busy.

She picked up Jack's anorak from the floor and walked through into the hall to hang it up. Maybe she could give Paul a ring and meet him for lunch. There wasn't much point staying here if Bronwyn had taken Jack to her mother's, and she wasn't meeting Julia at the gym until six. She had plenty of time. He'd be so pleased and surprised to see her on a Monday.

Normally she could only meet him on Fridays, when Jack was at nursery. Weekends and evenings were out, of course.

She punched the first three digits of Paul's office number, panicked, and hung up.

Stevie knew from past experience that, in her hands, a telephone could become a deadly weapon. She'd spent too many nostalgic evenings in the company of a bottle of white wine and a Carly Simon CD not to fear the consequences of picking up the phone on impulse. Ex-boyfriends were her particular weakness, although anyone she hadn't spoken to for at least a year was a potential target. One night, very drunk, she'd talked dirty for half an hour to a man she'd finished with because he was unbelievably boring. Twenty minutes after her phone call he'd come rushing round to her flat in a taxi, knocking enthusiastically on the door and waking all the neighbours up. She'd had to hide in the loo for two hours until he'd given up and gone home.

She hadn't been anywhere near Carly Simon this morning and Paul wasn't yet part of her ex-directory, but it was better to be safe than sorry. It was one of the first rules of being the Other Woman: never phone, unless you can put on a thousand and one different voices when his wife answers. She stared sternly at her reflection in the hall mirror. It's your own stupid fault you've turned into a craven moron. You went into this with your eyes open. You've only got one person to blame if it all goes horribly wrong.

She stuck out her tongue at herself, then peered a bit closer at the mirror. That looked suspiciously like the beginnings of a double chin. She lifted her baggy black sweater and scrutinised her waistline. How long exactly did it take for a chocolate to reach your hips? A day? A week? Or was it instantaneous transmission?

If only Paul didn't like his women like matchsticks. Unfortunately she was more Rubens than Lowry. Paul had already started to make pointed remarks about her usefulness in the event of a puncture.

She ran up the stairs in a sudden panic and leaped on the bathroom scales, then leaped quickly off again. The dial couldn't have been zeroed. She fiddled with it for a moment, then stepped on the scales again, more cautiously this time. She winced as the indicator passed the nine stone mark, closed her eyes and spent a minute trying to work out how much you had to deduct for the clothes you were wearing. After five-minutes' experimentation, she discovered that if she leaned forward, balanced her elbow on the soap dish and put her left foot in the bidet she could get the dial down to eight and a half stone, but it was hardly a long-term solution.

This skirt was on borrowed time. The saddest words in the English language – next to 'Can't we at least be friends?' – had to be 'I think you'd look better in a larger size.' Some Scarlet Woman she was. If she didn't watch out she'd end up wearing Laura Ashley.

'Are you absolutely sure this'll help?' Stevie asked doubtfully several hours later.

Julia propelled both herself and Stevie through the door to the gym. 'Look, do you want Paul to go back to his wife or not?'

'He hasn't exactly left her yet,' Stevie pointed out.

'And he's never going to if you keep eating chocolates and hiding in the changing rooms until the cooling-down exercises.' Julia's voice was stern. 'You have to do more than put on your leotard, you know. You actually have to join in some-times.'

'The only way I'm going to lose weight is by signing up on the next Space Shuttle mission,' Stevie sighed.

'Don't be a wimp.'

Slowly Stevie followed Julia's pert neon-pink lycra-clad bottom up the stairs to the aerobics gym, cursing her luck at having a raven-haired nymphet for best friend. On a good day, Stevie knew she could look rather fetching herself, but to achieve 'rather fetching' she had to work at it. She had to blow dry her shoulder-length unnatural blonde hair for an hour and a half, her head dangling upside down. She had to use half a tube of Clinique concealer to get rid of the shadows under her rather muddy blue eyes. She had to spend half an hour putting on her make-up to create the illusion that she wasn't wearing any. She had to encase her legs in 5-denier black ankle-enhancing stockings. She had to choose her clothes with the care of a military strategist to avoid looking pear-shaped, square-shaped or shapeless. Julia, on the other hand, could have a streaming cold, stay out until three in the morning, leave all last night's make-up on, get up after less than four hours' sleep, throw on a black bin-liner and still look absolutely ravishing.

Stevie arrived exhausted at the top of the stairs, wishing with every superfluous ounce of her being that the aerobics class wasn't mixed. A dozen svelte model-types were lounging decoratively around the gym, pretending to ignore the leering glances of the muscle-bound hunks casually tossing weights around as if they were juggling ping-pong balls. The women glared jealously at Julia as she entered the gym, their expressions turning to relief as they saw Stevie creeping in behind her and realised the light entertainment had arrived.

At six o'clock exactly the aerobics instructor entered the gym, turned on a tinny tape-recorder and the room was filled with Madonna as they all mounted a row of stationary exercise bikes and began pedalling in time to the music. Stevie watched the man next to her turn up his dial to 'mountain slope' and turned the tension of her own bike to 'downhill run'. Sweat rolled down her nose, and her heart felt as if it was going to burst. She must have been doing this for at least fifteen minutes by now. She glanced up at the clock and saw it was two minutes past six.

Stevie tried to divert her thoughts from suicide as she saw the man next to her pedalling halfway up Mount Everest.

11

She'd stay on this bike for another five minutes. Five minutes, she could easily do that.

At three minutes past six she got off the bike and lay exhausted on the rubber mat. She did her leg curls and thought about a double gin and tonic. She did her squat thrusts and thought about Paul. She did her arm stretches and thought about Paul's wife. She did her abdominal curls and thought about suicide.

She stood in the shower forty minutes later and examined her body. It was probably a medical miracle that she was alive at all. She was living on borrowed time.

She was still composing her funeral service and trying to decide between Jerusalem and the theme music to *Casualty* as she walked out of the shower and found Julia waiting outside, munching a packet of chocolate chip cookies. She waited until her flatmate had turned to talk to one of the other fitness goddesses and made a surprise attack on the biscuits. She'd got as far as the lockers before Julia caught up with her.

'I'm your best friend!' Stevie yelled. 'What happened to loyalty, kindness, do-unto-others?'

'It's for your own good,' Julia grunted, wresting the biscuits from Stevie's grasp. 'You'll thank me for this one day.'

Stevie doubted it. She had a sneaking suspicion Paul was not worth this much pain. And he certainly wasn't worth giving up the chocolate chip cookies.

'How many people have you slept with?'

'How many have you?'

'I asked first,' Julia said.

Stevie sat cross-legged on the end of her bed and stared across the hall at Julia, who was lying on her stomach on her own bed cradling a bottle of Liebfraumilch. They'd deliberately positioned their beds this way so that they could talk to each other from their own rooms without having to move.

'What, all of them?' Stevie asked. 'One-night stands, everything?'

'All of them.'

Stevie thought for a few moments, then started scribbling in the Care Bears notebook her mother had given her for Christmas. Julia took a swig of wine and waited for her to finish.

Ten minutes later Stevie had shown no sign of letting up. Julia watched in astonishment as Stevie turned the page for the second time.

'Shit, you're like a one-woman service station,' she said. 'How many have you got to so far?'

'I'm not telling you until you tell me. Go on, you write down all yours and we'll swap at the end.'

'Oh, all right.' Julia refilled her glass and started writing on the back of an envelope. After a few minutes she stopped.

'That's all?'

Julia nodded.

'But that's ridiculous. You haven't even got past the post-mark. Did you put in all the ones you didn't even enjoy?'

'Yes, and the ones who couldn't get it up. Seven altogether. Now come on, how many?'

'Twenty-six.'

'*Twenty-six?*'

'Well, Peter Davis got two entries, because we split up and got back together again. So it's twenty-five, really.'

'Twenty-five! You've been with Paul for the last two years, Stevie, so that's twenty-four other men between the ages of –?'

'Seventeen.'

'Thank you. Seventeen and twenty-two. That's nearly five men a year!'

Stevie looked miffed. 'If I was a man you wouldn't think twice about it. You'd be jealous.'

'How many do you admit to if a man asks you?' Julia said. 'What have you told Paul?'

Stevie reached out and took the wine bottle from Julia's out-stretched hand. 'Five.'

'Why five?'

'Well, he's never going to believe I'm a virgin, for a start. And men don't like to think you've only had one or two lovers before them, it makes them think you take sex too seriously, as if this is it and sleeping with them is a big commitment. And no matter what they tell you about being New Men and liking a woman with experience, no man wants to think everyone's had a swig of the bottle. Ten's too many, three's too few. So I tell them all five.'

'I don't know how you keep a straight face.'

'Here, let me see your list.'

'Only if I can see yours.'

They put their lists on either side of the wine bottle in the centre of the hall and swapped on the count of three.

Stevie dipped a Jaffa Cake in her glass of Liebfraumilch and wriggled back against the headboard. 'Has Hugo accepted your proposal yet?'

'I've tried everything. The first time I asked him was when we celebrated his new job on the steps of St Peter's in Rome with a bottle of champagne. He said it wasn't the right atmosphere. Then we risked our lives together rock-climbing in the South of France and I tried again, but apparently the very likely prospect of till death us do part didn't help. The third time was during a romantic candlelit meal in Venice – he said it was neither the time nor the place. I gave up after that.'

'He's bound to say yes some time,' Stevie said.

'I'm just terrified I'll spit it out on the 6.35 from East Croydon, or in the middle of a traffic jam on the M25. Hardly something you want to tell your grandchildren.'

'I'll be lucky if I even get that far with Paul.'

Julia curled her endless legs beneath her and swept back her curtain of silky dark hair. Stevie tried not to hate her.

'Why the hell do you put up with him? He's never going to leave Amy, you know,' said Julia.

'He might if I lost weight.'

'I'm serious, Stevie. Even if he leaves her – which he won't – you'll spend the rest of your life checking his pockets and calling his office to see if he's where he said he'd be.'

Stevie knew Julia was right. Being right was something Julia did well, along with remembering birthdays and never being overdrawn. It wasn't fair. Beautiful women were supposed to be dippy and forgetful, it was expected of them, to make the rest of womankind feel better. They certainly weren't meant to be practical, intelligent and level-headed as well as devastatingly attractive. Clearly someone had screwed up somewhere along the line.

Julia would never have got involved with someone like Paul. It wasn't that she had a big moral thing about it; she just had the sense to realise that for every man who actually left his wife, another hundred were waiting for the kids to grow up, the mortgage to be paid off, the kitchen extension to be finished, or the cat to get over its flu. Stevie knew that in the first spine-tingling glance across a crowded room, Julia would instantly have spotted the tell-tale gleam of a wedding ring and left Paul to share his quiche lorraine with someone else dumb enough to fall for his line in wifely misunderstanding. Someone like Stevie.

Stevie had never meant any of this to happen, of course. Unlike Julia, whose point of view was based on common sense and statistics rather than morality, Stevie had always despised women who had affairs with married men. She'd seen Bronwyn's tears and desperation and positively loathed the painted little tarts who'd caused them. She'd seen friends in the throes of a passionate love affair with a man who would – really *would* – leave his wife just as soon as he'd managed to transfer his assets out of the country, and watched them spend one miserable Christmas after another alone, sniffling uncom-

15

forted into lonely pillows as deadline after deadline passed, and had felt nothing but contempt and pity.

The first morning after she and Paul had slept together, she'd stared at her reflection in the mirror and tried to reconcile it with the image of the Other Woman, the Home Wrecker, the Superbitch, that her mother had brought her up to despise. Other Women didn't have roots and spare tyres, they didn't bite their nails or have spots the week before their period. But one night of – OK, she couldn't deny it – unbelievably fantastic sex had suddenly turned her into one, and even now she couldn't quite get used to the idea. She'd never wanted Paul to divorce Amy and marry her. Well, not at first. But recently she'd found she wanted him to *think* about it, at least.

She'd met Paul Whittington two years ago at one of Bronwyn and Robin's summer barbecues. They'd hardly spoken that first day – she hadn't been allowed to fraternise with the guests – but he'd caught her eye across the crowded lawn and given her a deep brown stare which had lasted four unflinching seconds. It was the nearest she'd ever been to sex without touching.

She'd known right from the beginning that he was married, but somehow it hadn't seemed important. His wife had been a nebulous shadow in the background, a little piece of gold on his left hand. When in the ensuing weeks they'd bumped into each other at bus stops and supermarket checkouts, with a frequency she'd found hard to put down to coincidence, they'd chatted about things anyone could safely have overheard – the baby, the weather, how England was doing at rugby – but they'd smiled a lot, and afterwards she'd always felt a little more excited than she should have. Paul had been thirty-six then, fourteen years older than her, a plausible, urbane sales representative for a company that manufactured screws. The irony hadn't occurred to her until later.

About three months after they'd first met, she'd found a note tucked beneath Damien the Fiat Panda's windscreen wiper: 'I need to talk to you. Can we meet? (Friends).'

It was the 'friends' bit that had given him away, a clever little distancing trick which had made clear that friendship was the last thing on his mind. But she'd met him for a drink anyway, and she'd watched the way his floppy blond hair curled over the edge of his collar and noticed the tiny gold hairs peeking out from the wrists of his snowy white shirt that someone else had ironed. She'd crossed and uncrossed her legs and tossed back her head when she laughed and accidentally let her hair sweep across the back of his hand when she leaned forward to pick up her drink. He'd smiled and let his eyes lock with hers every time she dared to meet them, and when his lips had brushed hers in farewell his kiss had tasted sweet and heady, like wine. He'd dropped her off at her flat in time for *News at Ten* without suggesting that he come in for coffee because they'd both known that this was only the start of it.

She'd lain in bed that first night and told herself that she was grown-up enough for a no-strings affair with an older man in a burnt-out marriage. Things always worked out if you tried hard enough. She could justify an affair. His marriage had been a mistake from the start. He'd been too young, they'd grown apart, his wife had her own life. For God's sake, they didn't even have sex any more. They hadn't had children. Children would have changed everything. Anyway, it was his responsibility, he'd be doing the cheating. She had no one to cheat on. It wasn't her problem: she was single.

Finally she'd slept with him on their sixth date. Afterwards, she'd watched him get up to throw the squishy condom down the loo and shower the scent of sex from his body, and known intuitively that everything had changed between them. Pre-Durex, Amy had been a problem they'd faced together, like Stevie's charming hesitation. Paul had been the one with the dead marriage, practically begging her to change his life. Now he had everything and she was forever at his mercy, pathetic-

ally grateful for a snatched half-hour or a hurried phone call –
always made by him – that invariably ended with an abrupt
'I've got to go' and the burr of the dead receiver in her ear.

She'd known it was serious last month, when she'd walked
into the newsagent's on the corner, picked up her usual copy
of *Cosmo*, and turned to the article about 'Divorce' before the
one about 'Multiple Orgasms'.

Stevie drained her wine glass. 'I know, I know, you're right,
Jules. I don't know why I put up with any of it.'

'Shit, I nearly forgot!' Julia leaped off her bed and ran into
the living room. Stevie could hear her opening and shutting
drawers as she raised her voice and carried on talking. 'I saw
an ad in *The Lady* last week when I was looking through the
house-sitting column for my sister, you know, the one with
nerves. I meant to tell you about it before. It sounds perfect for
you.'

Julia reappeared, leafing through the magazine. 'Here, listen
to this: "English couple living in Rome require nanny for baby
due September, age 22–27, non-smoker, driver, 2–3 years'
experience including newborn, flexible, organised and responsible. Own room and bathroom, use of car and private swimming pool, live-in maid also employed. Telephone Italy blah
blah." Bring your own Italian lover.'

'It doesn't really say that –'

Julia tossed the magazine on to Stevie's bed. 'Almost.'

Stevie stared at the magazine. 'Don't be ridiculous! I
couldn't possibly!'

'Why on earth not?'

Stevie hesitated. 'Well, Paul for a start. And you! What
about you? I couldn't go away and leave you on your own.
Who would you live with? Who'd help you open the child-
proof locks on your paracetamol?'

'Stevie, Prick Whittington is an out-and-out bastard who'll
never leave his wife. I'm earning enough commission at the
estate agent's now to pay your share of the rent too, and I'd

quite like the extra room. I might even be able to persuade Hugo to move in with me if he didn't think he'd have to face you without your make-up every morning. And your brother lives downstairs. Oliver can open the paracetamol for me.'

For a brief moment, Stevie imagined actually picking up the phone, arranging an interview, maybe even getting the job. Rome! Somewhere it didn't rain and you navigated your way home by the Colosseum and the Forum instead of the Fox and Hounds and the Bunch of Grapes. No more furtive dates with Paul in disgusting restaurants because all his friends went to the good ones. No more leaving the cinema halfway through a film because he'd just recognised some of Amy's friends in the ice-cream queue. She still didn't know who Hugh Grant had ended up with, and they'd been to see *Four Weddings and a Funeral* three times. No more raiding the rent money to pay the electricity bill before it was cut off; it would all be paid for. And think of all those gorgeous Italian men who went crazy at the merest glimpse of blonde hair! By the time they got far enough to find out hers wasn't real it'd be too late.

'I can't. They'd never give me the job.'

'Why not? You're the right age, you don't smoke – well, not cigarettes, anyway – you can drive, you've got experience and no one could say you're not flexible, not with twenty-five men under your belt.'

'But what about the "organised and responsible" bit?'

'You can lie, can't you?'

Stevie was struggling. 'But the job'll have gone by now. You said yourself it was last week's magazine.'

'For God's sake, Stevie, stop being so negative. You'll never know if you don't try.'

Stevie thought again of all the gorgeous Italian men just waiting for a glimpse of her highlights. Julia was right: she had all the right qualifications. She'd got her NNEB, she'd taken care of Jack since he was two weeks old. She could drive (ish), she was presentable – well, she would be if she had her own bathroom and two hours to spare every morning – and literate, and she didn't have any communicable diseases unless you counted a Crawley accent. Perhaps if she put some space between herself and Paul it'd be just the incentive he needed . . .

Two

Stevie lay absolutely motionless on the bed, her eyes closed. She could hear Paul moving around the bedroom and wondered what he was going to pour over her this time. She hoped it wasn't going to be Häagen-Das again. Never mind the adverts, that ice-cream had been fucking cold.

She tensed, waiting for whatever it was to touch her skin, acutely conscious of her nakedness. It was the most erotic sensation she'd ever experienced. Every nerve ending in her skin was charged with anticipation, the slightest breath of air against its surface magnified a hundredfold. By the time Paul was ready for her, she was in such a state of heightened awareness that she had no idea if what he poured over her was hot or cold, wet or dry. She gasped in shock as it hit her skin.

'What the *hell* was that?'

Paul laughed. 'Don't worry, it won't hurt.'

Stevie tried to relax and figure out what it was. It was cool, but not unpleasantly so. She felt it trickle across her breasts and over her shoulders. She turned her head to one side and stuck out her tongue to catch the drops. 'It's honey!'

'So are you, sweet stuff.'

She opened her eyes and watched as Paul poured the honey across her abdomen. She must be the only woman in history who'd find the missionary position a novelty.

Paul put down the jar and slid on to the bed next to her,

rubbing his hands across her honeyed body and licking his fingers. Stevie felt the honey dribble stickily on to his black satin sheets and thanked God she didn't have to wash them. What on earth did Paul's cleaning lady make of it all?

They were in Paul's secret bachelor pad in Islington, which even his wife didn't know about. He'd bought it several years ago, before he and Stevie had met, out of what he called his 'Divorce Account': the one that neither his wife – nor her lawyers if it ever came to that – knew existed. Even before he'd married Amy, he'd been stashing money away 'just in case'.

Stevie felt a twinge of unease. If he could lie to his wife, he could lie to her. She tried not to think about who else he'd brought to his flat, taken into his seven-foot-wide, custom-made Israeli bed. That way madness lay.

Her dark thoughts vanished as Paul bent his head and started to lick her breasts, cupping first one and then the other in his hand, his tongue playing with her hard pink nipples like a child with an ice-cream. She could feel the honey trickle slowly over her skin, pooling in little puddles beneath her body. She wanted to concentrate on the delicious sensations Paul was creating with his tongue and fingers, and all she could think about was how she was going to get it out of her hair. She preferred the Moët he'd used last week. That had just washed off.

Paul raised his head from her left breast, his smooth chin glistening with honey. 'Good?'

'Mmm, wonderful,' she lied.

Paul dipped his head between her legs. She felt a shiver of real pleasure as he opened her cunt and started to tease her with his tongue. She wound her fingers through his gold hair, pulling him in towards her. When he put his mind – or rather his tongue – to it, he could drive her wild. At times like this, she knew exactly why she'd fallen in love with him. If only he didn't insist on treating her like some sort of exotic smorgasbord.

22

She stopped wriggling with pleasure as something cool and slightly squidgy entered her. 'Paul –?'

'Just keep still, darling. I promise you'll enjoy it.'

No, Stevie thought, I have to draw the line at being fucked by an over-ripe banana, peeled or not.

She closed her legs firmly. 'I am not a fruit salad, Paul. I object to being treated like some sort of flesh-and-blood banana split.'

'Relax, babe. Don't be so uptight.'

'I am not uptight,' Stevie said tightly. 'I just wish we could go to bed one day without taking half of Sainsbury's with us.'

Paul slid his hand smoothly between her thighs and rubbed her clitoris, massaging the banana into her as he trailed sticky kisses across her breasts. 'I thought you could deal with this, Stevie.'

'I can –' It was difficult to concentrate when he was doing that. 'Only, sometimes, I wish you could be a bit more –'

The kisses stopped. 'Dull? Predictable?'

'No, of course not.' Suddenly she wished she'd never started this. 'Just a little more – well – romantic.'

'You don't think this is romantic?'

Stevie looked down the length of her body. Her hair was stuck together in clumps, and the banana was making her feel distinctly squidgy in certain areas. She felt cold and embarrassed and faintly ridiculous, and a very long way from romantic.

She snaked her body around his, feeling like a lump of blu-tack as she peeled herself away from the sheets. 'I was just thinking about the first time we made love, here, in this bed. You'd lit candles – remember? – and you spent an hour just kissing me, all over, even between my toes.' She wiped her sticky hand on the pillow. 'I just wanted it to be like that again.'

'I thought it was.'

'Oh, it is wonderful, of course it is, and I like it – I do, Paul,

I really do – but just, sometimes –'

'You know, you're beginning to sound like my wife,' Paul said. 'She never wants to try anything new either. But then, she doesn't love me. I thought you did.'

'I *do*.'

'Well, then. If you loved me –'

Paul picked up another banana from beside the bed and started to peel it. Stevie laid a restraining hand on his wrist, then hesitated. She'd meant to broach the subject after they'd made love, when he was in a good mood, but he'd already told her he had to get to a meeting. She had to tell him today. If it didn't work, she had nothing to lose. She couldn't stand this situation – the secrecy, the deceit, the sordidness of it all – any longer.

'Paul, I've been meaning to talk to you about something.' She crossed her fingers behind her back. It was now or never. 'I've been offered a job in Rome.'

There was a silence.

Then Paul said, 'I see.'

'Is that all you're going to say?'

'You seem to have made up your mind without me. When do you start?'

'I haven't actually accepted it yet.' Stevie hadn't even rung to apply for the job yet, but Paul didn't have to know that. 'I wanted to talk to you about it first.'

Paul reached for his packet of Marlboro on the bedside table and lit up, leaning back against the black satin padded head-board as he inhaled. 'You know, Stevie, Amy and I were talking last night. She's quite keen to go to Ireland this Easter to see her parents. I thought I'd stay behind and look after things. Amy knows I can't take any time off right now, we're too busy. But if you're going to cut me out of your life like this, I might as well go with her –'

'Paul, is she really going?' Suddenly Rome was a miserable crowded foreign city where they ate nothing but pasta and

Cornettos. 'How long will she be away for?'

'Three weeks.'

'Oh, Paul!'

'I don't know why I'm telling you. You'll probably be in Rome by then. And anyway, I'm not romantic enough for you, remember?'

'I'm sorry, darling, I didn't mean you weren't romantic.' She slid on top of him; her nipples, hardened by honey, brushed against the golden hairs on his chest. 'Of course I won't be going to Rome. I just get so frustrated, only seeing you once a week. I want us to be together all the time. Perhaps you should tell her about us when she gets back, Paul? I mean, she must know it's not right between you two. She's probably guessed you've found someone else anyway. Maybe this trip is her way of letting go gently.'

'Maybe.'

'I'm sure that's it.' Stevie took his cigarette out of his hand and guided his now semi-erect cock into her. 'She'll probably be just as happy as you to get it finally out in the open. It can't have been very pleasant for her either.'

Suddenly Stevie found it easy to feel benevolent towards her rival now that she was sure Amy's days were numbered. She'd never wanted to go to Rome anyway. It had worked, though. She smiled and kissed Paul, tasting the mingled sweetness of honey and banana and herself on his lips. She didn't like lying to him, but it was only a little white one. Just to make him realise how much he'd miss her. His hands gripped her hips as she slid up and down on him, their bodies sticking together like flypaper. She stared down at him, feeling his cock swell inside her. She was so lucky to have someone like him. She had to stop behaving like a gauche child, even if that's what he made her feel like sometimes. He was a sophisticated, experienced man; that's what had attracted her to him in the first place. He didn't just want a quick screw behind the bike sheds like most of the men she'd had. With Paul, sex was a gourmet experience

25

to be savoured, not a quick hamburger and chips on the run.

She just wished his interpretation wasn't always quite so literal, that's all.

'Oh, please, Stevie, not again!'

Julia clutched the duvet and tried to roll herself into it.

Stevie tugged on the other end. 'Jules. It's Saturday, I have to go to Sainsbury's today.'

'Can't you take my car?'

'I couldn't. Not a GTi, Jules, that'd be asking for trouble.'

Julia swung her tanned legs over the edge of the bed and stood up. Her purple Mickey Mouse T-shirt just about covered her skimpy pink knickers. She still managed to project an air of sophistication that Stevie knew she'd never achieve if she spent two days getting ready.

'This is the fourth day running, Stevie. I'm not doing it again. Either you get Damien's starter motor fixed or our friendship is over.'

'I promise, I promise. Monday, first thing. I'll take him in, get him fixed.' Stevie grabbed the fake Vuitton handbag she'd bought at a car boot sale and made for the front door.

'Where's the hammer?' Julia muttered.

Fifteen minutes later, after Julia's ministrations with the hammer, Damien roared into life.

'You have to drive without taking your foot off the accelerator,' she yelled. 'If you lose revs, it'll stall. How the hell are you going to get home again?'

'I'll take the hammer with me. I can always find someone to help. Anyway, Damien only does this in the morning, when he's cold. By the time I get to Sainsbury's, there'll be nothing wrong with him.'

She left Julia standing speechless in the driveway and by the time she reached Sainsbury's, Damien was purring like a kitten. She turned into the car park and automatically headed for the spaces nearest the supermarket which were set aside for shoppers with young children. Jack wasn't exactly on board, but his car seat was still in the back, which Stevie reckoned was near enough. She was just about to turn into the last available space when a large black four-wheel-drive Range Rover shot past her and parked.

Stevie furiously positioned Damien across the rear of her hijacked space and leaped out. She ran over to the Range Rover and banged angrily on the driver's window. 'Can't you read? This space is reserved for shoppers with children.'

The driver swung open his door without warning so that Stevie had to jump out of the way. He got out and pointed an automatic alarm-setter at the car. The locks shot down and a little red light flickered from the dashboard.

Stevie wished she'd kept her mouth shut when she saw how good-looking he was. It was clear he was the exception to her Ferrari-versus-Fuckability rule. His blue-black hair was long enough for her fingers to tingle with the urge to run through it. His blue eyes – pale as a husky's – burned into hers. 'I don't see any children with you,' he said.

She swallowed. 'It doesn't say you have to bring them with you. It just says you have to have them.' She pointed to Jack's car seat. 'See.'

'How do you know I haven't?'

Stevie pressed her nose against the back window of the Range Rover. 'You haven't got kids. There isn't a single sweet wrapper in your ashtray.'

He ignored her and started to walk away. 'If you haven't got anything better to do, Miss Marple, I have. Kindly move that eyesore out of my way by the time I return.'

'Eyesore – !'

'If it's not gone when I come back, I shall simply drive over it. It would probably be a blessing.'

Stevie stared after him. For a moment she thought about leaving Damien exactly where he was, but the arrogant bastard wouldn't think twice about carrying out his threat. With that macho monster he was driving Damien wouldn't stand a chance.

She parked in a 'Disabled' space and stalked towards the trolley rank. She pulled the nearest trolley towards her, cursing as its wheels locked with the one in front and jammed.

A fat woman pushed past her and took hold of the trolley handle. 'You've got to put a pound coin in, dear.'

'You didn't have to last week.'

'That's inflation for you.'

Stevie ignored this *non sequitur*. 'But I haven't got a pound coin.'

The woman shrugged. 'Sorry, dear. Can't help you. Only got one myself.'

Stevie emptied the contents of her handbag on the ground and watched as two Polos she'd been saving for when she was really desperate rolled away into the gutter. She found two crumpled passport photographs, a spare tampon, a Clinique lipstick labelled 'Just Raisin' with its top missing, a pair of broken sunglasses that had been there since last summer, the telephone bill she'd hidden to stop Julia finding it, a half-empty packet of Jellytots, three letters she'd forgotten to post from the days when a first-class stamp still cost 20p, a fish-hook she'd never seen in her life before, a packet of Donald Duck plasters for the blisters she got whenever she wore a pair of new shoes, the one and only love letter Paul had ever written to her – 'Milk's in the fridge. See you next week, love Paul' – the latest copy of *The Big Issue* which she didn't approve of but which she'd bought because she was scared to say no, a hundred pesetas from her last trip to Malaga and every coin of the realm issued since decimalisation except a pound coin.

'Use one of them ones wiv the blue 'andles.'

Stevie stopped shoving everything back into her handbag and looked up. A small boy of perhaps eight or nine was rounding up trolleys that other exasperated shoppers had abandoned, and wheeling them back to the rank to reclaim the pound coins still in them.

'They ain't got round to changin' 'em yet. You don' need a pound coin if you use one of them.'

'Oh, thanks.' She studied the contents of her handbag and decided all little boys liked fish-hooks. It was either that or the tampon. 'Here, have this,' she said.

The trolley had a distinct list to the left, but at least she didn't have to rob a bank in order to operate it. She managed to negotiate the revolving doors without serious mishap, and found herself in the midst of terrain she didn't recognise.

The fat woman she'd seen outside was busy sorting through a display of avocados. 'Changed everything in here too, they have. I don't know how I'm supposed to find the faggots now.'

Stevie fled down the aisle and paused by tinned goods to collect her thoughts. Normally, her version of shopping consisted of filling the trolley with anything that came to hand until it was full, but this week – under threat of death from Julia if she came home with one more jar of raspberry jam to add to the seven they already had – she'd spent half the previous night writing out a comprehensive list of everything they needed. She stared hard at the baked beans and remembered exactly where the list was. Next to the telephone at home. She'd just have to improvise. She chucked a few tins in her trolley and wished she'd had breakfast before she'd left. She always bought far too much when she shopped hungry.

She reached the coffee aisle and watched the bastard who'd pinched her parking space take the last jar of Nescafé. He wasn't fighting with a demonic trolley, either, he had a nice neat little wire basket filled with – she did a quick inventory – fresh salmon from the fish counter, a tub of black olives, three different types of lettuce, a bottle of white wine and two plain Greek yoghurts. She felt sorry for the other yoghurt-eater. He might be gorgeous, but he was a shit with it.

A spotty youth of about sixteen with a vacant expression

and a wispy ginger beard wandered past her with a crate of tea-bags. Stevie swung her trolley round and blocked his way.

'Do you have any more Nescafé?'

'Uh?'

'Nescafé? As in coffee?'

The boy still looked blank. Stevie took out the half-empty packet of Jellytots, emptied them into her hand and shook her closed fist by her ear, then held it out palm upwards in front of his nose. 'Like the adverts, remember?'

The boy backed away. 'I dunno about that.'

'Oh, for God's sake –' She pointed to the Bastard's basket. 'Look, like he's got.'

Understanding dawned. 'No, we ain't gone none of them. Run out.'

'But it's not even eleven o'clock yet,' Stevie exclaimed, her patience exhausted. 'How could you run out already? Has there been a sudden run on coffee I don't know about? The Brazilians had a revolution and burned their beans? Tea been banned in West Sussex, has it?'

The boy edged nervously down the aisle. 'Look, it ain't down to me. I just stack the shelves. Why don't you come back Monday, we might 'ave some by then.'

'Oh, great. I'll just wait around here for two days, shall I? Don't you worry about me. I'm just a customer who's going to get minced alive if I dare go home without it, that's all. You just look after your tea-bags –'

She broke off as she heard a voice she would have recognised in a catatonic coma.

She peered through the gap where the Nescafé should have been. Paul was standing in front of the pasta, evidently trying to decide between tagliatelle and those squirly curly things. Quickly Stevie applied a fresh coat of Clinique's Just Raisin and ran her fingers through her hair. She wished she hadn't worn her brother's rugby shirt to cover the holes in the crutch of her oldest, ugliest grey leggings. Next time she came shop-

30

ping she'd wear that little black number she'd been saving for the day she and Paul could finally go to a restaurant without having to wear paper bags over their heads.

She rounded the corner. 'Hello, Paul.'

Paul dropped the tagliatelle as if she'd stuck a red-hot poker up his bottom. 'Stevie!'

'I would've thought I'd find you by the Geest stall,' Stevie said slyly. 'Or is it lychees this week?'

'For Christ's sake, Stevie! Amy might hear you!'

It was Stevie's turn to look alarmed. 'Oh, shit. She's here?'

'She's looking for the tofu. She'll be back any minute.' Paul pushed her back towards her trolley and started to steer it along the aisle. 'I'll call you when she goes out this evening. Now please, go.'

'But Paul, hang on a minute. She doesn't know about us, does she? Even if she sees me talking to you, she won't have a clue who I am –'

'Trust me on this one, Stevie. She'd know.'

Stevie stood at the end of the aisle as Paul hurried back to his tagliatelle. She'd never seen Amy before, although Bronwyn had told her, in response to her discreet enquiries, that Mrs Paul Whittington was dark, pretty and far too nice for him. Stevie had often wondered what she looked like, but now that it came to it, she was scared to find out. Once she'd seen her, Amy would no longer be the shadowy figure in the background. She'd be a real person with a real life and a real husband, and every time she and Paul made love Stevie knew she'd see Amy's face floating in front of her.

She pushed her trolley down the aisle, fighting the desire to turn her head as she heard a woman call Paul's name behind her. She reached the dairy section and started searching for Jack's favourite fromage frais.

Twenty minutes later, her trolley having reached its plimsoll line, Stevie decided to call it a day. She studied the trolley thoughtfully. She had no idea what culinary delight Julia would come up with given a tin of refried beans, some smoked salmon, a jar of raspberry jam, a bottle of Lucozade, a packet of wild rice, some Wagon Wheels, a tub of cottage cheese (she had to pay lip service to her diet), a jumbo jar of peanut butter (but not all the time), two frozen Chicken Kievs, a packet of tortilla chips, some garlic bread, dried spaghetti, tinned spaghetti, fresh spaghetti from the pasta counter (the February issue of *Cosmo* had run an article that maintained pasta wasn't fattening, and Stevie wasn't taking any chances), a bottle of Tabasco and two fresh papayas because they were the one fruit Paul had never managed to work into their lovemaking. Everything else gave her too many ideas.

She had reached the wine section and was just trying to work out if a £1.19 bottle of white wine could possibly have any characteristics that marked it out as different from a bottle of battery acid, when she heard Paul desperately trying to divert his wife as she headed firmly towards the aisle where his mistress was standing.

'Amy, darling, we really don't need anything here. I'd rather go to Oddbins, they've got a much better selection –'

'Don't be silly, Paul. I'm sure we can get exactly the same wine here, and it means we don't have to make an extra journey into the village.'

Stevie glanced to her left for some means of escape, but the wine aisle finished in a dead end. She could hear Amy's foot-steps closing fast to her right. Tunnelling was out, but for a moment she debated scaling the shelves in front of her.

'Amy, darling, I'd much rather treat you to some decent wine –'

Stevie felt a gentle touch on her shoulder. 'Excuse me, would you mind if I took a look?' Paul's wife stood next to her.

'No, no, please,' Stevie mumbled to the wine label in front of her. 'Go ahead.'

She sidled sideways, her gaze never shifting from the bottles at the end of her nose. She kept going until she reached the end of the aisle and shot a quick glance at Amy's ankles – slender, black, 5-denier ankles – to see if she showed any signs of moving. The Italian leather-shod feet remained firmly in place. Stevie prayed the captivating ankles were God's way of balancing spots, a hook nose, inverted breasts and cellulite, and slowly turned round.

She saw immediately that, even in her normal condition, Amy's ankles were not so much a consolation prize as the icing on the cake. Her skin was radiant, her nose perfect, her breasts full and her legs endless. She was right up there with Julia on Stevie's why-can't-I-look-like-her death wish list. But Amy's condition was far from normal. Stevie suddenly knew exactly why Paul had been so desperate to avoid the encounter.

Amy was at least eight months pregnant.

'But it's so *humiliating*!' Stevie sobbed. 'To have your lover cheating on you with his own wife!'

'I always told you he was a no-good, lying, cheating, miserable ratfink son-of-a-bitch,' Julia said.

'You say that about all my boyfriends.'

'Well, that's because they are.'

'Julia, you're not helping.'

Julia started unpacking the plastic shopping bags Stevie had dumped on the kitchen table. 'Just think of all the things you can do now you're single again.'

'Like wanting to swat every couple you see snogging on the bus with a baseball bat, you mean.'

'No, I mean like you can wear tights instead of stockings – no Nescafé, I see – and you don't have to have sex if you don't want to –'

'I always want to.'

'– and you can do all the things he hated, like Immac-ing your legs in the sitting room in front of *EastEnders* –'

'At least I'll never have to spend all night arguing with you about why I'm still going out with him,' Stevie said.

'And you'll lose weight.'

Stevie perked up. 'Why?'

Julia shrugged. 'I don't know. But you always lose weight when you break up, it's in *Cosmo*.'

'Oh, that would be typical,' Stevie said, her gloom returning. 'I mean, now I haven't got a man to lose weight for I'll be a size eight by this time next month.'

Julia stared at the shopping on the table. 'Stevie, we'll all be losing weight on what you've bought. What the hell am I supposed to do with refried beans, a jumbo jar of peanut butter and six tons of spaghetti?'

'I don't know. You're the cook, I just wash up. Anyway, there's some Wagon Wheels and Tabasco in there somewhere.'

'Thank you. That is such a help.' Julia opened the cupboard over the sink and added an eighth jar of raspberry jam. 'Look, Stevie. Men cheat. It's true, it's widespread and the only reason it isn't universal is lack of opportunity. You just fell in love with a Grand Master.'

'It was being the Grand Mistress I liked,' Stevie said.

'There's always DIY. As Woody Allen said, don't knock it, it's sex with someone you love.'

Stevie opened the packet of tortilla chips and shoved a handful into her mouth. 'At least I won't have a minor nervous breakdown whenever my period's late.' She gave a despairing wail. 'Oh, Jules. What am I going to do?'

Julia dug around in the bin and pulled out the magazine Stevie had thrown away two days before. She brushed the remains of Stevie's Jaffa cakes off the cover. 'You're going to go to Rome, that's what you're going to do.'

Three

Stevie shifted uncomfortably on the sofa and wondered if her interview dress had somehow shrunk since she'd last worn it. Admittedly, that had been three years ago, but she'd always assumed that it was physically impossible for a deep purple, flower-sprigged Laura Ashley pinafore dress to be anything other than voluminous. The current evidence seemed to indicate otherwise: the dress was coming rather too close to figure-hugging for comfort. But her mother insisted it projected an aura of dependability and respectability she would never have achieved on merit.

Things weren't helped by the fact that, away from the temperate climes of southern Italy, the Mitchells were suffering from the usual freezing weather of an English March day. Mr Mitchell had evidently been at the central heating, and the temperature in the London hotel suite where they were conducting the interview was somewhere approaching tropical. Stevie could feel great rings of sweat forming beneath her armpits. She didn't *smell*, did she? Surreptitiously she pressed her chin to her chest and took a quick sniff. Either she was going mouldy, or she'd left this dress in mothballs too long.

'Excuse me, Miss Colvin, is something wrong?'

Stevie jumped as Mrs Mitchell addressed her. 'No, no, nothing at all. Just a slight – er – muscle cramp in my shoulder. Um, Mrs Mitchell, how long do you think you'll be in England?'

'Just long enough to find the right nanny.' Mrs Mitchell's pursed lips seemed to suggest that this event had not been brought any closer by meeting Stevie. 'We'll fly back to *Roma* as soon as we can. William hates to be away from his work for longer than is absolutely necessary.'

'What is it you do, Mr Mitchell?'

'My husband is *the* William Mitchell, dear,' Mrs Mitchell said.

Stevie was none the wiser. 'Oh, *The* William Mitchell. Really. I hadn't quite put two and two together until you said it like that. My mother will be thrilled.'

There was a pregnant pause, quite apt in the circumstances, Stevie thought hysterically. Not that pregnant was a good way to describe Mrs Mitchell, however accurate it might be in fact. *Beige* was more the word Stevie would have used. In her fawn suit, flesh-coloured tights, tan Hush Puppies and with her dull brown hair pulled back from her sepia-tinted face into an unflattering bun, she looked more like an old dry twig than a flowering bloom. Her husband was almost as bad in his mustard slacks and dark brown woollen tank top, the original train-spotter. She'd put money on his second name being Arnold.

The silence stretched into minutes. Stevie watched Mr Mitchell impose new degrees of suffering on her overloaded central heating system as she tried to think of something else to say. She was just about to resort to commenting on the remarkable greyness of the sky and the incredibly seasonal coldness of the day when Mr Mitchell provided a riveting diversion by returning to the stiff gilt chair next to his wife. His contribution to events was short-lived, however, as he proceeded to rest his hands on his knees and study the unpatterned carpet with an intensity the rest of the nation reserved for 8.10 on a Saturday evening when they consulted their lottery tickets to find out if It Could Be Them.

Mrs Mitchell opened a large folder, and extracted Stevie's

CV, her nose wrinkling in distaste at the jammy imprint of Jack's hand embossed on the back.

'So, Miss Colvin. It says here you have five – is this G-C-S-Es?' Her tone indicated that such qualifications were second only to muggers and rapists on her list of least desirable elements in society. 'I'm not quite sure I know –?'

'It's what you take now instead of O levels,' Stevie said.

'*Sort of* O levels. I see.' Stevie sincerely hoped she didn't. 'And what subjects were these in? I don't think you mention that here –'

Oh, shit. 'Just the usual handful,' Stevie said, praying she wouldn't take it any further.

She did. 'Maths? English?'

'Well, not as such, no –'

'History?'

'Um, sort of. Social science.'

'That's probably what they call history nowadays,' Mr Mitchell said helpfully. Stevie shot him a grateful – if startled – look. She thought he'd dozed off or died.

'So that's *sort of* history. I see. And?'

'Sociology, food and nutrition –'

'Cookery, dear,' Mr Mitchell put in.

Stevie hoped his wife wouldn't say 'I see' again. It was beginning to make her edgy. 'RE – that's religious education,' she added, beating Mr Mitchell to the punch by milliseconds. 'And drama. I got an A for that.'

'And your degree was in –?'

'It wasn't exactly a degree,' Stevie said uncomfortably. 'I qualified as a nanny, it's an NNEB rather than an Hons. But it's sort of the same thing, really.'

'*Sort of*. I see.'

Stevie decided it was time to break away from the thorny issue of her written qualifications. If she'd got a first from Oxford, she'd be writing bestselling novels, not trying to get a job as a nanny. 'After college, I spent a year at a nursery school in Sussex before the job I've got now. I've been with the Halfords for three years, ever since Jack was a few weeks old.'

'Why are you leaving, Miss Colvin?'

Stevie was ready for this one. 'Jack's going to nursery school full-time from next term. There really isn't enough for me to do at home without him. I feel it's time for a change –' Paul Whittington, you bastard '– and I would prefer to know a child right from the beginning, which is why I'd like a job with a small baby.'

'Oh, but it isn't just the baby,' Mrs Mitchell said. 'We already have a four-year-old boy. We'd expect you to look after them both.'

'You didn't mention that in your ad –'

'We didn't like to put it in,' Mr Mitchell said, lowering his voice as if to avoid being overheard. 'Ernest would have been most upset if he thought we were going to get someone to look after him. It's bad enough telling him we need a nanny for the new baby. Ernest doesn't really approve of nannies. He thinks parents should take full responsibility for their infants and not hand them over to strangers.'

'I see.' God, the woman had got her at it now.

Mrs Mitchell smiled indulgently. 'Oh, yes. Ernest's very advanced, isn't he, William dear? Didn't approve at all of the other nannies we interviewed. He's rejected nine already.'

'It's ten now, dear.'

'Ten.' She beamed as if this proved Ernest's genius beyond all reasonable doubt. 'There you are. So then we had to contact you, Miss Colvin.'

Charming. 'And is – er – Ernest here today?'

'He would have been, but he wanted to visit the Natural History Museum again, so his grandma has taken him there. He's been through your details, though. We'd have to refer it back to him, of course, if we decided to go ahead and employ you.'

Stevie wondered if this child prodigy had been consulted

before a decision was taken on the creation of further Mitchell progeny, and concluded that he probably had.

Six hours later, Stevie was staring dolefully into her glass of Frascati and bewailing her fate with an enthusiasm that would have done her drama teacher proud. 'That was the worst interview of my life.'

Julia giggled. 'I think you had a lucky escape.'

'Put like that –' Stevie helped herself to another chocolate finger from the Cadbury's tin box on the floor and dipped it into her Frascati. 'But Jules, this is serious. What am I going to do now? I can't keep working for Bronwyn and Robin, they're friends with the Whittingtons. Sooner or later I'm bound to bump into Paul and Amy with their little bundle of joy, and then I'm going to die, I just know it.'

She felt a pang somewhere in the region of her stomach as she said his name out loud. It had been eleven days and – hey she wasn't counting, she had no idea how many hours – since she'd seen Amy, radiant, beautiful and very pregnant, standing in the middle of Sainsbury's wine section without a care in the world. Even Paul hadn't been able to talk his way out of that one. Stevie might be Catholic, but she wasn't that gullible.

Paul had phoned her the next day, excuses tripping readily from his lying, cheating lips. 'I had to sleep with her sometimes,' he'd protested self-righteously. 'Don't you see? I did it for us. She'd have got suspicious otherwise. I didn't enjoy it, darling. It was like wanking into a test-tube. How was I to know she'd stopped taking her bloody pill?'

A treacherous part of her had longed to believe him, but for once her disbelief had refused point-blank to suspend itself. Even as he'd been talking, she remembered the adoring expression on Amy's face as she turned to ask her husband's advice about something as mundane as which overpriced, underwhelming bottle of cheap white wine she should choose. She'd known that the picture Paul had painted of an arid, bitter marriage which was over in all but name was very far from the truth.

Stevie had told him to fuck off, slammed the phone down and burst into tears.

She'd spent the next week in deep mourning, certain she was going to die from grief. She cried so much she'd made herself sick, she refused to eat – *Cosmo* and Julia were right, every lovesick cloud had a thinner lining – and she was so depressed she'd even found every line of *EastEnders* loaded with meaning. She'd taped the most miserable song she could think of – 'I can't live, if living is without you' – end-to-end on a 90-minute cassette, shut herself in her bedroom and played it over and over again until Julia had marched in, ripped the cassette out of the machine and distributed the shiny brown tape all over the room, accompanying her actions with unsubtle threats to do likewise with Stevie's limbs should she ever hear Nilsson's cheery tones again. After that, Stevie had wisely decided to nurse her agony in silence, but to her surprise, after ten days she'd started to get a bit fed up with being miserable and living in self-imposed purdah. She must be in denial, that was it. She'd read all about it in last month's *Cosmo*. She was deeply, fatally wounded – she knew the chances were she'd Never Dare To Love Again – but at the moment she must be in emotional shock. She had to get away from Paul before it wore off.

Julia read her mind, a feat Stevie greatly admired given that after twenty-four years, she still couldn't do it herself. 'I know you want to get away, Stevie, but it doesn't have to be quite as far away as Italy, does it?'

'I suppose not. I'd just fancied the idea of all those dishy Italians drooling over my blonde hair. I should've known it'd be too good to be true.'

Julia grinned. 'I might have guessed. There's me thinking you were keen to experience the culture and history of the most beautiful city in the world, and all the time you were hungry for some Italian crumpet.'

'Well, 'Crawley crumpet' doesn't have quite the same ring to it, does it?' Stevie paused and stared into the mirror on the kitchen wall. 'It's not fair, I seem to be going straight from acne to wrinkles. It's lack of sex, it's got to be.'

'I'd put my money on Kit-Kats and the sunbed,' Julia said.

'Oh, Jules, you know how to wound.'

Stevie stood up and disappeared in the direction of her bedroom. Julia wisely decided not to follow. Stevie's bedroom was a law unto itself, and Julia wasn't entirely sure if her jabs were up to date. Her friend had more cupboard space than Princess Diana, but it was hard to work out what might be in them, given that almost the entire contents of her wardrobe were scattered over the bed, chest-of-drawers, bedside table and, principally, the floor. If an archaeologist studied a side view slice of Stevie's room, Julia mused, it would give an excellent insight into a decade of late twentieth-century fashion: grunge on the top, power shoulders in the middle and flares somewhere near the bottom. Every so often Stevie would spend a rainy Sunday afternoon tidying up, but as she delved through each layer of clothes she'd come across so many interesting artefacts she thought she'd lost – the autobiography she'd written when she was eleven, her pogo stick, the photographs of Julia's sister's hen party in Torremolinos two years ago when they'd all worn T-shirts with SUE'S GETTING WED on the front and I'M NOT on the back – that she rarely got much further down than her ra-ra skirt and boob-tube era. From her position by the doorway, Julia could just make out the heaps of Estée Lauder and stale chocolate digestives on the windowsill. She sighed.

Stevie, now undressed, scrummaged around her unmade bed for a few moments, found her 'Don't Worry, Be Happy' nightshirt and yanked it over her head. 'It's all right for you, Jules. You've got Hugo. You don't know what it's like to be reluctantly celibate.'

'I wish you'd stop talking in *Cosmo* shout-lines,' Julia said. 'You're beginning to sound more American than Doctor Ruth.'

'There's probably a support group for people like me in America. I bet we're a protected minority there. You should feel sorry for me.'

Julia ignored her and picked Stevie's Laura Ashley dress up off the bedroom floor. 'I'm going to have to iron this. Your next interview's the day after tomorrow.'

'The fifteenth? Forget it. I'm doomed. I might as well give up now.'

'What are you talking about?'

Stevie padded into the kitchen and opened the fridge. 'Look, I might have got the lowest mark in Eng. Lit. GCSE ever recorded, but I do remember one thing from my *Julius Caesar*. The fifteenth of March was never a good idea.'

Two days later, Stevie smoothed the purple horror over her knees, wondering how Julia's crisp fresh ironing had managed to turn itself into dish-rag creases in the short time it had taken her to travel from Sussex to London on the Gatwick Express.

God knows why the Alexanders wanted to interview her in some poxy London hotel anyway. Julia said they actually lived in Sussex, quite near them in fact. Maybe they wanted to find out what Stevie was like before the neighbours saw her.

She glanced around the crowded hotel lobby, wondering if she had time to visit the Ladies. She always needed to go when she was nervous. The Alexanders were running twenty minutes late – bad sign, they'd probably found someone they wanted – but she daren't risk missing her slot. It was typical: she'd managed the minor miracle of arriving on time and in the right place, and they'd probably tell her they were sorry, but could she shut the door on her way out.

She crossed her legs and tried not to think about waterfalls and running water as she watched a small boy of about four or five who was clambering across a shit-brown leather sofa on the opposite side of the lobby, clearly with some ulterior motive in mind. Intrigued, she watched him creep up behind a man reading a newspaper on a sofa back to back with the boy's own. The child's grubby hand reached out and hovered over the man's head, then he turned and caught Stevie's eye as if daring her to intervene.

Suddenly he seized the man's rather badly fitting toupee, then ran like a bat out of hell.

Stevie leaped up and grabbed the boy as he passed her, shoving him down behind her own sofa before the outraged Samson had a chance to see who'd Delilahed him.

'Miss Colvin?'

Stevie jumped guiltily. 'Yes?'

'Mr and Mrs Alexander will see you now. Room 316. Please take the lift to the third floor, turn right into the corridor and it's halfway down on your left.'

Stevie followed the receptionist's directions, leaving the little boy to his fate, relieved to escape. Thank God the Alexanders were having a helpless, tiny newborn baby. She wouldn't fancy trying to keep a swine like that little boy out of mischief.

The lift stopped at the third floor and Stevie passed a fat, capable-looking woman in a tweed skirt and sensible brogues as she stepped into the corridor. Her spirits sank as she realised that this was probably the Alexanders' previous applicant. She needed to get this job. She didn't dare take any more time off work for interviews – Bronwyn was already beginning to question how many grandmothers one person could possibly lose inside a fortnight. And there was no way she could bear to wear this bloody dress again.

She knocked on the door of 316 and entered a small, characterless room whose designers had been unsparing with the ubiquitous red-and-gold flocked wallpaper and fringed pink lampshades so beloved of London hoteliers.

A man rose to greet her. 'Miss Colvin, I'm so sorry to have kept you waiting. I hope you weren't too bored.' He extended his hand. 'Patrick Alexander.'

My God, he seems almost normal, Stevie thought. She guessed he was about the same age as Paul, somewhere in his mid-thirties, but whereas Paul's age and experience had given him an aura of danger and sexual allure, her overwhelming impression as she shook Patrick Alexander's hand was one of reassurance. In some ways he reminded her of her father, though they didn't look alike. He was broad and solid, and she knew instinctively that his hugs would be reassuring and impregnable. He was quite good-looking, too, in an avuncular, newscasterish sort of way, and he had a nice smile that immediately made her feel less nervous. His best feature was definitely his eyes: deep-set and slightly hooded, they were an extraordinary colour that was exactly the same as her favourite king marble – the one she'd won from her brother, Oliver, when she was ten and for which he still hadn't forgiven her – sort of swirls of gold and brown and green all mixed in together.

As he turned to introduce his wife, Stevie noticed that the whole of the left side of his lightly tanned face was criss-crossed with tiny white scars, faint, but unmistakable. She wondered how he'd got them.

'Please excuse me if I don't get up.' Mrs Alexander pointed to her large pregnant bump. 'Would you like me to order you some tea, Miss Colvin? Patrick and I were just about to have some ourselves. Our previous applicant was a bit of a talker, I'm afraid. That's why we're running late.'

'My wife has a penchant for understatement,' Mr Alexander said. 'That woman could have wittered for Britain.'

Stevie mentally punched the air.

Mrs Alexander picked up the hotel phone. 'Lemon or milk?'

Stevie sensed immediately that Annabel Alexander was several degrees cooler than her husband. She looked sophisticated and together, the sort of woman whose knickers never went grey in the wash and whose nail varnish always matched her outfits. Did she have to re-do it every day?

She watched the older woman surreptitiously as she ordered room service. Mrs Alexander was probably the same age as her husband, though she could have passed for under thirty. She was wearing a baby-pink wool suit tailored for late pregnancy, its jacket buttoning neatly down to her discreet bump and then flaring tastefully around it. No Peter Pan collars or naff 'Baby on Board' T-shirts for her. Her ash-blonde hair was pulled into one of those french pleats only hairdressers and women with four arms could achieve. Stevie bet she never laddered her zero-denier stockings on the way out of the door.

Mrs Alexander replaced the telephone and smiled politely. 'Won't you sit down?'

Stevie sat in the armchair.

'Where would you like to start?' Mrs Alexander asked.

Salary and days off, Stevie thought. 'Perhaps it would be best if you could tell me when you'd want me to begin? Your advertisement didn't specify exactly when the baby was due.'

'The baby is due on April the first –'

'Two weeks from now? Are you sure?'

'I carry them very small,' Mrs Alexander said complacently. 'Patrick says I wasn't much bigger with the twins.'

Uh-oh, Stevie thought. 'Did you say twins?' she asked.

'Don't worry, you won't have to look after them,' Mr Alexander said, reading her mind. Stevie blushed. 'Jamie and Lily are five, they're at school full-time. I'm not quite sure what we'll do about the holidays – hire an au pair or something. We'll cross that bridge when we come to it.'

'I must say, we were impressed by your experience,' Mrs Alexander said, scanning Stevie's CV. 'You have looked after a small baby before, I see, and you've also done some nursery work. Which did you prefer?'

'I liked the variety of working in a nursery, but the children don't become a part of your life in the same way as if you have sole charge at home, and I miss that. I'd much rather be part of a family again.'

'I don't think you've lived in before, have you?' Mr Alexander asked. 'Do you think that would be a problem? Obviously you'll have your own room and bathroom, with TV and satellite and so on, and you'd have access to the rest of the house and the pool and gym unless we're entertaining. There's plenty of space, you could bring all your things.'

Julia would be hanging out the flags. 'No, no, that's fine. I don't mind at all. Transport won't be a problem either, I can drive.'

Stevie was puzzled by the sudden glance of amusement the Alexanders shared, but neither of them seemed about to explain.

'Is there anything else you'd like to know?' Mrs Alexander asked. She paused for a moment. 'Would you be prepared to sign a confidentiality agreement?'

'A confi-what?'

'It's just an agreement not to talk to the press about us, our household, anything that happens while you're with us,' Mr Alexander explained. 'I'm afraid it would have to be a condition of employment.'

What are these people, satanists? Stevie thought. Then she remembered the satellite and pool and gym. 'Yes, of course, no problem, absolutely.'

'That's everything, then Miss Colvin. We'll be making a decision over the next few days, so we'll let you know on Monday, if that's all right.'

Mrs Alexander pulled herself gracefully out of the armchair and reached for a plate of chocolate biscuits that room service had brought with her tea. 'Biscuit?' she offered.

Stevie couldn't say no, not after Mrs Alexander had gone to all the trouble of getting out of that chair to offer them to her. She smiled her thanks and reached out.

Her dress didn't.

'I told you the Ides of March was a bad idea,' Stevie howled six hours later. 'I've never been so embarrassed in all my life. What on earth must they have thought of me?'

'It could have happened to anyone,' Julia said soothingly.

'No it couldn't. Things like that only ever happen to me. I bet Annabel-bloody-Alexander has never even split a banana, never mind a dress.'

'I'm sure it won't make any difference –'

'Yes it will. You didn't see their faces. The Alexanders are just not the kind of people to hire a nanny whose dress divides in two like the Red Sea when she reaches for a chocolate digestive. They were terribly nice about it, of course – well, *he* was – but I could tell Mrs Alexander was thinking I was some kind of lunatic who'd been let out for the day. There's no way she'd trust me with a real live baby. And it had been going so well, too. I was certain they'd been about to offer me the job.' She groaned with remembered humiliation. 'I *would* have to be wearing my mauve Batman knickers. Mr Alexander must have been able to see right round to the Batmobile, the split was so big. Oh, God, it was so embarrassing. I had to walk out of the hotel with a towel wrapped round me. The porters must have had a field day.' She threw herself face down on the sofa. 'Oh, Jules, that's the second interview I've fucked up. What am I going to do now?'

Julia picked up her diary. 'Right then. Next Tuesday. Who do you think you can be burying this time?'

Four

Oliver Colvin had always enjoyed Sunday mornings. No law college, no waiting on tables at The Dome to supplement his pitiful grant, no sound of the perennial roadworks outside the house he shared with his sister Stevie and her friend, Julia. If Saturday night had gone as well as it usually did, it was rare for him even to wake up in his own bed. On the odd occasion he had to, he happily shared the duvet with several forests of newsprint until he got hungry enough to get up.

He listened to the sound of coffee being brewed and croissants being warmed and smiled. He'd had the most amazing sex of his twenty-two years last night, and what was more, he'd been sober enough to remember it. And now she was making him breakfast. What more could a man ask?

She came back into the bedroom with one of those Hollywood breakfast-in-bed trays on legs and put it down on the bed. Oliver was impressed. She'd obviously done this before. But then if last night was anything to go by, she'd done a lot of things before.

He just wished he could remember her name.

She whipped back the crisp white linen sheet covering his lean body and smiled. 'Mornin', cowboy.'

Shit, he'd forgotten she was American. No wonder she gave such good head. They had the mouths for it.

'Fixin' to start, honey?'

For a moment he wondered what she was asking and then he remembered the transatlantic language barrier and relaxed. 'Just say the word.'

She moved the tray on to the floor, undid the belt of her midnight-blue silk dressing-gown, slid on to the bed and reached for his cock. 'Come to Carrie, baby,' she murmured. 'Come to Mommy.'

Oliver leaned back against the pillows and closed his eyes as she stroked the inside of his thighs with her nails, snaking her body between his legs as she planted butterfly kisses across his groin. He could smell soap and shampoo and some heady, rich perfume – Giorgio, Poison maybe – overlaid with the unmistakable scent of sex. He moaned as her lips brushed the tip of his hard-on and wished she'd just open her wide American mouth and swallow him whole. He couldn't stand much more of this tease routine. Her tongue whirled around the base of his cock and he groaned again, winding his hands into her heavy blonde hair and pushing her face into his groin, desperate to sink himself into some moist, warm opening, he didn't particularly mind which, only for Christ's sake, let it be soon.

She disentangled herself and knelt up, her hair falling forward and obscuring her face so that all he could see were her full breasts dangling a few inches from his dry mouth. She dipped forward so that they brushed his lips and drew back as he tried to take the ripe cherry nipples in his mouth. They repeated this Tantalus dance a few more times, then Oliver caught hold of her hair and roughly held her still. He captured her breast between his lips, smiling with satisfaction as he felt her nipple instantly spring erect beneath his tongue. She might be ten years older than he was, but he'd been around the block a few times himself, he could teach her a thing or two. He sucked hungrily. God, but she tasted good. His free hand rolled the tip of her other nipple between his thumb and forefinger, his rock-hard cock pushing upwards against her smooth, hairless mound. He wondered curiously if all American women shaved there, or if it was just her. He'd found it slightly dis-concerting when she'd stripped for the first time last night and he'd seen her all-over – and he did mean *all* over – tan, but now he found it strangely erotic. It was something to do with the contrast between the baby-soft skin and damp grown-up cunt, dangerous stuff. He'd be going after little girls next.

He sat up and pushed her on to her back, then squeezed her large breasts together and took both nipples in his mouth as his knee spread her legs far enough apart for him to be able to move his long body between them. She let him take the lead as his fingers slid between her legs and sought her clitoris, her throaty sigh of appreciation telling him he'd found his target. He looked up and smiled as he read the desire in her eyes.

She pulled him hard against her. 'Let's fuck.'

He thought briefly of the Durex in his jeans pocket. Last night they'd both been too pissed and too randy to bother with them. He decided it was either too late or unnecessary now. He thrust his tongue into her mouth at the same moment as his cock entered her. He felt her hips rise to meet him. His kiss deepened as he drove into her, his hands planted on either side of her shoulders as he took his own weight, her breasts pillow-ing against his chest. God, but she was horny. He was going to come in a minute if he didn't watch out. He pulled back a lit-tle and counted to ten in German before plunging back into her, feeling her muscles clenching round his cock as if she had a pair of hands wanking him inside her.

He slid his hands beneath her buttocks and lifted her on to his lap, his cock still buried inside her. Moving carefully to make sure he didn't slip out, he eased towards the edge of her huge double bed, threw a pillow on to the floor, and gently leaned her over the edge until her head was resting on the pillow, her hips balanced on the edge of the bed. She hooked her legs over his muscled shoulders and moaned as the angle of their bodies enabled him to thrust steadily into her, deliber-ately holding himself back so that his climax built slowly in time with hers. After a while his back began to ache and he slid his feet to the floor on either side of her head, cradled her back, and stood up with her in his arms. He moved across the room towards the wardrobe, held her against the door and fucked her there. He picked her up, shifted to the wall, and fucked her again. Then he staggered towards the window, held her against the glass pane and fucked her in full view of the driver of the 438 bus. Playing to his audience, he curved his hand around her generous right breast and ostentatiously lifted it to his lips, sucking her nipple greedily as the bus driver ignored the green light and stayed to watch. Carrie groaned and clawed his back, making him suddenly overbalance, and he fell backwards on to her chest of drawers. Undeterred, she gripped the built-in mirror with both hands and watched herself for a moment as she rode him, then let go to cup her breasts, expertly fingering her nipples as Oliver struggled to regain the upper hand. He succeeded only in tumbling them both to the floor. The bus driver waited a few moments to see if they'd come back into view, then, disappointed, drove back to the bus depot and locked himself into the Gents for an hour with a copy of *Playboy*.

Oliver realised he couldn't hold back much longer. His hard-on felt like the rock of Gibraltar with a nuclear warhead buried inside it. He held Carrie's shoulders hard against the floor and finally gave up reciting transcripts of *The Crown* v. *Crippen* in his head.

'I'm going to come, I'm going to come –'

Carrie bucked beneath him. 'Sorry, cowboy. Ladies first!'

It was the first time he'd ever climaxed at the same time as a woman. It was a breathtaking, unbelievable, totally knackering experience. As soon as he'd come he collapsed on to the Habitat rug next to her and fell asleep.

When he came to twenty minutes later, she was calmly sitting up in bed eating her croissant and skimming the *Mail on Sunday*. 'Better now?'

'Oh, shit, I'm sorry. You were so fantastic. I can't think why

I fell asleep – too many late nights –'

She shrugged. 'Forget it. I hate all that talking shit after a fuck. Like, at that precise moment, you really give a damn about how it was for the other person?'

Oliver scrambled on to the bed beside her and drained the glass of orange juice she held out. 'You're really something, you know that?'

'Don't go and get mushy on me.' She waved her left hand under his nose. 'I'm a married woman, remember? We agreed last night, this is just a Welcome to England fuck, OK? No strings, no telephone numbers.'

Oliver bit back his disappointment. She'd made her terms quite clear when he'd picked her up at the pub, but he'd been unable to stop himself from hoping last night had changed her mind.

'OK, OK. No mushy stuff.' His finger trailed a path across her collarbone and down her arm. 'Am I allowed to tell you that not only are you the most beautiful woman I've ever met, but you're a fantastic lay as well?'

She laughed. 'I guess you can tell me that.' She stood up and wrapped her silk dressing-gown around her body. 'I just got to go call my mother. It's her birthday today, and she'll be going out later. Have another croissant, I'll be back soon.'

As Oliver watched her walk out of the room, the satisfaction weighing down his limbs was replaced by a renewed surge of lust as his eyes followed the sway of her firm buttocks. Shit, he was ready to go again! He'd never met a woman who'd had this effect on him before. Why the hell did she have to be married?

He waited five minutes before deciding that if this was going to be a one night stand, he wasn't missing any more of it than he had to. He got up and made his way into the living room, tripping over a dog's water bowl and splashing his bare feet as he did so. She glanced up as he entered the room, smiled and carried on talking. Oliver hadn't missed the quick once-over she'd given him, nor the way her gaze had lingered on his groin. Swiftly he moved behind her, bent her forwards over the back of the couch, lifted the blue silk of her dressing-gown and shoved his cock deep into her.

Somehow Carrie managed to turn her groan of appreciation into a cough. 'Listen, Mom, I gotta go. Something just came up –'

His hands reached forward and cupped her breasts, his breath hot on her neck as he rolled her nipples between his fingers.

'No, Mom, nothing's wrong –'

He slid out of her so that only the tip of his cock was still inside her.

'Mom, there's something I have to finish right away – no, it can't wait – ' he drove into her again – 'it's really getting to me – ' and out – 'you know what I'm like when I'm on a job – ' and in. 'Bye, Mom.'

She dropped the phone on the sofa and Oliver quickly pressed the cradle to make sure Carrie's Mom didn't get to hear exactly what kind of job her daughter was on. They fell over the sofa at the precise moment Carrie climaxed.

She slid off him and buried her face between his legs. 'Your turn, cowboy. Let me show you what an all-American gal can do when she puts her mouth to it.'

He sank back against the sofa cushions, his arms out-stretched across its back, his head thrown back and his eyes closed. Carrie wasn't kidding. Jesus, she could tie knots in cherry stalks with her tongue, she was that good.

He cursed as the telephone rang again.

Carrie stopped tonguing him. 'It might be my husband. I'd better get it, just in case. He'll wonder where the hell I am at ten-thirty on a Sunday morning if I don't. I'll take it in the bed-room. Stay there, I'll be back in five.'

He prayed she meant five seconds, not five minutes. He doubted he'd last much longer.

He didn't have to. He felt her lips around his cock almost before he'd had time to realise she'd gone. Her tongue whirled around the tip and along his length, her hair brushing silkily against the inside of his thighs. He moaned softly. He couldn't decide if he liked the fucking or the blowjob more. It was one hell of a dilemma to be in.

He could feel his climax building as she sucked him greedily, his entire body centred on the sensation in his groin. He didn't care what she said, he had to have this woman again.

'It was just my Mom again. She wanted to know if we'd had a crossed line, she said she could hear some strange noises in the background –'

Oliver froze. Either Carrie had mastered the art of talking with her mouth full or –

He opened his eyes wide. Carrie was standing in the doorway, staring at him with the strangest expression he'd ever seen. He swung his gaze towards his groin.

Between his legs, Carrie's Alsatian stared back at him.

Julia sighed as she opened the door. 'Hello, Oliver. Good, was she?'

'Let me put it this way. Bed, wardrobe, window, floor, wall,' he said.

'Another notch on the bedpost. You're such a bastard.'

'I think I was a notch on hers, actually.'

Oliver ducked his head as he folded his tall frame through the doorway into their sitting room. 'Where is Stevie, anyway?'

'She's your sister. You tell me.'

'She can't still be in bed. It's nearly two o'clock. She'll miss the *EastEnders* omnibus.' Oliver flopped into the battered orange armchair Stevie usually commandeered. 'Thank God. I can watch the Grand Prix on your telly. Mine's finally given up the ghost.'

'Can I do anything else for you while you're here to make

your stay more pleasurable? Tea, coffee, perhaps?'

'A beer'd be nice, but only if it's cold.' He threw his long legs over the side of the armchair and reached for the remote control. 'And I wouldn't mind some chocolate digestives. I'm starving. I know Stevie'll have some hidden somewhere.'

'She didn't feed you, then?'

'Who? Oh, yes, last night.' He grinned. 'You don't want to know what she did. You'd only get jealous.'

'I'll try to hold myself in check.'

Julia stepped over the not-so-little black dress Stevie had carelessly deposited in the kitchen doorway on her way to bed last night and opened the fridge. She wrenched a can of Budweiser from the plastic six-pack at the back. Oliver's Sunday afternoon hear-it-and-weep sessions on their sofa were becoming quite a little routine. Some time after midday Julia would hear the door to his basement flat slam as he either returned from a night on the tiles or let out Saturday night's conquest. A few minutes later he'd bound up the stairs to their flat three at a time with some pathetic excuse – like today's, running out of Weetabix – to make sure they saw that he was still in yesterday evening's crumpled, lipsticked clothes, then make frequent references to how tired he was and what a long night it had been. It was all a game to him, a sort of X-rated conkers. She wondered if, once he'd bonked a woman, he added her score to his.

Oliver caught the can she tossed him and pulled back the tab. 'Cheers. The Brazilian race should be good today. First Grand Prix they've had over there since Ayrton Senna bought it. I'd put my money on Schumacher now. He's a bloody genius.'

'I can't wait.'

'What I wouldn't give to be a racing driver,' Oliver murmured reverently.

'Oh please. You'd really want to give up law to spend your days driving round and round in a circle at 120 miles an hour?'

'You're a girl. You wouldn't understand.'

'You're a boy. You'll never grow up.'

'Point of information, Your Honour –'

'I take it we're back to last night again?'

He grinned. 'I wish.'

Julia bit back a sharp retort. Oliver wasn't quite the hard-bitten cocksman he liked to make out. She had no doubt about his pulling power – she'd listened to the evidence through the paper-thin floor often enough – but she suspected he cared about the women he screwed more than he liked to admit. The fact that most of them became his friends even after he'd dumped them was evidence enough of that. But sooner or later, Oliver would meet his match and get his heart broken, and then perhaps he'd stop using and discarding women like Kleenexes. Until then, no amount of scolding from his older sister's best friend was going to make any difference.

She eyed him surreptitiously. It was still difficult for her to look at him without seeing the obnoxious spotty maggot who'd put worms in her school lunchbox and made loud sucking noises whenever he'd caught her on the sofa with a boyfriend, but to a poor, unsuspecting woman who hadn't grown up with him, he might seem quite good-looking – sexy, even, if you liked them six-foot two and crumpled in a Hugh Grant sort of way. For all his bravado there was an endearing boyishness about him. Every time he pushed his hair out of his eyes, she was reminded of the ten-year-old boy who'd been scared of wasps and hated to be left alone in the dark.

'So, where *was* Stevie last night, then?'

Julia jumped. 'Sorry? Oh, we went down to Brighton, tried out this new club Hugo's found. Bit of a rave, really. Stevie was drowning her sorrows.'

'She's still upset over that married wanker she was seeing?'

'A succinct but apt description, counsellor,' Julia said. 'I don't think she's so much hurt as humiliated. You and I knew he was a lying toad, but unfortunately, Stevie believed the corny old lines he fed her. Now she feels a right prat.'

'Well, she was.' Oliver handed her his empty can, doing his best to look helpless. Julia gritted her teeth and wondered what it was about him that got otherwise intelligent, independent women like her to run around after him as if he was Neanderthal Man and she his cavewoman.

'Shit, Damon's got pole position. Michael Schumacher's got it all to do.' Oliver tore his attention away from the screen with difficulty. 'Thanks, Julia. What happened with Bronwyn and Robin, then?'

'To be honest, Oliver, the job situation isn't helping . . .'

She broke off as the living-room door slowly swung open without any apparent human agency behind it. She wondered briefly if they'd got ghosts, then realised Stevie was crawling along on her hands and knees.

'Oh, God, I'm going to die.'

'Don't be ridiculous. You've just got a hangover. It's not likely to prove fatal.'

'Don't tell me that. It's only the thought of dying that's keeping me hanging on.'

Oliver held out his beer. 'Hair of the dog?'

'Now I know I'm going to be sick.'

When Stevie returned five minutes later, her Yogi Bear T-shirt bore two new large damp stains of dubious origin on the front, but her skin was no longer the deathly pale it had been for her first appearance, and she was able to claw herself into a semi-upright position against the sofa. She put her sun-glasses on and groaned. 'Never again. From now on, it's orange juice all the way.'

'That's what you said last Sunday,' Oliver said.

'And every Sunday before that,' Julia added.

'It's your fault, Jules. You shouldn't have let me have that last tequila slammer. I was all right till then.'

'Shouldn't have *let* you?' Julia said indignantly. 'You were wringing out the barman's sleeve for drips.'

Stevie was about to protest when she saw her brother polishing off the last of her chocolate digestives. 'Oliver, you bastard! I was saving those for later. I don't know why you can't stay for lunch with your Saturday night pick-up instead of coming round here and eating all my biscuits.'

'Their husbands tend to want them back by lunchtime,' Oliver said. 'Look, can you shut up now, Stevie, the race is about to start.'

Stevie was about to tell him exactly what he could do with his Grand Prix when she discovered a hitherto unsuspected interest in motor-racing. 'Omigod, Oliver, who's *he*?'

'Who? Oh, him. Rafe Dussi.'

Oliver took full advantage of the opportunity to show off his knowledge in front of Woman. 'It'll be interesting to see how he does. This is his first season in Formula One, but he's been pretty good in practice. Only about twenty-six or twenty-seven, but everyone says he could be the new Ayrton Senna. Schumacher hates him. Quisling Mild/Terroni snapped him up for their team as their number two driver.' He nodded sagely. 'You know, I reckon the Terroni team have a good chance this season. They're right up there with the Benetton and Williams teams, particularly now that Charles Cusack is managing them. If they can play Michael Schumacher and Damon Hill off against each other –'

'I was thinking more along the lines of his address and phone number,' Stevie said.

'Dream on, sister. He's way out of your league. Anyway, he's probably a tax exile in Monaco. Follow the smell of burning rubber.'

'Don't mind her, Oliver,' Julia said. 'She hasn't been the same since she went for that job in Rome. All she can think about is Italian crumpet.'

'Will you shut up? They're about to start!' Oliver cursed as the phone rang. 'Shit, what now?'

'Don't mind us, it's just our flat,' Julia said.

58

'Are you going to answer it or what?'

Stevie held her head. 'Quit bickering. I'll take it in the hall. It's probably Mum, anyway.'

She disappeared into the hallway. The ringing stopped, and the room was filled with the irritating whine of twenty-six racing cars swarming around the track. Julia resigned herself to the fact that Oliver was going to occupy their sitting room for the next seventy-one laps or so, and went out into the kitchen to put the kettle on. She opened the fridge to get out the milk and forced herself to study its noxious shelves, wondering whether to attempt to clear out the worst of it before Hugo arrived. He hated having to cram his Moët – he always brought Moët on Sundays, one of the charming little things she loved about him – between half-eaten McDonald's Chicken McNuggets and Stevie's Death by Chocolate. In fact, Hugo hated most things about their flat, including her flatmate. But then, that was fair enough, she herself had always hated Prick Whittington.

She had known the double-dealing, two-timing, ratfink bastard for what he was the first time she'd met him, but she'd also known that there was no way Stevie was going to believe he was anything other than Prince Charming whose Cinderella didn't understand him. She'd done exactly what any best friend worthy of the title should do in such circumstances: she'd shut up and stockpiled tissues for when the end came.

She opened a glass jar filled with Typhoo One-Cup and tried to find an unused tea-bag. She wished Stevie wouldn't keep on putting the old ones back in again once she'd dried them out on the windowsill. No wonder Hugo hated coming here. He was so . . . fastidious. Maybe if Stevie got a job somewhere else and moved out, she'd have more chance of getting Hugo to propose.

She did wonder if the problem wasn't that Hugo was not the marrying type, but that he just wasn't the marrying-*her* type. They'd been going out for nearly five years, and she still hadn't been home to meet his parents. Hugo was a bit of a dark horse. In fact, if she was going to be accurate about this, he was a whole stable full of them. Beyond the fact that he did something in the City, wore two pairs of jeans to hide his thin legs and threw up if he ate mussels, the range of her knowledge about him was somewhat limited.

The kettle clicked off and Julia picked it up to pour just as Stevie let out a blood-curdling scream, threw her sunglasses in the air and leaped enthusiastically on to the sofa. 'I've got it! I've got it! Yahoooo! I've got it! The baby was early. They want me to start straight away! Tomorrow!'

Oliver managed to tear himself away from the television. 'What job is this?'

'God, I feel sick again.'

'Sit down, Stevie, for God's sake.'

Stevie sat down. 'Mr and Mrs Alexander. They've decided they want me after all.'

'You mean the people you saw when you split your Laura Ashley?' Julia said incredulously. 'They're going to trust you with their baby? Are they completely mad?'

'Must be,' Stevie said. 'It was their little boy who clinched it. He thinks I'm wonderful.'

'What little boy? I thought you said you were being interviewed to look after a baby?'

'It's a long story. There was this little boy in the reception of the hotel –'

'Where do these people live?' Oliver interrupted.

'Near here, I can't remember where exactly, but pretty close. Edenfield, I think. They're sending me a driver to pick me up with enough clothes to last me the week. I'll fetch Damien and the rest of my stuff next weekend.'

'What does this Mr Alexander do?'

'Oh.' She paused, surprised. 'I never thought to ask. They wanted me to sign some sort of agreement though, saying I'd never talk to the press. Must be something to do with the government.'

'Starting tomorrow? Are you sure about all this?' Julia said hesitantly. 'You don't know where they live or what they do or anything about them. You don't think this is all a bit – well, sudden?'

Stevie stopped bouncing up and down on the sofa. 'Oh, shit. Bronwyn. I'm going to have to tell Bronwyn.'

'She'll kill you,' Oliver said cheerfully.

'Kill me? She'll eat me alive. She'll chew me up and spit out the bits. Oh *shit*.' Stevie thought for a moment. 'There's only one way round this, Jules. If I'm going to have to face Bronwyn tomorrow morning, I'm just going to have to get absolutely off my head tonight.'

Five

For the second morning running, Stevie found herself on intimate terms with the inside of a toilet bowl.

She retched, tears streaming down her cheeks. God, she couldn't throw up again, she just couldn't. There was nothing more left. She sank back on her bare haunches and clung to the toilet seat, wishing for the hundredth time that they'd changed it for one that wasn't Day-Glo orange. Julia insisted it wasn't their responsibility, it was up to their landlord, but at the end of the day, it wasn't the landlord who had to throw up into it. In Stevie's opinion, on mornings like this, a plain ordinary white one would have been a worthwhile investment.

She waited a few moments to make sure that really was it, emptied the half-Domestos bottle they used to catch drips from the leaky cistern into the loo, then stood up on wobbly legs and leaned against the toilet-roll holder as she reached for the old-fashioned loo chain. For some reason known only to God and Armitage Shanks, it was the only way their bog would flush. She gripped the edge of the washbasin and, sticking her head under the cold tap, turned it on and let the slightly musty water spill over her face and open mouth. Please God, let me die. I promise never, ever to drink again. It's the wagon all the way.

She lifted her head and faced the mirror. She looked awful. Her skin was an appealing shade somewhere between uncooked dough and the colour make-up artists used for bloated corpses dragged out of the river in *Death Wish* movies, a comparison rendered even more telling by her red-rimmed eyes and runny nose. Great.

'Stevie, are you OK in there?'

She heard a rattle and then a gentle thunk as Julia prodded the brass key out of the keyhole and bent to call through it. 'Didn't you say your car was going to be here at nine? It's already ten to. If you want me to tackle Bronwyn for you, I've got to go.'

'Don't worry, I'll be fine. You just go on, don't fret about me. I'll just curl up and die here on my own.'

'Stevie, you're not going to die so stop feeling sorry for yourself. It's just a hangover. I'll see you at the weekend, OK? Good luck.'

It's going to take more than good luck to get me through this, Stevie thought. She listened to the sound of the front door slamming and, moments later, Julia's GTi pulling out of the drive. She was going to have to slather on the old Black & Decker to hide all these spots. Maybe a hat with a really big, floppy brim –

She heard the front doorbell ring and panicked. She hadn't even started packing yet.

'Just a minute!'

She picked up the key that Julia had pushed out of the lock, inserted it and yanked open the door, thanking a slightly forgiving God for not letting it jam shut for half an hour as it usually did on these occasions. She ran into her bedroom. Saint Julia had already left her expensive new leather holdall on the bed for Stevie to borrow. She started picking up clothes from the piles scattered around her single bed and flung them heedlessly into the holdall. She just hoped there were some clean knickers in there somewhere. She couldn't sleep in a strange bed without knickers on.

The doorbell rang again and she dashed over to her bedroom window, holding the curtain across her body so that she was

63

not revealed to the Alexanders' driver in all her naked glory as she yelled through the open fanlight. 'Look, I'll be five minutes, OK? Could you just wait in the car until I come out?'

She heard the gravel crunch underfoot as the driver returned to his car. Tugging a comb through her tangles with her left hand, she searched feverishly along the windowsill for her quick-set emergency foundation, then leaned over her dressing table and started to slap it on straight from the tube. This was not the time to start blending on the inside of your wrist and messing about with damp sponges. After a few moments she realised that her Torremolinos tan must have faded since she'd last worn this particular make-up, which was looking a rather startling shade of orange against the unhealthy white of her skin. Jamming the holdall against the edge of the dressing table, she swept the contents in on top of her clothes then zipped up the bag as the driver revved his engine outside. What the hell was he driving, a Formula One racing car? She was being as quick as she could.

She threw in her Chelsea boots and an extra pair of knickers, grabbed the holdall and ran. She didn't have time to mess about, she could collect everything else at the weekend. Checking she had her keys, she shut the door to the flat behind her and ran downstairs to the main front door they shared with Oliver. It wasn't until she saw her reflection in its glass that she realised that, apart from the luminous orange foundation, she was still stark naked.

Stevie said a silent prayer of thanks to whichever god had prompted her to check she'd still got her keys before she'd left the flat, rather than after. Her hands modestly covering her rear just in case the driver came back to the front door, she ran back upstairs, let herself in and started looking for something to wear.

Ten minutes later, grabbing her battered old teddy, she left the flat for the second time that morning. As she reached the main front door a sudden wave of doubt and fear assailed her.

She *was* doing the right thing, wasn't she? She had been right to chuck in her job with Bronwyn and Robin and Jack – little Jack – and go to work for these people? She felt the tears prick at the back of her eyes. What if Bronwyn forgot to leave his Old-Woman-Who-Lived-In-A-Shoe night light on? He'd always been scared of the dark. And last week he'd decided he hated beetroot, he said it made him feel sick – she'd forgotten to tell Bronwyn that. She'd have to ring her as soon as she got to the Alexanders' –

She jumped as the driver sat on his horn again. Pull yourself together, Stevie. If it doesn't work out, you can always come back.

She stopped short as she reached the main road. Instead of the battered Volvo estate or Renault Espace she'd been expecting, a brand-new silver N-reg open-topped Porsche was parked at the end of the drive.

And sitting at the wheel, smiling at her from behind his shades, was Quisling Mild/Terroni's number two Formula One driver, Rafe Dussi.

Annabel Alexander stared critically at her reflection in the full-length mirror. She loved Nicole Farhi, but the designer did tend towards those rather conservative, subtle colours so beloved of certain English women to whom daring meant wearing a pair of earrings other than the pearl studs they'd received from their grandmothers on their eighteenth birthdays. At least she was getting her figure back. After nine months of maternity clothes, it was a joy to wear anything pretty. The dress she had on now was a soft, creamy biscuit shade that set off her colouring perfectly, but it did need a little something around the neck to brighten it up. She opened the cupboard where she kept her accessories and sifted through a shimmering heap of Hermès silk scarves before selecting a ruby, cream and gold one that had cost her £120 more than three years ago. She moved back towards the mirror and deftly

65

arranged it over her shoulders. Perfect. No one would ever guess she'd had a baby six days ago.

She slipped her stockinged feet into the low-heeled beige leather shoes she'd already selected from the dozens in her walk-in shoe cupboard, checked the reflection of her back in the mirror to make sure there were no marks she'd missed or stray pieces of cotton on the back of her dress – so many women forgot to bother with the back, yet most people saw that side of you just as often as the front – and, satisfied, left her dressing room. She might only be dressing to receive the new nanny, but that was no excuse to let standards slip.

She picked up her gold watch from the dressing table where she'd left it while she showered. 'Patrick, have you seen my Cartier bracelet?'

Her husband smiled up at her as he finished tying the laces of his tennis trainers. 'That pretty charm bracelet you wore to meet me at the airport last night? I put it back in the safe. You really shouldn't leave it out overnight.'

'Oh, Patrick. I wanted to wear it again today. You know how awkward it is to get things in and out of that safe.'

'That's the idea, darling. If it's difficult for you to reach, one hopes the same holds true for any burglars. I'll get it out for you.'

Annabel followed her husband as he moved towards the oak-panelled wall at the far end of their bedroom. 'Rosie's had her safe put in behind that little Matisse print in her study,' she said. 'You can just move the picture and there you are. No crawling about in filthy attics getting covered in cobwebs and dirt.'

'And no second guesses where any thief worth his salt would try first either.'

She watched her husband lean against a section of the old oak panelling and wait as it swung slowly inwards, revealing a dark, narrow passageway perhaps ten feet long and three feet wide. The room had been constructed as a priest's hole four centuries before, during the reign of Protestant Elizabeth I, when the manor house had been owned by a Catholic family who wanted to practise their forbidden faith in secret. Annabel hated it. The filth and gloom was bad enough, but if she was honest, it was the ghosts she feared more.

She would never have admitted it to Patrick, but even in broad daylight, Annabel wouldn't open this door alone. Local legend held that the narrow room was haunted by the ghost of a young Jesuit priest, fresh from the Seminary at Douai, who had been trapped there in the summer of 1580 when the house had been raided by the Queen's agents as he was celebrating Mass. Loyal servants of the host had managed to hide him, but, certain that the Jesuit was concealed somewhere in the house, the Queen's men had arrested every member of the household and sealed the building for a month. No one had been able to enter and no one had been able to leave. The Jesuit, unable to open the panelling from the inside, had slowly starved to death.

Annabel wondered if it was true that Patrick's own grandfather had discovered the young priest's skeleton himself when he bought the manor house back in the 1930s. Knowing Francis Alban Alexander, he would have just stepped over it.

'Thank you, darling.' Annabel fastened the bracelet around her wrist as Patrick emerged from the dusty passageway. 'Heavens, you're filthy. Your hair is full of cobwebs. I hope you're going to clean up before you go out.'

'I'm playing a game of tennis, not meeting the Prince of Wales for lunch.' He laughed as he saw her expression. 'OK, OK.'

'Darling, you're not going out until the new nanny gets here, are you?' Annabel called as Patrick disappeared into the bathroom. 'I think we should both be here to welcome her.'

'Damn. I'm sorry, I didn't realise she was coming this morning. I've got a tennis lesson booked, I can't cancel it now.'

'But Rafe's already gone to get her. How will it look if you've gone out when he gets back?'

'Rafe? When was he here?'

'Half an hour ago, just after I came back from running the twins to school,' Annabel said. 'You were still asleep and I didn't want to wake you. Arcor came up to the house to tell me he'd managed to do something to his back putting up the tomato cloches or something. Anyway, he can't drive today, so as Rafe was here he offered to pick Stephanie up.'

Patrick grinned. 'Hasn't that boy got a home to go to?'

'He *is* your team-mate, Patrick. His family are all back in Italy. We're probably the closest he has –'

'I know, I know. I'm only teasing. I like to have him around, you know that.'

Patrick shut the bathroom door and, moments later, Annabel heard the sound of the shower. She moved towards the mullioned bedroom windows and stared out across the wide, sweeping driveway lined with beeches, their bare branches clutching at the pale March sky. Sometimes she found it difficult to know when Patrick was being serious. He was such a hard man to read. He kept so many of his inner thoughts hidden, even from her. They had been married for almost ten years, yet even now she could only guess sometimes at his motivation.

Annabel had known almost every biographical detail of his life barely twenty-four hours after she'd first met Patrick Alexander at a Live Aid charity ball in 1985. She hadn't had a clue who he was when he'd asked her to dance, but her mother had instantly recognised one of the youngest and most eligible racing drivers ever to win a Grand Prix. By the time Annabel had met him again for dinner the following evening, she'd read and memorised every cutting the local library and her mother could produce.

She'd learned a tragic history. Patrick was an only child, brought up at Edenfield Manor by his paternal grandfather, a widower, after his parents had died in a car crash when he was three. According to the *Brighton Evening Argus*, James, Patrick's father, had been driving. He had skidded out of control on a bend one wet, stormy January night in 1963 as he had returned with his wife and young son from an evening out with friends. It was an accident that could have happened to anyone, except that James Alexander had been the holder of the FIA Formula One World Championship at the time. Somehow it made the tragedy seem even more shocking to Annabel. All those races without a scratch, and then to die like that, at the wheel of an old Vauxhall Cresta on a B-road somewhere between Brighton and Edenfield. James had been killed instantly; Elizabeth, Patrick's mother, had died in the ambulance on the way to hospital.

The newspapers had said that Patrick himself had been thrown clear. Rescuers had found the three-year-old huddled beneath a tree twenty feet from the wrecked car, his arms wrapped tightly around himself, his eyes wide and staring. There hadn't been a mark on him, but according to old Mrs Arcor, the housekeeper, the little boy hadn't spoken a word for ten months after the accident. Even now he sometimes woke in the middle of the night, drenched in sweat, sobbing and screaming for his mother.

Annabel had long since realised that Patrick's need to replicate his father's life had been his way of coming to terms with the accident. Mrs Arcor said he'd lived, breathed and dreamed motor racing from the moment he was old enough to say 'car'. His heroes had been Stirling Moss and Graham Hill, his childish vocabulary littered with terms like 'RPM' and 'skid block'. He'd started racing himself before he was even in his teens, telling his grandfather he was spending the weekend with his best friend, Charles Lytton, while the two of them sneaked out to go-kart rallies and later stock-car races. He'd been twenty when he'd first started in Formula Three; within eighteen months he had become a test driver for Quisling Mild/Terroni, racing F1 cars around the track at Silverstone or Estoril in Portugal while Terroni's team of mechanics took notes and adjusted their championship drivers' cars accordingly. By the time she and Patrick met three years later, he'd been Terroni's number two driver, and the following year he'd been moved to their number one slot. Now, not yet thirty-five, he was Terroni's veteran; Rafe Dussi was the young blood of the team, with Martin Romaine, their twenty-four-year-old test driver, hot on his heels.

The eldest of three daughters in a loving, if slightly strait-laced, family that extended to many dozens of cousins, aunts and uncles, Annabel had tried and failed to imagine what it must have been like to grow up alone at Edenfield Manor, a withdrawn, isolated little boy with only an old man for company. Francis Alexander had been Patrick's only living relative. He could not have been an easy man to live with. A formidable businessman who had made his fortune smuggling Irish malt into America during the years of Prohibition, he had still been alive when Annabel and Patrick had first met – he'd died two years later from testicular cancer at the age of eighty-one. Annabel remembered him as distant and forbidding. He'd made it clear that he disapproved of what his dead son and grandson had chosen to do with their lives. His demands on Patrick had been exacting, his standards almost impossibly high. Annabel had no doubt that if Francis Alexander's code had not demanded that his grandson receive a proper education – by which he meant the discipline of a distant boarding-school – Patrick would have grown up a deeply disturbed and isolated young man. But if he had not been able to learn what love was from a family of his own, at least he had had the chance to observe it at second hand in those of his peers.

Annabel was not much given to introspection; she had been brought up to believe in appearances, the tangible signs of a successful life – a beautiful house, exquisite clothes, a doting husband and children. She rarely stopped to consider the shadows beneath the surface, the forces that shaped people and made them what they were. But she knew exactly what it was that had made Patrick Alexander fall in love with her.

She had been twenty-two when they'd met, two years younger than Patrick; already a beautiful woman, she had been charming, poised and amusing. As a child she had realised she would never be intellectually gifted, but she had worked hard at being accomplished: she spoke conversational French and Italian, she knew which wine to serve with lobster and in which months oysters could safely be eaten, she skied well and played tennis better. But it had not been her mastery of choux pastry or her piano playing that had prompted Patrick to ask her to marry him over the spinach soufflé at Langans a mere ten days after they'd met. It had been her sense of family, her confidence, her belief in herself that came from having had the stable, loving upbringing that had eluded Patrick. He had wanted to be part of it more than he'd ever wanted anything in his life.

Their marriage four months later had worked, perhaps because she had needed to be needed as much as he'd needed to be loved. Unlike so many of the suitable, chinless young men she'd met at hunt balls or on the ski slopes at Klosters, Patrick had not wanted an accessory, a glossy asset to be acquired along with the house in Tite Street or membership of the Garrick. He loved her for who she was, not what she could do, and if he'd never been able to tell her in so many words, she knew. She was the calm stillness at the centre of his turbulent life, the rock from which he could strike out in any direction. She had given him the family he had so craved: the twins, James and Elizabeth – named after his parents – and now Henry. The nightmares when he woke sobbing for his mother were fewer now.

She watched as the gardener and odd-job man, Arcor, trudged slowly towards the sunken rose garden behind the clipped yew hedge on the far side of the lawn, his ancient wheelbarrow crunching on the gravel. All this time, and yet she sometimes felt as if she knew the real Patrick no better now than she had the first time they'd danced.

She shifted the delicate Dresden china shepherdess a fraction to the left on the windowsill. She had no reason to complain. Her marriage had brought her a great deal, not least of it a man she loved. She lived in one of the finest privately owned fifteenth-century manor houses in Sussex. Its panelled rooms included the King's Room, where Charles II had reputedly stayed during his flight to France in 1651, and a unique *trompe l'oeil* Painted Room which had been decorated for his triumphant return visit ten years later. Annabel never tired of walking through its beautiful rooms. Patrick gave her free rein when it came to running the house, as he did with everything else he considered her domain. He had never once queried the amount she spent on clothes; he had never failed to buy her some exquisite piece of jewellery for her birthday.

She heard the baby crying over the intercom and left the bedroom, her heels tapping softly on the wooden floor which had been burnished to a soft gold by centuries of beeswax and polish. This uncharacteristic restlessness was probably her hormones, nothing more. It was the baby blues, she'd get over it. She lifted the iron latch and entered the nursery, the floorboards creaking beneath her feet. Henry stared up at her as she bent over the cradle that had rocked four generations of Alexanders, his deep blue gaze unwavering. She picked him up, feeling her breasts tighten uncomfortably as he snuffled against her shoulder for milk. With her free hand, she switched on the bottle warmer on the baby table and waited for it to heat. It was all very well saying breast was best, but she didn't want hers hanging down to her knees by the time she was forty.

The bottle warmer clicked off just as she heard the spin of wheels in the drive. She picked up Henry's milk and headed downstairs, ducking her head to avoid the low beam on the half-landing and feeling an unexpected twinge of unease at

Patrick's absence as she glimpsed Rafe through the landing window. If she'd been alone with Martin Romaine, Patrick's sweet young test driver, she wouldn't have minded at all. He was only a boy, and anyway, he was practically family now. He'd worked with Patrick for years, ever since he'd left school. But Rafe Dussi was different. She barely knew him. He wasn't much older than Martin, but she found him disturbing for reasons she didn't want to analyse. She fought to control herself as she opened the front door. She was being silly – Patrick was only upstairs, she was hardly alone – and anyway, what could possibly happen here, in her own home?

She summoned a bright smile. 'Hello, Rafe. Perfect timing.'

'As always.'

She glanced through the open doorway as the new nanny followed him into the hall. 'You two look a bit wet. I didn't realise it was raining.'

'We're fine,' Rafe said. 'It only started a few minutes ago.'

'Would you like me to take the baby, Mrs Alexander?'

'Oh, thank you, Stephanie.' Annabel handed him over and slightly self-consciously rearranged her Hermès scarf. 'He needs feeding –' She broke off as she saw Stevie clearly for the first time. 'Are you feeling quite all right? You do look the strangest colour –'

'I think it was my driving, actually,' Rafe interrupted. 'I'm sure she will be fine just as soon as her stomach returns to its normal place.'

Stevie shot him a grateful look.

'You Italians,' Annabel said lightly. 'You think every road is la Monza.'

'You English. Even when you're driving you queue.'

'Um, Mrs Alexander?' Stevie glanced round the shadowed hallway. 'Is there anywhere I could take the baby? I think he might need changing.'

Annabel pointed towards the stairs. 'If you go straight on up and turn right, his nursery is at the end of the corridor. I'm sorry to throw you in at the deep end, Stephanie, but it's been a difficult morning. If you come back down when you've finished, I'll show you round the rest of the house and leave you to settle in properly.'

She watched as Stevie cradled the baby carefully against her shoulder as she went up the stairs, her touch gentle and confident. The girl had the strangest taste in clothes she'd ever seen – God alone knew why she needed a hood over her head now that she was indoors, and her jeans had to be at least two sizes too small and were covered in paint – but she seemed to know what she was doing with Harry. Annabel hoped they'd made the right decision in hiring her. She had rather liked the quiet little thing from East Anglia whom they'd interviewed last week, but James had been absolutely set on Stephanie. Even Patrick had unexpectedly volunteered his opinion on a subject he normally considered wholly Annabel's domain, reminding her that children and animals were supposed to be the best judges of a person's character. It was probably just as well Stephanie was slightly unconventional. She would be working in an extremely unconventional household.

'Any danger of a coffee, Annabel?'

'Oh, I'm sorry, Rafe. I was miles away.' She turned and headed down the dark passageway towards the huge flag-stoned kitchen. 'As long as Mrs Arcor hasn't made off with my supplies again.'

Rafe followed her into the kitchen and leaned against the warmth of the Aga, his arms folded across his chest as he watched Annabel spoon coffee grounds into a small copper coffee pot. 'I don't know why you keep them on. I don't think I have ever seen either of them actually do any work.'

'Not so much a couple who do as a couple who don't,' Annabel said.

'I'm sorry?'

She waved her hand. 'English humour. Never mind.'

She reached past him to lift the heavy cover over the Aga's

hotplate. Rafe didn't move. The back of her neck prickled beneath his stare. She could smell the spicy tang of his after-shave and the damp wool of his fisherman's sweater as it steamed in the heat of the kitchen. Her limbs felt suddenly liquid as she leaned across him again to place the coffee pot on the hotplate. She knew he knew exactly what he was doing to her.

She pulled back abruptly, anger and confusion in her eyes. 'Rafe –'

They both turned as the back door opened.

'It's fucking pouring out there.' Rosie Knighton shook her tangle of curly black hair, spattering raindrops all over the kitchen. 'Your drive's a bog, you know that? I nearly disappeared in it for good.'

Annabel flurried round her, glad of the excuse to put some distance between herself and Rafe. 'Why on earth did you walk in this weather? Why didn't you drive?'

'Laurie's car is out of action, and he needed mine to visit a patient. I hope the bloody thing breaks down on him –' She broke off as she saw Rafe. 'Well, hello *you*.'

'Oh, sorry, haven't you met Rafe yet?'

'Annabel, honey, I'd remember if I had.'

'Rosie Knighton, this is Rafe Dussi.'

'Rosie.' He held her hand for a fraction longer than was necessary. 'A beautiful name for a beautiful woman.'

'A beautiful *married* woman,' Annabel put in, unable to suppress a surprising pang of jealousy.

'If a man can't hold on to his wife, he does not deserve to have her,' Rafe said.

Unaware of the tension snapping between Rafe and Annabel, Rosie shrugged off her bright yellow waterproof mackintosh and threw it over the back of a chair. A sudden hiss filled the kitchen and all three of them turned towards the Aga.

'Bugger it. Your coffee's boiling over.' Rosie grabbed a dishcloth and picked up the coffee pot, hot brown liquid frothing over its sides. 'Is there somewhere I could put this, Annabel?'

'Here, stand it on some newspaper. The *Mail on Sunday* has to be good for something –' She jumped as she heard the front door slam. 'Damn. I'd forgotten Patrick was going to play tennis. That must be him leaving now.'

'I need to see him before the team meeting this afternoon,' Rafe said. 'Is he taking the Range Rover? Good, maybe I can catch him by the stable block. I'm sorry about the coffee, Annabel, another time, OK? *Ciao*.'

Annabel was glad to see him go. She reached up to the top shelf of the pine dresser opposite the Aga. 'Fancy a Hobnob?'

'I can tell you what I do fancy, Annabel Alexander, and it isn't a biscuit,' Rosie said. 'You witch. You didn't tell me you had a secret stash of gorgeous Italian racing drivers in your kitchen – he is *the* Rafe Dussi, I take it? I'd have been beating a path to your door if I'd known.' She grinned. 'Or is he already taken?'

'For heaven's sake, Rosie. Just because you cheat on that poor dear man of yours, it doesn't mean everyone else is doing the same.'

'Oh-ho, it's like *that*, is it?'

'And what's that supposed to mean?'

'Come on, Annie. This is me you're talking to. Unless you've gone blind in the last twenty-four hours, I can't believe you haven't noticed Rafe Dussi's the horniest guy to hit Sussex since William the Conqueror.' She took a sip of coffee. 'What's he doing down here in the sticks anyway?' she asked.

'Rafe is Patrick's new team-mate,' Annabel said. 'Now Charles Cusack's the team manager, he thought it made sense for Rafe to be in the same place as Patrick and Martin and the rest of the team, so they can work on cars or strategy or whatever it is they do together. Rafe's staying down at the Gate House until the end of the season. If it works out with Terroni, 'he'll probably find his own place down here for next year.'

'He's sitting on my doorstep for the next eight months? Thank you God, it must be Christmas.'

'Rosie, you're terrible. What about poor Laurie?'

'What *about* poor Laurie?'

'I don't know why he puts up with you,' Annabel said. 'He's such a nice man, and you treat him so appallingly.'

'Oh, come on. You think he doesn't have affairs?'

'You know perfectly well he doesn't. You only pretend you think he does to justify what you get up to. It would serve you right if he did leave you for his secretary –'

Rosie sat up, spilling her coffee. 'God, he isn't having an affair with her, is he? You would tell me if he was, wouldn't you? I couldn't bear the humiliation of being the last to know –'

'Calm down, Rosie, for God's sake,' Annabel said crossly. 'Of course he isn't. I don't even know if he's got a secretary. But the way you play around, it'd be no more than you deserve if he was.'

Rosie Knighton was a law unto herself. In her early forties, she wrote racy bodice-rippers that sold well, and over the years she had quite deliberately created a media image of herself as an *outré*, uninhibited author willing to do or say anything outrageous. Sometimes Annabel thought Rosie almost believed in her own illusion. It was as if she could no longer distinguish between the reality of her life as a village doctor's wife and the fantasies she wrote about in her books. She even dressed the part – today she was wearing a thigh-skimming black mohair dress, opaque black tights, Doc Martens and a dozen silver bangles clanking halfway up each arm. Why Laurie Knighton tolerated her numerous affairs Annabel had no idea.

Rosie brushed biscuit crumbs off the front of her black mohair. 'Tell me, Annie. Haven't you ever been the least, *tiny* bit tempted to cheat on Patrick?'

77

'Of course I haven't. I love him. Why would I need anybody else?'

Rosie didn't miss Annabel's blush. 'Are you asking me or telling me?'

'I couldn't cheat on him, Rosie. It would destroy him.'

'I hope you mean that.'

Annabel shifted under Rosie's shrewd gaze. 'Of course I do. Why?'

'Because if you don't have Rafe Dussi, sooner or later some woman round here will. I hope you're strong enough to stand by and watch.'

Six

Stevie lay on her back and watched the shadows of the leaves outside her bedroom window dance across the sunlit walls. Sunday morning without a hangover. This had to be a first.

She pushed the heavy sheets and blankets away – she still hadn't got used to life without a duvet – and leaned up on one elbow. It was hard to believe she was really here. Julia would have a fit when she saw her bedroom. It was like something out of one of those expensive hotel guides which had 'Children Are Banned' written in invisible ink across the cover.

Her huge double bed was the best bit. As soon as Annabel had left her to 'freshen up' on her first morning, she'd raced the length of her bedroom and launched herself on to it, nearly braining herself on a supporting beam crossing the room roughly five and a half feet from the floor. For the first time in her life she'd thanked God that she wasn't as tall as Julia, or her mother would be dithering between 'The Lord Is My Shepherd' and 'Jerusalem' now. At the last minute she'd managed to swerve and land on the carved wedding chest at the foot of the bed, bruising her ribs and scattering dried lavender and faded rose petals across the room as she sent a china bowl of pot-pourri flying. She'd been so relieved the bowl hadn't broken and indentured her to the Alexanders for the next sixty years that she'd happily spent the following hour and a half crawling around on the floor picking bits of dead flowers out of the carpet.

After that, she hadn't even dared touch the willow-patterned basin and ewer on the chest of drawers. She'd washed out of her toothbrush mug for two days before she'd discovered the bathroom door, hidden behind the wardrobe which she'd moved when she was picking up the pot-pourri. Not only was there a wonderful deep claw-footed tub in which she'd spent hours wallowing in the best the Body Shop could provide, but a glitzy American power shower that was a far cry from the pathetic dribble she and Julia had shared. She could spit faster than their old shower had been able to produce water.

Her room was at the back of the house; she could see the dew-grey lawns sloping down to the silver birch woods bordering Edenfield Manor, now shrouded in early morning mist. Beyond them, the last soft orange streaks of dawn were being washed away by the early morning sunshine. This was the time she was normally going to bed.

Stevie wriggled forward until her cheek was pressed against the cool glass. From this angle she could just see the Gate House at the end of the sweeping drive, perhaps half a mile away. For all she knew, Rafe might be awake too, looking out of his own bedroom window towards her right now.

Rafe Dussi. She couldn't believe she'd actually met him, let alone sat next to him in his Porsche for sixteen and a half minutes. If only she hadn't wasted most of them. She'd been in a state of shock for the first four, unable even to understand what he was saying, let alone spit out any of the witty replies she'd typically thought of the minute he'd gone. She'd only come to when her oxygen-starved brain had demanded that she breathe again before she turned blue, at which point she'd caught sight of herself in the wing mirror and spent the next seven minutes alternately gasping for air and burning with humiliation that she had to have met this sex god when she looked like Freddie Kruger's mother on a bad hair day.

Eventually she'd managed to summon just enough wit to appreciate the glory of her position, even if her sole contribution to the conversation had been a strangled squeak when he'd asked her if she'd seen yesterday's Grand Prix. Seemingly unaware of her lust-induced laryngitis, Rafe had chatted about the Brazilian race as he'd driven at unbelievable speed along the narrow winding lanes towards Edenfield, clearly under the impression that he was still on the Interlagos circuit. She'd stolen quick, thrilling glances at him as he talked, his excellent English spoken with a sexy Italian accent turning his story about some complicated scandal over petrol – *petrol*? – into the most erotic sweet nothings she'd ever heard. She could have listened to his description of Damon Hill's rear suspension failure for ever as her eyes lingered over the tiny golden hairs on the back of his tanned wrist and the way his dark hair curled at the nape of his neck. She ached to follow it with her fingers, slide her hand beneath the rough cream wool of his fisherman's sweater, to rip his tight black jeans off and fuck his brains out.

She sighed and rolled away from the window. Rafe Dussi didn't even know she existed. He probably smiled that slow, lazy smile at every woman he came across. It must be an Italian thing, like the way he had deliberately held her gaze when he'd helped her out of the car and run his finger lightly down her spine as Annabel had opened the front door.

It was probably just as well she hadn't seen him again since she'd arrived. She had serious work to do on her diet for a start, and anyway, she'd had enough to get her head around once she'd realised that Patrick Alexander was *the* internationally famous Formula One racing driver. Oliver would cream his jeans when he found out.

She closed her eyes, then opened them again. It was no good, she'd never get back to sleep now she'd got herself going over Rafe. She stood up and headed towards the bathroom, turning on the shower and letting it run for a few moments so that the hot water would come through. This was an unbelievable job, but it did take some getting used to. She pulled off her 'Hey Mon No Problem' T-shirt and tested the water with her hand as she considered her new employers. She'd really liked Patrick at the interview, but that was before she'd realised he was famous. She felt a bit scared of him now. He certainly didn't make a big deal of it – he still seemed really kind and thoughtful – but he'd just come second in the bloody Grand Prix, for God's sake. He'd even been on ITN last week. Stevie now felt rather in awe of him.

She wasn't quite sure about Annabel Alexander. She kept calling her Stephanie, for a start. Nicknames and abbreviations were obviously about as popular as polyester and white stilettos in Annabel's household. Stevie had never met anyone so much in control, both of herself and of everything around her. Annabel could switch from organising a dinner party for six-teen to providing quotes on the significance of the change in this season's F1 engine from 3.5 litres to 3000cc with scarcely a pause. She even knew what a cc *was*. She never raised her voice or lost her temper, and she always looked so bloody per-fect. Just when Stevie was feeling quite good about life, having finally got her jeans to zip, her hair to curl under and her con-cealer actually to conceal, Annabel would waft past in some designer outfit looking like she'd just stepped off the cover of *Vogue*, leaving Stevie only too aware of straining buttons and baby puke on her shoulder. The only thing Annabel conspicu-ously lacked was a sense of humour; but then, she didn't have to look at Stevie's reflection in the mirror every morning.

Mrs Arcor hadn't helped bolster her fragile self-esteem either. On Stevie's first afternoon at the Alexanders', the housekeeper had given her a double portion of home-made fruitcake – 'I can tell you're a girl who likes her food, love' – while she'd recounted the trials and tribulations they'd endured with the twins' previous nanny, who had clearly been a cross between Claudia Schiffer and Zuleika Dobson. She'd peppered her recital with many a reference to painted trollops and those who were No Better Than They Ought To Be, concluding with another huge piece of fruitcake and heartfelt expressions of relief that the menfolk of Edenfield would at least be safe with Stevie.

Sunshine was already streaming through the window, illuminating tiny motes of dust in the air and casting golden diamond blocks on to the floor. Stevie curled up in the deep flower-sprigged chintz armchair and towel-dried her hair. It was still only eight o'clock in the morning. She had the whole day to herself. Maybe she'd take Jamie and Lily for a walk in the woods. She had promised, and Jamie had been begging her to come looking for bluebells for days.

She threw aside her towels, pulled on a pair of greying knickers that must have shrunk in the wash – why else were they suddenly two sizes too small? – and opened the wardrobe to get out a pair of clean, freshly ironed black leggings. Annabel complained that Mrs Arcor spent her whole day ironing so that she didn't have to do any real work, but as far as Stevie was concerned, she already owed the housekeeper two boxes of Milk Tray. She yanked the leggings on and pulled a dusky pink sweater over her head, then scrabbled around under the bed for her black Chelsea boots. Jamie had already asked for a pair exactly the same for his sixth birthday. God knew what Annabel would say.

She dragged a comb through her damp hair and left her room, remembering to duck for once as she reached the low beam on the half-landing. Her triumph at being up in what was effectively the middle of the night suddenly faded as she walked into the kitchen and saw Annabel standing at the Aga stirring a home-made casserole, casually chic in worn cream jodhpurs and an ancient hacking jacket. Stevie had lived in Sussex long enough to know that in matters of equestrian sartorial elegance, the older and more dilapidated the better.

'Good morning, Stephanie. I didn't expect to see you up this

83

early on your day off.'

'Oh, I hate to miss too much of the day,' Stevie said brazenly. She hovered self-consciously near the kettle, dying for a cup of tea but unwilling to brave Annabel's disapproval when she saw how she made it. Typhoo One-Cup with milk and sugar was probably social death in this house. 'Anyway, I think Harry's got me into the habit of getting up early. He's been waking up at six all week.'

'Really? He didn't wake up at all last night. He's still asleep now, in fact, so I thought I'd go for a quick ride before I set to in the rose garden.'

Bloody typical, Stevie thought. On the hour every hour when I'm on duty, and I have a night off and the little sod sleeps for twelve hours straight through.

'Did you want a cup of tea, Stephanie? There's a new box of Earl Grey leaves in the store cupboard, I think we must have finished the last one.'

'No, no, I'm fine.'

'Oh, well. I'd better go before it gets too late.'

'Are Jamie and Lily up yet?'

'Oh, yes, of course. They've had breakfast. You're taking them for a walk this morning, aren't you?' Annabel rummaged through the heap of wellington boots near the warm range. 'I brought their boots in to dry them yesterday, they got soaked playing in the garden. James's are the yellow ones, Elizabeth's are red. Don't let them tell you otherwise – James's feet are a fraction bigger and he ends up with blisters if he wears Elizabeth's boots.'

She picked up her riding crop and opened the back door. 'They should be down in a few minutes. If you have any problems, speak to Patrick. I'll see you later.'

As soon as Annabel shut the door, Stevie switched on the kettle and headed for Mrs Arcor's secret store of tea-bags. She opened the kitchen door while she waited for the kettle to boil and stared suspiciously at the watery blue sky. She didn't mind getting wet, she just liked to know, that was all.

'Stevie, Stevie! Can we go now? Can I put my boots on?'

'Can we jump in the puddles?'

'Is it going to rain?'

'Will we find some bluebells?'

'Can I get some conkers?'

Stevie laughed at the eruption of noise behind her. 'Boots, puddles and bluebells yes. I'm afraid you'll have to wait for the conkers, Jamie, they don't come until autumn.'

'When's autumn?'

Lily tossed her blonde curls scornfully. 'September-octobernovember.'

Stevie bent down and waved two KitKats at the twins. 'The first one into their boots gets to choose which one of these they want.'

Jamie giggled. 'That's silly. They're both the same.'

She sipped her tea as she watched the twins sit on the steps and squabble over their boots. What was it Annabel had said, yellow for Lily and red for Jamie? They were twins, so how could they have different-sized feet? They were so alike; Lily wore her golden curls long and was slightly more thoughtful than her rather impulsive brother, but in almost every other respect they were identical. She grinned as she saw them settle the problem by each putting on one red and one yellow wellington. She should lend them to the UN, they could solve a lot of problems.

She handed them each a KitKat and helped them on with their Barbours, then squirmed into her own antique blue cagoule – she had a feeling equestrian reverse chic didn't apply to C&A plastic anoraks – and took one chubby little hand in each of hers as they headed across the lawn towards the birch woods. The air smelt clean, a gentle breeze whipping their coats and lifting their hair, bringing with it the scent of damp earth and leaf mould. They reached the fence encircling the woods and Stevie clambered over the stile, wiping her grimy hands on her leggings before helping the twins wriggle through the bars.

'Mind out for the stinging nettles,' she called as the twins darted off. 'And don't go too far off the path. You don't want to get lost.'

'I seen a squirrel!' Jamie cried. 'Stevie, I seen a squirrel!'

'I saw a squirrel,' Stevie corrected.

'Me too!' Jamie said. 'Do you think he'll come back?'

The twins ran along the path, shrieking and laughing as they pointed out flowers and butterflies. Every so often one of them would run back to her with their latest find, pressing funny-shaped stones and wet, bent daffodils into her hands for her to save before dashing off to discover something else. The path grew more overgrown and muddy as they moved deeper into the wood, layers of wet leaves covering the forest floor and muffling the sound of rainwater dripping off the trees. It was darker and cooler here, the birches so close together in places that few bars of watery April sunshine were able to penetrate the gloom to dapple the path in front of them. Several times Stevie had to hold back brambles or stinging nettles for the twins to pass, leaping quickly out of the way herself as she let go and they sprang back into place.

She had to jog to keep up with the twins as they raced away, her feet squelching in the mulch covering the path. She paused for a moment to catch her breath and looked behind her, shocked at how different the wood seemed viewed from the opposite direction. Other paths she hadn't seen on the way into the wood were suddenly visible from this angle, so that it was difficult to be sure which track was the one they'd followed here. She hoped they were going to be able to find their way back OK. They'd already been walking for an hour, and a fine mist of rain had started to fall again. The last thing she needed was for them to get lost.

'Stevie, Stevie, we found a princess!' The twins came running back.

'Where? In a castle?'

'No, a wicked king had tied her to a tree and wouldn't let her go,' Jamie said. 'He cast spells on her to make her love him but she didn't.'

'I want to be a princess,' Lily said.

'I'm going to shoot you! Ack-ack-ack-ack! Ack-ack-ack-ack!'

Lily started to cry. 'I'm not dead! Stevie, tell him I'm not dead.'

'Of course you aren't dead, Lily, Jamie was only pretending.' Stevie reached up and helped him climb down off a fallen birch tree. 'Come on, Jamie. It's time to go back.'

She took one of the twins' hands in each of hers and glanced around to get her bearings. The path had almost disappeared here. The air felt cold and smelt of rotting leaves; the foliage was so dense that in places the sheltered track was still dry. They were standing near the top of an incline; ahead of them, the path dipped down into the forest and then rose again, climbing a hill. It seemed much clearer on the other side of the dip. She decided it would be easier to go forward and try to circle back to Edenfield Manor rather than fight their way back through the nettles and brambles. She started to walk forward.

'Hey, you! Stop!'

Stevie looked up, startled. Twenty feet ahead of her, on the facing slope, a man dressed in a Barbour and mud-spattered boots stood straddling the path, a shotgun breeched over his forearm. An Irish wolfhound stood guard behind him. 'Don't come any further!'

'We were only walking –'

'This is private land! You're trespassing!'

Stevie bridled as the twins cowered behind her. 'Look, I'm sorry, I didn't see any signs.'

'How many times do I have to tell you? Just get back.'

'I don't think you have to be so unpleasant. They're only children –'

'So teach them some manners.'

You could do with learning a few yourself, Stevie thought angrily. She stood her ground for a moment, grappling with a strange feeling that she'd seen this man before. He was too far away for her to be certain, but he seemed younger than she'd first thought, maybe mid-thirties. He was soaking wet from the rain, his dark hair slicked back against his head, rivulets of water running down his face and gathering in small pools in the wrinkles of his waxed jacket. She realised it was raining hard and that she and the twins were getting extremely wet.

'Come on. Let's get back home before we catch our death of cold.' She pushed the twins ahead of her. 'As soon as we get home we can have some hot chocolate and some of Mrs Arcor's cake.'

She glanced briefly over her shoulder as they left to see if the man was still there. Again she felt that same sense of uneasy familiarity as she met his unsmiling gaze. She *had* seen him somewhere before, she was certain of it. She just hoped she didn't ever have to see him again.

'D'you think they saw us?'

Rosie Knighton giggled. 'I'm sure they did. We've probably given them a complex for life.'

Martin Romaine ran his hand along her collarbone and down between her bare breasts, smiling with satisfaction as her dark nipples quivered beneath his touch. 'You're enough to give any man a complex.'

Rosie squirmed against the trunk of the silver birch to which he'd tied her, as the rope he'd used to bind her wrists behind her back dug into her flesh. She was completely naked, her legs splayed slightly apart, her arms wrenched round behind the tree, unable to do more than move her head a few degrees either side to follow him as he circled around her. She felt vulnerable and exposed and incredibly aroused. Even though they hadn't recognised her, seeing the children peering at her through the bushes had heightened the delicious fear of discovery to an almost unbearable erotic pitch. She arched her back towards Martin, straining against her bonds, her full breasts jutting towards him as if to tempt him to drink.

Martin stood naked in front of her, stroking his erection, his eyes riveted to the dark tangle of hair at the top of her thighs. 'Is this what you want?'

'*For Christ's sake*, Marty.'

He smiled, then planted his hands on either side of her head and kissed her mouth, firmly closing his own as she tried to slide her tongue between his lips. His kisses were chaste, delicate, deliberately frustrating. He could smell her need, feel the tension in her body as she undulated against him. He held himself away from her so that the only part of his body touching hers was his mouth, that touch so delicate she could scarcely be certain it was there.

He broke their kiss and dodged out of her range behind the silver birch. She heard the rustle of leaves as he knelt on the ground and took the little finger of her bound left hand in his mouth. His tongue described circles around and around the first joint, licking the fold of skin between her little finger and its neighbour before returning back to suck the tip. She felt as if that finger was connected to her cunt and every time he sucked it her whole body vibrated with need. He took another finger in his mouth and then another. Her hands had become an erogenous zone, her skin flaming as his lips moved past the rough hemp he'd tied her with and along the underside of her arm. She felt her knees buckle, but her bonds held her rigid against the tree. She felt as if she'd explode if he didn't fuck her within the next thirty seconds. Who would have imagined Martin Romaine could be such an exciting lover? He'd always seemed so quiet and unassuming, his smooth round face and white-blond curls reminding her more of a Renaissance cherub than a Formula One test driver.

She'd seen him hundreds of times, of course, he'd hung

89

around Edenfield Manor messing about with Patrick's cars ever since he'd left school, but until he'd stopped by the surgery this morning to collect his repeat hay fever prescription she'd barely noticed him. Laurie had been called away to deal with a case of acute peritonitis, and she'd put her hand on Martin's knee more because she was bored and to see what he'd do than for any other reason. She certainly hadn't expected him to push her back against the sofa, unfasten her lace bra and slip his hand up beneath her tight skirt and black silk panties in one deft movement. Just as she'd been about to throw caution to the winds and fuck him there and then in Laurie's waiting room without even bothering to lock the door, he'd stood up, grabbed her hand and pulled her outside to his battered old VW beetle. Fifteen minutes later she'd been standing naked tied to a silver birch tree in the middle of the woods in broad daylight on a Sunday morning.

She was so hot for him now she'd have fucked him if the entire church choir had been with them watching. She stared at his cock, her cunt twingeing with excitement. A splash of water from the branches above her landed on her left breast and she couldn't suppress a throaty groan.

'Jesus, Martin.'

Without even realising what she was doing, she spread her legs wider and tilted her hips upward, offering herself to him. He could see her arousal glistening on the inside of her thighs, her whole body trembling with need. He stood between her legs, his cock one desperate millimetre away from her skin, his pale body motionless as she strained forward. He'd known he was going to fuck her the moment he'd walked into the waiting room that morning. He knew all about Rosie Knighton. Even if he hadn't been aware of her reputation in the village, he'd seen the same look of cupidity on his mother's face every time she'd taken a new lover. Now he was the one in control, and he was going to make her beg for it.

He bent his head and took her nipple between his teeth, bit-ing her just hard enough to make her gasp without giving her so much pain that he broke the spell of lust. His fingers sought the cleft between her buttocks and he pulled them apart, his body rock hard as she lifted her legs and twined them around his waist. He found her clitoris with his thumbs so that she bucked against him.

'Marty, untie me, for God's sake,' Rosie panted. 'I can't stand any more of this.'

His thumbs stopped moving.

'Oh, God, don't stop, please don't stop!'

He shoved her back against the tree, ignoring her whimper of pain as the bark dug into her bare skin. Wrenching her legs away from his waist, he stepped back and tilted her chin up so that his grey eyes met her angry black gaze.

'If you move or make a single sound, I'm just going to walk away from here and leave you,' he said quietly. 'If you're very, very good, I might give you what you want. But only if I want to. Do you understand, Mrs Knighton?'

'You *bastard*.'

Martin picked up the neat pile of clothes protected from the rain beneath his yellow anorak and started to put on his shirt. 'I wonder how long it'll be before they find you,' he said conversationally, reaching for his jeans. 'Maybe if you really yell those kids will hear you and come back. But then again, maybe they won't.'

Rosie watched him for a moment longer, desire fighting with humiliation and anger. It was an unequal battle. 'OK, OK. Whatever you want.'

'You mean you'll do anything to get me to fuck you?'

She nodded, her cheeks burning.

'Say it.'

'I want you to fuck me, OK? I want you to fuck me so bloody much I don't care if you bring the whole village along to watch.'

Without bothering to remove his shirt, he strode back towards her and knelt between her thighs. 'If you move, if you say anything, I shall just walk away.'

Gently he parted her legs and slipped his tongue between her lips, licking her clitoris with quick, darting movements. He could feel the tension stiffening her body as she forced herself to remain motionless. He sucked her softly, his hands reaching up towards her breasts as he cupped them in his hands, rolling her engorged nipples between his thumbs and forefingers as he drank her juices. Slowly he stood up, his lips trailing sticky kisses across her stomach as he moved, his cock just brushing against the inside of her thighs. When he was finally upright, he positioned himself at the entrance to her cunt, feeling her muscles opening around him, desperate to yield.

'Any time I want, I can have you,' he murmured in her ear. 'Any time. Say it.'

'Yes. Any time,' Rosie whispered.

'Any time, any place, anywhere.'

She moaned as he slid himself an inch inside her. 'Yes, yes. Any time, any place, anywhere.'

'You hot bitch,' Martin whispered. 'I could take you right now in front of your husband, couldn't I?

'Oh, yes, oh yes, oh yes!'

Another inch. 'You don't care who's watching, you don't care who else I fuck.'

'No! I don't care.'

'Tell me I can fuck your daughter.'

Her eyes flashed open. *Portia*? She's only a child!'

'She's sixteen. She's nearer my age than you are, Mrs Knighton. Tell me I can fuck her.'

'No!'

He started to pull out of her. Rosie moaned and writhed against the ropes, desperately trying to hold him inside her.

'Tell me I can fuck your daughter.'

'Yes! Yes! Anyone! Please, Martin, don't stop!'

He laughed. He didn't give a damn about her daughter, he'd never even met her, but he knew Rosie did. He had her. He was in control. He smiled as he started to fuck her hard against the silver birch. Even the thrill of racing didn't match up to this.

Martin could still taste the doctor's wife on his tongue an hour later as he walked into Nigel Purvis's study for the Terroni team meeting. He pulled out a black vinyl chair and sat down, savouring the ache in his thighs. She was a faithless, amoral bitch, but she knew how to fuck. He was already looking forward to repeating the experience.

'You're late.'

'Nigel, there's no one else here yet.'

'Yes, well.' Nigel removed a noxious-looking cheroot from between his thin lips and gestured towards the chrome and Perspex clock on the wall. 'I would have thought punctuality is a common courtesy whatever the circumstances.'

Lillian, Nigel's wife, stuck her head round the door. 'Hello, Martin. Can I get you a cup of tea?'

'Thanks.'

'For heaven's sake, Lillian,' Nigel snapped. 'Wait until everyone is here. I don't want you flapping in and out with tea and biscuits all afternoon.'

Martin felt an intense wave of dislike for the other man as his wife fled from the room. Nigel Purvis was an obnoxious, opinionated bastard. Unfortunately, he was also the senior marketing executive with Quisling Mild, the cigarette company who sponsored the Terroni team, and as such he pulled all their strings. Without Quisling's money, there would be no Formula One team. Much as Martin might want to punch Nigel on the nose, it would be professional suicide. He was only a test driver now, driving prototype cars round an empty circuit whilst the engineering boffins took notes on its performance, but sooner or later he'd break into Formula One himself and need sponsorship. In motor racing these days it wasn't how you drove that mattered, but whose logo was on your underpants when you took a piss afterwards.

Nigel eased his tall frame from behind the glass slab he used as a desk and paced towards the window, twitching the red velour curtains to one side to peer out into the street like a paid-up member of Neighbourhood Watch. Martin dropped his gaze to the orange floral swirls on the carpet. How on earth had Nigel managed to turn his study into such a revolting mix of Seventies kitsch and sterile Eighties modernism? Lava lamps jostled for space with steel-balls-on-string executive toys, a heap of battered LPs in torn paper covers were shoved on top of a glossy black CD system that made the cockpit of Concorde look like a *Blue Peter* bog-roll-and-sticky-backed-plastic creation, and just the existence of the lurid purple sofa made it guilty of harassment.

Nigel was a pretty revolting mix himself, Martin decided. He was a bit like one of those middle-aged women who still stuck to the hairstyle and make-up they'd had when they were young and attractive – he dressed like a yuppie, complete with red braces and Filofax, though he had to be pushing forty by now. His dirty-blond hair was swept back from a receding hairline and just brushed the edge of his white-collared blue shirt, neither short nor long. His narrow face was as sharp as his baggy designer knock-off suit, his grey eyes cold and humourless. He had an irritating habit of shooting his cuffs to reveal flashy amethyst cufflinks and a chunky fake gold Rolex he'd probably picked up somewhere like Thailand or Hong Kong. Martin bet he'd never been further than the brochure of the Old School whose tie he was currently sporting, either. The only genuine thing about Nigel Purvis was his vicious temper.

'Patrick, Rafe, at last. Trouble finding the way?' Nigel said peevishly. His four-bedroomed redbrick was less than a mile from Edenfield bloody Manor, he saw it every time he looked out of his white-netted bathroom window. You'd have thought Patrick, at least, could make it on time.

'Annabel was late. The Vintner cast a shoe up on the Downs, she had to walk him home,' Patrick said. 'It's our

94

nanny's day off, so I had to hold the fort. Sorry, Nigel.'

'I don't suppose you know if anyone else is bothering to turn up?'

'No idea about Humphrey. Tammy can't make it, she's working on the set-up with the mechanics this afternoon. Terroni want a full report on the monocoque problem before they'll commit themselves to any changes.'

'Tammy's our race manager,' Nigel said petulantly. 'She's supposed to be here.'

'She will be more useful at the workshop,' Rafe said. 'If she needs to know anything else, Patrick and I can tell her later.'

Nigel ignored the young Italian. He disliked all the racing drivers on the Terroni team on principle for being richer, more famous and better-looking than he was, but he reserved his most bitter hatred for Rafe Dussi. The little shit had had everything handed to him on a golden plate. Emmanuele Terroni himself had insisted that Dussi be part of their team this season, and the worst of it was, when the fucker was on form he was better than anyone on the grid. He knew it, too. He flaunted his youth and success in Nigel's face, dangling an ever-changing string of beautiful women under his nose as if he were some kind of superstud. At least Martin and Patrick had the grace to keep a low profile. Nigel burned as he watched Rafe throw himself into the purple sofa, his body lithe and muscular beneath a white T-shirt and tight black Levis. Rafe Dussi thought he was God's bloody gift. Well, he only had to make one mistake – *one* – and he'd have him, he'd have the bastard.

The door opened again. 'Nigel, sorry I'm late. I had terrible trouble getting here, you wouldn't believe –'

Nigel turned the full force of his venom on the hapless newcomer. 'Where the fuck have you been, Humphrey?'

Humphrey Prince, Patrick and Rafe's new sponsorship agent, visibly trembled. 'I'm so sorry, but you see, Susan had to take the car to get Edmund to his violin lesson, and I was supposed to be getting a lift from Rosie Knighton, but for some reason she didn't answer her phone, so then I tried the Hamiltons, but Sheila's in Yugoslavia and Freddie doesn't drive, and Patrick must have already left –'

'For God's sake, Humphrey,' Nigel exploded.

'Oh, sorry, am I going on?' Humphrey said. 'What a nice sofa, Nigel. Susan wanted a brown leather one, but I said to her –'

'Look, can we get on with things?' Nigel demanded. 'We haven't got all day.'

'Cusack isn't here yet,' Martin pointed out.

'Oh. Yes. So he isn't.'

Martin suppressed a smile. Nigel was as transparent as that piece of glass under his elbows. The only reason he gave Charles Lytton, manager of the team, the time of day was because he was also – according to his current entry in *Debrett's People of Today* – the 7th Earl of Cusack, 9th Baronet, Viscount of Lytton, Lord Edenfield and Gore, Baron Cusack and Baron Lingbridge, son of the 6th Earl of Cusack, KT, DSO, MC, and the Hon. Dame Eleanor, née Bower, DBE, JP, daughter of the 3rd Baron Rosedale. Nigel was a sucker for a title. His self-abasement in front of Cusack was almost as revolting as the way he treated his wife Lillian.

'Well, we'd better give him five minutes as he is the team manager. Lillian!' Nigel scowled as his wife appeared in the doorway. 'Aren't you going to offer anyone tea or coffee? Do I have to do everything myself?'

'I thought you said you wanted me to wait until everyone was here, dear –'

'Listen to her. She thinks the whole restaurant has to be full before she serves a table. Tea, Lillian. And get a move on, we're all dying of thirst.'

Charles Cusack walked into the room and threw his mud-spattered Barbour over the back of a chair as Lillian scuttled away. 'Do you have to be so fucking rude to your wife, Nigel?' he asked.

'There speaks a man who has never married,' Nigel said, forcing a stillborn laugh.

'I wouldn't talk to a marketing executive the way you talk to Lillian,' Cusack said.

There was an embarrassed silence. Rafe and Patrick looked away. Neither of them liked Nigel, but it was painful to watch him squirm on the other end of Cusack's cold blue stare. Martin returned his gaze to the garish carpet, lost in his own world. Only Humphrey had the grace to laugh as if Cusack had been joking.

'Yes, well, let's make a start, shall we?' Nigel said at last. 'Now, if we're all here –'

'Forget the roll call,' Cusack said. 'First of all, I think Patrick and Rafe should be congratulated for both making the points in Sunday's race. It gives us an excellent shot at the Constructors' Championship, quite apart from the individual –'

'Um.' Humphrey put up his hand like a child in class. 'Excuse me, Your Lordship –'

Cusack winced. 'Just Cusack will do.'

'Oh, yes, of course. I'm sorry to interrupt, your – Cusack, but what do you mean exactly, "making the points"?'

'Forgive me, Humphrey,' Cusack drawled. 'I was assuming that as a sponsorship agent for two racing drivers, you were acquainted with the basic principles of Formula One. Clearly I was being over-optimistic.'

'I only took over this account on Tuesday,' Humphrey whined. 'I was happy with looking after quiz show hosts, I didn't get asked if I wanted to be moved to sport. They only did it because Gary's still in the clinic and I live here. Susan doesn't like sport. She says it'll make me rough and brutal. I'm not even allowed to watch Wimbledon in case I get carried away.'

Martin tried and failed to imagine this eventuality.

'I suppose a copy of *Motor Sport* isn't allowed to cross the threshold either?' Cusack asked drily.

'Oh, no. She even takes off the back pages of the *Daily Mail* because of the sport,' Humphrey said. 'It's a bit annoying because they're joined to the front pages, so I always have to start on page seven –'

'For God's sake, Humphrey, Cusack doesn't want chapter and verse,' Nigel exclaimed.

'Somebody tell him and put him out of his misery,' Cusack said.

'The Grand Prix championship is determined on points Humphrey,' Martin explained, talking slowly and clearly. 'There are seventeen Grand Prix this season at various tracks across the world instead of the usual sixteen. The top six drivers in each race get awarded points – ten for first place, six for second, four for third, three for fourth, two for fifth and one for sixth. The rest don't get any. Whoever has the most points at the end of the last race wins.'

'If we can end the elementary maths lesson, I think the only thing we really need to discuss today is Patrick's monocoque problem,' Cusack said. 'Rafe, if you're happy with the rest of your set-up –'

Humphrey raised his hand. 'Um –?'

'The monocoque is the cockpit. The set-up is the way a car is put together,' Martin said before Charles could bollock Humphrey again. 'You see, a Formula One car isn't like your average Fiat Panda. It doesn't get built on an assembly line and stay built like that until it falls apart. There are computers on board a Grand Prix car that record and assess every single aspect of its performance during the race. Based on that assessment, and the testing I do, the mechanics take the car apart at the end of each race to try and improve on it for the next one. Twisting a nut ten degrees can make a difference of half a second. That could be the difference between first and second place on a Grand Prix circuit.'

'Er, Cusack, if I *could* intervene?' Nigel said.

'Please, be my guest. What was it you wanted to know? How many cars on the grid? How many drivers in each team?'

98

'Twenty-six and two,' Martin whispered.

'No, no, it's nothing like that,' Nigel laughed matily. 'It's just that we have a little problem with Patrick's collar. He is supposed to wear it done up when he's interviewed so that you can read Quisling Mild properly. On Sunday, all you could see was Qu-ild. After all, we are paying him half a million pounds a year to do it properly.'

Cusack shot Patrick a warning glance. Neither man enjoyed having to subscribe to the logo-for-cash brigade, but they had no choice. No car manufacturers – including Terroni – could afford to finance a Formula One motor-racing team alone; they had to find sponsors to spread the cost. Patrick's contract with Terroni obliged him not only to race, but to parade in front of the cameras wearing whichever borrowed feathers Terroni chose – he wore a Quisling Mild baseball cap before a race, a Goodyear one afterwards, he had Pioneer on his collar, Agip on his breast pocket. Two hours before a race, he might have to shoot a promotional video for Sony; ten minutes after one, he could be doing an ad with Canon. He'd been in Formula One for more than a decade, and it got worse every year.

'OK, Nigel,' Cusack said tersely. 'Patrick, let's talk about the monocoque problem.'

'If you recall, I told you at Christmas that the new chassis was a little snug,' Patrick said. 'When I tried it again at Estoril during the pre-season test, I said it would take more than a quick fix to get it right.'

'You did come second in Brazil, Patrick,' Nigel intervened. 'It can't have been that bad.'

'When the adrenalin is pumping and your mind is focused on what you're doing, you don't notice the full extent of the discomfort,' Patrick said irritably. 'I could hardly bloody walk on Monday. The monocoque is too small, Nigel. That's all there is to it.'

'That's what comes of having a woman as race manager,' Nigel muttered. 'I knew we should've hired a man.'

'Tammy has nothing to do with this,' Patrick argued. 'She's a first-rate mechanic. This is a design problem, not a question of logistics.'

'If the panel modification didn't work, there's only one solution. We'll have to redesign the monocoque from scratch,' Cusack said.

'You can't do that!' Nigel gasped. 'Quite apart from the cost, the public will think we're all incompetent. What will that kind of image do for Quisling Mild?'

'We can't alter the existing design without compromising its structural integrity,' Cusack said. 'I'm not putting Patrick's life at risk with a botched rebuild.'

Automatically Patrick's hand went to the left side of his face and across the lattice of tiny raised scars. He could almost smell the petrol, feel the heat scorching his skin. At night when he closed his eyes, he never knew which nightmare would come to haunt him: whether he would be three years old or twenty-nine, watching his father desperately trying to wrest the wheel back towards the road, or taking the corner at Monte Carlo too fast and careering out of control towards the crowd. His earliest memory was of unimaginable terror; instead of love, fear – nameless, unreasoning – had become the backbone of his childhood. It infected every aspect of his life so that there had never been a moment when he was unafraid. He'd learned to know it in all its forms: the nagging doubt, the crawling churn of concern, the paralysing terror that petrified his limbs and left his body drenched in sweat. It had become a presence so constant he could no longer live without it. He understood fear. He lived with it by challenging it, again and again; every time he conquered it, he felt as if his existence was vindicated. He couldn't imagine how he would live if he couldn't race. What had happened to Charles Cusack was his biggest fear of all.

'I want to know who's responsible for this fuck-up,' Nigel demanded, breaking into Patrick's thoughts.

'It's no one's fault,' Martin said. 'You're talking about tiny dimensions here. There's no point starting a witch hunt.'

'You're the test driver,' Nigel snarled. 'You should've found this out before now.'

'I test the car's performance. I can't test the way it fits another driver any more than I can test a condom for him. It either fits or it doesn't.'

'Terroni are already mapping out a new monocoque,' Cusack said, unrolling a sheaf of shiny papers. 'They faxed this across this morning. Patrick?'

Patrick forced himself to concentrate. 'At the moment there's not enough room to work the wheel and it's too tight on my hip-bones. The bottom line is that the chassis needs to be about 20 millimetres wider.'

'I think we can get the new monocoque completed by the time we get to Monaco in May,' Cusack said. 'But you've got three races between now and then.'

Patrick bit his lip. 'I can't not race. I'll just have to live with it.'

'Let me see,' Martin said.

Excluded from the inner circle, Rafe watched them for a moment, then stood up to open the door in response to the rattle of china on the other side. Lillian edged sideways through the doorway bearing a large wooden tray laden with cups and saucers.

Rafe had come fifth in the first Grand Prix of the season, placing him just four points behind Patrick with sixteen races to go. Patrick would be fighting a losing battle for the next three, maybe longer if the monocoque problem continued. Rafe liked and respected the older driver – he particularly liked his wife – but it wouldn't do him any harm to build up a good lead over Terroni's Number One driver while he had the chance.

Not if he meant to have that position himself by the end of the season.

Seven

Stevie had forgotten quite how exhausting a three-week-old baby could be. She tiptoed out of Harry's nursery, closed the door and slumped against it. The little swine had been awake all night for no reason that she could fathom other than to knacker her so thoroughly she'd never look at another man again. First he'd puked all down his nightgown – Annabel would no more put her child in a Mothercare babygro than wear one herself – then he'd puked all over her T-shirt, then he'd puked all down his clean nightgown again. She'd had to change Harry's terry nappy – no Pampers, what a surprise – twice, which meant two more nightgowns because she still hadn't mastered the art of pinning the sodding thing on before he peed in a neat golden arc all over everywhere.

As she dumped the four dirty nightgowns into the laundry basket in the children's bathroom, she caught sight of herself in the mirror. Well, didn't she look gorgeous this morning. Those attractive black bags underneath her eyes really offset her red eyeballs nicely. It was amazing how well they matched her dark roots, which were growing through so fast she looked like one of those two-tone rocket ice-lollies. Jamie was right, the zits on her chin *did* look like an aeroplane with wobbly wings, particularly now he'd joined them with his blue felt-tip like the dot-to-dots in his colouring book. But it was the seductive little pink winceyette number and orange woolly bed-socks that really did it. Move over Linda and Naomi, Stevie Colvin has arrived.

'Oh, my Lord, Stevie. What happened to you?'

Stevie shuffled into the kitchen and warmed her bottom on the Aga. 'Don't ask.'

Mrs Arcor immediately went into crisis mode, whipping a psychedelic green-and-purple knitted teacosy off the teapot and pouring Stevie a steaming mug of tea so strong you could tan leather in it. Stevie watched helplessly as Mrs Arcor added four generous spoonfuls of sugar and stirred. Clearly the housekeeper was of the kill or cure school.

She sat down and pulled the chipped mug towards her. 'I don't think Harry ever sleeps, at least not when I'm on duty,' she said. 'I don't know where he gets the energy. I'm knackered, and it's only Tuesday morning.'

'It won't last long, love. You try getting a teenager out of bed and you'll see what I mean.' Mrs Arcor opened two new packets of Annabel's Hobnobs and shamelessly emptied them into the staff biscuit tin. 'That baby will be going straight through the night the minute he goes on to solids.'

'Oh, yes please, God! When do I break open the Weetabix?'

'Soon as he's twelve pounds or twelve weeks, that's what we always did.'

Stevie buried her head in her arms. 'Oh, well, that's it then. Annabel weighs him in kilograms.'

Mrs Arcor pointedly ignored the silver polish and clean yellow cloth Annabel had left out on the kitchen table and disappeared into the scullery to fetch the ironing board. 'You should go out more, that's your trouble,' she called over her shoulder. 'It'd pick you up a bit, give you something to look forward to. You've been here two weeks and I still haven't seen your young man –?'

Stevie smiled despite herself. 'I didn't say I had one, Mrs Arcor.'

'Oh, dear. Well, never mind, there's someone for everyone,

love, don't you worry. Beauty is in the eye of the beholder, so they say. It's what's inside that matters.'

Thanks a bunch, Stevie thought. The housekeeper had clearly discounted the remote possibility that any man might actually fancy her, relegating her to the not-exactly-an-oil-painting division whose only hope of marital success lay in their mastery of flaky pastry and bread-and-butter pudding.

Mrs Arcor hauled the ironing board back into the kitchen, her purple Crimplene trousers stretched to breaking point across her huge bottom as she reversed out of the dusty scullery. Stevie glanced briefly at the vast expanse of white bristly leg between orange bedsock and pink winceyette and wondered how long it would take her to learn to make treacle pudding and custard.

'Ooof, this blessed thing.' Mrs Arcor's tight blue curls frizzed even tighter around her shiny pink face as she wrestled with the ironing board. 'I keep telling Mrs Alexander to get a new one. It was Mrs Elizabeth as bought this, and she's been dead thirty years.'

Mrs Arcor upended the board and Stevie stood on it, clinging to the kitchen door-handle for support as the housekeeper struggled to pull out the rusty iron legs. 'I don't know how you've managed with it this long,' Stevie grumbled.

'Practice, love,' Mrs Arcor panted. 'It's been a few years.'

'How many?'

'More than I care to remember.' She pressed her hand into the aching small of her back as she straightened up to catch her breath. 'Lord, it must be nearly fifty years now. It don't seem yesterday me mum sent me up here for the job of kitchen maid. Terrified of me own shadow, I was. Of course, things was very different here then. Old Mr Alexander – that's Mr Patrick's grandfather as died – he kept a good house. Not like today, though I dare say Mrs Annabel does her best.' She sniffed eloquently. 'Three gardeners we had in them days, proper gardeners, not flowery bits like that young Peter from London

– you've not met him yet, love, you'll see what I mean – and a housekeeper and cook and two maids as well as me. There was a nanny for Mr James, too, though old Mr Alexander got rid of her after he sent the lad off to boarding-school. It broke his heart when he came back and found she'd gone.'

Stevie had a sudden image of her Jack wandering alone through long empty corridors, unable to understand why his nanny didn't come when he called, why there were no warm arms to scoop him up when he fell and cut his knee, no reassuring kisses when he awoke from a nightmare in the middle of the night. Her heart ached for that lonely little boy.

'I don't mean to be ungrateful, love, but are you going to stand on that ironing board all day?' Mrs Arcor gave the legs a yank as Stevie pulled, grunting with satisfaction as they finally slid into place. 'There we are, it's a knack.' She stepped over the bucket and mop Annabel had thoughtfully left by the sink and arranged an embroidered white pillowcase over the ironing board. 'Mr Patrick was different from his father, more able to cope, somehow. He was never scared of old Mr Alexander, for a start. He always knew what he wanted, though he never made no song and dance about it. He just went out and got it.' She smiled reminiscently. 'The times he'd sneak in here after he'd been out to them go-cart races with old Lord Cusack's son. They was of an age, them two, got into mischief like you wouldn't believe. Old Mr Alexander would've had a heart attack if he knew.'

'I can't imagine him getting into mischief,' Stevie said. 'He seems so calm and sensible –'

'Oh, yes, very sensible to go charging round in a circle at hundreds of miles an hour with all them foreign drivers, I don't think.' Mrs Arcor shook her head. 'He's a strange one, all right. He was the same as a boy. Most of the time he was cool as you'd like, nothing much seemed to reach him. But if you crossed him, there was fireworks like you've never seen –' She broke off abruptly as Annabel entered the kitchen, her arms full of freshly cut flowers from the garden. She ran cold water into the sink and stood the flowers in it. 'Mrs Arcor, do you really have to do the ironing *again*?'

'I take too much upon myself, Mrs Alexander, I know that, but I take a pride in my work. I don't mind doing a bit extra where it's needed, never have, you know that.'

'That's not quite what I – oh, never mind.' Annabel deftly arranged the flowers in an elegant Nick Munro glass vase while she talked, each bloom perfectly placed. Stevie bet the damn woman could juggle too. 'Stephanie, I have to spend the day in London now; my fitting with Caroline Charles has been changed to 2.15 this afternoon. Would you mind picking up the twins from school? I'll never be back by 3.30.' She glanced at her watch. 'I must dash if I'm to catch my train. Mrs Arcor, if you could just check the state of the silver, we have a dinner party on Friday. Stephanie, the laundry basket in the children's bathroom is a little full.'

Mrs Arcor waited until Annabel had gone, then settled herself comfortably at the kitchen table and pulled the teapot towards her. 'She does too much, that one. Never get nowhere by rushing all the time.'

Stevie decided Mrs Arcor was a woman after her own heart. She pushed her mug across the table for a refill and frowned with concentration as she opened the biscuit tin and tried to decide between a Hobnob and a chocolate digestive.

'Excuse me?'

They both jumped guiltily as a willowy blonde girl dressed in cream trousers and a tailored navy jacket stuck her head around the back door. 'Is this Edenfield Manor?'

'Who might be asking?' Mrs Arcor said warily.

The girl held out her hand. 'Christie Bradley. I'm the reporter with INN.' She looked from one blank face to the other. 'International News Network? I'm here to interview Patrick Alexander. My crew should be along in a bit, they had to stop off to get some wide shots of the house.'

'You'd better see if Mrs Alexander's left yet on your way upstairs,' Mrs Arcor whispered loudly.

Stevie suddenly realised she was still in her nightie. 'Oh, God. Yes, yes, of course.' She glanced once more at the blonde girl, who had already earned Mrs Arcor's undying gratitude by providing an unimpeachable blue-chip excuse to avoid the washing up. Stevie recognised her now. She was only about twenty-nine but she was already mega-famous, Stevie had seen her on the late news standing in shell-holes and bomb craters everywhere, from Sarajevo to Somalia.

Stevie opened the front door just in time to see Annabel's shiny new Range Rover disappear down the drive. Bugger it, she'd have to go and find Patrick herself. That meant she'd have to get dressed first, she didn't want him thinking she was trying to seduce him in her saucy little winceyette number. She ran upstairs to her bedroom and yanked on the first pair of leggings and sweatshirt she could find. Gianni Versace didn't have a problem with shocking pink and traffic-cone orange, so she wasn't going to worry about it.

'Mr Alexander?' Stevie called, poking her head round the Alexanders' bedroom door and modestly averting her gaze from the bed. 'There's a television crew here.'

'Shit, I'd forgotten about them,' Patrick yelled from the bathroom. 'Could you tell them to set up in the drawing room? I'll be down in five minutes.'

By the time Stevie returned to the kitchen, the camera crew had arrived and were happily ensconced around the table with big slabs of Mrs Arcor's home-made fruitcake in their hands. The housekeeper had abandoned any pretence of working as she handed out pint mugs of stewed tea with the air of one who has been through the Blitz and is Ready For Anything. The crew stood up as Stevie entered, not so much out of politeness as disbelief.

'You do look a bit luminous, love,' Mrs Arcor said, awed.

'I'm volunteering for Sarajevo next time,' Mickey, the

107

cameraman, grumbled. 'You get danger money there.'

Christie put her mug down. 'OK, guys. Time to work.'

Stevie led them towards the drawing room and stood back as they all trooped in. She loved this room. It was part of the west wing of the house that had been added to the original Tudor timber-framed building in the late seventeenth century, following the Restoration of Charles II – local legend held that the work had been paid for by the King himself in return for favours rendered by the lady of the house. The room was bright and high-ceilinged, pale April sunshine filtering through the french windows. The walls were covered in lemon silk that had faded to a soft, creamy primrose with the passage of time, the sofa and armchairs upholstered in a pale yellow fabric that brought out the warmth of the deep stone fireplace. Family photographs in silver frames stood on several delicate walnut marquetry occasional tables. The scent of Annabel's freshly cut flowers mingled with the woody, spicy smell of pine logs in a wicker basket by the fireplace.

Christie swung round to face Stevie, her gold bobbed hair swishing softly against her nauseatingly flawless chin. 'Great. The light's perfect.'

Stevie watched enthralled as the two men carted three huge silver boxes into the room, unrolling armfuls of cables and shifting furniture that probably hadn't been moved since the reign of Queen Anne, and certainly not during the reign of Mrs Arcor. This was television in the making. She'd never realised it was so complicated. She'd always assumed you just pointed a camera and asked a few questions, but everyone here seemed to be taking it terribly seriously. Christie perched on the basket of logs and scribbled in a notebook. The crew erected two six-foot-high spindly lights on either side of the cream armchair Christie had selected for the interview, switching them on and flooding the area with bright white light.

Mickey balanced his camera on top of a tripod and bent his tall frame to check the shot. 'Mind standing in for a minute?'

108

Trying to look as if she did this sort of thing every day, Stevie picked her way carefully over the cables Andy was gaffer-taping to the floor – Annabel would have a fit when she saw what they'd done to her french polish – and sat down. She tilted her chin and tried to look mysterious.

'You'll have to shift the flowers on that table thing, Christie. They look like they're growing right out of her head. Can I have a white balance?'

Christie held a clean page of her notebook in front of the camera and Mickey fiddled for twenty seconds, then gave Christie a quick thumbs-up.

Stevie reluctantly stood up, eyeing the wall socket where a cluster of plugs and adaptors were piled crazily on top of each other like distressed Lego. She just hoped they didn't burn the place down. Annabel would be sure to think she was at the bottom of it.

Patrick walked in wearing a faded denim shirt and jeans, his hair still damp from the shower. 'Sorry to keep you,' he said, shaking hands with Christie. 'I only just flew in from Argentina yesterday, I was catching up on my sleep.'

'The newsdesk want this for the lunchtime bulletin, that's why there's a bit of a rush,' Christie apologised.

Patrick sat in the armchair Stevie had just vacated. She watched agog as Andy snaked a microphone lead beneath his shirt, hoping they wouldn't notice she was still here. God, this was so exciting!

'OK for level,' Andy said.

Mickey nodded. 'Ready when you are, Christie.'

Christie sat forward. 'Mr Alexander –'

'Patrick, please.'

Stevie watched him soften beneath the reporter's smile and wished she could have that effect on men. Christie Bradley was doubly lucky, being both beautiful and sickeningly intelligent, but if Stevie was given the choice to be just one of the two, she knew exactly which one she'd go for. Bugger Mensa.

109

She wouldn't ever follow the bimbo's time-honoured routine and ask to be taken seriously, either. She wasn't now, so she might as well be a Page Three Stunna and have done with it.

'I wanted to talk about Sunday's race first of all,' Christie began. 'You started off in pole position, but you had to retire after just eighteen laps –?'

Patrick nodded. 'It was a difficult race all round. I started well, but an electrical problem with my car showed up almost immediately, and the combination of that and the basic monocoque problem forced me out on the eighteenth lap.'

'Your team-mate, Rafe Dussi, came in second behind Damon Hill and pushed Schumacher into third place,' Christie said. 'That puts Rafe two ahead of you in the championship points. Does that bother you?'

'Rafe had an excellent race. He is a brilliant driver, he deserves his place up there with two of the world's best.' Patrick grinned disarmingly. 'And don't forget, there are still fifteen races to go.'

'What's the situation with the new cockpit?'

Stevie watched from the doorway, enthralled, as the interview continued, until she was distracted by a soft footfall behind her. She turned and saw Rafe Dussi standing by the front door, which was wedged open by the camera crew's empty silver boxes. She felt a flock of seagulls take flight and bat around her stomach as she drowned in his dark eyes.

'Hello, Stevie. Can I come in?'

God, he was so bloody gorgeous. She just wanted to rip his clothes off and fuck him stupid. The way he stood there, his arm casually resting on the door-jamb next to his dark head so that his collarless cream shirt rose above the waistband of his jeans and exposed three inches of tanned, taut stomach, whorls of dark hair just visible –

'Stevie?' Rafe's breath was warm and sweet as he whispered in Stevie's ear. 'What has happened?'

'She, um. Television,' Stevie burbled. 'It's the television

Patrick for people. Um, I mean, the television people for Patrick.' Get a grip, girl, for God's sake. 'They wanted to interview Mr Alexander.'

'Oh, yes.'

Christie grinned across at Rafe. 'Rafe Dussi, I take it? Or are there lots of gorgeous Italians wandering around this part of the world?'

Stevie watched as Rafe kissed her lightly on both cheeks, his dark glance filled with casual desire as he followed the reporter through into the drawing room. If only *she* had the confidence to talk to him like that. Whenever he was around she seemed to turn into a gibbering wreck.

She heard the baby begin to cry and headed disconsolately upstairs. Mrs Arcor was right. Some women were born to be beautiful and talented and to inspire devotion and lust simply by breathing. Others were destined to have roots and spare tyres and inspire very little. She was wasting her time even thinking about Rafe Dussi, he was out of her league.

She entered the nursery and picked up Harry, cooing softly to soothe him as she switched on his bottle warmer. He had a stinking nappy again.

The telephone rang as the bottle warmer clicked off. Stevie waited for someone to answer it but it carried on ringing. They must all be busy with the interview. She ran downstairs as quickly as she dared, wondering how to juggle bottle, baby and telephone without dropping any of them. In the end she jammed the bottle into Harry's mouth and grabbed the receiver with her left hand. 'Hello?'

'Christie?'

'Um, no. This is Stevie.'

'Can you tell her to call Ollie urgently? It's about the AIDS piece she's doing this afternoon.'

'Ollie, urgent, AIDS.'

'Thanks.'

The man rang off before she could say goodbye. Stevie

glowed. She had an important message to convey. She was part of it all, a cog in the wheel, a link in the chain. She dashed down the hall, Harry and the bottle still tucked under her arm.

'Miss Bradley, Miss Bradley –'

The cameraman waved furiously at her to stand back and keep quiet as she burst in. Chastened, she shut the drawing-room door behind her and edged carefully around the makeshift set the INN crew had created. Patrick, Rafe and Christie were all standing now, facing the camera. Through the french windows she could see a white van parked in the drive, lots of whirly aerial things on the top and electronic bits and pieces visible through its open side door. She stared at it as she manoeuvred closer to Christie. It had little television screens in it, and loads of wires all criss-crossing each other and going to different places like a 1930s telephone switchboard in an Agatha Christie film. She was so busy wondering how they didn't get muddled up that she failed to notice the rats' nest of cables at her feet.

Patrick caught the full force of Stevie as she tripped and cannoned into him. They both tumbled back into the armchair in a chaotic tangle of baby, bottle and luminous pink lycra.

'I think perhaps we should return to the studio,' Christie said calmly to camera. 'Victoria?'

Stevie sank down on the stone steps at the bottom of the rose garden and hugged her psychedelic pink knees to herself. This could only have happened to her. Patrick would sack her now – that's if he didn't have her arrested. She couldn't really blame him. It would've been bad enough if the interview had been recorded. She'd never forget the expression on his face as he'd sat there with baby puke dripping down one shoulder, hot milk down the other and a revolting, squidgy, bright yellow nappy leaking all over his hands – but at least they could've edited it out, bribed the camera crew, vandalised the tape or something. But no, she had to do it live in front of half the

nation. It was one thing making a complete fool of herself –
that was par for the course – but it was quite another humiliating your employer in front of three million people. And Rafe!
For a moment she'd forgotten he was there too. He must think
she was an absolute moron. Oh, God, how could she have been
so *stupid*?

'Do you mind if I join you?'

She peered through her fingers without looking up. Two
black Italian leather-clad feet stood on the step next to her. Oh
God, this was all she needed, for him to come and gloat.

She shuffled her bottom across the step to make room for
him, her head still buried against her knees.

'Hey, *cara*, come here.'

She gasped as Rafe put his arm round her and pulled her
against his shoulder. She felt as if someone had just stuck her
finger into a wall socket. Tingly shivers of electricity rippled
round her shoulders and along the arm where he was touching
her. She tried to relax casually against him at the same time as
holding herself rigidly in check so that he didn't have to take
her full weight.

'Oh, Rafe!' Stevie said, and burst into tears.

Rafe held her comfortably while she sobbed into his soft
suede jacket, rubbing her back every so often when she got
stuck on the hiccups as if she were a baby trying to bring up
wind. Eventually she pulled away from him and hung her head
so that he wouldn't see her running nose and blotchy eyes.

'I'm so, *so* sorry.'

Rafe handed her a soft red silk handkerchief. 'It's nothing.
Don't worry about it.' Gently he brushed the tears from her
cheeks with his thumb. 'It was an accident. No one thinks it is
your fault. Tomorrow you will laugh about all of this.'

Stevie gazed helplessly into his dark eyes, desperately aware
of his hand against her cheek, the warm, spicy male scent of
him as he sat next to her on the step. Her heart pounded. She
felt as if she'd just run the hundred metres; her breath was

coming in quick little gulps. Oh, God, he was so bloody handsome. She couldn't move, she couldn't speak, she couldn't do anything. His soft mobile mouth was just inches away from hers. If only he'd lean forward and kiss her. If only he'd throw her down in the flowerbed and –

'Stevie, do you feel all right?'

She scrabbled away from him like a trapped kitten. 'Yes, yes, fine. Well, no, actually, I feel like a complete berk, but I'm getting used to it.' She sighed gustily. 'I should think Mr Alexander wants to kill me.'

'Patrick has a good sense of humour. He'll see the funny side.' Rafe said.

'Oh, you don't know what it's *like*,' Stevie wailed. 'This sort of thing only happens to me. Have you ever got trapped in a revolving door at John Lewis and had to be cut out by Emergency Rescue? Well, I have. I lock myself out so often the fire brigade have the spare key. Julia says I'm a walking blackspot, I should be sectioned off by cones.'

'I think you're wonderful. Crazy, but wonderful.'

'Don't be nice to me, it just makes me feel worse.'

'I wasn't being nice to you,' Rafe said. 'I mean it.'

She stared suspiciously at him. He was smiling, but it was an amused, mischievous grin that invited her to laugh with him. She rubbed her nose with his red silk handkerchief and gave a watery smile. 'I've spoilt this now.'

'Good. My grandmother gave it to me for Christmas and I hate it.'

Stevie giggled. 'My mother has a special cupboard at home that she keeps things in that people give her that she doesn't like – you know, like picture frames with shells on and those horrible pink lamps with knobbly fringes – and then when they come to visit she gets them all out so they won't be offended. The only thing is, you have to remember who gave you what so you don't get them muddled up.'

'When one of my grandmothers comes to stay we all have

114

to rush round the villa hiding photographs of the other grand-mother because they hate each other.'

'What happens if they both come together?'

'We hide in the kitchen.'

Stevie laughed.

'That's better,' Rafe smiled. 'I like it when you laugh.'

Stevie flushed with pleasure. 'Do you miss your home very much?'

'A little.' He shrugged. 'My parents divorced when I was five. My mother lives in America, I haven't seen her for years. My father is very busy, he works all the time. There isn't very much for me to miss.'

'What does your father do?'

'He makes cars,' Rafe said shortly.

Stevie was aware she'd ventured on to forbidden ground. She sensed Rafe withdraw from her, the easy smile of a few minutes ago replaced by a guarded look. *Shit*. What the hell did she have to go and say that for?

'Rafe, what the bloody hell are you doing out here?'

They swung round as Charles Cusack strode across the lawn towards them. Rafe stood up. 'Cusack. I didn't realise anyone was looking for me.'

'Well, of course they bloody well are,' Cusack said irritably, his blue eyes glinting. 'The phone's been red-hot since that fiasco on INN. Half the tabloid press want an interview with you. We're going to have to do some bloody fancy footwork to avoid the whole team being made to look complete bloody morons. I don't know what that stupid girl thought she was doing.'

'It was an accident,' Rafe said.

Stevie leaped up. 'No, no, he's quite right, I should never have been there in the first place. I'm not surprised everyone's so cross –' She stared at Cusack. 'It's *you*!'

'Oh, Jesus. I might have known. The trespasser.'

'I did *not* trespass,' Stevie said heatedly. 'There were no

115

signs in that wood. How was I to know it belonged to you?'

'I should have thought that was obvious –'

'Do you two know each other?' Rafe said, puzzled.

'In a manner of speaking,' Cusack replied. 'She barricades me into car-park spaces at Sainsbury's and trespasses all over my land in her spare time.'

Suddenly Stevie realised why he'd seemed so familiar when she'd met him in the woods. He was the arrogant bastard who'd threatened to run over Damien in his sodding great Range Rover and then nicked the last jar of Nescafé on the shelves. The penny clunked down another couple of notches. *Cusack*. He was also her boss's boss and childhood friend, and a lord or an earl or something to boot. Oh, great.

'I'd love to stand and chat, but some of us have work to do,' Cusack said. 'Rafe –?'

Rafe scowled. Unexpectedly, Stevie sensed a strong dislike between the two men that was not explained by the interview cock-up or Cusack's general bloody-mindedness and bad temper.

'I should go,' Rafe murmured to her. 'I'll see you soon.'

'Oh, yes, please!'

He patted her cheek. 'And don't worry. OK?'

'OK.'

She touched her face reverently as she watched the two men walk away. They couldn't have been more different. Rafe was as warm and golden and glowing as Cusack was cold and pale and arrogant. There was something strangely compelling about Charles Cusack, though. Stevie found her eyes drawn to him as he walked towards the house, and for the first time she noticed his limp. How strange that she hadn't seen that before. He was still a bastard, though. Maybe their shared sense of grievance against him would unite her and Rafe . . .

She sighed as she trudged back to face the music.

Annabel Alexander had been trying to get Rafe Dussi out of

her mind for two weeks. Ever since that day in the kitchen, she hadn't been able to stop thinking about him. His mocking smile filled her dreams; when she closed her eyes, she could still feel the warmth emanating from his body as she'd leaned across him to heat the coffee. Every time Patrick reached for her she couldn't help imagining it was Rafe and she hated herself for it. She felt as if her body were betraying her. She didn't want to feel this way. She loved Patrick. In ten years of marriage she had never even looked at another man. She wasn't like Rosie Knighton. There was no place in her life for an affair. Her world was safe, comfortable, secure; she didn't want it to change.

Wearily she climbed out of the Range Rover, gathering her chic paper shopping bags to her chest as she backed out of the converted stable block and shot the bolts across the garage door. She had done nothing wrong, she reflected, and yet her life seemed shot through with a thousand tiny lies already. Every time Patrick smiled at her, his expression filled with love, she was twisted by remorse at her longing for the younger man. She could no longer meet his eyes. She was so confused. Part of her wished she'd never met Rafe Dussi. The other part of her wished she'd met him ten years before.

She walked round to the side of the house, feeling her way in the dark. It was nearly 9.30. She was much later than she'd expected; her train had been marooned halfway between Victoria and Clapham Junction for two hours because of a bomb scare. She wished Elizabeth and James would still be up. The love you had for your children could never be called into doubt. Suddenly she needed their reassuring noise and warmth to remind her of what really mattered in her life.

She let herself into the darkened kitchen and dumped her bags on the table, shrugging off her Armani blazer and warming her hands against the Aga. She had a wonderful husband, three beautiful children, a gorgeous house, a lifestyle that many women would envy. She had a bit of a crush on Rafe, that was all. She'd grow out of it. She just needed to keep her distance from him until she'd sorted out her feelings.

'Hello, Annabel.'

She uttered a small cry.

He stood up and moved towards her, his dark eyes glittering in the dim light. 'Did I frighten you?'

'I – I didn't expect anyone to be here.' She turned away from him. 'You startled me. Did you want to see Patrick?'

'I wanted to see you.'

She fiddled with the tea-towels draped along the rail of the Aga. 'Why?'

'I think you know the answer to that,' Rafe whispered.

His jacket rasped against the white silk of her shirt as he moved to stand behind her. She didn't move, her body trembling with tension as he gently smoothed her hair away from the back of her neck and bent to kiss it. As she felt his warm lips press against her skin she couldn't suppress a soft moan of wanting. She bowed her head as he kissed her neck again, offering no resistance as he turned her in his arms. She couldn't stop him. She didn't want to stop him.

'Annabel?'

They sprang apart as Patrick walked into the kitchen and turned the light on. 'Rafe! I thought you'd gone hours ago.'

'I was on my way out when I heard a noise in the kitchen. Annabel was just coming in. We got talking.'

'In the dark?'

'We didn't really notice,' Annabel said, summoning a smile.

Patrick slipped his arm loosely around his wife's shoulder and grinned at Rafe. 'You're lucky she listens to you. She just tells me to shut up.'

'A wife's privilege,' Rafe said blandly.

'Did you want some coffee?' Annabel's voice was shaky.

Rafe shook his head. 'It's late. Another time.' He let himself out into the darkness.

Patrick could feel Annabel's tension as she held herself rigid beside him. He was suddenly acutely aware of her separateness from him, and for the first time in many years, he wondered what she was feeling. She was usually so easy to read, so constant, so controlled. He knew she found his moods difficult to understand, but he could have predicted her reaction to almost any given set of circumstances with almost perfect accuracy. But not tonight. He glanced at the taut set of her face, saw the shadows beneath her eyes. He felt as if he were looking at the face of a total stranger.

Eight

'Hey, waiter! Another Bacardi and Coke!' Julia yelled.

'Julia, *please*,' Stevie hissed. 'We *are* in San Lorenzo's.'

'There's Cindy Crawford!' shrieked Julia. 'Hi Cindy! Isn't Richard with you?'

Stevie wanted to crawl under the table along with the chic little flower arrangement Julia had already sent flying. It had been a serious mistake to let her drink somewhere so posh the mood she was in, but Julia had insisted. After all, it was where Hugo had brought Camilla for lunch, and if it was good enough for his cheap bit on the side, it was good enough for *her*.

'Why did he do it to me, Stevie?' Julia wailed. 'What's she got that I haven't?'

'A rich daddy with letters after his name?' Stevie suggested.

'Aubergine hair,' Julia said. 'She's got aubergine hair. And a mouth like the Dartford Tunnel and no tits. We have five years of bliss and then he dumps me for a titless wonder. There's no justice in the world.'

'He was probably bottle-fed. He's got low expectations.'

'Well, she bloody well hasn't. You should have seen his Amex bill.'

'You're better off without him, Jules. He's a complete wimp.'

Julia poured a hefty slug of Frascati into her water glass and drained it in one go. 'I know. Men are such bastards. Hugo couldn't even tell me he'd got someone else to my face. He made bloody sure I found out for myself though. He started off by telling me he had to go out on Thursday with this guy from the office. He *never* goes out with anyone from the office. Then he changed his story and said he was seeing a friend. Then when he was sure I was really suspicious he called me when he knew I'd be at aerobics and left a message on my answering machine telling me to call him back urgently. So I did. All bloody night. It was four o'clock in the morning before I realised the bastard had set me up.'

'What you have to realise, Jules, is that men hate verbal confrontation. The words "We need to talk" strike fear into their craven breasts.'

Julia viciously snapped a breadstick in half. Stevie noticed a middle-aged man at the next table wince. 'I'm sure he left his briefcase behind on purpose, too. I spent the rest of the night going through his credit card statements. They read like the *Good Food Guide*. Five years we were together, and the bastard never took me to San Lorenzo's or Langan's at £200 a throw. I swear the woman must be a bloody horse, the amount she eats.'

'And you never guessed a thing?'

'Well, I must admit I thought it was a bit funny when he came home from that trip to Birmingham last summer with a suntan.' She drained another glass.

Stevie sighed. If Julia – all raven-haired, five-foot-eleven, size ten, 36–24–36 of her – couldn't keep a pathetic, charmless anorak like Hugo faithful, there wasn't much hope for those with less perfect proportions. 'Did you confront him with it?'

'I tried. But when I tracked him down, he just threw up his hands and said –'

'Threw up his hands? How do you know? I thought you were calling him on the phone?'

'Well, he only lives ten minutes away, so I went over there and – um – sort of messed him up a bit.'

Stevie groaned. 'Just tell me he was alive when you left?'

'I've always found it a bit difficult to tell,' Julia said thoughtfully.

'Why the bloody hell did you stay with him, then?'

'I suppose it's because he never fancied me.'

Stevie took Julia's wine glass out of her hand and drained it. 'I'm sorry, Jules. You've got me there. Who is this Camilla tart, anyway?'

'He met her at his handicrafts evening class. She's a mosaicist, for God's sake.'

'More like a sado-mosaicist if you ask me.'

Julia poured herself another glass of wine. 'Maybe I should become a lesbian.'

'I wish I was a lesbian,' Stevie said wistfully. 'I could have chocolate cake for dinner every night and still get laid. Other women empathise with cellulite and bad hair days.'

'A woman knows what another woman wants,' Julia said.

'Totally non-fattening zero-calorie spaghetti carbonara, chocolate chip ice-cream and roast potatoes.'

'Painless bikini waxes.'

'Tom Cruise's home telephone number.'

'Multiple orgasms on multiple occasions,' Julia giggled.

'A cold day, a warm bed and a hot man. Right now.'

A po-faced waiter materialised on cue at Stevie's elbow. 'Was Madam the Dover Sole or the Stuffed Chicken?'

Stevie stared at the little piece of lemon wrapped in muslin at the side of her plate, then stabbed futilely at it with her fish fork.

'You're supposed to squeeze it over the fish, Stevie, not hack it to death. The muslin's to stop the pips coming out.'

'Takes all the fun out of it,' Stevie said.

'So come on,' Julia said. 'How far have you got with Rafe Dussi, then? Four? Five?'

Years of exchanging all the sordid details of the previous night's exploits over their Rice Krispies in the morning had led to the development of a very precise shorthand system of reference. At the bottom of the scale, scoring one point, was holding hands and kissing, moving through french kissing (two), above the waist and above the clothes (three), above the waist and below the clothes (four), below the waist above the clothes (five), below the waist below the clothes (six), heavy petting (seven), oral sex (eight), and All The Way (nine). The ultimate score, ten, was reserved for bestiality, three-in-a-bed and anything involving hot chestnuts or Welsh men.

Stevie grimaced. 'Zero. He doesn't even know I exist. It's more than two weeks since I saw him in the rose garden and I've hardly spoken to him since. I'm sure he was only nice to me out of pity.'

'I thought he said he wanted to see you again?'

'Well, he has. Buried beneath a pile of dirty nappies and looking rather like one of them most of the time.'

'You've got an attitude problem, that's what,' Julia said firmly. 'You look at Rafe and think "What could a gorgeous, available, mouthwatering sex god like that want with me?" when what you should be thinking is "What would an exciting, voluptuous, sex-crazed woman who can speak English like me want with a greasy foreign dago like him?" '

'I hadn't thought of it like that.'

'Well, start trying. When will you be seeing him again, anyway?'

'Patrick and Rafe are racing in San Marino on Sunday, so I suppose they'll be back around Tuesday. I'm just amazed Patrick didn't sack me after what I did. He was actually very nice about it,' Stevie said through a mouthful of calories. 'Unlike that miserable bastard Lord bloody Cusack. I heard him tell Patrick that after meeting me he had a sneaking sympathy for Lord Lucan.'

Julia snorted. 'I rather like the sound of him.' She paused

suddenly, her spoon in mid-air. 'I've heard his name before. I think he used to race himself, didn't he?'

Stevie shrugged.

'No, I'm sure he did. There was a terrible accident a couple of years ago – God, I can't remember. Maybe Oliver would know.' She put down her spoon and pushed her plate away. 'God, I'm full.'

'I dread to think how we're going to pay for all this.'

'We aren't. Hugo is.' Julia grinned. 'He forgot his cheque-book was in his briefcase. He shouldn't have such a poncey signature. I've been forging it all round London.'

Stevie giggled. 'Oh, Jules. You're terrible.'

'And about to be more so.' She scribbled a cheque and stood up unsteadily. 'So. Which do you fancy first? Harrods or Harvey Nicks?'

Oliver forced his way through the crush of people towards the makeshift bar, desperate for a glass of water. It was the main trouble with raves, you got so bloody thirsty. He could murder a beer, but these places never served anything but water. With the amount of drugs going down, they couldn't risk it. If you drank alcohol when you were on E, you could kill yourself.

He pushed his way past a teenager wearing a hooded Stüssy sweatshirt and a blank expression, threw down a pound coin and grabbed a full plastic litre bottle of lukewarm water. He emptied it without pausing for breath and headed back to the dance floor.

They were playing hardcore, a soulless, mindless cacophony of noise that sounded like a jazzed-up version of saucepans falling on the floor. The din reverberated off the concrete walls of the warehouse cellar as the DJ mixed and remixed the records on his two decks. This was a 12K rave, pretty good. The higher the wattage of the speakers, the better. On his way here he'd seen a flyer for a 15K at the Brighton Centre on Sunday. He'd ripped it off the telegraph pole and stuffed it in his pocket. These things were fast becoming collector's items.

In the last couple of months, Oliver had been going to raves almost every weekend. It had started the week after Carrie had gone back to her rich husband in New York, and he just hadn't been in the mood to hit the usual clubs and pick up someone else. He'd missed Carrie far more than he'd expected, and it wasn't a feeling he liked. The rave scene wasn't really him – the kids were usually quite a bit younger than he was for a start, and he hated their hip conformity: the weird trousers, the DMs, the lank hair washed with soap so that it wouldn't shine. But the raves gave him the chance to block everything out and lose himself in the noise. No one wanted to talk, no one was interested in who he was or what he did. He spent the rest of the week being responsible and achieving, forcing his brain round a shitload of facts: tort, libel, case law, appeals. At a rave you could just let your brain coast along in neutral. The drugs helped, of course, but it was the atmosphere that gave him the real high. Every so often he just needed to cut loose.

It was OK for Stevie. Ever since they'd been kids, Stevie had been the dippy one, getting into trouble, losing things, failing everything from her cycling proficiency test to her Brownie first-aid badge. Everyone had sort of got used to her screwing up. Even though he was two years younger, Oliver had looked out for her rather than the other way round. He'd pulled her out of the duckpond when she'd fallen through the ice the February he'd turned nine; he'd scrambled over the roof of a four-storey condemned building they'd been exploring to get in through the skylight when she'd locked herself in the loo. No one had ever expected anything of Stevie except visits to Casualty. It had all been down to him. *He* was the academic one, *he* was the one who'd got thirteen straight As in his GCSEs, *he* was the one with four A levels and a first in law from Oxford. Everyone was so used to him sailing through his exams and coming top in everything, no one took him seriously when he said he was scared he'd fail. Even his parents thought he was just covering himself in case he didn't get 100 per cent this time.

He thought of his law books sitting on his desk at his flat, unopened. The exams started in just over a month. The pass rate was less than 50 per cent, and this included A-grade students who were all as talented as he was. He wasn't just scared this time. He was fucking terrified.

A tiny dark-haired girl in a grubby white skinny-rib and torn hipster jeans deliberately pressed her body against his as they danced, her head thrown back and her eyes half-closed as she raised her arms over her head and pulled invisible bell ropes in time to the beat. Oliver caught brief glimpses of small, springy white breasts as her skinny-rib lifted with each movement. Suddenly he needed more than just the music.

He bent and put his lips against her ear, smelling her sweat. 'Got any tabs?'

The girl nodded towards the fire exit. A skinny blond boy wearing a filthy Joe Bloggs sweatshirt was standing in the half-open doorway with two kids, taking quick, furtive glances around him as they talked. He couldn't have been more than seventeen. Oliver saw the boy palm some notes and hand something to the other two, who slapped him a high five and walked away. He eased through the press of gyrating bodies and tapped the dealer on the shoulder.

'Yeah?'

'You got something?'

'Seven quid each.'

Oliver dug around in the pocket of his jeans. 'Give me a couple.'

The boy raked his dirty blond dreadlocks back from his face. 'You want something stronger, man? I got some Angel Dust, it's the real stuff. They're really mean. I can get you as much as you want, fifteen quid a tablet.'

'I never heard of it. Good stuff?'

The boy shrugged. 'It's the business. But you gotta make

sure you don't do more than half a tablet, you can lose your marbles, know what I mean? You know when you do too much acid? Well, it's the same – but worse.' His eyes flickered across the dance floor and he licked his lips. 'The good thing is, if you imagine you're in a pile of female bodies, you'll feel them, know what I mean? But you gotta be real careful, man, these things are brain fuckers.'

Oliver shook his head. He just wanted something to juice him up, not blow his mind. 'Maybe another time. Just give me the tabs for now.'

'Whatever you want, man.'

Oliver took the two tiny pieces of blotting paper patterned with smiling suns and placed one on his tongue as he looked around for the girl. It was impossible to see her in the mass of sweating, heaving bodies. He edged along the wall, feeling the noise suck him in as the acid started to do its work. He knew it would be dawn before he stopped dancing.

'You score?'

Oliver handed the girl the other tab. He realised she was younger than he'd first thought, maybe sixteen. Too young for him. She slipped the tab under her tongue without a word of thanks and glanced back at the dealer. 'He try to get you to buy anything else?'

'Yeah. Some new stuff he was pushing.'

'Angel Dust?'

Oliver nodded. 'You done it?'

'No way. Angel Dust's a killer.' She pushed her dark hair behind her ears and scowled. 'Jake's a bastard. You sell that stuff, you end up getting people dead. I heard what it did to kids in America. They think they're Superman, they start trying to headbutt trains and fly off buildings. It fucks with your mind. One kid gouged out his own eyes. Jake's too dumb and too stoned to know what he's selling. He just pushes whatever he's given.'

Oliver glanced back. The young dealer was now talking to

an older man who was standing just outside the fire-exit doorway, his features obscured by shadow. Oliver watched him take a bundle of notes from the blond boy, then hand him a small polythene bag. Clearly the older man was the boy's supplier. Oliver felt sick. Selling Es or acid was one thing, but this bastard was getting the kid to push something much more dangerous. You went to a rave, you just wanted a good time, a bit of juice to keep you going. Most of the kids here weren't ready for what this guy was selling.

The older man looked up suddenly, and for the briefest of moments, their eyes met. Oliver felt a flash of recognition. He knew this man. Shit, who the hell *was* he?

'You glued to the floor?'

Oliver looked at the girl. Her eyes were already bright, her body jumping. It would be hours before she came down. Despite the acid he'd taken, he suddenly felt very old and tired.

'Another time, OK?'

She shrugged. 'Your funeral.'

Oliver watched as the girl disappeared into the crush. He worked his way towards the door. Saturday night and he was on his way home before midnight. He must be losing his touch.

Portia Knighton felt a brief flare of annoyance as the guy who'd bought her the tab faded out, then it was gone. She was feeling too good to care for long. The music was really intense, the sound pulsing hot and fiery through her body like she'd been IV'd with vodka. She danced for hours, pressing her narrow little hips into the groin of first one guy and then another. It was the best thing about raves, you were free to float, there was no question of ownership. It was kind of a communal thing. You could arrive on your own, lose yourself in the music without speaking to anyone, but you were never alone, you were all part of everyone else's experience. She liked the way acid made her feel, too, as if she could fuck the world and fly.

'Portia?'

She turned her head but kept on dancing. 'Yeah?'

'Want a ride?'

'I want a drink.'

She shoved her way towards the bar without stopping to check if Will Purvis was behind her. She picked up a bottle of water without paying and glugged half of it back, then looked up at him. Shit, he was tall. Not bad looking, either. She wouldn't have minded fucking Will. There was something about him, a kind of amused knowingness in his deep-set grey eyes. He was only seventeen but it was like he'd got the world taped already. 'What's it to you, anyway?'

'Save you a taxi.'

'What makes you think I'm going home?'

'Yeah, right.'

Portia scowled. Will was a nice guy – a lot nicer than his father, Nigel Purvis – but she wasn't in the mood. 'I'm not a kid, you know.'

'Sweet sixteen, never been kissed.'

'Fuck you.'

'You wish.'

Portia tried to push past him, but he blocked her path. 'Look, Will, give me a break. What makes you think you're my fucking keeper, anyway?'

'Just looking out for you, OK?'

'Well, don't. I can look after myself.'

Will shrugged and stepped aside. 'You get grounded by Rosie, don't come crying to me.'

'Fuck Rosie.'

'I'm sure she'll get round to me.'

He didn't even see the blow coming. Will reeled back. She could see the red imprint of her hand already spreading across his cheek. 'You say anything like that again, I'll fucking kill you, OK?'

'*Jesus*, Portia.'

She let go and turned her back on him, not wanting him to

see her tears of pain and rage. It wasn't fair to take it out on Will, but she'd had enough. Every time she walked into the village shop, her ears burned. Everyone knew her mother was a tart. In Edenfield gossip spread like butter on newly baked bread. Rosie wasn't even discreet about it. You could always tell when she'd started a new affair. She'd disappear up to London and return with a new hairstyle and a bootful of designer shopping bags, then lock herself in the bathroom for hours and come out smelling like a brothel. Instead of her usual grey M&S bras and knickers draped on radiators all over the house, there'd be minuscule silk teddies and camiknickers drying flat in the airing cupboard in accordance with the instructions on their expensive labels.

Rosie would come home from meetings with her publisher hours late, her hair dishevelled, her clothes crumpled, reeking of sex, and give some wild excuse about trains running late or losing her purse in the woods. The whole charade would go on for about two or three months, then suddenly the singing in the bath and the dropped telephone calls would stop, and Rosie wouldn't get dressed for days, mooching around the house in her candlewick dressing-gown and refusing to wash her hair. Eventually Laurie would coax her out of her depression and she'd throw herself into her work, tossing off another novel and dutifully playing the role of wife and mother. Until the next time.

For most of her childhood, Portia had been terrified her parents would divorce. Every time she heard them rowing she'd cry herself to sleep, convinced that in the morning she'd wake up to find one of them gone. Sometimes they wouldn't speak to each other for days, then suddenly they'd be all over each other and she'd have to bang on their bedroom door to get them out of bed long enough to run her to school. The uncertainty had frightened and undermined her over the years. Petrified it was somehow her fault, she'd tried her hardest to be good, getting top marks at school, captaining the netball team, winning the Art Prize, never staying out late and tidying her room without being asked. At twelve years old, she'd been a pale, withdrawn child, unnaturally polite and well behaved.

At thirteen, she'd come home early from school and walked into the kitchen to find her mother pressed up against the fridge, her long brown legs wrapped round her tennis coach as he'd pumped away between her thighs. Later, her mother had come into her bedroom and carefully shut the door, explaining as Portia sobbed into her pillows that it didn't matter, she wasn't going to leave Daddy, she was just having some fun, surely Portia was grown up enough to understand that?

Portia was quite grown up enough to understand the two £20 notes her mother had left on her dressing table 'to spoil yourself for a change, darling'. She'd quickly learned that any mention of her father closely followed by reference to a pair of jeans she liked or a party she wanted to go to was instantly met with shopping bags or cash for the taxi home. But despite her veiled threats, Portia had actually worried herself sick trying to cover up for Rosie, inventing excuses for her when she was late, hiding the watch one of her lovers had left in the bathroom by mistake, terrified her father would find out about the affairs and they'd split up after all.

In the end, about a year after the tennis coach incident, Portia had let the cat out of the bag herself. Her father had stopped her as she'd been on her way out wearing yet another new outfit – this time an expensive pair of black leather Versace jeans – and accused her of shoplifting. Caught unawares, Portia had blurted out that Rosie had given her the money, and it hadn't taken long for the whole story to come tumbling out. Laurie had cuddled her as she'd sobbed into his scratchy tweed jacket, not saying anything. Suddenly she'd stopped crying and pulled away from him.

'You *know*!'

Laurie nodded.

'For how long?' Portia had whispered.

'She's been having affairs since we married. I've always known.'

She'd stared at her father in disbelief. 'Why don't you do something? Why don't you stop her?'

'Your mother is a dramaholic,' Laurie had said quietly. 'She doesn't live in the real world like the rest of us. She lives in a world inhabited by grand passions and star-crossed lovers, that's why she's so obsessed with those bloody American soap operas and magazine problem pages. Sometimes she can't tell the difference between one of her plots and real life.'

'But why do you put up with it?' Portia had shouted. 'Why don't you *make* her see the difference?'

'It never lasts long. She can't help it. I have my work, and she needs more attention than one man can give her.'

Portia had gone very pale. 'But if she's been doing it since you married, how can you be sure –'

'That I'm your father?' For the first time then she saw the pain and bitterness Laurie had been hiding. 'Oh, I'm sure. That was one thing I wasn't leaving to chance. I took her to a deserted Greek island for a month on our second wedding anniversary and didn't let her out of my sight. You're mine, all right.'

Portia hadn't forgiven her mother. She'd hated her, and with the narcissistic logic of a child, she'd hated herself. She was half-Rosie, and Rosie was bad. That made her half-bad already. She'd started staying out late, playing truant, not handing in work. She'd slept with the first boy who'd asked her two weeks before her fifteenth birthday, and when she'd discovered how popular it had made her, she'd spread her favours around. It wasn't her fault if she was a tart. It was in her genes.

She felt slightly drunk as she staggered back on to the dance floor. It must be the tab she'd taken. She caught a brief glimpse of Will as he left, and for a moment she wished she'd gone with him. She really liked Will, she'd known him for years and he'd always looked out for her. He was like the big brother she'd never had. Now he probably thought she was no better than her mother.

She felt a pair of arms slide round her waist and someone's chin nuzzle her neck. 'How you doin', babe?'

'Get off me, Jake.'

The young dealer laughed and pressed his groin against the small of her back. 'Hey, honey, don't be like that.'

'*Jake* –'

'Excuse me, is he giving you trouble?'

She pushed Jake away as the older man who'd been talking to him earlier came over. She realised he wasn't so old, maybe twenty-five, twenty-six.

'Nothing I can't handle.'

'I was only trying to be friendly –' Jake protested.

'No harm done, eh?' He squeezed Jake's shoulder as if in warning. 'We're all friends here, right?'

Portia nodded uncertainly. For some reason she was having trouble focusing on anything.

The older man put his arm protectively around her shoulder. 'Look, do you want to sit down for a bit?'

She found herself being steered towards the back room of the warehouse, the older man's arm still round her, Jake following close behind them. She knew what the room was for. She'd seen enough people disappear in there before. 'Look, I don't even know your name –'

'Call me Mace. Everyone else does.'

Portia knew he'd given her his street name, not his real one.

Mace shut the door behind them. 'Hey, this is supposed to be a party. I think we need some champagne, Jake.'

'I like champagne,' Portia said, her voice overbright.

Mace laughed. 'Everyone likes champagne. And the best thing is, it has no calories.' He was leading her towards a huge heap of cushions in the centre of the small room. Portia stumbled and half fell on to them. Mace settled easily beside

133

her, his arm suddenly comfortable and familiar around her neck. She started to relax as Jake opened a small fridge in the corner of the room, took out a chilled bottle of Moët and handed it to Mace to open. They were just having a good time, that was all. Nothing heavy. She glanced hazily around the room, wondering if it really was this dim or if it was just her. She could barely make out their faces.

The room wasn't much bigger than a store cupboard, its walls and ceiling painted the same dark shade of red as the deep-pile carpet. It must have been soundproofed, because she could barely hear the music next door, though she could feel its beat throbbing through the walls like a distant heartbeat. She felt warm and safe and drowsy, as if she were in some kind of underwater dream. Mace handed her a glass of champagne and she drank it and spilled some of it down her chin. She barely even noticed Jake refill her glass, stroking her calves as he settled down beside them.

'You're a babe, Portia. A real babe,' he said.

Mace was stroking the bare strip of flesh between the bottom of her skinny-rib and her low-slung flared jeans. Portia lay back against the cushions, smiling dopily up at him and stroking his hair. She felt so warm and sexy, her body tingling like little fishes were nibbling at it.

Mace slipped his hand beneath her top and rubbed the palm of his hand against her springy little breasts. Portia finished her third glass of champagne and Jake took it from her and placed it on the floor as Mace started to kiss her neck, gently rolling her nipple between his thumb and forefinger. Jake undid the laces of her DMs and slipped off her shoes, his hands caressing her legs beneath the loose denim of her jeans. Portia could feel someone undoing the buckle of her belt but Mace was kissing her mouth now, his tongue sliding between her lips, hot and sweet. A sense of incredible warmth and well-being spread through her as her jeans slid away from her body. She felt suddenly free and light without her clothes. She kissed Mace back, barely registering the sound of Jake undressing.

Mace broke the kiss, his hands smoothing down from her breasts across her flat stomach, pressing the ball of his thumb against her mound, feeling her warmth and wetness through the gauzy fabric of her panties. Jake bent over her, his matted blond hair tickling her cheek as he kissed her, his mouth cool and soft and slightly smoky. Mace was sliding out of his clothes, kissing her feet, working his way up between her legs as Jake pushed up her top and sucked at her breasts. She could feel four hands, two tongues, roaming all over her body except where she wanted them most.

Jake suddenly pushed himself up on his forearms and entered her. Portia wrapped her skinny legs around him as Mace licked and bit her breasts, then manoeuvred his way around so that his cock was over her face, his body spread crosswise across her torso as Jake fucked her. She took him in her mouth as she teased his balls with her hand. Mace expertly fingered her clit as Jake thrust against her and she felt as if she was going to explode with desire. She tasted salt as Mace started to come, then abruptly he pulled out of her mouth and moved behind her, slipping his hands beneath her armpits and lifting her so that she was on her knees, Jake still buried deep inside her as he took her weight. He leaned backwards so that Portia was on top of him; hungrily he sucked her tiny, pointy breasts as he rocked her hard and fast against him. For such a skinny guy he had an incredibly wide cock, Portia thought irrelevantly. She heard a rustle of paper and then Mace forced her forward, hard against Jake's chest. She tried to push herself upright, but Jake had caught her arms in his hands, holding her against his chest as he kissed her. Mace spread her legs from behind and knelt between them, and as he pushed her buttocks wide she realised with a flare of excitement and fear what he was going to do.

'Don't worry, baby,' Mace whispered hotly in her ear. 'I'm using something. You're OK.'

He lunged forward and forced his cock so deep into her anus she felt as though she was being ripped apart inside, a hot, fiery pain flashing through her. Jake arched his back beneath her, driving his cock hard and high into her as he squeezed her breasts. Portia thought she'd never experienced such agony. And then, suddenly, she felt the pleasure sweep over her, an ecstasy so acute it hurt almost more than the pain. Her whole body shook with the strength of her climax, and she dimly felt the two men grip her hard, holding her down as they came.

Portia collapsed, a limp rag between them. She felt utterly drained, as if they'd sucked the life out of her and spat away the pieces. She flopped against the cushions as Mace pulled out of her and flung the spent condom into the bin. A tiny flicker of triumph burned deep inside her.

She was her mother's daughter, all right.

Nine

Two weeks after she had forcibly removed Julia from the Fine Jewellery department of Harrods where she'd been attempting to buy a £17,000 diamond Cartier necklace on Hugo's American Express card, Stevie walked into Annabel's kitchen and stopped short. She stared at the vision of hectic industry in disbelief. It was 8.30 on a Tuesday morning and Mrs Arcor was already at the sink, under Annabel's eagle eye, doing last night's washing-up, her purple back rigid with indignation at having been firmly parted from the ironing board.

Peter Appleby, the 'flowery bit from London' loosely responsible for the estate, was sulkily arranging the masses of flowers Annabel had brought in from the gardens.

A pungent wave of Giorgio swept through the back door, bearing with it a tiny bleached blonde of about forty who probably weighed six stone soaking wet, wearing a bright pink denim jacket, stonewashed shrink-to-fit jeans and four-inch clear plastic jelly shoes. A beer-bellied man twice her height and four times her girth appeared behind her clutching a heavy, linen-draped metal tray.

' 'Allo, love,' George Cobbit said cheerily to Annabel as she stood surveying the disgruntled industry around her. 'Where d'you want these ors doovrays, then?'

Annabel winced at both endearment and pronunciation. 'If

you could put the trays in the pantry, George, it should keep them fresh until tonight.'

'Right you are then, love.'

Annabel fiddled with the row of pearls at the neck of her beige silk blouse and pretended she hadn't heard. The Cobbits ran a dreadful fake Tudor pub called The Gilt Edge in the village and were appallingly over-familiar, but George could cook like a dream, for which she forgave him much. 'Sharon, the ramekins for the cheese soufflés are over here. Mrs Arcor is just washing them up now.' She tried not to flinch as the housekeeper made her views on the subject eminently clear. 'Oh, dear. Stephanie, the dustpan and brush are in the scullery. Perhaps you could show Mrs Cobbit where everything else is. You might start with the china in the dining room.'

'Oooh, ain't they nice flowers!' Sharon enthused as she tottered after Stevie. 'Such pretty colours. Look, George. Ain't the flowers nice?'

Peter Appleby scowled and savagely jabbed another pink peony into the crowded vase.

Stevie tugged her grubby Mexx T-shirt down over her bottom as she crouched and swept up the broken crockery. Thank God she was wearing knickers. One of these days she'd manage to get fully dressed before the entire world arrived on her doorstep. Bloody Annabel and her dinner parties. She usually held them on a Saturday night, when Stevie was safely out of the way. Why she had to go and pick a Tuesday now, Stevie had no idea. She wasn't very good on Tuesdays. She was still recovering from the weekend until at least Wednesday.

She emptied the dustpan into the bin and led Sharon through the hall into the vast dining room, one of the few rooms Patrick had refused to let Annabel touch. As a result, it was an eclectic mix of the varying tastes of generations of Alexanders: Jacobean paintings, chinoiserie wallpaper, Chippendale side-tables, Venetian glass lamps, Aubusson rugs and Georgian brocade curtains. Burnished silver chafing dishes stood on top of the ugly Victorian sideboard at the end of the room, a huge twenty-four-seat Regency dining table and chairs dominating the centre. It was not the room for a purist. Peter Appleby had had to go and lie down the first time he'd seen it, but Stevie rather liked it. It seemed to have grown in a leisurely way over the centuries, rather like the oaks and silver birches outside. Nothing matched. Everything glowed with the soft, dull patina of age and use.

Sharon Cobbit tilted her shingled peroxide head to one side and clucked. 'Don't suppose they can afford much new stuff, looking after a place this size,' she said sympathetically. 'Not even a proper wall-to-wall. I'll give you a tip, love: if you put plastic runners down, the carpet lasts much longer. I don't let no one into the 'ouse with their shoes on.'

Stevie tried and failed to imagine two-inch cream shag pile beneath the spindly Chippendale legs.

Sharon ran a scarlet talon over one of the dining chairs whose rose-and-cream upholstery had been softened by centuries of wear. 'I got some great polyester floral chair covers from John Lewis I could bring down. Ever so smart they are. They'd look much nicer than these faded old things.' She glanced round doubtfully. 'Mind you, they might make the rest of the place look a bit tatty.'

'Probably best to leave it,' Stevie said as she opened the sideboard.

'I'll never find twelve matching place settings out of this lot,' Sharon complained as she saw the exquisite assortment of eighteenth-century porcelain. 'If I'd known they only 'ad second-'and I'd 'ave brought me own stuff.'

'Oh, I forgot to tell you. It might be more people than that coming. Mrs Alexander said something about Lord Cusack changing his mind.'

Sharon rolled her eyes, no mean feat given the amount of mascara she was wearing. 'Oh, blimey. Better make sure I get the fish knives on the right side then. It's going to bugger up Mrs A's seating plan, though, she'll be a woman short.'

'He's probably bringing someone –'

'Well, 'e don't usually bother,' Sharon said. 'Can't say I blame 'im, given the type of women 'e 'as to put up with. I've met 'em when we've done the caterin' up at the Castle. No sense of 'umour and not a tit or bum between them. He must get pretty sick of all these toffee-nosed anorexic types stickin' their fingers down their throats. Men want something real to get 'old of, not one of these fragile pieces you just sit and look at. They've got enough of that with their bleedin' furniture. You look at Prince Charles, he's got a fashion plate sitting at 'ome and yet 'e goes after that Camilla. You've got to admit, she's 'ad a bit of wear and tear.'

'I suppose so,' Stevie said faintly.

Sharon carelessly picked up a pile of priceless side plates and started counting them with a crimson fingernail. 'Four, five, six . . . Maybe they'll ask you to make up the numbers, love. Better than having an empty place . . . ten, eleven. I knew it. Two short.'

'Annabel would never ask me anywhere near the Waterford,' Stevie said gloomily. 'I'm too much of a liability.'

Sharon was already pulling out another heap of plates. 'I shouldn't take it personal, love. It's more likely they just 'aven't got enough forks.'

At six o'clock that evening, Stevie was lying in the bath and frantically reviewing her wardrobe as she tried to decide what to wear. Cinderella still hadn't been invited to the ball – Annabel had decided to place Cusack between her rapaciously eligible younger sister, Candida, and Patrick and Rafe's agent, Humphrey Prince, on the grounds that Humphrey was the closest she could get to sexually neutral – but Patrick had suddenly decreed that the twins could stay up until dinner was served at eight, which meant that Stevie would be front of house. And Rafe Dussi was one of the guests.

She ran the hot tap again to top up the bathwater and added another hefty slug of Radox. It wasn't quite Chanel No. 5, but it was better than the elderberry bath oil Bronwyn had given her last Christmas. She had to wonder about Bronwyn's motives.

She submerged herself and sucked in her stomach until only her nostrils and toes were above the waterline. She almost looked a size ten from this angle. Well, a size twelve, anyway. She released her breath and watched as her breasts shot back up to the surface like two underwater barrage balloons cut free from the seabed. Her stomach rose slowly into view, a glistening pink mountain topped with bubbles. What with her nipples, her stomach and her knees, she was almost an archipelago.

She sat up, sending a tidal wave sluicing over the side, and reached for her razor. She'd better get a move on, she had a lot of work to do. Tonight was The Night. She was going to pull out all the stops and see if Rafe noticed. If she could really make an impact on him tonight, maybe, *maybe*, he'd even ask her out. Julia was right: all she needed was a positive attitude. It was cheaper than plastic surgery.

What the hell was she going to wear? Her favourite red sequined number was out, it was hardly your average putting-the-kids-to-bed outfit. Ditto the bottle-green stretch velvet dress, her pink lycra hotpants and the little black tunic whose matching trousers she'd lost somewhere between Gatwick and Ibiza.

She opened a tub of henna hair wax and sniffed it. God, this stuff stank worse than the elderberry bath oil. It'd better bloody do her hair good. She scooped out a gritty, slippery handful and started to smear it all over her hair. Did 'Work through to the roots' mean the dry, grotty blonde bits at the end or the dark greasy bits near her scalp? She never could work it out. She dolloped on another handful to cover herself and wrapped the whole gunky mess in a towel. The things she did for love.

Once out of the bath she opened the bathroom cabinet and poked around six months' salary-worth of creams, revitalisers, softeners, firmers and tonics. You'd have thought there'd be something here that would improve her appearance. But there didn't seem to be a St Jude Miracle Face Mask for Hopeless Cases.

Padding naked back into her bedroom, she threw open the doors of the wardrobe and began to work cotton wool between her toes as she contemplated its contents. They divided neatly into two categories: clothes she wore to work, which consisted mainly of faded T-shirts and tatty leggings over which more children had puked and chucked Ribena than she cared to remember; and those she wore when she was on the pull, which were mainly low cut, highly strung and extremely indecent. Nothing seemed suitable for this evening. She didn't even have any demure meeting-the-in-laws outfits she could wear, thanks to Paul. It had been the one good thing about bonking a married man: she hadn't had to put up with his mother at Christmas.

She unscrewed the top of her red nail varnish and bent double over her toes, trying not to dislodge the turban on her head. Was it just her, or did you have to be a contortionist to paint your toenails?

There was always the white dress, she supposed. She'd bought it a few years ago when she'd been going through her Pre-Raphaelite phase. She'd tried to grow her hair long and look romantic, but every time she'd worn the dress so many people had asked her when it was due that she'd put it in the back of her wardrobe. It was sleeveless and a bit light for the middle of May, but it was either that or her dressing-gown.

A blood-curdling shriek at the end of the corridor made her jump out of her skin and spatter red nail varnish all over her bare feet. She leaped up and grabbed a towel to cover herself

142

as she hurtled into the twins' playroom.

She found Lily crouched over a tiny bundle of fluff on the floor, tears pouring down her peachy cheeks. 'Saddam's dead! He's killed Saddam!'

'Oh, dear. What happened?'

'Jamie sat on him!' Lily sobbed. 'He said Clinton and Saddam wanted to play, so we let them out, and then he went and sat on Saddam!'

'I didn't do it on purpose,' Jamie cried. 'It was an accident. He went behind me. I didn't mean to squash him.'

'Can't you make him better, Stevie?' Lily asked tearfully.

Stevie could see that the UN of the gerbil world would be hanging out the flags. 'I don't think so, Lily, but I'm sure he's gone to Heaven.' More than his namesake would do, she thought privately. 'He was a very good gerbil.'

'Where's Clinton?' Jamie asked suddenly.

'Quick, Lily, shut the door before he gets out too,' Stevie said. 'Your mother will have a fit if she sees him.'

The three of them started crawling on all fours round the room, calling Clinton's name. Stevie clutched at her towel and prayed no one would come in and see her half-naked, her hair in a turban, nail varnish spattered all over her feet, as she crawled on the floor and called for America's President.

'Look! He's under the bed!' Jamie shouted.

Of course, Stevie thought. Where else would he be with a name like that?

After a great deal of coaxing, they managed to get Clinton out from under the bed and back into his cage. Stevie put the late Saddam in a shoebox and sent Jamie downstairs to give him to Mr Arcor to bury. By the time she'd settled the twins in front of a Power Rangers video and returned to her room, it was already ten to eight, and she hadn't even started on her make-up yet. She wondered if she'd done something truly awful in a former life to deserve all this. She must have been Lucrezia Borgia at the very least. It was the only reasonable explanation.

143

'Bloody hell, how many people have they asked?' Nigel Purvis exclaimed as they swung into the courtyard in front of the Alexanders' stable block and saw the row of parked cars.

'I don't think it can be that many,' Lillian said placatingly. 'Cusack, Rafe and Martin are coming, of course, and Humphrey and his wife. I think that apart from them, Annabel's only asked her sister and the Knightons, just to make up numbers.'

Nigel scowled as he deliberately slewed their Mercedes across two parking spaces. 'That sodding Volvo doesn't belong to anyone we know.'

'I think it might be Humphrey's,' Lillian ventured.

'Precisely my point,' Nigel said nastily.

'It was you who suggested a dinner party so everyone in the team could get to know each other.'

'I didn't realise it was going to turn into a bloody circus,' Nigel snarled.

She winced as Nigel slammed the car door and stalked towards the house, his baggy Armani knock-off flapping around his skinny frame. He'd been in a vile temper ever since the Spanish Grand Prix on Sunday, when both Rafe and Patrick had been forced to retire with engine trouble. It was Monaco in a fortnight, *the* social race of the Grand Prix season when all the sponsors turned up with their wives and mistresses to rub shoulders with the rich and famous in Hospitality. Nigel would go spare if neither of his drivers ended up in the points at Monte Carlo.

Lillian tugged the hem of her discreet little black number with a skirt that ended nicely at mid-knee and wished she was anywhere else but here. She'd much rather have stayed at home and finished her poem. She liked Annabel and Patrick, but she did find these social situations terribly trying. She was always acutely aware that people weren't really interested in what a frumpy old housewife had to say and were only making small talk to be polite until they could get to the glamorous blonde on the other side of the room. Nigel would spend the whole time staring at the other women's breasts and then tell her how much she was letting herself go when they got home.

She sighed as she followed her husband into the house. Only another three hours and they could go home again. You never knew, she might even think up the last line to her poem while she was here.

'Portia, would you please ask your father to turn the radio down,' Rosie Knighton said tightly.

'Would you tell your mother I'm trying to listen to the news,' Laurie snapped.

'Tell your father we've already had the headlines twice and I've got a headache.'

'Tell your mother that some of us happen to be interested in what's going on around us, even if others couldn't give a damn if the whole world goes up in flames.'

'For God's sake!' Portia yelled. 'How long are you two going to keep this up?'

Her parents stared stiffly through the windscreen as Laurie manoeuvred their Citroën around the burnt-orange Mercedes blocking half the courtyard. They hadn't been talking for three days, ever since Laurie had marched Rosie and her new Herve Leger dress straight back to Harrods and cancelled her charge cards. He was prepared to put up with her affairs, he'd told Portia, but he was buggered if he was going to finance them as well.

Portia leaped out of the car and plumped up her small breasts against the gold Vivienne Westwood corset she'd pinched from her mother's wardrobe. This dinner party was going to be a right bundle of laughs. She wouldn't normally be seen dead with all these wrinklies, but her parents had completely grounded her ever since she'd stumbled in with the milk after that rave a couple of weeks ago, and she needed to earn a few Brownie points if she was going to get the ban lifted. She hadn't said a word when her father had told her she was coming with them whether she liked it or not. At least it meant she didn't have to sit at home listening to them arguing through her all night.

She followed her parents into the house and hovered near the door as she scanned the other guests. She almost fell off her platform shoes when she recognised the man standing opposite her.

What the hell was Mace doing here?

Annabel walked anticlockwise round the dining table, mentally ticking people off against the seating plan in her hand. She'd put that slimy toad Nigel Purvis on her right because she knew that's where he'd expect to be, but she'd given herself Laurie Knighton on the other side to balance Nigel out. Lillian Purvis was on his left because she was the nicest person coming to the dinner party and Annabel thought Laurie deserved some fun.

Annabel's hands trembled as she reached Rafe's chair. She hadn't dared to sit Rafe next to her, much as she'd longed to. Instead she'd put him where she could barely see him, on the curve of the table between the unattractive Susan Prince and Portia, Rosie and Laurie's teenage daughter, on the premise that they were the two safest women at the table.

She jumped as Patrick stuck his head round the door. 'Everyone's arriving, Annabel. You'd better come through.'

'I'm just checking the table,' Annabel said. 'I'll be with you in a moment.'

She glanced quickly at her reflection in the antique pier glass near the fireplace. She knew she'd never looked more beautiful. Her bare shoulders rose creamily from a cloud of soft silver chiffon that skimmed her perfect figure and fell in a cobweb swirl around her ankles. Her heavy white-gold hair was pulled back into a delicate silver snood, an exquisite platinum filigree necklace studded with grey pearls wreathing

146

her pale throat. The diamond drop earrings Patrick had given her when the twins were born sparkled at each ear. Her cheeks were stained with a faint guilty flush, and her blue eyes glittered with excitement. She knew she'd dressed for Rafe this evening.

She drew the dining-room doors shut behind her and pinned a bright smile to her face as she swept into the drawing room. 'Humphrey, Susan! So glad you could make it.'

Humphrey flushed to the top of his appalling bow-tie. 'Annabel. You're looking ever so nice, if you don't mind me saying so.'

'I brought the details of the Women Against Rape appeal for Bosnia,' Susan said earnestly as she and Annabel brushed cheeks. 'Should I give them out now?'

'Don't you think we should wait until everyone's had a drink first?' Humphrey mumbled.

Annabel slipped away on the pretext of checking the ice-bucket and stood by the open window for a moment, the evening breeze cool against her skin. Her mind was whirling, she couldn't concentrate on anything. Her whole body was trembling with anticipation. This was ridiculous. She was a grown woman of thirty-two with three children. A grown *married* woman. So why the hell did she feel like a teenager on her first date?

She jumped as an arm slipped around her waist and drew her into the window embrasure. She could smell Rafe's mixture of expensive cologne and newly washed shirt. His lips were barely inches from her ear. 'Annabel. I missed you.'

'Rafe, for heaven's sake. Someone might see –'

'Tell me you don't want me,' Rafe's breath was hot against her cheek. 'Tell me and I'll leave you. I'll never look at you again.'

She turned and stared at him, her eyes huge violet smudges in her small, delicate face. 'Don't do this to me, Rafe.'

'What's he been doing to you, darling?' Patrick said, as he

entered the room. 'Not boring you with motor racing again?'

'We were just talking about Monaco,' Rafe said. 'Annabel said she was thinking of coming with us.'

Patrick looked surprised. 'I thought you hated being on the road?'

'Yes, I do, but I – I thought maybe I should give it another go,' Annabel said hastily. 'After all, everyone seems to enjoy Monte Carlo. And the children would love it.'

'What about school?'

'They can miss a few days. Stephanie can come with me, we can all have a little holiday.'

Patrick shrugged. 'Of course, I'd love you to come, if that's what you want. But I'll be pretty busy, I won't have time to show you round.'

Patrick held out his arms to the twins as they raced into the drawing room ahead of Stevie. 'Do you want to come and watch Daddy racing?'

Annabel watched them as they threw themselves headlong into their father's embrace. What on earth had possessed her to agree that they all go to Monaco? The last thing she needed was to be anywhere near Rafe. Then she caught his eye over Patrick's head and knew exactly what had possessed her.

Stevie stood by the door of the drawing room as everyone made a fuss of the twins, hoping she didn't look too awful in her frilly white dress. She saw Portia flirting lightly with Martin Romaine, and wished she'd had that kind of confidence when she was sixteen. That gold corset thing looked marvellous on her, and even the clumpy platform shoes just seemed like a witty fashion exclamation mark. If she'd worn them she'd have looked more like a full stop.

She felt slightly cheered as she spotted Rosie Knighton, who was trapped in a corner with Susan Prince and sending meaningful glances towards her daughter, who was blithely ignoring them. If she had breasts that old and saggy, she certainly wouldn't wander round in sheer Indian cotton blouses without a bra. The woman's nipples must be level with her navel. Stevie hoped they weren't having button mushrooms for dinner, or someone might make a terrible mistake.

No one could accuse Mrs Prince of being too daring, Stevie thought, as Rosie finally escaped over to Portia and Martin and Susan turned to confiscate her husband's glass of sweet sherry. Beneath her saucy little navy-blue-and-lemon rayon shirt-waister all you could see were ropes and rigging. No wonder Humphrey looked so depressed.

Lillian Purvis smiled warmly as she spotted Stevie skulking in the corner. 'Hello, Stevie. You're looking very nice this evening.'

Stevie loved her for bothering to lie. 'Thank you, Mrs Purvis. So are you.'

'Oh, call me Lillian.' She took Stevie's arm and propelled her towards the centre of the room as Susan bore down, waving her leaflets. 'Quick, quick, talk to me, or I'll be stuck with that woman for hours.'

Stevie giggled. Before she had a chance to say anything, a stunning ice-blonde in a revealing white Versace dress sashayed across the room towards them and put her hand detainingly on Lillian's arm. Stevie watched every man's head swivel towards her and hated her on sight.

'Out of the frying pan . . .' Lillian murmured.

'It's Mrs Purvis, isn't it?' the girl gushed. 'Candida Mornay, Annabel's sister. Her *younger* sister,' she added quickly.

'Oh, Candida, of course. We met at Christmas. This is Stevie Colvin, Annabel and Patrick's new nanny –'

'Really?' Candida didn't even glance Stevie's way. 'I'm so glad to have a chance to talk to you, Mrs Purvis. I understand you'll be going to Monaco this season? I was only saying to Jeremy last week – Jeremy Irons, that is – there really is only one race one wants to go to . . .'

God, what a bitch, Stevie thought as Candida triumphantly bore Lillian away. Annabel might have a slight sense of humour failure, but her sister was a bloody rattlesnake. She didn't know how Patrick stood these parties. Lillian Purvis was terribly nice, all plump and motherly, and so was Dr Knighton – he seemed so solid and dependable, with his silvery-grey hair and those lovely kind eyes – but most of this lot were a dead loss. She watched as Candida carelessly abandoned Lillian to Susan Prince's tender mercies the moment Charles Cusack entered the room, hooking her arm possessively through his and chattering brightly as he glowered beside her, unable to escape. Stevie hated to admit it, but they did look good together. Cusack was an arrogant bastard, but he was also strangely attractive, with his deep blue-black hair, hawk-like nose and that pale, dramatic face. He didn't seem over-impressed with Candida, though, stiffening almost imperceptibly every time she touched his arm to make a point. His dark blue eyes looked around the room, clearly not listening to a word she was saying. Stevie couldn't imagine how he and Patrick were such good friends. They seemed so different. Patrick had his arm round Portia now, playfully flirting with her and laughing as the twins pulled him into an armchair and clambered all over him. He was so warm and full of fun. Cusack was like a block of ice beside him.

Cusack abruptly turned his unsmiling gaze on her almost as if he could read her mind. Stevie flushed. He made her feel about two inches tall. What a pig.

She turned away. Behind her, Patrick had escaped the twins only to be trapped in a corner by Susan Prince, who was haranguing him on the subject of the ozone layer as he tried unsuccessfully to look interested.

'– so we hardly ever use the Volvo, although we have had a catalytic converter fitted,' Susan was saying.

Martin Romaine intercepted Patrick's silent plea and came to the rescue, his platinum curls gleaming in the light. 'Did you say you never use your vulva?' he asked wickedly.

Susan frowned. 'Well, not very often –'

150

Stevie managed to turn her snort of laughter into a cough as Martin winked at her behind Susan's back.

'And how many people can you get in it at once?'

'Oh, it's very economical, six or seven if they all squash in together –'

'Stevie, would you take Lily and James up to bed now,' Patrick interrupted hastily.

Stevie collected the twins, waiting patiently as they strung out their bedtime by insisting on kissing everyone in the room at least twice. They kept coming back for more and claiming to have missed someone out, until eventually Patrick laughingly scooped them up himself and marched towards the door. 'I'll take them up, Stevie, or they'll never settle down,' he said. 'Why don't you have a break and watch television, and come back and join us in the drawing room for a coffee after dinner?'

Oh no, Stevie thought. If she went anywhere near all that priceless china and hot coffee, it was bound to lead to trouble. Judging by the frozen expression on Annabel's face, she was thinking the same. 'Thank you, but I don't think I should –'

'Oh, please do,' Lillian implored. 'It seems such a shame to miss everything.'

'Poor little Cinderella,' Rafe smiled. Stevie's legs turned to water.

Annabel realised she was outnumbered. 'Please do join us, Stephanie,' she said politely.

Panic and excitement swept through Stevie in equal measure as she left the drawing room. The last thing she wanted was to have to make small talk in this sodding frilly white dress while Annabel and Candida wafted around like supermodels in their chiffon and Versace numbers. If she'd known she was going to be taking them on, she'd have brought out the big guns. That scarlet sequined number would've given them a run for their money. But it didn't really matter, Rafe had noticed her anyway. She gave a little jump of glee in the corridor. Rafe wanted her to join them for coffee! He'd actually called her Cinderella and smiled at her! Maybe he was just waiting for the right opportunity to ask her out. Perhaps he thought Annabel wouldn't approve of him going out with her nanny. She was sure Patrick wouldn't mind, though; he wasn't as fussy as Annabel about mixing with the staff.

She dodged as Sharon Cobbit backed out of the kitchen into the hall with a huge tray of cheese soufflés. She'd changed out of her jeans and jelly shoes, and was now wearing a neat, knee-length black skirt and high-necked white blouse, although the sober effect was somewhat diluted by teetering black stilettos and half a dozen gold chain necklaces at her throat.

'They all gone in?' Sharon whispered.

Stevie nodded. 'Patrick's just put the twins to bed, I saw him come back a minute ago.'

'Thank God for that. George'll go potty if 'is cheese sooflays is spoiled.'

She winked and tottered into the dining room. The soufflés smelt so delicious, Stevie suddenly felt rather hungry. She decided to head for the kitchen and raid the fridge. Sharon had promised she'd put something by, and Stevie needed to settle the butterflies in her stomach before she joined everyone for coffee. Mr and Mrs Arcor and Peter Appleby were already ensconced at the kitchen table as George bustled between the sink and the Aga, his huge face scarlet with heat and exertion. He grinned as he saw Stevie hovering by the door.

'Come on in, love, make yerself at 'ome. Everyone else 'as.'

Stevie plonked herself down next to Mrs Arcor. 'It all smells delicious.'

'Tastes delicious an' all,' George said, patting his vast stomach. ''Ow d'you think I got like this, then?'

Sharon returned ten minutes later with the empty soufflé ramekins and a detailed report on the state of play in the dining room. Stevie almost fell off her chair with laughter when she heard that Nigel Purvis had caused havoc by dropping a spoonful of hot cheese soufflé down Portia's Vivienne Westwood basque in his eagerness to get a better look at her teenage breasts.

For the next two hours, Sharon kept them entertained with frequent updates on the antics next door, and by the time George's magnificent Queen of Puddings had been demolished and he'd reluctantly started to perk the coffee, Stevie almost didn't want to leave the warm kitchen for the social minefield awaiting her in the drawing room. Mrs Arcor had happily worked her way through the best part of the Christmas pudding brandy and was offering to read the hand of anyone who crossed her palm with a full glass. Mr Arcor was snoring in front of the Aga, and Peter Appleby was describing in intimate and salacious detail some of the more notorious celebrity bedrooms he'd seen. Stevie decided she'd much rather stay here than go next door and have Candida & Co. staring down their aristocratic long noses at her.

She was just wondering how she could get out of it when the kitchen door opened and Rafe sauntered in. 'So, this is what my little Cinderella does when no one is looking.'

Stevie turned pink. 'Hi. We were just – um – chatting,' she said.

'I think you have been having more fun than the rest of us,' Rafe said. 'Now you will have to join us for coffee.'

'Do you think anyone will mind me coming?'

'I think I will mind if you don't,' Rafe smiled.

Stevie's stomach tilted and she suddenly wished she hadn't eaten that second portion of Queen of Puddings. This was it, this was *It*. She tried to find something to say, but her mind had suddenly gone completely blank. Oh, God, think of something interesting, she told herself. This could be your last chance. 'Wasn't the pudding nice?'

Rafe laughed. 'Yes, it was.'

This is ridiculous, Stevie thought. You were fine a minute ago in the kitchen when everyone else was there. Just talk to him, he won't bite. They had reached the drawing room. In another minute it would be too late. He still hadn't said anything about seeing her again. Stevie tried not to care. What did you expect him to do, throw himself at your feet and profess undying love? She was an idiot to ever think he could be interested in her. God, this was so embarrassing. He must think she was a complete prat. She reached out to open the door, unable to look at him.

Rafe reached past her and held the door closed. 'I think you'll be coming with us to Monaco for the Grand Prix in a few weeks,' he said. 'Perhaps we can explore Monte Carlo together?'

'Oh, yes, please!' Stevie gasped.

Rafe laughed at her delighted expression. 'It is what I like about you. You make everything seem such fun.'

Stevie floated into the drawing room on a cloud. He'd actually asked her out! They were going to Monte Carlo! She collapsed on to a spindly chair near the door, too happy to do anything but smile stupidly. He'd told her she was nice and said it would've been more fun at dinner with her instead of all these people, even that beautiful cow Candida, who was still draped all over Cusack. Stevie even managed to feel a bit sorry for *him*. He did look rather beleaguered, especially when Susan Prince started going on about him opening her WI fête.

'Stevie, would you like some coffee?' Patrick asked, making her jump.

'Oh, yes, thank you.' She got up and moved over to the side-table for cream and sugar, her head still in the clouds, then turned as Lillian broke off from exchanging Shakespearian sonnets with Laurie Knighton and caught her elbow. 'Stevie –'

'Yes?'

'Your skirt.'

Stevie looked down at her dress, puzzled. She hadn't spilt anything on it, it hadn't split or anything. She glanced up at Lillian. 'Is something the matter?'

There was a tinkly little laugh from the other side of the

room. 'Oh, my God,' Candida sang out. 'She doesn't even *realise.*'

Everyone stopped talking and turned to look at Candida. Cusack abruptly caught her elbow and started to propel her towards the window embrasure with more animation than he'd shown all evening. Candida shook him off. 'Someone's got to tell her,' she said loudly.

'Shut up,' Cusack hissed.

Stevie glanced round at the row of embarrassed faces. Portia was frantically pointing to the back of her own minuscule purple leather skirt as Rosie took advantage of her husband and daughter's distraction to slip her hand down Martin's trousers. Stevie suddenly caught on to what Portia was trying to say and twisted round to look at the back of her skirt. In the centre of the creased white cotton was a huge, unmistakable, red stain.

'Well, at least we know she's not pregnant,' Candida tittered.

Lillian moved towards her, but Stevie backed away, ashen-faced. It was simply the most appalling, embarrassing thing that had ever happened to her in her entire life. The delirious happiness she'd experienced only a moment before seemed a lifetime ago. She ran out of the room, tears pouring down her cheeks. She'd made an impact on Rafe tonight, all right. Whatever he might have felt for her before, he certainly wouldn't want anything to do with her now.

She threw herself down on her bed, sobbing as if her heart would break.

Ten

Patrick's hands sweated inside his flame-proof gloves as he gripped the wheel and waited for the Monaco Grand Prix to start. No matter how many times he raced, in these final moments before they moved on to the grid he always felt sick with fear. He knew that every race could be his last. The deaths of Ayrton Senna and Roland Ratzenberger at Imola the previous season had proved that. The FIA had revised the Imola circuit and tried to slow down the cars in an attempt to make Formula One safer, but they were missing the point. Accidents happened. You couldn't legislate against them. Ayrton had survived crashes far worse than the one that had killed him. Reducing the engine capacity from 3.5 to 3 litres, limiting the size of the rear wing, putting in chicanes before the lethal Tamburello corner; airbags, safety fences, tyre barriers – in the end, none of it mattered. You either accepted the danger, and the fear that went with it, or you stopped racing. It was as simple as that.

His mouth was dry as he completed the parade lap with the other twenty-five Formula One cars, weaving backwards and forwards behind the safety car to keep his tyres hot so that they'd grip the track better. He fought the impulse to floor the accelerator and break free. You weren't allowed to overtake or change position on the parade lap. The weather was fine, so he was using slicks: treadless tyres so soft that when they'd warmed up after a few laps you could push your finger into them and leave a dent as if they were soft toffee. If the threatened rain materialised, he'd have to switch to wets, which did have treads so that any rainwater on the track could be squeegeed away in the gaps.

The cars moved slowly on to the grid in the order determined by the preceding two days' qualifying races. Damon Hill had got the fastest time yesterday and was now at the front of the field in pole position. Patrick was in fifth place; immediately behind him was Rafe in sixth.

It was an important race to win. At this stage in the championship, after four of the seventeen races of the Grand Prix season, Michael Schumacher was in the lead with twenty-four points, just one point ahead of Damon Hill; Gerhard Berger was third with thirteen points, then Patrick himself with twelve, and Rafe was in fifth place with eleven. With ten points on the track for a win, the Monaco race would probably determine whether the '95 season would simply be a battle of the Titans between Schumacher and Hill, or whether it would open out and become a much less predictable championship. Patrick knew that if he wanted to stay in contention, a place in the high points now was vital.

He eased his elbows slightly away from his body as the last cars slotted into their places on the grid behind him, sweat soaking the flame-proof all-in-one body suit he wore beneath his overalls. Shit, he was hot. These body suits were worse than thermals. Thank God Terroni had got their act together and delivered his new cockpit in record time. If he'd had this car two weeks ago during the Spanish Grand Prix in Barcelona, he'd probably have been able to deal with the engine problem that had developed early on and managed to stay in the race. He'd simply been too cramped in the small cockpit to pick up the change in the feel of the engine as swiftly as he should have done, and had ended up having to retire after eighteen laps. Rafe had been forced out on the forty-second with gearbox trouble; their problems had been totally disconnected, although Nigel Purvis hadn't seen it that way. As far as Nigel was concerned, the two of them had done it on purpose.

Patrick glanced in his mirror. The race marshal at the back of the grid still hadn't waved the green flag to signal that the twenty-six cars were all in place. He hated the Monaco circuit. Unlike most of the Grand Prix fixtures, Monte Carlo had no specially built race track. The streets of the town were simply closed and the Formula One cars sent hurtling through them. If the Monaco Grand Prix hadn't become such a glamorous tradition – particularly amongst the rubbernecking sponsors whose money kept the whole thing going – it would never have been allowed, for safety reasons alone. It made Patrick feel like a bullet in a concrete gun. On either side of him, flats, apartments and hotels overshadowed the track, Quisling Mild and Marlboro flags fluttering from balconies and windows. The streets were so narrow it was almost impossible to over-take. The road surface was bumpy and uneven, the corners sharp. It didn't leave much room for error.

Still no green flag. Dammit, how much longer were they going to keep them sitting here? It was the waiting that drove him crazy. It gave him too much time to think. Too much time to remember. The knot of fear in his stomach tightened. This circuit had nearly killed him once already, and had as good as killed his best friend. He'd raced here half a dozen times since then, but time and familiarity had done nothing to erase the terrible memories.

It had been the second day of qualifiers for the '89 Monaco Grand Prix. He was going into the hairpin Virage Anc Gare corner just before the notorious tunnel section, Charlie Lytton, his then team-mate with Terroni, just ahead of him, holding the corner so tight it was impossible for Patrick to find a way through. He saw again the car skimming suddenly between them, coming out of nowhere; felt the panic as he lost control, his car spinning round a full 360 degrees and skidding across the track into Charlie. He could hear the sickening sound of ripping carbon fibre as the two cars tangled together and plunged towards the concrete wall at the side of the track; he could smell the smoke, feel the heat; he remembered the paralysing terror that had frozen him to his seat, and the searing relief as hands had suddenly released the steering wheel trapping him and pulled him free.

His face had been lacerated by shards of broken plastic from his shattered visor – he still bore the scars – but otherwise he had been miraculously uninjured. He'd sat bleeding by the side of the track, watching them cut his best friend out of the wreckage, and known as soon as he saw Charlie's bloody, mutilated leg that his team-mate would never race again.

Charlie Lytton had effectively died when they'd amputated his foot to get him out before he bled to death. The man who had hobbled out of hospital on crutches six weeks later, his trouser leg flapping eerily in the wind where his right foot should have been, had not been the Charlie Lytton Patrick had known all his life. That brilliant, laughing, supremely confident young man had gone for ever, wiped out by a split-second error on the track at Monte Carlo. In his place stood a bitter, cold, hostile stranger.

Charlie and Patrick had been friends since they were three years old. Barely two months separated them in age, and less than a mile in geography. Charlie's father, the 6th Earl of Cusack, had been a contemporary of Patrick's grandfather, Francis Alexander; Alastair Cusack, a widower twice over, had been nearly fifty-four years old when his third wife, Eleanor, had finally given him the long-awaited heir after a succession of much-loved but genealogically useless daughters. Charlie Lytton had been one of the few boys Francis Alexander had considered a suitable friend for his orphaned grandson. Living so close to each other, growing up together, attending the same prep and boarding-schools, the two boys had become closer than brothers. Both had had to deal with an authoritarian, elderly, out-of-touch parent, although thanks to his mother's discreet intervention, Charlie had been allowed freedoms – such as girlfriends – denied to Patrick. He'd frequently used Charlie as an excuse when he wanted to go somewhere his grandfather disapproved of or stay out late; it had gone against the grain of his natural honesty to lie, but the alternative had been little better than a gaol sentence. Eleanor Cusack had never once betrayed him when Francis had telephoned to check up on him. Patrick had envied Charlie many things – his adoring sisters, his mesmerising good looks, his incredible confidence – but most of all, he had envied him his mother. The only thing in which Eleanor had refused to support her son was his racing.

It was Patrick who'd got Charlie involved in racing in the first place. It had been the year they'd both turned fourteen; Patrick had been taking part in kart rallies for almost a year by then, using Charlie as his cover, stashing the many trophies he'd won under his friend's bed at Cusack Castle so that his grandfather wouldn't find out what he was up to. One Sunday there'd been a beginners' rally in Brighton, and after much persuasion Charlie had agreed to enter, more for the sake of a quiet life than anything else. The moment he'd seen Charlie race, Patrick had known that although he was good, Charlie was better. When Charlie sat behind the wheel, he didn't just control his car, he became part of it. He raced effortlessly, guided by intuition and instinct.

What gave Patrick the edge over his friend was his hunger to win. He put everything he had into his racing, driven by the desperate, irrational need to match his dead father's accomplishments. All he'd ever wanted to do was race. To Charlie, the whole thing was a game, something he could do without really trying. Much as he enjoyed racing, he was never really prepared to work at it. Unlike Patrick, he'd had nothing to prove. There were times when Rafe Dussi reminded Patrick of the way Charlie had once raced. They were both brilliant drivers, unbeatable when they were on top form, but erratic and unpredictable. It meant that despite the fact that Charlie was the better driver, Patrick was the one who won.

By 1989, Patrick had been Terroni's number one driver for three years. It had only been Charlie's first season in Formula One as Terroni's number two, but by the time of the fateful Monaco Grand Prix, only a few races into the '89 Championship, Charlie had already proved that when he wanted to, he could out-perform everyone on the grid. Patrick had known that it was only a matter of time before Charlie won the World Championship, simply because he'd been the best there was.

And then there had been that terrible moment on the track at Monte Carlo, and everything that Charlie had been until that point had been swept away.

With a supreme effort of will, Patrick forced himself to forget the accident and concentrate on the race ahead of him. At the rear of the field, behind the last car on the grid, a race marshal finally waved a green flag to indicate that everything was in order. The start marshal flicked a switch and a red traffic light glowed at the head of the field. Every driver knew that within a few seconds the light would change.

The moment he saw the green light, Patrick felt his fear evaporate. He shot forward, his mind wholly on the next corner, the next curve. Everything else was forgotten. For approximately the next hour and fifty-five minutes, the only thing that mattered was this race.

Stevie had never realised it was possible to feel so exhilarated and so terrified at the same time. The race hadn't even started yet, but the atmosphere was incredible. She'd always found motor racing excruciatingly boring when Oliver had insisted on watching it on television – second only to snooker in black and white – but this was completely different. It was hardly surprising it seemed dull on television, twenty-six cars just driving round and round in a circle for two hours. Television couldn't possibly capture the buzz, the excitement, the smell of petrol and rubber, the crowd's electric sense of anticipation. She leaned forward over the side of the huge yacht Nigel Purvis had hired on behalf of Quisling Mild, holding tightly to the brass rails so that she wouldn't fall into the harbour as she craned her neck for a better view. It had to be tempting fate, putting her and water in such close proximity. Annabel was either an eternal optimist or secretly plotting some sort of revenge.

Stevie had not expected to be here after the débâcle at Annabel's dinner party two weeks ago. She hadn't been able to bear the thought of facing everyone afterwards and had immediately handed in her notice. Patrick had been very sweet, hugging her and telling her that although they'd be sorry to lose her, if that's what she wanted, they understood. But Annabel had refused to accept it. She hadn't made light of what had happened or told Stevie that it didn't matter; she'd simply said that if Stevie ran away now she'd never be able to shake off the feeling of failure. She had to learn to live with what had happened and move on. Stevie had had the strange feeling that somehow Annabel knew what she was talking about. She'd realised then that there was a great deal more to Annabel than the beautiful, controlled woman which was all she allowed the world to see.

She glanced along the deck. Annabel was sitting chatting to Lillian Purvis, her face hidden by the brim of her cream straw hat. The baby was asleep in his carrycot in the shade, the twins playing happily at being captain on the bridge with the poor sod who was responsible for this boat. Stevie was suddenly glad she hadn't resigned. Somewhat to her surprise, she was actually beginning to quite like Annabel: in the last few weeks there'd been something – nothing Stevie could quite put her finger on, just something – about her that was different. She

162

was still her usual calm, competent self, but she seemed less critical, a bit less demanding, as if she'd finally discovered that not everyone was as perfect as she was – or as if she'd realised that she wasn't quite perfect herself.

Stevie squinted back at the track. Nothing much seemed to be happening at the moment. She sank back down on her heels and stared into the muddy brown water between the side of the yacht and the quay. God, she really hoped she didn't fall in, she'd probably catch legionnaires' disease or salmonella or something. Monte Carlo harbour was not exactly your typical glittering blue Mediterranean sea. But she had to admit they had the most unbelievable view of the track. It curved right round the edge of the harbour, following the coast road, barely feet away. When the cars had gone round on the parade lap earlier, they'd been so close she could almost see the expressions in the drivers' eyes. One false move and they'd be on board the yacht with her. This had to be the only place in the world where it was more terrifying to be a spectator than a driver.

She shaded her eyes with her hands and wished she'd thought to bring her sunglasses. It was probably pissing it down in England right now. The last twenty-four hours had been unbelievable. The flight from Heathrow to Nice had been relatively uneventful – if you discounted Jamie accidentally inflating the life-jacket under his seat and sparking a major security alert by hiding his water pistol at the bottom of Stevie's bag – but then when they'd arrived, Annabel had decided to get a helicopter transfer to Monaco. It had been Stevie's first time in a helicopter, and it would be her last, even if she had to crawl on her hands and knees all the way back to England. Planes were OK, particularly nice big 747s – you could fool yourself into thinking you weren't really in the air at all; but a helicopter was something else. It dipped and wobbled all over the place, and there was no getting away from the fact that you were suspended in mid-air with nothing but luck holding you up. The twins had loved every minute of it, but Stevie had spent the entire flight with her head between her knees, alternately terrified the thing would crash and kill her, and feeling so sick she hoped something would. All that kept her going was the thought of the warm, safe, comfortable, motionless hotel bed waiting for her at the end of the journey.

She'd nearly died when they finally arrived on the quayside last night and Annabel had told her they were staying – *sleeping* – on-board the Quisling yacht. She hadn't cared that it had cost a fortune to hire or that Nigel had had to bribe the harbour-master for one of the most sought-after mooring positions in the world with a brand new Terroni soft-top sports car complete with requisite seventeen-year-old blonde draped over the passenger seat. The only thing Stevie had cared about had been her stomach, which had been in a state of extreme delicacy. The thought of bobbing up and down on some boat for two days had nearly made her throw up on the spot. Only one thing had got her up the gangplank at all: the bittersweet knowledge that Rafe would be sleeping just a few cabins away from her.

She hadn't seen Rafe since the night of the dinner party. He'd flown to Italy early the next morning with Cusack, Martin Romaine and Patrick for some important meeting with Terroni, and he hadn't bothered to phone her. She'd known then that it – whatever 'it' might have been – was over between them. In a way she was glad she hadn't had to face him. It would have only made it hurt more.

Whether by accident or design, Annabel had kept her too busy washing, ironing, folding and packing the ninety-four outfits the twins and Harry were bound to need in the three days they'd be in Monaco to think about Rafe. Much. She'd managed to put him out of her mind during the day by ruthlessly refusing herself the indulgence of thinking about him, but at night, when she lay tossing and turning alone in her huge bed, a hot, urgent pulse of desire throbbing between her thighs, it was impossible to forget him. God, she wanted him. Every time she closed her eyes she saw his slow, lazy smile, that warm, inviting dark gaze. She knew it was hopeless, but just the thought that he'd only be a few feet away from her – albeit separated by several rather substantial bulkheads – for three whole nights was better than nothing.

She wished the race would hurry up and start. All this waiting around was making her feel hungry. If only they'd serve some proper food instead of all these olives and minuscule bits of bread and caviare. She hated caviare. God knows why people got so excited about it, it was only fish eggs when all was said and done, and it tasted worse than a blow job. But it was the most expensive food you could buy, so Nigel had insisted on it. She glanced over to where he was talking to some of the sponsors and Terroni executives he'd invited on board. He'd gone completely overboard – she eyed the murky water again: if only – on this whole thing. The yacht had been painted in the Quisling Mild colours, purple and gold, and draped in bunting and flags. Even the poor waiters sidling round with trays of Martinis looked like cigarette packets in their purple uniforms and gold sashes. The seats round the edge of the deck had been upholstered in white leather, with inch-thick violet carpeting and huge whirlpool baths down below. If it hadn't been for the ominous rock-and-roll every time another damn speedboat whizzed in and out of the harbour ferrying VIPs to and from yachts anchored further out, she'd never have guessed she was even on a boat. Nigel himself was got up like a dog's dinner in baggy white linen trousers, a loose white shirt open halfway down his chest, fake mirrored RayBans and white leather shoes. Perhaps he hoped that if he was sitting down he'd blend in with the seats and Lillian wouldn't notice if he had his hand halfway up some bimbo's skirt.

Stevie saw him nearly tip his Martini down his white trousers as a stunning redhead walked past their yacht and into the Paddock, the vast enclosure along one side of the harbour filled with luxurious motor homes and tents decked out in the various sponsors' colours. The redhead turned to pose for the paparazzi and Nigel couldn't keep his eyes off her. That'd teach him to ponce around on some huge yacht, far away from the action.

She did a double-take as Tom Cruise and Nicole Kidman entered the Paddock, followed by the actor Patrick Barlow and his glamorous pregnant wife, Louise, then Mike Mills and Jefferson Holt from the rock group R.E.M. Poor old Nigel, he must be spitting blood. There were more famous faces here than in a year's issues of *Hello*! Julia would die when Stevie told her she'd actually seen Tom Cruise with her own eyes, even if he *was* half a mile away. A host of minders were strictly monitoring the entrance and turning back anyone who didn't have the right passes, however famous they claimed to be. According to Annabel, it was harder to get into the Paddock at Monte Carlo than Wimbledon's Centre Court on Finals day. Stevie grinned as some tarted-up bimbo was unceremoniously sent packing. She still wasn't thrilled with this boat, but it was pretty cool to be able to stand here and watch soap stars and big-name football players getting turned away.

The place was packed out. Annabel had been complaining all day about the *tifósi*, and it was some time before Stevie had realised she wasn't talking about a new vegetarian soya substitute but the hordes of Italian motor racing fans wandering around Monte Carlo dressed in Terroni and Ferrari colours. It was funny how the Italians coined all these words – paparazzi, *tifósi*, mafiosi – to describe specialists at the national pastime of aimlessly hanging around in groups watching everybody else. Martin Romaine called it the Iron Filing Syndrome, because they all seemed to be magnetically drawn to some unspecified point where they clustered for no apparent reason.

There was a sudden roar from the crowd and Stevie swung back to the track. Almost immediately the expectant hush gave way to a groan of disappointment. A couple of cars shot by, but even Stevie could tell that they weren't racing.

'Bugger. False start.'

Stevie jumped. She hadn't heard Charles Cusack come out on deck. He was leaning against the rails a few feet from her, his eyes on the far horizon, holding a small two-way radio against his ear. She realised he wasn't talking to her, just thinking out loud.

'Red flag. Must have been an accident.'

'Is it – is it bad?'

He glanced round in surprise, as if he hadn't noticed anyone else was there. 'David Coulthard tangled with the two Ferraris on the way into the Devote corner,' he said after a moment. 'Doesn't seem too bad. They'll restart in their spare cars. Shouldn't take long.'

He ignored her and went back to his radio. Rude bastard. He was always so bloody bad-tempered. God knows why anyone bothered to talk to him. She glanced at him out of the corner of her eye as he pressed the radio to his ear. Even leaning against the rails, his weight noticeably on his left leg – she remembered he had a limp – she could see he was extremely tall, easily six-four or six-five. He was wearing jeans and an ancient, shapeless Barbour more suited to rambling through his woods than across the deck of a luxury yacht in Monte Carlo, the sleeves carelessly shoved halfway up his forearms so that she could see the frayed cuffs of his faded denim shirt. He had strong forearms, she noticed in surprise, tanned and well muscled, the hand gripping the rail firm and masculine. Somehow it was not at all what she'd expected.

There was a sudden burst of static and a few indistinguishable words from the radio. 'Shit, Tammy, you're breaking up,' Cusack shouted into the two-way. 'Say that again.'

The radio crackled once more, then died. 'I should be in the pits with them, not stuck on this sodding boat massaging Nigel's fucking ego,' Cusack muttered angrily. 'Tammy, for Christ's sake, *talk* to me.'

Stevie tried to look simultaneously inconspicuous and deaf as he paced backwards and forwards behind her trying to get some sense out of his radio, his eyes chips of flint in his pale face. Eventually he swore again and gave up, shoving the radio into one of his deep pockets and coming back to the rail.

'I hate these fucking people,' he said suddenly. 'Bloody wankers and arse-lickers, the lot of them.'

Stevie wasn't sure if he was talking to himself or to her. She wished he'd go away. His presence was dark and unsettling, like a black cloud looming on the horizon. He made her feel awkward and uncomfortable.

Abruptly he turned towards her. His cold blue gaze studied her without any real interest. His expression was bored and faintly scornful. 'So. What misfortune drags you here?'

'Me? Oh, um. Well, Annabel, I suppose.'

He looked away again. 'Fucking waste of time.'

'What, the racing?'

'No, all this. The fucking boats and parties and drinks and the rest of the shit we have to go through to get enough money to get on the track. Turns the lot of us into whores.'

Oh, sod off, Stevie thought. 'Why do you come if you hate it that much?' she asked.

'I should never have let Patrick talk me into it,' Cusack muttered sourly.

'Into what?'

'Coming back into racing. Taking this lot on again. I'd forgotten how bad it could be. And this time I don't even get to race. Team fucking manager. I must be fucking mad.'

'Did you race before?' Stevie said, surprised.

Cusack hunched forward over the rails, his expression unreadable. 'It was a long time ago.'

Stevie vaguely remembered Julia saying something about him once being a racing driver himself. 'Why did you stop?'

'Why do you think?' Cusack said coldly. 'Because I had a fucking accident, right here in Monte Carlo as a matter of fact.

A "bad" fucking accident, as you would say.'

'I'm sorry – I didn't know –'

It was too late. She had an uneasy feeling she'd lit the blue touchpaper, and retired. 'Jesus, if I could race, don't you think I'd be out there with them?' Cusack said. 'Do you really think I'd be trapped on board this floating Christmas tree with a load of has-beens and never-will-bes?'

'Look, I *said* I'm sorry,' said Stevie. 'You don't have to be so bloody rude –'

'And what would you know about what I have to be?' Cusack snapped. 'What would you know about being trapped in a heap of twisted, smoking metal that might explode at any minute while two doctors stand beside you calmly debating whether to cut off your foot or not? And all because of some-one else's stupid fucking mistake?'

'Well, you certainly know all about self-pity,' Stevie snapped back.

Cusack brought his temper under control with a visible effort. 'Oh, I see. You think I should pull myself together, get on with life, is that it?'

'Well, why not?' Stevie said defiantly.

'Really. Well, thank you for pointing that out to me, Miss Amateur Psychologist. There was everyone else treating me with kid gloves and all that nonsense, but you managed to get straight to the heart of the problem, didn't you? Got to be cruel to be kind, isn't that how it goes?'

Stevie flushed. 'No, I –'

'And with your vast experience, you decided to put it all right and say what no one else dared to,' Cusack drawled. 'Shock horror all round, then suddenly the poor misguided fool realises she's right, he has to move on, put it all behind him. Life will never be the same, but suddenly it has meaning again. After six years, he can pick up the pieces and live happily ever after.'

'I didn't mean that –'

'No, no, forgive me.' He held up his hand. 'I forgot the most important part, the bit where I look into the eyes of the woman who's saved me from myself and realise the debt I owe her and tell her I can never repay her, but if only she'll marry me she'll make me the happiest man alive.'

'I wouldn't marry you if you were the last man on earth and you crawled to me on your hands and knees begging me!' Stevie burned with anger and humiliation. '*You* were the one who started all this, remember. I didn't ask you to start telling me the story of your life. I don't give a toss what you think or what you feel, to be honest.'

He laughed shortly. 'Oh yes, you've made that clear enough.'

'I could almost feel sorry for you, if you weren't doing such a good job of it yourself.'

'Got the answer to everything, haven't you?'

'Oh, get a life,' Stevie spat.

'You little bitch.' Cusack steadied himself against the rail with one hand.

Stevie instantly felt ashamed of herself. He was an arrogant bastard, she couldn't stand the sight of him, but even she realised it must be hard, having to come back to Monte Carlo of all places and watch Patrick and Rafe race when he couldn't. And he was right about one thing: Nigel and the others like him *were* complete wankers. It was no wonder he was so angry all the time, though he didn't have to take it out on her. She felt a twinge of guilt. It had been partly her fault. Julia *had* mentioned some sort of accident, she shouldn't have asked such a stupid question. Stevie glanced at him as he leaned on the rail, his jaw tense and trembling, his knuckles white. Shit, shit and double shit. He wasn't the kind of person to start bleeding all over the nearest stranger, he must have really been upset to blow his top like that and say as much as he had, particularly to her. She wished she could take back what she'd said, even if it was all true.

She braced herself for another outburst. 'Look, I know I'm probably saying all the wrong things, but –'

She broke off as she saw Candida Mornay walking towards them, wearing a stunning cream dress that hugged her curves and showed off her long, tanned legs. Bloody hell, this was all she needed.

'Cusack, *darling*,' Candida gushed, slipping her arm through his and ignoring his lack of response. 'We were just talking about the new engines and Nigel said they shouldn't make any difference to a skilled driver, but Emmanuele said it will, and we really need you to settle the argument.'

'Nigel can fuck off,' Cusack said, disengaging his arm.

Candida laughed lightly. 'I really don't think I'd better tell him that –'

'I don't give a flying fuck what you think,' Cusack muttered.

If Candida heard him, she gave no sign. Stevie decided it was about time he was rude to someone else and edged away as Candida effectively blocked Cusack's only escape route, determined not to be shaken off.

'Oh, dear, I don't know what Stevie's been saying to get you so angry,' Candida said as the twins spotted Stevie and rushed over to her. 'Terribly sweet, of course, but hardly *Mastermind* material, is she? And she's not exactly much to look at, poor darling. Rather unfortunate nose, and with her skin, I don't think I'd eat so much chocolate. It's no wonder she's a tad overweight.'

Cusack looked bored. 'I hadn't noticed.'

'Well, no one could call her attractive, poor thing –'

'I don't find criticism of other women attractive, Candida, whoever they are.'

'Goodness, I wasn't criticising, whatever made you think that?' Candida said quickly. 'Stevie's a sweetie, really. I'm *terribly* fond of her, of course. But she could do so much more with herself, don't you think? Perhaps a different hairstyle, or a few smart clothes, though with her figure ... Really, I'm only thinking of her.'

Cusack was silent.

'Darling, you're terribly quiet. Has she driven you quite, *quite* mad –?'

'Actually, I was thinking she had a lovely smile.'

Candida was momentarily shocked into silence. 'Well, I'd no idea things had gone this far,' she said gaily, recovering her composure. 'Who would have thought it? Falling in love with the nanny, how terribly convenient! You won't have to hire one.'

'Don't be ridiculous –'

'No, no, let me be the first to congratulate you. Lady Stevie, how terribly quaint. And of course she will fit in so well with your family, I can quite see her entertaining up at the Castle. You can teach her to ride to hounds, and she'll introduce you to the pleasures of *Coronation Street* and bingo. Very Eliza Dolittle. How terribly egalitarian of you.'

Cusack pushed past her. 'I've had enough of this nonsense. I'm going to the pits. You can tell Nigel that's where I'll be.'

Stevie had heard none of this exchange but glanced round as Cusack stormed to the gap in the rails and jumped awkwardly down on to the quay. God, he looked furious. Candida didn't look exactly thrilled either as she stalked back to rejoin Nigel and the other sponsors. Stevie bit her lip guiltily and pulled Lily on to her lap, pointing towards the track as the safety car drove past. Sod Lord bloody Cusack. She had more important things to worry about.

'Where the hell are you going?' Nigel shouted to Cusack as the race restarted. 'I wanted you to stay on board –'

Cusack carried on walking. Nigel flushed with anger, furious at being so publicly ignored. '*Signor* Terroni, I can't apologise enough –'

Emmanuele Terroni waved his hand. 'Let him go.'

'I can't think what the problem is. There must be something

172

urgent he has to deal with – he's not normally *this* rude.'

Not much, Stevie thought. She studied Emmanuele Terroni with interest as he turned away from Nigel and started talking to Lillian. This was the man Patrick and Rafe worked for, the owner of their racing team and the Terroni car empire. Even to someone as inexperienced as she was, he seemed to emanate power, raw and dangerous. He looked a bit like a Hollywood Mafia mobster, a cross between Robert de Niro and Chazz Palminteri. Stevie guessed he was somewhere in his mid-fifties, though it was difficult to tell. He was a big man, not just tall but broad-shouldered and heavy. There was no trace of grey in the dark hair slicked back from his high forehead into a small ponytail; his eyes were like black olives as they darted from one person to another, seeing everything and missing nothing. He was far from conventionally good-looking, but there was something about him – strength, ruthlessness – that was attractive. Stevie guessed he wouldn't be a good man to cross.

Jamie broke her reverie, kneeling up beside her, his chin on the rails. 'Where's Daddy? Is he winning yet?'

'He's that purple car, Jamie, see? The one with the four on the front.'

Lily squirmed in her lap to get a better look. 'There's two purple cars.'

'The other one is Rafe,' Stevie said. 'He's got a number fifteen on his, see?'

Annabel sat down beside her. The cars raced past them, so close that Stevie flinched. The noise was deafening and a strong smell of burnt rubber and exhaust fumes filled the air. Lily suddenly burst into tears, burying her head in Stevie's shoulder. 'I don't like it! I don't like it!'

Jamie looked scornful. 'You're just a stupid girl.'

'Ssh, Jamie,' Stevie said as she hugged the sobbing girl, stroking her hair. Annabel watched helplessly. 'Come on, now, Lily. What's the matter?'

'I want my daddy to be here! I don't want him to be killed!'

'Oh, Lily. He's not going to be killed,' Stevie said. 'Whoever told you such a dreadful thing?'

'Anya at school. She said lots of people have crashes and get killed.' She started crying again. 'I don't want my daddy to be dead.'

'Your daddy is a very good driver, Lily, nothing's going to happen to him –'

Lily twisted in Stevie's arms and glared at her mother. 'I hate you, I hate you! It's all your fault! If you loved Daddy you wouldn't let him race and then he wouldn't be hurt! You don't love him any more!'

Annabel gasped. '*Elizabeth*!'

'Go away! Go away, we don't want you! You don't love us! You don't love Daddy!'

Stevie rocked Lily in her arms, surprised by the uncharacteristic outburst but not dismayed. Most five-year-old girls were jealous of their mothers and wanted their fathers all to themselves. It was something they all went through and soon grew out of. She glanced up at Annabel, her smile of reassurance fading as she saw the shocked expression on the older woman's pale face. Annabel's beautiful blue eyes held pain – and something else Stevie couldn't quite identify. If she hadn't known better, she would almost have thought it was guilt.

Stevie was scarlet with excitement by the time the cars shot past the Quisling yacht for the seventy-sixth time and began the penultimate lap. It had been a breathtaking Grand Prix. The lead had switched back and forth between Patrick, Rafe, Michael Schumacher and Damon Hill as each of the drivers had been forced into the pits to change tyres and refuel. It was only now, in the final stages of the race, that everything rested on the drivers' skills.

Stevie had had no idea how much strategy was involved in

winning a Formula One Grand Prix. She'd just assumed the drivers lined up and raced round the circuit, and whoever drove the fastest and managed not to crash won. But no, nothing that involved advertisers and television ratings could be that simple. If racing was all that happened in a Grand Prix, it would long since have knocked bowls off the number one position in the most suicidally boring televised sport listings. The FIA had introduced a number of otherwise pointless rules to jazz things up a bit, one of which limited petrol tank size and forced the drivers to stop to refuel at least once. These days the teams had to make a tactical decision before the race started: whether to carry as much fuel as possible, the weight of which would initially slow the car down but mean only one stop in the pits, or take on less fuel and risk the delay of more than one pitstop. In a sport in which the difference between first and second place was a matter of seconds and a team spent millions of pounds on a gadget that might save half a second per lap, the length of time spent in the pits was crucial.

Even with an extremely personal (six-foot Italian) interest in the race, after the first few laps Stevie had found it hard to get excited just watching the cars just whizz round and round. She had to admit the refuelling stops livened things up a bit, even though it seemed that in the end, the race came down to who got their nuts off quicker in the pits – shame that wasn't as exciting as it sounded – rather than who was the better driver. They might as well abolish the driving bit altogether and just have the mechanics racing each other changing tyres and pumping petrol, sort of like a Grand Prix *It's a Knockout*.

Damon Hill had initially led the restarted race, but both Patrick and Rafe had stayed with him, Michael Schumacher – running a heavier fuel load – not far behind. Damon had lost his early lead during his second stop in the pits, enabling Schumacher to dominate the latter half of the race with Patrick, Rafe and Jean Alesi close behind. Alesi had crashed out during the forty-first lap, and then – to unsporting cheers from the

Quisling mob – Schumacher had had to make an unscheduled stop in the pits with gearbox trouble, giving Patrick the chance to go into the lead. He'd taken it and somehow managed to hold on to it, despite the best attempts of Rafe and Schumacher to wrest it back.

Rafe was a fraction of a second behind his team-mate as the two purple Terroni cars swept by the yacht to begin the last lap, so close to Patrick they were almost touching. Stevie hopped up and down as they passed, too excited even to cheer. Next to her, Nigel Purvis nervously chomped hard on his cigar and yelped as he nearly bit through his tongue.

'Patrick's going to win! He's going to win!' Stevie gasped, halfway over the rails with enthusiasm.

'Oh, Stevie, don't tempt fate,' Lillian Purvis groaned.

Stevie let go of Lily's patient little hand to grab Jamie by the collar of his blue polo shirt as he saw a fish swim past and nearly went overboard trying to net it. 'Only one more lap! I can't watch.'

'When I grow up I'm going to be a racing driver too,' Jamie announced proudly. 'I'm going to have a purple car and win and everyone's going to cheer.'

'Oh no you won't,' Annabel muttered. 'I'm not going through this with you as well. It's bad enough with your father.'

'Looks like Terroni will end up with first and second place,' Nigel said greasily to Emmanuele Terroni. 'Should give you a good shot at the Constructors' Championship as well as the Drivers'. I always knew Patrick wouldn't let us down –'

'Two weeks ago you were quite prepared to demand his replacement next season if he didn't start winning,' Terroni said coolly.

Nigel shifted uneasily beneath Annabel's wintry stare. 'I think perhaps there's been a bit of a misunderstanding. Maybe the language barrier –'

'I understand you perfectly,' Terroni said.

'Oh my God! Rafe's trying to overtake!' Stevie cried.

Annabel moved forward, pushing her way between Stevie and Nigel Purvis. She gripped the brass rail of the yacht, her face pale, her knuckles white.

'What the fuck is Rafe playing at?' Nigel snapped. 'He hasn't got room. He'll knock them both out and screw everything. It's the same bloody corner Patrick crashed last time.'

Stevie felt the fear rising inside her as she pulled Jamie towards her and held him securely. She could almost taste the tension on board the yacht. Her stomach was filled with butterflies and her mouth was dry as the two cars shot towards the tunnel entrance, purple blurs in the distance. Annabel stood motionless beside her. Lily looked in bewilderment from one person to another and started to cry again. Lillian Purvis glanced briefly at Annabel's frozen, unresponsive face and pulled the frightened child towards her, hugging her and stroking her hair as she murmured words of reassurance.

Nigel grabbed his portable radio from the bridge and turned up the volume so that everyone could hear.

'*Alexander's still in the lead, but Dussi's right behind him!*' the commentator shrilled. '*There's only one place left he can overtake now, they're coming into the Virage Anc Gare corner – that's where Patrick Alexander and Charlie Lytton crashed out so spectacularly six years ago –*'

Annabel swayed slightly.

'*Of course, this is Charlie Lytton's first season back in motor racing since that tragic accident. This time he's team manager, and what a team he's managing! Unless something goes very, very wrong, it looks like Terroni will be walking away with first and second place!*'

'Annabel, you must be thrilled,' Candida murmured.

Annabel looked at her sister sharply. 'I just want Patrick home safely.'

Candida smiled infuriatingly. 'Of course you do.'

'*Dussi's very close now!*' the commentator shrieked. '*But there's less than half a lap to go!'*

'He's not going to try to overtake, surely?' Lillian Purvis murmured over Lily's head. 'It's so dangerous, he can't be.'

'He bloody is,' Nigel said furiously.

The commentator was beside himself. *'If he's going to do it, this is the moment!'*

'No,' Annabel whispered.

'Yes!' the commentator screamed.

Jamie yelled and broke away as Stevie gripped his hand tight with terror. Sunlight dazzled her eyes so that it was impossible to separate the distant purple blur into two cars. For an endless moment they seemed to merge together, and then suddenly one of them shot forward into the mouth of the tunnel alone.

'Dussi's done it!' the commentator cried. *'He's through!'*

Annabel sank down on to the white leather seating. Stevie felt a flicker of surprise as she saw her expression. She didn't look too disappointed that her husband had come within an ace of winning his first Grand Prix of the season and ten vital championship points, only to lose it all at the last minute to his own team-mate. If anything, she looked pleased. It must be the relief that Patrick was going to be all right.

'Rafe Dussi has won the 1995 Monaco Grand Prix, his first ever Grand Prix win!' the commentator on the radio cried. *'What an unbelievable race! This will put Dussi in third place in the championship with twenty-one points, just five points behind the leader, Michael Schumacher!'*

'I knew he could do it,' Nigel said to Emmanuele Terroni. 'Rafe's an excellent driver, I've always thought so.'

'Shut up,' Terroni said mildly.

'But all is not lost for Patrick Alexander, who now lies in fourth place with eighteen points. With another twelve races to go between now and the final Grand Prix in Adelaide on November the twelfth, it's still anybody's championship. But what a day for Terroni!'

'Heavens, won't Cusack be pleased?' Candida said brightly. 'First and second place. He really is a jolly good manager, don't you think?'

'Bloody brilliant,' Nigel said quickly. 'Absolutely right to go down to the pits earlier, good decision, back him all the way.'

Lillian stood up and took Lily back to her mother. 'I'm ever so sorry, Annabel,' she murmured. 'I know how much this race meant to Patrick. It was jolly bad luck to be pipped at the post like that.'

Annabel smiled. 'Yes. Wasn't it?'

Eleven

Stevie closed the door to the twins' cabin with a sigh of relief. After the excitement of the race it had been almost impossible to get them to settle down. So much for Patrick's blithe promise at the interview that she'd only be looking after the baby – not that she really minded. She adored Harry, but at two months old he wasn't exactly a thrill a minute. All he did was feed, shit and sleep. The twins were exhausting, but she couldn't complain they were dull. Last week Jamie had climbed on to a priceless Hanoverian occasional table in the drawing room which had fortunately survived the experience, lifted down from its place over the mantelpiece the Samurai sword his great-grandfather had brought back from one of his trips to the Far East in the Thirties, and ceremoniously beheaded every single flower in his mother's rose garden. When Annabel had discovered what he'd done and made clear exactly what his immediate future held by way of solitary confinement and stops on his pocket money, he'd attempted to repair the damage by Sellotaping the severed blooms back on to their stalks. Stevie was just thankful he hadn't decided to practise his sword strokes on one of Mrs Arcor's cats.

'*Ciao*, Stevie.'

Stevie jumped as Rafe came down the narrow corridor. A hot blush washed over her as she remembered the last humiliating time she'd seen him. He must remember it too. He had to think she was a complete moron. God, would she ever live that dinner party down?

'So, is everything OK?'

'Oh, yes. Fine,' Stevie said awkwardly. 'Um, congratulations on winning the race. You did really well.'

'I was just lucky.'

'No, you were very brave. I'm sure you deserved it.'

He shrugged. 'I was pleased.'

Stevie shifted uncomfortably, trying to think of something to say. This was so embarrassing. He must know how much she fancied him, she'd made it plain enough the night of the party. He was probably just as embarrassed himself for ever suggesting they look round Monte Carlo together. She bet he was trying to think up an excuse to get out of it right now. She squirmed inwardly. If only she could turn the clock back. She must have been seriously evil in a former life for God to do this to her. Jezebel or Wallis Simpson at least. After the fool she'd made of herself, no wonder Rafe was trying to forget the whole thing. She ought to do the same, she was only making it worse. If only he wasn't so *bloody* handsome.

Rafe leaned comfortably against the wall beside her, his weight resting on one hand. He seemed to fill the entire space as he loomed over her, six feet of pure, unadulterated sex on legs. Bugger, bugger, *bugger*. Why did she have to fall for someone so far out of her reach?

She suddenly realised Rafe was staring strangely at her. 'Stevie, your face –'

What now? Stevie thought wildly. Purple rashes? Orange spots? Alien life-forms bursting through her skin?

He grinned. 'I think maybe the twins had – what do you call it? – Marmite for tea?'

Stevie's eyes locked helplessly with his as he licked his thumb and gently rubbed Jamie's Marmite fingerprints from her cheek. He touched me! Stevie thought ecstatically, falling back against the cabin wall for support. Oh, Jamie, I owe you one. Flying saucers, gobstoppers, white chocolate mice, anything you want. OK, Rafe rubbing her face clean might not be the hot passionate sex of her dreams, but it seemed it was the closest she was going to get. Suddenly her legs felt weak and rubbery as if she'd just got up after a week in bed with flu. She was breathless, literally winded with wanting him as if she'd been punched in the stomach.

'*Perfetto*.' He stopped rubbing her cheek but made no move away from her. 'So, *cara*. Why aren't you in the Paddock celebrating with everyone else?'

She tried to breathe again. 'I was just –' Her voice was dry, papery. She swallowed and cleared her throat. 'I was just putting the twins to bed.'

'Did they enjoy the race?'

'I think so. Well, Jamie did, anyway. I'm not so sure about Lily. The noise frightened her a bit –'

He was openly studying her face as she spoke. His gaze slowly travelled down the rest of her body as her voice trailed away. Stevie blushed under his scrutiny, helpless with longing. He could have stuck pins in her and she wouldn't have been able to object.

'And you, Stevie? Did *you* enjoy it?'

If she hadn't known better, she'd have thought he was teasing her. Did he have any idea what he was doing to her? Her whole body was flaming beneath his gaze, her nipples standing out like organ stops.

She nodded, enthralled. 'Oh, yes.'

'It excited you?'

This time there was no mistaking his tone. He knew exactly what he was doing to her. She didn't have time to wonder why, she was too busy trying to stay upright.

She trembled as his fingers brushed across her face again. 'I think –' his thumb trailed across her cheekbone – 'it is time –' and down her neck – 'for the victor –' and along her collarbone – 'to claim his spoils.'

182

His eyes never left hers as his body closed in on her. She could feel his heat, smell the spicy tang of aftershave, the faint aroma of petrol and burnt rubber that still clung to his leather jacket. His lips were warm and dry as they brushed swiftly, lightly against hers.

'I think you promised me that we would explore Monte Carlo together,' he murmured. 'Can I hold you to your promise?'

'Oh, yes, please!'

He glanced at the chunky steel Breitling on his wrist. 'OK. It is nearly seven now. I will meet you in the bar of the Hôtel de Paris in one hour. It is very easy to find, just ask for Casino Square.'

'Hôtel de Paris, Casino Square,' Stevie repeated dazedly.

'Eight o'clock.'

Stevie watched him walk down the ill-lit corridor, too stupefied to move. Her whole body was aching with the unfinished passions his kiss had stirred, her mind whirling with confusion. She should be racing round her cabin, running a bath, painting her toenails, choosing her clothes, sorting – her body tingled deliciously at the thought – through her underwear for something lacy and seductive to wear tonight, just in case. Instead all she could do was watch his retreating leather back and think how much she wanted him.

She closed her eyes ecstatically. 'Oh, God. Roll on eight o'clock.'

'Eight o'clock,' Rafe said.

Annabel gripped the deck rails and stared straight ahead of her. The town of Monte Carlo was alive with excitement, clusters of people talking and laughing on every corner. Crazy kids in VW Beetles and on motor scooters tore through the streets that only hours ago had been a Formula One Grand Prix circuit. Lights glittered all along the coast, their reflections smeared in the jet-black water of the harbour. She could feel the anticipation rising from the city like steam from a Turkish bath.

She bowed her head, staring at the inky gap between the yacht and the quay. 'I can't, Rafe.'

She felt him move behind her, his body hard against her back as he rested his hands on the rail on either side of hers. 'If you want to, you can. Patrick is busy tonight. You're free. Do you want to, Annabel?'

Annabel was silent. For the first time, she admitted to herself how much she *did* want to. In those split seconds this afternoon when the purple blurs that were Rafe and her husband had merged together on the lethal corner before the tunnel entrance, she'd been able to read her feelings with the clarity of someone who'd been fumbling endlessly in the dark and then suddenly found the room flooded with light. Her first desperate fear had been not for her husband of ten years, the father of her children, but for Rafe. She still loved Patrick, of course, but her feelings for him were conscious, deliberate feelings based on years of loyalty and friendship, on a decade of shared lives and experiences. Her feelings for Rafe were primitive, instinctive, overwhelming.

'Do you want to, Annabel?'

It took all her willpower not to turn round and fold herself in his arms. 'I can't,' she repeated.

His breath was hot and sweet against her cheek. 'That isn't what I asked.'

'For God's sake!' Annabel cried, twisting round. 'What do you *expect* me to say? I'm married, I have three children who need me. What do you want from me?'

'I want the truth.'

Something snapped inside her. 'All right, yes, I want to be with you! Does that satisfy you? I want you so badly I can't think of anything else! I lie awake at night and imagine it's you beside me, I let my husband make love to me and it's your face I see!' Her voice was anguished. 'Is that what you wanted to know? Are you happy now?'

Rafe caught her arms and pinned them against her sides as

184

his mouth drove down on to hers, crushing her lips against her teeth so hard she tasted her own blood. She struggled to break free, refusing to open her mouth to admit his tongue. His kiss deepened, and lust scorched through her, withering her resolution. Suddenly she no longer had the will to fight it. She groaned her submission, her lips opening beneath his. He released her arms and she pulled him against her, her heat rising as she felt his erection pressing into the soft curve of her belly.

Rafe broke the kiss, his dark eyes unreadable as he looked down into hers. 'Meet me, Annabel.'

She nodded, unable to speak.

He touched her cheek gently as he turned away. 'Oh, Annabel. It is so hard to leave you.'

Annabel watched him walk to the gap in the rails and jump lightly down on to the quay. Instead of the fear and guilt she'd expected, there was only relief that the battle with her conscience was over, even if it meant she'd lost. Until she'd met Rafe, she'd always thought her relationship with Patrick was secure and unassailable; but Rafe had breached it effortlessly. It terrified her. For the first time in her life, she wasn't able to control her feelings. The more she'd run from them, the more they'd seemed to overwhelm her. She hadn't been able to sleep or concentrate on anything. The months of fighting herself had completely drained her until she was no longer sure of anything. At least now she'd made the decision, for better or worse. She refused to think about what would happen after tonight. The excitement buzzing through her veins drowned out the tiny voice telling her she was insane to risk everything – her home, her marriage, the happiness of her children – for a man she scarcely knew.

Her stomach fluttered as she glanced round. The boat was deserted. Stephanie had already gone into town – probably to meet some man, judging by the rapturous expression on her face – and everyone else was in the Paddock where Nigel was busy holding court. She ran lightly down the stairs to the deck below, entering the cabin she shared with Patrick and locking the door behind her. Crossing to the wardrobe, she pulled out an ankle-length beige chiffon dress embroidered with thousands of tiny amber, bronze and gold beads sewn into the shape of grapes and vine leaves. When she wore it, it looked as if she was naked but for the beaded leaves twisting and curling all over her like ivy around a neglected statue. It was an Armani and it had cost her – Patrick – nearly £10,000; the most expensive outfit she'd ever bought. She hadn't allowed herself to acknowledge why she was packing it two days ago. Now she admitted to herself that she'd known since the dinner party what she'd wanted to happen in Monaco.

She laid the dress on the bed and ran her bath. Rafe had known she'd be on her own tonight: Nigel Purvis had demanded Patrick's attendance at a Quisling Mild dinner, Monaco being one of the few chances the company's fat cat executives had to mingle with the rich and famous. She wasn't expected herself; she'd given Stephanie the night off as soon as she'd heard about the dinner so that she'd have an excuse not to go. She hated these sponsorship dinners with their *nouveau riche* clients and timid little wives. But Patrick couldn't get out of it. Annabel loathed Nigel Purvis, but right now she could have kissed him.

The dinner wouldn't finish until at least midnight; she'd be fine as long as she was back on the yacht by 11.30. No one would ever know.

She suddenly realised that, without Stephanie, she had no babysitter. What in heaven's name was she going to do? She couldn't ask anyone else; they were all going to the dinner, and if they dropped out to babysit for her, *she'd* have to go to the wretched thing. She was in a Catch-22.

It was funny how quickly the adulterous mind adapted to a life of deceit. Once she'd made the decision to cheat, the rest seemed to be following almost without conscious thought: the lies, the ruses, the excuses. Rosie had always said –

Of course! Martin Romaine was still on board. He had a bad cold and Nigel had banned him from the Quisling dinner – the stupid man was paranoid about catching something and getting ill. She'd tell Martin she was meeting a girlfriend Patrick didn't like her to see, or something. He had no reason to disbelieve her story, but even if he did she knew he wouldn't say anything, Rosie would see to that. After all the covering up she'd done for her in the past, Rosie owed her one.

After her bath she pulled on a tiny pair of coffee silk La Perla panties edged with Chantilly lace, hooking a matching bra behind her back. Her nipples hardened as she imagined Rafe removing them in a few short hours' time. She smoothed her cream Fogal stockings – £35 a pair, but worth it – over her legs and stepped into the Armani dress, deftly hooking the tiny row of loops over the buttons at the side. The delicate chiffon swirled around her ankles as she slipped on the matching beaded pumps she'd bought with the dress and studied her reflection in the mirror. Hair up or down? Down, she decided. It made her seem softer, more vulnerable. She shouldn't forget that Rafe was four or five years younger than she was. She didn't want to appear too sophisticated. No make-up tonight, then; she didn't need it anyway. Her pale blue eyes were bright with anticipation, her cheeks flushed, her complexion glowing. She looked twenty-two, not thirty-two.

She sprayed a cloud of Chanel into the air in front of her and walked through it the way her mother had taught her – 'Never directly on to the skin, dear, too overpowering and dreadfully common' – and glanced at her wristwatch as she left her cabin. Five to eight. Patrick and the others would be safely at the Beach Plaza by now.

She knocked on Martin Romaine's cabin door.

Martin stared at her as he opened the door. 'Annabel, you look stunning,' he said. 'I didn't realise you were going to the dinner too. I think –' he broke off to sneeze. 'Sorry. I think you've missed the others –'

'Yes, I know.' Nervously she shut the door behind her and busied herself straightening a hideous nautical print on the wall so that she wouldn't have to look him in the eye. 'Actually, Martin, I was wondering if you could do me a bit of a favour. A – a girlfriend of mine lives here in Monaco, and I've rather promised I'd meet up with her. I don't see her very often and she's going through a bit of a difficult time, her husband's left her, you see, and she's feeling rather down –' Annabel was aware she was saying too much, but the slightly sceptical expression on Martin's face was making her feel nervous. 'Well, you see, it's Stephanie's night off, and I was wondering –'

'You'd like me to mind the kids?' He leaned back against the bulkhead, his platinum curls gleaming in the spotlight above his head. 'Sure, I'm not going anywhere. Who's the girl-friend?'

'Just an – an old schoolfriend.'

'Couldn't she come over to the yacht?'

'Well, you see, it's a bit awkward. Patrick doesn't really like her very much –'

'Ah.'

Annabel smiled brightly. 'Silly, I know; but I don't want to make a fuss. I thought I'd just pop out now and see her. I won't be back late.'

'That really is a very beautiful dress, Annabel.'

They stared at each other. Annabel knew immediately that Martin had realised she was lying. She wouldn't wear a dress like this to meet a girlfriend. She hoped he didn't guess who she *was* meeting. It wouldn't take him long to work out that if Patrick discovered what she was up to, Rafe would almost certainly be thrown out of the Terroni team and that would leave one very convenient vacancy from the point of view of an ambitious test driver.

'Have a good time,' Martin said lightly, picking up his book again.

Annabel felt a surge of relief as she left his cabin. So far, so good. By the time her taxi reached the Hôtel de Paris, her stomach was churning. She paid the driver, ridiculously over-tipping him, and darted up the shallow steps to the front entrance. She walked into the main lobby, scanning it nervously. She didn't know how on earth Rosie did this all the time; any minute now she'd feel a hand on her shoulder. She tried to appear calm and relaxed as she walked through into the bar and perched on one of the stools. No one was going to see her, they were all safely on the other side of Monte Carlo. She ordered a margarita and sipped it slowly, her heartbeat return-ing to normal as she studied the lobby carefully. He wasn't here yet.

She almost spilled her drink into her lap when Stevie sat down on the stool next to her.

'Hello, Mrs Alexander. I thought it was you when I came out of the loo.'

'Stephanie!' Annabel stared at her in shock. 'What are you doing here?'

Stevie blushed. 'Oh, um. I'm meeting someone. Well, I hope so, anyway. I've been waiting ages and he isn't here yet.'

The girl was actually looking rather sweet tonight, Annabel thought distractedly. She was wearing some sort of stretchy little black dress – rather unexciting, but safe, and it made her look slimmer than usual even if it was a trifle short. She'd obviously made a bit of an effort with her hair, it looked quite smooth and glossy for once. The awful bleached bits seemed to be growing out at last; her natural hair colour was a surpris-ingly rich brown, chestnut with cinnamon highlights. Her make-up was a little on the heavy side, of course, but at least it hid the worst of her spots, and her eyes looked huge and bright, she was positively glowing. She did have a rather pretty mouth, Annabel reflected, soft and slightly vulnerable. Some

189

men might find her really quite attractive.

'What are you doing here, Mrs Alexander? I thought you were babysitting?'

Annabel thought frantically. 'Um, I'm –'

Stevie suddenly leaped off her stool, sending a small dish of peanuts flying. 'Oh, God. He's come.'

Annabel swung round. She didn't know who Stephanie was talking about, but Rafe had just arrived too. Her stomach flipped as she wondered how on earth they could get rid of Stephanie. Perhaps she should pretend to be surprised and just chat casually to him until Stephanie's date turned up. Annabel hoped for all their sakes that whoever he was he didn't stand the poor girl up.

She deliberately busied herself with her glass so that she would look more relaxed when Rafe finally spotted her. When she felt a hand on her shoulder she swung round, an expression of pleasant surprise already on her face.

She clutched the bar in shock and disbelief. '*Patrick*!'

Her husband grinned. 'So this is what you get up to when my back's turned.'

Annabel stared dumbly at him.

'Don't I get a kiss?'

Numbly she proffered her cheek. 'What – what are you doing here?'

'Thanking you two for getting me out of a lousy dinner,' Patrick laughed. He waved the barman over and turned to Rafe behind him. 'Gin and tonic for me. Another margarita, darling?'

'No, thanks.' She turned to Rafe, her expression dazed. 'I don't quite follow –'

'I met Patrick and Nigel in the Paddock earlier and we got talking,' Rafe said smoothly. 'I just happened to mention that Lily looked a bit off colour this afternoon, then Lillian Purvis started going on about some measles epidemic.' He shrugged. 'You know Nigel. He immediately banned Patrick from the dinner. We thought it would be a nice surprise for you if I didn't say anything about Patrick coming and just arranged to meet you here myself.'

'It – it was,' Annabel said faintly.

Patrick smiled at his wife. 'I knew you'd be pleased. It was terribly sweet of you to offer to stay and babysit, darling, but it was hardly a fun way to spend your first night in Monte Carlo.'

Stevie sat silent and bewildered, on her bar seat.

Annabel barely registered Charles Cusack as he stalked into the bar. She felt hot and faint, although she was sure it was cooler in here than it seemed. They'd come so close to being discovered. Thank God Rafe had had the presence of mind to cover for her. She'd have given the game away if it hadn't been for him.

Next to her, Cusack scowled into his glass. 'Fucking awful day.'

'Terrible,' Patrick agreed. 'First and second places, could hardly have been worse.'

'It could have been a lot worse thanks to that bloody idiot,' Cusack exploded suddenly, slamming down his drink and turning on Rafe. 'What the *hell* did you think you were playing at, overtaking like that?'

'It was perfectly safe.'

'You could have both been killed! What does it take to get through to you? Didn't you do enough damage last time?'

There was a tense silence.

Then, 'I don't think this is the time to talk about work,' Rafe said.

'Let's just enjoy this evening, shall we?' Patrick murmured. 'We're supposed to be celebrating.'

Cusack knocked back the gin and tonic he'd ordered and turned his back on them to order another.

Rafe put his arm round Stevie's shoulder and smiled. 'I'm afraid we must go. We have a date.'

Annabel's grip on her glass tightened as she watched Rafe and Stevie leave the bar together. Stephanie had been meeting *Rafe*. She felt as if someone had thrown a bucket of cold water in her face as she realised the significance of that. Stephanie had come to say goodbye to her on the yacht all dressed up and full of blushes before Annabel had even spoken to Rafe herself. That meant Rafe must have arranged to meet the girl *before* he'd beguiled Annabel with kisses and sweet talk out on the deck. Her mind whirled with confusion. Was Rafe playing some sort of sadistic game, deliberately tricking her into agreeing to betray her husband so that he could have the satisfaction of standing her up? No, there must be more to it, something she didn't know about. Rafe couldn't possibly choose Stephanie over her. The girl hadn't got a clue how to interest a man like Rafe. Look what she was wearing, for a start. Sweet little dress, but hardly an Armani. The girl didn't know the first thing about how to sparkle in conversation. Rafe must be using her as cover to stop Patrick becoming suspicious. It was the only explanation.

She saw Rafe pull Stevie towards him and drop a kiss on to the top of her head as the doorman leaped forward to open the door and she quelled a flare of jealousy. She should feel sorry for her, really. Rafe didn't care about the girl. He was just using her. It didn't mean anything. How could it, when it was Annabel he really wanted?

He's got his arm round me, he's got his arm round me, and everyone's watching, Stevie thought exultantly. She straightened her shoulders and resisted the temptation to stick her tongue out at the French doorman as they left the hotel. It had taken her ten minutes to convince the snooty bastard she wasn't a journalist or a hooker – either clearly equally unsavoury in his mind – and let her into the hotel when she'd arrived to meet Rafe. Now he was running round opening doors and bowing and calling her *Mademoiselle* because she was with Rafe Dussi. She felt like Julia Roberts in *Pretty Woman* when she went back to the posh boutique that had refused to serve her and waved all her shopping bags in their faces, taunting them because they worked on commission. 'Big mistake,' Julia had said. 'Big. Huge.'

'Did you say something?' Rafe said.

Stevie blushed. 'No, nothing. I must've been thinking out loud.'

'You didn't say something about a mistake –?'

She shook her head and Rafe gave a mock sigh of relief. 'Good. For a moment I thought you'd changed your mind about coming out with me.'

The doorman snapped his fingers and opened the door of a taxi as it drew up beside them. Stevie started to climb in, then stopped suddenly and turned to Rafe, her cheeks scarlet. It was no good, she had to know now, before she got too carried away. It would be much worse if she built this evening up into something special and he was only doing it out of kindness. 'Rafe, look, if – if it's just this evening, I'll understand,' she said hurriedly. 'It's really very nice of you to take me out at all. You didn't have to come. To be honest, I didn't think you would.' Her blush deepened. 'After what happened last time, I wouldn't have blamed you.'

'Oh, Stevie.' His dark eyes softened. 'I was only late because I met Patrick. Really, I *want* to be with you. And not just for tonight.'

Stevie felt giddy with delight and relief as she settled into the back of the taxi. He really *did* see this as a date, she hadn't got it wrong. She'd been so afraid he hadn't really meant to ask her out. Even when she'd been getting ready she'd kept telling herself not to get too excited in case she'd got the wrong end of the stick. She'd been too scared of tempting fate to spend hours on her hair and make-up, and anyway, there hadn't been time. She'd thrown on the only decent thing she'd brought to wear, a crumple-proof black velvet dress from French

Connection that she'd got half-price in a sale, brushed her hair, slicked on some red lipstick and almost run out of the door before Rafe could come back and tell her he'd changed his mind. She hadn't even had time to bung on any perfume. She'd arrived at the hotel half an hour early, fought her way past the doorman, and then sat hunched over a Bacardi and Coke miserably eating her way through a dish of peanuts, laughing hollowly at herself for having been so stupid as to have put her diaphragm in her handbag along with her lipstick and Amplex breath fresheners. She'd been to the loo twice already with nerves. When Annabel had arrived at a quarter past eight and there'd still been no sign of Rafe, she'd been certain she'd mis-understood somehow; he was meeting the others, not her. She still couldn't quite believe she was actually alone on a date with him.

And not just for tonight, he'd said. Oh God!

A cluster of fans outside the hotel entrance suddenly spotted Rafe and started to run towards them, shouting his name. Rafe bent and stuck his head inside the taxi. 'Stevie, would you like to go to the Casino instead? It's probably the only place in Monte Carlo where I won't have to spend the whole night sign-ing autographs.'

'Oh yes – that is –'

'It's OK, I only ever gamble with other people's money. This evening is on Nigel. Next time perhaps he won't be so quick to take up my bet when I say I'm going to win.' He leaned past her and carelessly threw a 20-franc note through the window of the taxi to compensate the driver for his wasted time. 'We don't need a cab, we can walk. It's not far, the Casino's just across the square from here –'

He broke off abruptly. Stevie stared up at him for a moment, puzzled, then peered through the window of the taxi. Cusack had just walked out of the hotel and was standing on the steps watching them. He held her stare for a long moment, then dug his hands into the pockets of his jacket, swivelled on his heel and marched in the opposite direction.

Stevie's heart sank as she clambered out of the car. This was her fault. 'Um, Rafe –'

'Don't worry, you look beautiful,' Rafe smiled, ducking round the side of the hotel and dragging her with him as the fans ran after the empty taxi, thinking he was still in it. 'Everyone will love you.'

'No, it's not that –' She bit her lip. 'The thing is, Rafe, I think it's me who's got you into trouble with Lord Cusack.'

He stopped walking. '*You*?'

'We had a bit of an argument this afternoon,' Stevie said awkwardly. 'I mean, I know he argues with everyone, but he really went ballistic today. He probably freaked out at the hotel because you're with me –'

'It is nothing to do with you,' Rafe said quietly.

'And even if we hadn't argued, I bet he doesn't approve of you taking his friend's nanny out,' Stevie rattled on. 'He probably thinks it reflects badly on the whole team –'

'Stevie, I told you, it has nothing to do with you.'

She stopped talking. She hadn't missed the dark light in his eyes. She recalled the tension she'd sensed between the two men when they'd all met in the rose garden after she'd screwed up Patrick's television interview with INN. Rafe wasn't just trying to spare her feelings, he was telling the truth. Whatever bad blood was between them had been there long before she'd come on the scene.

'What *is* it with you two, then?' she said curiously. 'Anyone would think you hate each other, the way you carry on.'

Rafe started walking again. 'Look, forget it, OK? It doesn't matter.'

'*Does* he hate you?' She darted in front of him, forcing him to stop and face her. 'He does, doesn't he?'

Rafe shrugged. 'It's not important.'

'Of course it's important! He's your manager, Rafe, he's responsible for you when you're out on that track. Supposing he tried to – well, to do something –'

'Like what?'

She flushed. 'Well, you know, your car –'

'Sabotage?' Rafe shook his head, laughing. 'Oh, Stevie, racing's a dirty game, I'll give you that, there's no such thing as a fair fight, but Cusack wouldn't try that sort of stunt. The mechanics go over every inch of those cars before each race. And it's not his style. He might try to ruin me, but he'd make damn sure he'd do it fairly and legally. It's the way he is.'

'Ruin you? Why would he want to do that?'

Rafe's smile faded. 'You don't give up, do you?'

'Not a hope. Ask my friend Julia, I drive her potty sometimes.'

'I'm beginning to see why,' Rafe said drily. He turned away, rubbing his forehead with one hand as if trying to obliterate memories he didn't want to see. 'There was a terrible crash here at Monaco six years ago,' he said finally. 'Patrick and Cusack nearly died –'

'Yes, I know, he told me about it.'

He took a deep breath. 'There is no easy way to say this. I was involved in that crash too.'

'You?'

Rafe nodded.

'But I don't understand. Why hasn't anyone said anything before? Cusack didn't even mention you. I thought this was your first season in Formula One?'

'Yes. As Rafe Dussi, it is.'

Stevie gaped. 'That's not your real name?'

'Stevie, when the accident happened I was just twenty-one, driving for a small Italian team called Brindizi. You won't have heard of them, they only lasted half a season. You have to understand, motor racing is incredibly expensive. It's OK for the big teams, they get sponsorship deals – if you win, you'll get thousands of pounds' worth of free tyres, engine-makers work with you for nothing, the sponsors come to you.'

'Like Quisling Mild?'

Rafe nodded. 'It's hard for the small teams to compete. If it was left to market forces, only three or four big teams like Ferrari and Terroni would ever get cars on the grid. The FIA don't want that, it would make for a very boring race. So they pay the teams just to turn up. You get almost as much for taking part as you do for winning. Every year there is a crap team on the back of the grid who come last every single race. In 1989, it was Brindizi.' Rafe pulled out a pack of cigarettes and lit one, his mind lost in the past. 'But we could have caught up. We were getting better. With a bit more time –'

'What happened?' Stevie interrupted.

Rafe blew out a long stream of smoke and finally turned to face her. 'It was the second day of qualifiers. I was coming into the corner before the tunnel – the same place I overtook today. Patrick and Cusack – he was Charlie Lytton then, this was before his father died – were racing for Terroni. They were both ahead of me. I was so certain I could get through between them.' He shook his head. 'I still don't know what happened. I passed Patrick, then he seemed to swerve and hit Charlie's car –'

'And Cusack blamed you,' Stevie said softly.

'He was so bitter, I suppose he had to blame someone. Patrick was his best friend, so instead he blamed me.' Rafe's voice hardened. 'Cusack claimed I was deliberately reckless. My licence was suspended while the FIA investigated. Brindizi's sponsors didn't wait for the outcome, they withdrew immediately. By the time I was cleared, Brindizi had folded. I had my licence back but no one to race for.'

There was a brief silence.

'What is your real name?' Stevie asked quietly.

'Dussi is my mother's maiden name. My real name is Raphael Terroni.'

'*Terroni*?'

'Emmanuele Terroni is my father.'

Stevie instantly pictured the big Italian, and the sense of raw, ruthless power that seemed to emanate from him. She felt an unexpected surge of pity for Rafe.

'He was the one who made sure that Charlie's accusations never reached the press,' Rafe said. 'It had only been a routine qualifier – no one caught the crash on camera, and apart from Patrick and Charlie no one was aware I was involved in the accident. With my father's power and influence it wasn't hard to keep me out of it. The FIA knew, of course, but since their private inquiry cleared me, it didn't matter. Of course, by the time that happened it was all too late.'

'But if the FIA cleared you,' Stevie said, 'why couldn't you find another team?'

'My father could deal with the press, but he couldn't stop the gossip,' Rafe said. 'Charlie Lytton – Cusack – was a brilliant driver. Advertisers and sponsors wouldn't touch me.' His voice was bitter. 'In the end it always comes down to money. I spent five years trying to convince someone else to take me on without a single offer.'

'I don't understand. Why didn't you go to your father to begin with?'

'You don't know my father,' Rafe said shortly. 'He controlled everything, he had to own everyone, body and soul. That was why my mother left him in the end and went back to America. Brindizi had been my one chance to be independent, to prove I could succeed without him. Cusack forced me to go crawling back to him on my hands and knees, to say he'd been right and I'd been wrong. I did it because in the end, it was either that or never race again. I couldn't bear that.' He drew deeply on his cigarette. 'My one condition was that I didn't use his name. I couldn't bear everyone thinking that I was only on the team because I was his son. Some of the old hands on the circuit know who I am, but the press and sponsorship people have short memories. They know me as Rafe Dussi, they don't ask any further.'

'Does Nigel Purvis know?'

Rafe shook his head. 'He'd drop Terroni if he knew there were any skeletons in our cupboard. It's in my father's interest as much as mine to keep it quiet.'

'But how can you bear to work with Patrick and Cusack now, after all they've done?'

'It was never Patrick,' Rafe said quickly. 'He's always been fair. He refused to blame me until after the inquiry reached its verdict, and afterwards, he accepted what they'd decided. He's always acted as though it never happened. As for Cusack –' he shrugged. 'Neither of us have a choice. We either work together for Terroni, or we don't work at all.'

'But it's so *unfair*!' Stevie cried hotly. 'It was all Cusack's fault! Can't you do something about it, tell someone? Cusack can't just go round ruining people's careers –'

Rafe smoothed her hair back from her forehead with both hands, framing her face. 'Oh, Stevie. You're so loyal. When I'm with you I forget all the bad things in my life. I wish I had met you before all – before.'

'You're with me now,' Stevie smiled. Her heart thudded with love.

'Yes, I am.' Rafe released her, finishing his cigarette and grinding it out beneath his foot, his mood suddenly lifting. 'And we're supposed to be celebrating, remember? I've just won my first Grand Prix, and I want to share this evening with you. No more bad memories.'

Stevie let him take her hand and drag her across the road towards the Casino, dazedly trying to absorb what he'd told her. No wonder he and Cusack barely spoke to each other. What a bastard! Of course it was terrible that he'd lost his foot and couldn't race any more, but that was no excuse to take it out on Rafe when it wasn't his fault. The FIA inquiry had cleared him; Cusack should have apologised, put the record straight and stopped the gossip. He probably had no idea of the damage he'd caused, although if he had he wouldn't care. He was too wrapped up in self-pity to think about anyone else.

Rafe was laughing as he pulled her up the steps towards the Casino entrance, as if he'd already forgotten their conversation. Must be his Latin temperament, angry one minute, laughing the next. She laughed back, catching his mood. Whatever had happened in the past, Rafe had just won his first Grand Prix fair and square and no one could take that away from him. He was right: this was no time to dwell on bad memories.

She half-fell as Rafe propelled her through the front door ahead of him and a uniformed flunkey immediately blocked her way, his expression openly contemptuous as he assessed her cheap velvet dress, plastic Swatchwatch and scuffed suede heels.

'Excuse me, *Mademoiselle*, are you here to meet someone –?'

Rafe strode forward, his presence instantly cloaking her in the equivalent of a Chanel cocktail dress. 'She's with me.'

'Ah, *Monsieur* Dussi, of course.' The flunkey awarded them both a brilliant smile which gave no indication that Rafe's leather jacket, white T-shirt and black Levis broke every aspect of the Casino's strict dress code. 'Welcome back. Many congratulations on this afternoon's win. A superb race, if I may say so. Would you like a drink at the bar before you go through?'

'No.' He grinned at Stevie. 'We have a bank to break.'

The doorman smiled obsequiously and beckoned to an underling. 'Of course. François, show *Monsieur* Dussi and *Mademoiselle* through to the Casino.'

Stevie slowed her steps, staring around in disbelief as they entered the vast Casino hall. She had never seen so much opulence, so much wealth. The Casino itself was magnificent, solid mahogany gambling tables covered in green baize stretching for miles across an ocean of deep red carpeting. Chandeliers glittered high above her head, throwing off prisms

200

of light reflected in dozens of huge gilt mirrors. She could hear the click of roulette balls skittering into slots, the chatter of hundreds of lost chips being raked in across the baize, the discreet murmur of voices as card players doubled their stakes or stuck on nineteen. The men were wearing black tie, the women Lagerfeld, St Laurent or D'Alfonsi. The diamonds at their necks, ears and wrists didn't just glitter anonymously when the light caught them; they were so huge you could actually see what shape they were.

'My God. It's amazing,' Stevie breathed.

'What would you like to play first?' Rafe asked, enjoying her reaction.

Stevie turned a full 360 degrees. 'I don't know. What do you think?'

'First, we need some chips.' Rafe took her hand and led her over to a glassed-in cage in the corner. 'You can take half, and I'll take half. Let's see who lasts the longest before we run out.'

'You mean lose it all?'

'Never come to a casino and expect to win,' Rafe said, casually handing the cashier what looked like a wad of several thousand dollars. 'If you do win, all it means is that you'll get a little bit longer here before you lose it again and have to go home. At the end of the day, the Casino always wins.'

Stevie picked up one of the flat round discs embossed with the Casino name. 'How much is this worth?'

'Five thousand francs – that's about £700.'

'*Seven hundred pounds?*'

Rafe counted out her chips. 'Those ones are about £135, these are £270, you've got the 700s, and these two are 10,000-franc chips – about £1400.' He laughed at her expression. 'Either be very sure you're going to win when you place those, or stand next to Robert Redford and hope he makes you an indecent proposal.'

Stevie glanced behind her as if half-expecting Redford to

walk past. 'I'm sorry, Rafe, I couldn't do it,' she said, staring at her chips. 'Even the little ones are more than I earn in a week. It's just too much.'

'Stevie, do you really want to tell our grandchildren that you came to the Casino at Monte Carlo and didn't dare put a single chip on the table?' Rafe said sternly. 'There are some things you have to do before you die, like having a love affair in Paris or showering naked under a waterfall. Or playing roulette at Monte Carlo.'

Our grandchildren, Stevie thought ecstatically.

Rafe took her arm and guided her towards the roulette table. 'Let's keep this simple to begin with. Red or black?'

'Um. Red.' She paused. 'No, black. No, no, red, red.'

'I'm glad I didn't ask you to pick a number between one and thirty-five,' Rafe said. 'Are you sure you want red?'

'Yes. Red.'

'OK. Put your chip down on that square there.'

Stevie studied the tube of discs in her hand. 'You're sure there isn't anything smaller?'

'*Stevie* –'

'OK, OK.' She took a deep breath. 'One of these on black.'

'I thought you said red?'

'I changed my mind.'

The croupier looked up as Stevie reluctantly committed her chip to the section of baize representing black. '*Faites vos jeux, mesdames et messieurs.*'

Stevie gripped Rafe's hand and closed her eyes. 'I can't watch.' She listened as the ball clattered around the wheel, then opened her eyes again. The square of baize marked out with the numbers on the roulette wheel was heaped with chips, most of them worth far more than the one she'd put on. How could these people bear to lose this kind of money? It was more than she'd ever earn if she lived to be a hundred.

'Six, black, *mesdames et messieurs.*'

'You've won,' Rafe murmured.

Stevie stared as the croupier raked in the lost chips and distributed others to those who'd won. 'A hundred and thirty-five pounds!' she said reverently. 'Just like that!'

'Just like that.' He smiled. 'OK. Now this time you can choose a number.'

'Everything on just one number?'

Rafe nodded.

'Twenty-nine,' Stevie said without hesitation.

'That was easier than I expected. Why twenty-nine?'

'The twenty-ninth of September is the twins' birthday.'

He laughed. 'Place your bet, then.'

Stevie started to push another small chip forward, then looked at Rafe, grinned, and placed a 2000-franc chip on twenty-nine. She watched as a young Chinese man next to her picked up ten silvery chips and put them beside hers.

'How much are those worth?' she whispered to Rafe as the croupier spun the roulette wheel again.

'A hundred thousand francs – about £14,000 each.'

One hundred and forty thousand pounds on one spin of the wheel. You could buy a four-bedroomed house in Edenfield for that. These people didn't live on the same planet.

'Thirty-two, black, *mesdames et messieurs.*'

The Chinese man shrugged as the croupier raked in his chips and counted out another ten, pushing them back on to twenty-nine. Stevie stared in disbelief.

'Would you like to try something a bit more within your control?' Rafe said, amused.

Stevie nodded.

'OK, then. Let's go and play cards.'

Stevie snuggled closer into Rafe's leather jacket as they came out of the Casino and stood on the steps, staring out across the bay as the first fingers of dawn pinked the grey sky. She had had the most wonderful, magical evening of her life. She didn't want it to end, she wanted to stretch every moment into an hour and make it last for ever. She was scared that if she closed her eyes, the spell would break and this evening would be nothing but a dream.

She clenched her palm around the chip in her hand, feeling its hard edge dig in. Rafe had kept it back specially and given it to her as they'd left. She could have cashed it in for over a hundred pounds, but it meant far more than that to her. It was her proof that tonight had really happened.

Rafe had been right, they'd lost all their chips by the end of the evening – but it had been worth it. They'd drunk champagne, they'd chatted to film stars (wait till Jules found out Brad Pitt had actually spoken to her, even if it was just to ask her to get off his foot); they'd shared peanuts with royalty (she wasn't nearly as dippy as everyone said, and she hadn't been sick once) and she'd even been asked to blow on some Greek shipping millionaire's dice to bring him luck. It hadn't, he'd lost, but that wasn't the point. She'd been part of it all, the glamour, the excitement. She'd even been £1000 up herself at one point. *A thousand pounds*. It hadn't seemed like real money, it had been like playing Monopoly. Nothing seemed real this evening. She half expected the clock to chime midnight and Rafe to turn back into a mouse, leaving her alone on the steps in her rags with only a pumpkin for company.

'I don't want tonight to end,' Rafe murmured.

'Oh, me neither,' Stevie whispered fervently.

'Stay with me?'

Stevie nodded, her eyes shining.

Rafe smiled, wrapping his arm round her as they started walking back towards the yacht. A faint breeze lifted his hair and chilled her arms. Rafe stopped and slipped off his jacket, placing it over her shoulders. It was warm and smelt of him. Stevie pulled it tightly around her. Anticipation fizzed through her. She wanted this to happen so much she felt sick. By the time they reached the quayside, she was jumping with nerves.

As Rafe stepped aboard the Quisling yacht and held out his

hand to help her, she stumbled slightly as a soft swell rocked the boat, and fell against him. Rafe steadied her but didn't let her go. Instead, he kissed her. It wasn't like the chaste kiss with which he'd said farewell earlier that evening. It was electrifying. She held tightly on to his jacket as his tongue slid between her lips, probing, tasting, exploring. She could feel the power held in check, the raw hunger behind his tenderness. Her stomach flipped as if she'd just gone over a hump-backed bridge, her nipples hardening beneath the thin velvet of her dress.

Rafe separated himself from her. 'Not here,' he whispered hoarsely. 'I want it to be right for you.'

He took her hand and led the way down the steps to the lower deck and along the narrow corridor towards his cabin. Her legs felt like wet string knotting beneath her short skirt and she jumped as his jacket caught a picture frame and it clattered against the cabin wall. Rafe stopped and glanced back, listening. There was no sound to indicate that anyone had woken. He put his finger to his lips in warning, then opened his cabin door.

Stevie slipped his jacket from her shoulders and stood holding it nervously in the centre of the room. Rafe moved to the bedside cabinet and switched the side-light on, then turned off the overhead glare. Through the dark porthole she could see the reflection of the full moon rippling across the surface of the sea.

Rafe walked over and stood directly in front of her, close but not touching. Stevie stared down at his boots, thinking how beautiful they were. The black leather seemed to cling to his feet like a second skin, soft and supple. That was the Italians for you, they made beautiful shoes; Annabel said their belts and handbags were the best in the world, they accessorised brilliantly . . .

'Stevie, there is nothing to be afraid of,' Rafe said, interrupting the hysterical flow of her thoughts. 'Nothing is going to happen that you don't want to.'

'Oh, I *do* want to!' Stevie exclaimed.

He smiled. 'I want to, too.'

'I have to – um, the bathroom – I'll be back in a minute,' Stevie gabbled.

She threw his jacket on the bed and locked herself in the tiny bathroom at the end of his cabin. God, she wouldn't want to have a hangover in here, all this gold and purple was making her feel stoned. She sat down on the loo seat and opened her bag, her hands shaking. She hated putting her diaphragm in, it was like trying to get a cork with a life of its own back into the bottle, but she'd been hopeless with the pill. She'd kept on forgetting it and having to start again. A diaphragm was much safer; at least you knew when it was in. She unscrewed the top of her tiny travel tube of spermicide – her Tart's Tube, Julia called it – and squeezed it round the rim of the diaphragm. Shit, she was so nervous there were squiggles everywhere, it looked like she was trying to decorate a cake. Bugger it, it'd have to do. No one was going to see it except the sperm, and they weren't going to live to tell the tale. Just as she thought she'd got it in place, she lost her cream-greased grip on it and it sprang out of her hands across the bathroom floor.

There was a soft knock on the door. 'Is everything all right, Stevie?'

'Yes, yes, fine,' Stevie panted. Where had the sodding thing gone now? 'Be out in a moment.'

She heard Rafe put on R.E.M. as she scrabbled behind the loo, looking for her diaphragm.

She used two hands this time and managed to get the bloody thing up and in before the spring released. Please God, let me be OK, don't let him be disappointed, don't let me make any squelchy noises or anything. And please, *please* don't let him notice my stomach.

Rafe was wearing only his black jeans when she emerged. She stared at him, drinking him in. His torso gleamed like burnished gold in the soft side-light, firm and muscular. Dark whorls of hair were just visible above his jeans. His bare feet made no sound on the thick carpet as he led her towards the centre of the room and stood behind her.

'First, I am going to kiss you, Stevie,' he whispered softly in her ear. 'I am going to taste you, the sweetness of you, feel the warmth of your mouth opening beneath mine. I am going to suck your lips, slip between them and enjoy their softness, explore every part of your mouth with my tongue, dip into you again and again.'

His words sent shivers across her skin. Moisture flooded between her legs and she clenched her cunt, frustration and excitement shooting along her limbs. When he turned her towards him and kissed her she had to hold on to him for support.

'I am going to peel your clothes away from your body and love every part of you, piece by piece,' Rafe murmured as he rained kisses on her face. 'I am going to slowly, slowly roll your dress down to your waist, kissing your shoulders, your collarbone, that sweet, small hollow in your throat. I am going to suck your nipples through that lacy bra until you're begging me to take it off so that you can feel my mouth against your hot skin. I will stroke your beautiful full breasts and then, when you can't bear it any more, then I will unhook your bra and suck and kiss and bite them –'

Stevie groaned as he started to ease her French Connection dress away from her shoulders.

'– and then when you are so hot with desire you are almost melting in my hands, I will slide your dress down further,' Rafe continued, his lips trailing across her collarbone. 'I will kiss your belly, my mouth will burn through your panties as I pull the dress down more, a little more, until it is around your ankles and you are trapped, exposed –'

He slid her dress from her shoulders to expose her black lacy bra. For the first time in her life she didn't care what she looked like or if he'd noticed the bulgy bit under her bra or what she should be doing; her whole mind was focused on his words. She had never experienced anything so erotic. The pictures he conjured up turned her on so much that by the time he did what he'd just described her body was charged with anticipation. He was fucking her in her mind long before he touched her body.

'– and then I will pull down your panties, and you will long for me to suck between your legs. Picture yourself, Stevie. You will be standing there, naked, your dress around your ankles, your panties around your knees. You can't run, you can't hide. The door is unlocked. Anyone might come in. But you won't care, Stevie, will you?' She barely felt him reach round behind her back to unhook her bra, her brain was whirling with a hundred erotic images. 'I am kneeling at your feet, Stevie, and you are standing there for me, giving yourself to me, your soft body gleaming in the moonlight, your breasts full and ripe and heavy, your nipples dark and hard. And between your legs is a secret darkness, Stevie, so wet and damp –'

His mouth descended on her breast. Stevie shuddered, her nipples burning as he sucked them. She twined her fingers in his hair, holding his head against her breast, but he eluded her, his hands deftly rolling her dress over her hips as he painted his erotic pictures.

'You will want me to fuck you, Stevie, you'll beg me to, but you will have to wait. I will stroke your breasts as my tongue dives between your legs, teasing and licking that little pink bud, and you will try to bury my head deeper in your beautiful hungry bush, desperate for my cock to take you.'

Her dress slipped to the floor. She throbbed as his lips trailed across her belly to the lacy black fabric of her panties.

'I will watch your face as you orgasm,' Rafe said, tilting his head back to look at her. 'And then I will pick you up and lay you on the bed, and you will rub your hands across your breasts and between your thighs as you watch me undress, you will moan and beg me to fuck you, you will want me so much you will not care what you have to do or say –'

He hooked his fingers through her panties and tugged them down to her knees, breathing in the musky scent of her as he bit the soft insides of her thighs. She nearly exploded as his tongue found her clitoris and flicked across it. She felt the deep-rooted throbbing begin within her and swayed as Rafe knelt on the floor and held her steady.

'Rafe, I'm going to come,' she gasped. 'Please, I want you to be inside me.'

'No. I want to watch you come.'

Stevie couldn't argue, it was too late. She gripped his shoulders as her orgasm broke over her, moaning his name over and over. Rafe stood up and pushed her backwards on to the bed. She stared at him as he stood naked before her, his cock rearing proudly from the tangle of dark hair at the top of his thighs. His golden body was firm and lean, his stomach flat, his buttocks hard and taut. But it was his eyes that drove her wild. She had never had a man look at her with such desire, and it turned her on more than anything he could have said. His hands roamed over her body, caressing, stroking, savouring her flesh, and suddenly she didn't feel fat any more, she felt voluptuous and soft and eminently desirable.

Rafe smiled as he thrust into her, taking her with quick, hard strokes. 'I am going to . . .' he murmured.

And did.

Twelve

Rosie Knighton slammed her wine glass down on the mantelpiece so hard the fragile stem almost shattered. 'Don't lie to me, Martin! I saw the way you looked at her!'

'For Christ's sake, Rosie!' Martin shouted. 'She's your daughter, what do you expect me to do? Ignore her?'

'*Ignore* her? You couldn't keep your *eyes* off her!'

'I met her in the street! We were just talking –'

'Oh, so you've got time to talk to *her*?' Rosie cried. 'You came back from Monte Carlo more than two and a half weeks ago and you haven't come to talk to me, you haven't even bothered to phone me once!'

Martin threw up his hands. 'This is ridiculous. I can't believe we're arguing over something as stupid as this.'

'You *told* me you wanted her,' Rosie hissed.

He stared at her. '*I* told you? What the hell are you talking about?'

'In the woods, remember?' Her voice dropped to a dangerous whisper. 'You made me say you could fuck my daughter. You were fucking me, you bastard, you actually had your cock inside me, but you still made me say you could have my sixteen-year-old daughter too.'

Martin felt a brief echo of lust as he remembered taking her against the tree, then it was replaced by a surge of irritation. He hadn't heard Rosie objecting at the time. She'd have agreed to anything, she'd been so desperate. Stupid bitch, she must have known it had all been part of the game, like the ropes and the outdoor venue. He didn't want her damn daughter, he wasn't into schoolgirls, not even prick-teasers like Portia Knighton; but if he *had* been serious about seducing the kid, she'd have got precious little protection from her mother. Rosie was more concerned about her own interests than those of her daughter.

He watched Rosie stalk on spiky black heels towards the drinks cabinet and pour herself another glass of wine. Her black eyes glittered with malice as she glared at him over the rim. Jealousy was never attractive, but in this context it was particularly pathetic. A middle-aged married woman accusing her toy-boy lover of making eyes at her teenage daughter. It was like something out of one of Rosie's bloody novels. No wonder her husband let her do her own thing, he probably got sick and tired of playing a walk-on part in Rosie's private soap opera.

'Marty –'

Christ, he hated it when she whined like that. He'd rather she was angry; at least there was some dignity to that. He turned away as she came towards him and stared out through the wide bay window at the front of the house, wishing he hadn't parked his VW half a mile away to prevent gossip when he saw that it had started to rain. A few drops spattered against his face through the open window. This Thursday afternoon thing had to end. It had seemed convenient enough at first – Laurie Knighton worked a shift at the hospital A&E department in East Grinstead on Thursday afternoons – but it was rapidly becoming a millstone round his neck. The grief Rosie gave him wasn't worth the fuck any more. He'd avoided her for the last fortnight, not even bothering to phone with an excuse and hoping she'd get the message. He'd realised when she'd called today and demanded he come round that he'd have to spell it out. He should just tell her now and have done with it.

She touched his arm. 'Marty, talk to me.'

He let her drag him back from the window, knowing he was about to duck it again. He just couldn't face the scene he knew would follow. 'Rosie, look, I have to go. Patrick and Rafe just got back from Canada this afternoon, I'm supposed to be testing with them.'

'Can't it wait?'

'You know it can't. The French Grand Prix isn't much more than two weeks away.'

She wound her arms round his neck and nuzzled his shoulder. Her breasts felt warm and pliant against his chest. 'Not even for me?'

'I'm sorry, Rosie.' Martin disengaged her arms and bent to pick up his leather jacket from the sofa. She really shouldn't wear skirts that short at her age. From this angle he could see the black lace top of her stockings. 'I have to go.'

'*Why*?'

'I've told you already.'

'Martin, I'm not some bimbo you can just pat on the head in the hope I'll go away,' Rosie pouted. 'I'm not a fool. If you'd bother to tell me what's going on I might be able to understand what you're doing a bit better.'

'What's the point? You hate motor racing. You don't give a damn about what I do.'

'How do you know? You never give me a chance.' She slipped her arms round his waist, her tone suddenly cajoling. 'Why don't you tell me about your work instead of assuming I don't care? I want to care. I love you.'

'No, Rosie, you don't. You just want to think you do.'

Rosie insinuated herself between his thighs, her breasts pressing against his chest. She wasn't wearing a bra beneath her tight red T-shirt. Her nipples were like two small hard buttons digging into him. Despite himself, Martin felt his cock stiffen. 'I do, I *do* love you,' Rosie whispered. 'You love me too, I know you do. I can feel it.'

His mouth was suddenly dry. Jesus, what was it about her?

212

He didn't even like her. He'd only screwed her in the first place to prove a point. She was a selfish, jealous, unprincipled bitch, she was probably out to get him – and he wanted to fuck her brains out. 'I have to go,' he repeated weakly.

Her hand tugged open the buttons of his Levis so that his cock sprang free. 'All this coming and going. It can't be good for you.' He sucked in a deep breath as she slid down between his legs and took him in her mouth. He had to stop her. He had to stop this now.

'If you're that interested, Patrick came third in Canada, Rafe got knocked out of the race on the opening lap when Mika Hakkinen's McLaren T-boned him,' he said, staring down at the top of her hennaed head and making no move to pull her away. 'That puts Patrick in third place in the championship behind Schumacher and Hill, with twenty-two points. Rafe's just one point behind him with twenty-one –'

She stood up and pushed him back down on the sofa, hiking up her tartan miniskirt so that he could see she was wearing nothing beneath it but her lacy black stockings. His limbs were suddenly weak and bloodless as she sat astride his lap and slid her wet cunt tantalisingly up and down his exposed cock without taking him inside her.

'So what happens next?' Rosie said politely, as if they were sitting chatting in a bar.

'*What*?'

'I said, what happens next, Marty.'

'It's – it's – the French – Grand Prix on July the second,' he managed to gasp, distantly wondering how and when he had lost control of this game as she reached for his balls. 'The team managers are already looking around at the drivers for next season. Patrick's doing OK now, but if he starts to lose ground to Rafe, Terroni will probably decide not to renew his contract – *Jesus*, Rosie. Oh, Jesus.'

'And if they decide not to renew?' Rosie murmured, kneeling up on the sofa.

He stared transfixed at her black bush as she thrust him deftly inside her. 'Then Rafe will probably – *shit, Rosie, ohh, yes* – be their number one driver next season –'

Rosie pulled her T-shirt over her head and yanked his platinum head towards her naked breasts. 'Which means?'

'They'll – *uuunh, yes* – have a vacancy which needs to be filled.'

'Don't we all,' Rosie murmured.

'You bitch,' Martin panted. 'I'm going to come. Oh, Jesus, you bitch.'

'But what if Patrick does well?'

He groaned as she knelt up on the sofa again, almost pulling him out of her. He struggled to keep hold of his orgasm, but the bitch had pushed it just out of his reach.

'Come on, Marty. You're not even trying. Keep your mind on the job.'

'Fuck you, Rosie.'

'When you answer the question.'

'You slut,' Martin gasped, giving in. 'Patrick has to do better than well. He has to beat Rafe, prove he's not too old for the game. And Rafe has to beat Patrick to show he's got what it takes. They can't both win. Terroni will dump the loser. Please, Rosie. *Ohhh, yes.*' She was thrusting herself hard against his cock now, driving down on him, forcing him to keep still and drawing his orgasm out of him almost against his will. 'Either way – *ohhh, Jesus* – either way, there'll be a space for me. I can't lose.'

'Oh, I wouldn't say that,' Rosie whispered as he bucked and came beneath her.

Portia backed away from the open window. She'd seen them at it the moment she walked up the garden path. She didn't know why she felt so shocked – it was hardly the first time she'd caught her mother in the middle of it. She could still picture the hard arse of the tennis coach as he'd fucked her mother against

214

the fridge. She should be surprised Rosie hadn't waved and invited her in to watch. The way the slag was going, Playboy TV could set up a regular afternoon live link from Edenfield without paying a penny. Scheming, cheating, lying, poisonous *bitch*! Of course she knew her mother screwed around – who didn't? – but to do it in her husband's own living room, in broad daylight on his own sofa! And she'd be sitting right there on the damp patch when Daddy came home, all smiles and sweetness and light, as if butter wouldn't melt. What a complete tart! There was Daddy working all the hours God made, doing holiday work, double shifts, locum cover, to pay for this stupid big house they didn't need, and the Bitch was just soaking up money and fucking around behind his back. Jesus Christ, and with Martin Romaine! He was only twenty-four, young enough to be her son! Didn't Rosie realise how ridiculous she was making herself look? The whole village probably knew about it and was laughing at them all. If her mother had to fuck around, couldn't she at least find someone her own age?

Portia chucked her school rucksack behind the hedge as she ran back down the garden path, heedless of the rain soaking through her thin summer uniform. Her dark hair hung in rats' tails around her face, her white blouse and navy gym skirt clinging wetly to her narrow frame. She didn't really blame Martin, it wasn't his fault. Rosie had probably lured him over to the surgery with some pathetic sob story like the car not starting, and he'd fallen for it. Once she'd got him there, he wouldn't have had a hope. Rosie must've practically raped him. She was like some disgusting black widow spider at the centre of her web, snaring any man who came too near. It was no wonder Portia herself hadn't got a steady boyfriend – if she dared to bring one home, her mother would probably eat him for breakfast. Even Will Purvis hardly ever came round any more. She hadn't seen him since the night of the rave.

She turned into the road, heading back towards the village, hardly aware of the tears mingling with the rainwater on her cheeks. Maybe she'd catch the bus into Crawley and hit the Mall, exercise her bitch mother's plastic a bit. She was pretty good at forging Rosie's signature now, she'd had enough practice. Slag Knighton. It had a good ring to it.

She walked along the edge of the ditch, cursing as mud squelched over her Caterpillar boots. What was wrong with a pavement, for fuck's sake? She hated living out in the sticks. This wouldn't happen in London. She hated this whole place. She sidestepped a puddle, wondering suddenly if her father knew about Martin. Probably; he'd known about all the others. Why the fuck didn't he do something about it? They'd both be much better off without Rosie. When would he realise she wasn't worth it? Men were so stupid. Thinking with their dicks. What was it about Rosie that men found so bloody irresistible, anyway? Even Will couldn't keep his eyes off her. OK, she had a good figure and huge fucking tits, but she was over forty, she was *old*, for God's sake!

She heard a car behind her and automatically stepped closer to the hedge. A huge burnt orange Mercedes whooshed past, sending a spray of water across her calves, then suddenly the car stopped and reversed. Portia recognised Will's father, Nigel, as he pressed a button to open the electric window and leaned out to call to her.

'Portia Knighton, isn't it? I thought so. You look soaking, do you want a ride?'

Portia didn't miss the way his eyes clung to her wet blouse. Dirty old bastard. She was about to tell him to sod off, then something made her shrug and nod.

Nigel stretched across the passenger seat and opened the door. 'Hop in.'

'Thanks.'

She climbed in and pulled the seat-belt across her shoulder. Nigel slipped the car into first and pulled back out into the

216

road, his eyes lingering on her bare knees a fraction too long. 'Where can I drop you?'

'Wherever. I'll let you know.'

They drove in silence for a few minutes. Portia glanced at him out of the corner of her eye. He wasn't bad looking, actually, sort of an older, more blurry version of Will. She liked his suit, it looked expensive, though she wasn't so keen on the huge purple rocks in his shirt cuffs and the gold watch; a bit poncey for her liking. At least he wasn't treating her like a kid, asking her if her mother knew she was out – what a joke! – or how school was going. She hated being asked about her GCSEs, like that was all she ever thought about.

'You want to dry off before you head wherever you're going?'

She felt the warm blast of the car's heating across her knees and suddenly shivered. Bloody English weather, and they called this summer? 'I don't –'

'Lillian – my wife – and Will have gone to Bristol, they're checking out campuses before Will decides which universities to apply to,' Nigel said casually. 'Lillian's sister lives in Bath, they're spending the night there.'

She leaned forward to reposition the heating ducts before her knees blistered. At the same time – what a coincidence – Nigel reached for the gearstick to change down as they approached the level crossing outside the village. His hand covered hers for a moment before sliding smoothly across to her thigh. Portia didn't stop him. 'You really are a most stunning woman,' Nigel murmured, encouraged by her silence.

Portia scowled. 'Everyone else seems to think I'm just a kid.'

'Then that's their loss.'

She looked at him. His pale blue eyes held hers for a moment, then slid down her face to her springy breasts, her bra clearly visible beneath the transparent wet blouse, and on to the moulded navy triangle at the top of her thighs. She felt herself weakening. He was a real man, not some kid who didn't know any better. He was rich, good-looking, successful – and, she realised suddenly, Martin's boss. Her mother could have the monkey. She was going with the organ-grinder.

She crossed her legs so that her wrap-around skirt opened to reveal six inches of creamy damp thigh, and smiled. 'What was that you were saying about a ride?'

Oliver Colvin swore and danced backwards as the burnt orange Mercedes shot past The Gilt Edge pub, sending up a spray of water. 'Fucking idiot! What the hell does he think he's playing at?'

'That's Nigel Purvis,' Stevie said, rolling her eyes. 'He always drives like that.'

'Jesus. Does everyone around here think they're on a Grand Prix circuit?' Oliver carefully placed the tray of drinks he'd been carrying on the wooden picnic table outside the pub and chucked Stevie a packet of Bovril crisps. 'That prat made me spill a bit, so watch out the glasses don't drip all over you.'

Julia grinned. 'Don't tell Stevie that, you know how she hates to waste good alcohol.'

'Charming,' Stevie sniffed.

'Hey, I wasn't the one who spent four hours emptying ninety-six miniature chocolate liqueurs into a glass when we ran out of wine last Christmas.'

'Don't remind me, I feel sick just thinking about it,' Stevie groaned. 'Take it from me, Tia Maria does not go well with Grand Marnier, vodka and Harvey's Bristol Cream.'

'Yeah, I know. I was the one who had to mop up afterwards, remember?' Julia half-stood and felt her bottom. 'These seats are still damp. My dress is soaking. Who was it said living in England is like living in the middle of a damp lettuce?'

'Anyone who's lived through an English summer, I should think,' Oliver said.

'It serves you right for being so rude to me,' said Stevie.

'Just be thankful it's not still raining.'

'I don't see why you want to sit outside, anyway,' Julia grumbled. 'I blame the French and their bloody pavement cafés, it's given everyone ideas. The EU can make as many rules as they like, they'll never get our weather to be the same as theirs. In years to come, it'll be our one stand of defiance against the continent.'

'You just hate the French because you were sick on the ferry going over to Calais,' Stevie said.

Oliver swung his long legs over the bench and slid them under the picnic table. Shaking his floppy blond hair out of his eyes, he opened a packet of peanuts, tossed one up into the air and caught it in his mouth. 'I think Stevie's just getting in training for when loverboy takes her home to visit the folks in Rome,' he said slyly.

Julia nearly dropped her glass. 'Stevie, you *haven't*? You *cow*, why didn't you say before?'

'I've been *dying* to tell you, you silly tart, ever since I got back from Monte Carlo, but you were off on some jolly in Blackpool –'

'Do you mind?' Julia protested. 'It wasn't a jolly, it was a conference on the problems of Negative Equity in a Stagnant Housing Market.'

'Give it as many capital letters as you like, I still don't know how you made it last two weeks,' Stevie said.

Julia grinned. 'You didn't see the guy from Repossessions & Arrears.'

'Don't tell me. He gazumped you.'

'I wish. I spent four nights working on him before I found out he was gay.' She giggled. 'All right, all right. Now, are you going to stop looking smug and tell me about *Signor* Wonderful or not?'

Stevie flicked a damp beer mat at her brother. 'I don't know how *you* found out. How long have you known?'

Oliver dodged. 'Mmmm – about thirty seconds.'

219

Stevie sighed. 'God, why do I always fall for it?'

'Never mind all that,' Julia said impatiently. '*So*?'

'So what?'

'*So*, how far did you get?'

'Oh, don't mind me, girls,' Oliver said. 'I'll just drink my beer and try not to feel inadequate.'

'Your brother is a typical man, sex glands in his eyes and Page Three in his heart,' Julia said scathingly. 'He thinks all we care about is the size of a man's willy.'

'Let's forget about it,' Stevie interrupted airily. 'I'm sure you'd be bored hearing all about my nights of Latin passion anyway. Isn't it warm for the time of year –'

'*Stephanie Colvin* –'

Stevie giggled. 'OK, OK. Nine.'

'Nine – you *slept* with him? What have I told you about bonking a man on the first date?'

'I know, I know, but he's different, Jules. I wouldn't normally do it, but –'

'Are you kidding? I used to bring you up two teas on a Sunday morning and had to guess the sugars because I never knew who you'd be in bed with.'

'Look, Mother Teresa, do you want to know about it or not?'

'Tell me *everything*. From the beginning.'

Stevie hunched forward across the table in Serious Girl Talk mode.

'God, I don't believe it,' Julia breathed at the end of her recital. 'It's like something out of a Mills & Boon.'

'Well, I can tell you one thing,' Stevie grinned. 'Barbara Cartland it wasn't.'

Oliver gave up trying to pretend he wasn't interested in girly chat. He'd missed his Sunday afternoon kiss-and-tell sessions with Stevie and Julia; they'd taught him more about women than his six years of exploratory and undeniably investigative sex. 'So is this a regular leg-over situation or just a one-night stand?'

'You pig,' Julia said.

'Actually, Rafe's been a bit busy since Monaco,' Stevie said self-consciously. 'He was only home a few days before he had to go off and do the Canadian Grand Prix, but he should be back this evening.'

'It must be love, you're bloody glowing,' Julia said. 'You lucky girl. A glamorous racing driver, good-looking, rich, famous –'

'Unbelievable in bed –'

Julia stuck her fingers down her throat. 'Oh, go away. You make me sick.'

'It'll end in tears,' Oliver prophesied mournfully. 'You know what they say about Italians.'

'And what might that be?'

Oliver turned, as an amused, accented voice spoke behind him. Before he could say anything, Stevie had leaped up in rapturous welcome, sending her Bacardi and Coke flying. Oliver hid a smile as Stevie quickly ran her fingers through her damp hair and smoothed crisp crumbs off the front of one of the old England rugby shirts she'd appropriated from her brother years ago.

Rafe mopped up the remainder of the drink on the table with his handkerchief. 'Don't worry, I always seem to have this effect on her.'

'I can see why,' Julia murmured.

'I wasn't expecting you,' Stevie said, flustered. 'I thought you were testing down at the track with Patrick and Martin this afternoon?'

Rafe shrugged. 'Martin did not show up, so Cusack called it off. Mrs Arcor told me you were down here with your friends. I thought perhaps I could join you – that's if you do not mind drinking with a lousy Italian?' he grinned.

'Introduce us, Stevie,' Julia hissed.

'Oh, um. This is my best friend, Julia, and this rude pig is my brother, Oliver,' Stevie said. 'Don't mind him, he's just terrified the EU will abolish his beer or turn it into litres or something.'

'Can you blame me after what they did to cheese? You know it doesn't taste the same in kilos.'

'Oliver, you're only twenty-two, you weren't even born until after decimalisation,' Stevie said. 'I bet you don't even know how many ounces are in a pound.'

'That's not the point. It's the principle of the thing,' Oliver said firmly.

'*Precisamente*,' Rafe said. 'You should see what they want to do with our pasta. I blame the French.'

'A man after my own heart,' Julia said.

Oliver watched Rafe as he sat astride the wooden bench next to Stevie, one tanned knee poking through the rip in his Levis, his brown leather flying jacket hooked on one finger over his shoulder. He couldn't help feeling a vague stirring of familiarity, as if he'd met Rafe before. It was weird, seeing someone you'd come to know through television. You felt like you were already old friends. It was rather like the time he'd seen a man he'd been certain he knew sitting having a coffee at the next table in a café. He'd been about to go over and say hello when he'd realised the man was a soap star he'd seen almost daily on television but never met.

Rafe murmured something in Stevie's ear and gently smoothed her hair back from her face. Oliver couldn't help admiring the way the guy operated. Rafe had barely seemed to notice Julia. Oliver still found it difficult to look at his sister's friend without seeing the bossy little madam who'd punched him in the balls when he'd drawn felt-tip breasts on her George Michael poster, but to a poor, unsuspecting man who hadn't grown up with her, she must seem quite attractive – sexy, even, if you liked them tall and sultry in a Winona Ryder kind of way. Even Oliver could see she looked pretty sensational today in that sort of tight orange halter-neck dress, it gave her a fantastic cleavage. Her legs weren't bad, either, he thought, surprised. Most men meeting her would at least have given her a quick once-over. The fact that Rafe hadn't even smiled her way in front of Stevie told Oliver that this guy was very, *very* used to dealing with women.

Rafe turned Stevie's hand over and kissed the inside of her wrist. 'So, *cara*. Are you free today?'

Stevie blushed delightedly. 'Annabel took the children over to see her mother, so she gave me the afternoon off to meet up with Oliver and Jules.'

'No work for you either?' Rafe said, turning to the others.

'I'm in the middle of law exams,' Oliver said. 'This is what you might call free study.'

'Jules just bunked off,' Stevie added.

'I did not,' Julia said. 'I had a new property to check out in Copthorne before we put it on the market. I work at an estate agent's in Crawley,' she explained.

'She uses the term "work" loosely,' Oliver drawled.

' "*I am ashamed the law is such an ass*",' Julia quoted back swiftly.

'Are you two married or something?' Rafe asked, amused.

'Ignore them. They love each other really.' Stevie grinned blissfully up at him, thrilled at the chance to show him off. 'I can't believe you're back this early. I'm off tomorrow, too, Annabel's staying at her mother's until the weekend. We could go somewhere –'

'Patrick didn't mention anything about going away for the weekend,' Rafe interrupted.

'I don't think he's going,' Stevie said. She glanced around suspiciously as if *News of the World* journalists were lurking behind the soggy canvas pub umbrellas. 'To be honest, I think she and Patrick aren't getting on terribly well at the moment. Things have been a bit cool between them lately. I wish they'd have a row or something, clear the air.'

'Why do you think anything is wrong?' Rafe said lightly.

'You're right, it's probably nothing –'

223

'Come on, Stevie,' Oliver said, recognising the signs. 'Spill. You know you want to.'

'*Well* –' She paused dramatically. 'The other day, Annabel was on the phone to someone from the drawing room – no one ever normally uses that phone – and I was tiptoeing in because Jamie had spilt some lemonade on the carpet in front of the fire, and I'd promised him I'd clear it up before anyone found out about it – after the business with the Samurai sword, he was terrified Annabel would keep his birthday money for damages –'

'Stevie,' Julia said. 'The abridged version?'

'Sorry, sorry. Anyway, I was trying not to make a big song and dance about it for Jamie's sake, so Annabel didn't hear me come in. She was talking really quietly, like she didn't want anyone to hear, and she looked awfully upset.'

'Who was she talking to?' Julia asked.

Stevie shook her head. 'No idea. I just heard her saying something about being set up or something, and then she said, "But why go with *her*?" and he said –'

'What makes you think it was a "he" she was talking to?' Julia interrupted. 'It could have been her sister, or anyone.'

'No, I'm sure it was a man, there was something about the way she was talking.' Stevie shrugged. 'To be honest, though, I wouldn't really have thought anything of it, if it hadn't been for Patrick –'

Rafe looked up sharply.

'I didn't want Annabel to see me, you see, in case she thought I was earwigging, so I legged it back to the kitchen, and when I walked in, Patrick was just putting down the extension. He must've been listening to her conversation. Surely he'd only do that if he thought something was going on?'

'Maybe he wanted to make a call and didn't realise she was on the line until he picked it up?' Julia suggested.

'Maybe,' Stevie said doubtfully.

'It does sound a bit odd,' Oliver said, tossing peanuts into

Stevie's empty glass. 'Didn't you say she was in that hotel bar in Monaco when she was supposed to be babysitting? What was she doing there?'

Stevie frowned. 'She never actually said.'

'Maybe she does have someone else, then. What with Patrick away so much –'

'Who do you think the mystery man might be?' Rafe said, picking up some peanuts and matching Oliver shot for shot.

'Can't be that many to choose from,' Oliver said. 'Bugger, missed. Adultery is like murder: it's usually with someone the person already knows.'

Rafe scored again and smiled triumphantly at Oliver. 'Any suggestions?'

'Mmm – how about this Lord Cusack you keep talking about? Plenty of opportunity, they're from similar backgrounds, move in the same circles – it would be easy to meet up without anyone knowing.'

'The bastard!' Stevie exclaimed. 'That's just the sort of thing he'd do, steal his best friend's wife. I might have guessed it would be *him* –'

'Hang on a minute, you don't know it's him, it could be anyone,' Julia said. 'You don't even know Annabel's having an affair in the first place, this is all sheer guesswork.'

'Well, if she *is*, I bet it's all Cusack's fault.' Stevie was undeterred. 'He probably only did it to score one up on Patrick. Can't beat him driving, so screw his wife. Typical man, thinks sex is the answer to everything.'

'I think that's a bit unfair,' Oliver protested.

'You can't talk. You're the worst of the lot,' Julia said.

'I live like a monk.'

'Yeah. Rasputin.'

There was a clatter of heels as Sharon Cobbit tottered over to their table. Oliver wondered idly if she cleaned the loo in a tight pencil skirt and four-inch stilettos. It was all he'd ever seen her wear. 'Can I get you anythin', loves?'

Rafe stood up. 'Not for me. I'm afraid I have to go.'

'But I thought you were free this afternoon?' Stevie said, her face falling.

'*Cara*, forgive me.' Rafe bent and kissed her cheek. 'I have just remembered, I have to go back to the track to talk to Tammy. I will see you tomorrow, OK?'

'But where –?'

'I will call you, don't worry. *Ciao*, Julia, Oliver. It was good to meet you.'

'You done all right there, love,' Sharon whispered loudly to Stevie as Rafe walked away. 'I wouldn't say no to a bit of that meself. Always loved Italians, smooth as glass, they are. Dead romantic, got all the chat.' She glared at George as he cheerily hefted some crates around the side of the pub. 'They know 'ow to make a girl feel special, unlike some I could name.' She sighed. 'Mind you, they've 'ad a lot of practice, that's always the trouble.'

No wonder Stevie had fallen for the racing driver, Oliver thought, watching his sister glow with pride and adoration. Rafe was an easy man to like. He had a certain something about him. Maybe that's what made him seem so familiar. His sex appeal probably wasn't dented by the fact that he was a dashing Formula One racing driver, either. Oliver just hoped Rafe was as keen on Stevie as she clearly was on him. He loved his sister, but he had to admit she wasn't quite the person he'd have expected someone like Rafe to be with. If competitiveness ran in your DNA, Rafe must have the relevant gene in spades. He couldn't even chuck peanuts in a glass without turning it into a competition. But maybe he was being unfair and there was more to Rafe than met the eye. Perhaps he wanted a real relationship, someone he could be comfortable with. Stevie was very real. If that was what Rafe needed, perhaps it would work out.

Rafe turned and waved as he reached the turn in the road that led up to Edenfield Manor. Oliver stared at him as the pieces suddenly slotted into place. The way he smiled, the angle of his face –

He *had* seen Rafe Dussi somewhere before.

Oliver unlocked the main front door of the house he now shared only with Julia and stepped over a heap of mail lying on the mat. He picked it up and sifted through it as he kicked the door shut and headed towards the front door of his downstairs flat. Some junk mail for Stevie – she'd told him to chuck it all straight in the bin – a handwritten letter for Julia – he sniffed it: not Hugo, the prat had always sprayed his letters with *Egoiste* aftershave, for some reason he'd thought it was cool – and a bunch of envelopes for him, all but one of them brown. He put Julia's letter on the hall table so that she'd see it when she got back from her evening out with Stevie, and opened his lone white envelope as he let himself into his flat. Barclaycard, refusing his application for a higher credit limit, great. And that was the good news.

He opened the fridge. Ripping the tab off a can of Budweiser, he stared at the heap of brown envelopes. He didn't have to open them to know what they contained. Final demands for electricity, gas, the garage bill for the new alternator he'd had to get for his B-reg Ford – God knows how much longer the car was going to last, it was on its last legs already – council tax, telephone, his personal contribution to the National Debt. He guessed there was a letter from the bank in there somewhere too; he was already paying interest on the interest on his student loan, and Barclays were now probably charging him twenty quid for the privilege of sending him a letter telling him what he already knew: that working all the spare hours God gave waiting on tables at The Dome was not proving a satisfactory bulwark between him and bankruptcy.

Thank God he didn't have to pay rent on top of all this or he'd be out on his ear by now. His and Stevie's parents had bought this house for them several years ago when Stevie had been doing her NNEB course, splitting it into two flats, one for each of them. The deal was that neither of them would have to pay anything until they were earning, at which point their rent would be put towards paying off the mortgage on the property, which they would one day end up owning. In the meantime, if he had to sleep on bare boards and eat baked beans cold from the tin, at least he had a roof over his head.

He wandered into the sitting room, ignoring the pile of unopened books on his desk, and stared out of the window. Despite the earlier downpour, it was turning into a beautiful summer evening, sun glinting across the tops of the houses opposite and bathing them in a soft glow. He opened the sash window and the scent of damp roses from the flowerbeds outside filtered into the room. In the distance, he could hear children shrieking and the occasional ting of a bicycle bell. He felt a powerful longing to be back sitting outside The Gilt Edge, enjoying the balmy evening. June was always the same; tempting him outside when he should be studying. Every summer for ten years he'd been stuck inside some library, revising for one set of exams after another – GCSEs, A levels, First-Year Mods, Finals – watching sunshine stream in through grimy library windows, knowing that if he gave in to temptation and took an afternoon off, he'd feel guilty the entire time he was away from his books. He longed for July, but it was never the same once the exams were over. It was like that extra ten minutes in bed after the alarm had gone off: you only appreciated it because you knew you had to get up.

He leaned his head back against the wall and took a swallow of beer. A gentle breeze soughed through the uncurtained window and fluttered the pages of a TV guide that had fallen on to the floor and Oliver's glance travelled guiltily back to the unopened law books on his desk. He shouldn't have bunked off to see Stevie this afternoon, he should have been revising. He'd kept putting it off, aware that the moment he started studying, he'd realise how much he still didn't know. The two exams on Monday were his best subjects, but for that reason he hadn't given them the attention he should have done, concentrating instead on bringing the others up to scratch. He was going to have to spend the next three days buried in his books if he wanted to have any hope of decent marks. Jesus, he was sick of studying.

He felt a brief flare of envy for Stevie, jetting all over the world at someone else's expense without a care in the world. Saying you were a nanny might not impress everyone – why was it that anything to do with children was automatically downgraded? – but at the end of the day, without a real GCSE to her name, she was living rent free in a fantastic house he'd probably never be able to afford even if he made it to silk, with no bills to pay, free travel, mixing with glamorous people she couldn't have hoped to meet otherwise. Whereas he, for all his A levels and Oxford degree and bloody law college, was trapped inside this flat on a warm, sunny summer evening, scared shitless about his exams, and up to his ears in debt. Talk about the hand that rocks the cradle rules the world.

For a brief moment, he wondered if he ought to tell Stevie about Rafe. She was clearly mad about him; perhaps it was something she should know. He remembered again the way she'd looked at him when he'd arrived, and decided against it. It wasn't that big a deal, and anyway, it wasn't up to him to interfere. If it worked out between them, she'd find out soon enough. If it didn't, why cause her unnecessary worry for nothing?

In the meantime he was tired, pissed off and broke. It seemed a long time since he'd just cut loose and had a good time.

Fuck it. He stood up suddenly, sending a heap of back issues of *FHM* and *Marie Claire* – thank God Stevie had forgotten to cancel her subscription when she'd moved out, he could never have brought himself to go into a newsagent's and buy a women's magazine – sliding from the windowseat on to the floor. What he needed was a break. He picked up the telephone from the floor and balanced it on his lap as he opened his Psion address book. Switching it on, he typed in 'Women' and waited for it to call up the relevant files. Scrolling quickly down through 'Married', 'Never Again', and 'Potential', he stopped the cursor on 'Sure Thing'. He didn't want to mess about tonight, he just needed a good shag. He was about to enter the file, then he stopped. What he needed first was a pick-me-up. Right now he didn't have the energy to raise a smile, let alone anything else.

He knew exactly where to go to get what he wanted; if he played his cards right, he might find a way to make a bit of money into the bargain. He hadn't been back to the club for a few weeks, but he had the feeling that Mace would remember him.

Throwing on a clean, faded denim shirt, he grabbed his wallet, shoved it deep into his jeans pocket and left the flat.

Thirteen

Annabel smoothed a sweep of cold cream across her face as she watched Patrick undress in the mirror. She couldn't see his face, but the stiff set of his shoulders as he unbuttoned his shirt told her that nothing had changed since their argument that morning.

The row had been over nothing: he'd forgotten to go to the dry cleaner's to pick up the black Ralph Lauren trousers she'd wanted to wear at the Silverstone Grand Prix tomorrow, and when she'd complained, had snapped that he had more important things to think about. His anger had ignited hers. She'd told him that if he couldn't be bothered to think about her, she couldn't be bothered to watch him race. He'd stormed out of the house without saying another word, and she'd let him go, the apology hovering on her lips left unsaid.

She tipped her bottle of Clinique toner against a ball of cotton wool and began to cleanse her face with quick, upward strokes. Her mother's acid voice echoed in her head: Never cleanse downwards, Annabel, gravity does quite enough damage. For a brief moment she wondered what Katherine Mornay would have had to say on the subject of adultery. Sex – illicit or otherwise – was not something that had ever been discussed in the Mornay household. Like God and bankruptcy, its existence was tacitly acknowledged but never mentioned in polite company. That was left to the lower orders and the red-

231

top Sunday newspapers.

Her eye caught Patrick's as she bent to throw the dirty ball of cotton wool into the waste-paper bin beneath her dressing table. He held her gaze for a few moments, then looked away again without smiling. Six months ago, Patrick would have apologised for forgetting her trousers and laughingly told her to dig something else out of her meagre, six-cupboard wardrobe. Six months ago, she'd have laughed with him and found something else to wear.

A cold chill settled in the pit of her stomach. She couldn't remember the last time they'd laughed together. In the seven weeks since Monaco, the easy, familiar rapport they'd shared for more than ten years had cooled into a stiff, formal wall of politeness neither of them seemed able to breach. They tiptoed around each other, as courteous as strangers – would you like to use the bathroom first? Do you mind if I watch the news? – as if unwilling to risk shattering the fragile, unspoken truce their marriage had become. Sex had become part of the ritual holding the whole precarious edifice together, performed by tacit mutual consent just often enough for its absence not to become remarkable. Annabel felt as if they were standing on the edge of an abyss that had abruptly opened beneath their feet, and for the first time she wondered if they would ever be able to find their way back.

Divorce. The word slithered into her mind, prying opening a door she'd been struggling to keep shut. She felt a jolt of shock, her stomach lurching as if she'd just gone over a hump-backed bridge. Had it really come to that? She and Patrick had had a relatively easy ride so far, but it wasn't as if they hadn't had their moments in the past. That time, six years ago, after the accident at Monte Carlo: five months pregnant with the twins, she'd begged Patrick to stop racing and stormed home to her mother's when he'd refused point-blank even to consider it. She'd sworn she never wanted to see him again, but when he'd come round and laid siege to her old bedroom, vowing he wouldn't leave until he'd spoken to her, she'd taken one look at his poor, bandaged face and collapsed sobbing into his arms.

Annabel picked up her jar of moisturiser. She was being melodramatic. They'd come through far worse than a row over a pair of trousers; it was hardly time to consult the lawyers. In a few days they wouldn't even be able to remember what this argument had been about . . .

She started as she heard the click of the bedroom door shutting. For one shocked moment she thought Patrick was going out to sleep in the guest room, then she heard the sound of the shower and felt a quick surge of relief. It hadn't quite come to that, then. In ten years together, unless separated by Patrick's work, they'd never slept alone no matter how big the row. The chill in her stomach seeped along her limbs as she tasted that word again. *Divorce.* If their relationship could have deteriorated so far so fast, almost before she'd realised what was happening, what had once seemed unthinkable could become a reality frighteningly quickly.

Why are you so surprised? she asked herself mockingly. Where did you think this was going to end? *You* were the one who arranged to meet Rafe Dussi in Monte Carlo. Did you think you could have your nice, safe husband and an exciting love affair without paying some sort of price? You can't have them both. Sooner or later, you'll have to choose.

For the first time, she realised she couldn't sit in her comfortable marriage and weigh the options for ever. She hadn't even slept with Rafe, and already her feelings for him were eating away at her relationship with Patrick, driving a wedge of fear, guilt and mistrust between them. She had no idea if Rafe had been right when he'd called a month ago to warn her that Patrick was checking up on her, but in the end it didn't make any difference. The lines of communication between them had already shut down.

She tried for a moment to imagine life without Patrick. With

233

a sick feeling, she realised how much she depended on him; not just for financial security – although she knew that even with maintenance payments and a generous settlement, she would never have a lifestyle that encompassed £10,000 Armani dresses on her own – but for her own sense of identity. She *was* Mrs Patrick Alexander. It wasn't just the celebrity, although she enjoyed being photographed whenever she left San Lorenzo's. It was the fact that she was able to sign their Christmas cards 'Annabel & Patrick', that she had a strong, black-jacketed arm to lean on at balls and parties, that there was someone else to take the ultimate responsibility in her life. She didn't want to be one of those bitter ex-wives who was never invited to dinner parties because it unbalanced the numbers and whose married friends quietly dropped her, fearing for their own husbands. She had never worked in her life. If she wasn't Mrs Alexander, who was she?

She heard Patrick come back into the room and swivelled round on her dressing stool, the blue glass jar of moisturiser still in her hand. Clinique Turnaround Cream. She wished she could rub it on to her marriage instead of her face.

'Patrick –'

He looked up, his expression immediately guarded.

'Patrick, I –' She struggled to find the words, to grope her way carefully back from the edge of the precipice to safety. 'I'm sorry about this morning. I flew off the handle, it was ridiculous.'

For a moment, Patrick's face softened, then he bent forward and tugged off his slipper. 'It doesn't matter.'

'Yes, it *does* matter,' Annabel said, surprising herself with the urgency of her tone. 'Patrick, please, you *must* talk to me. We must talk to each other. We can't let this – this silent war go on. There's no point pretending everything is all right any more when it isn't. You know it isn't.'

'Look, I'm tired. It's nearly midnight, and I have an important race tomorrow.'

234

She knelt in front of him. He raised his head as she touched his hand and she stared at him, seeing for the first time the weariness in his eyes, the lines scoring the sides of his mouth. As her gaze traced the scars along his cheek she remembered the time when she'd cared so passionately about what happened to him that she'd run home to her mother out of fear for him.

'Annabel, I don't know what's going on in your life, and right now I don't want to know,' Patrick said quietly. 'But I will tell you this. I won't be second-best. I'm not a consolation prize, someone to make do with. I love you more than anything else in the world, but I don't want to be someone you settle for. I would rather you left if you can't love me any more.'

'I *do* love you –'

Angrily he pulled away from her. 'Don't just repeat it back to me like a parrot. I want it to come from the heart. I want to know if you love me; *me*, not all this –' he waved his hand around them. 'The house, the money, the life. You can have it, I don't care, you know I'd make sure you got whatever you wanted. You don't have to stay with me to keep it. I just want to know the truth. *Do you love me?*'

Annabel realised that she had never dared to ask herself the question that should have come first, before everything. She forced herself to ask it now. She cared about him, yes, she wanted to be married to him for so many reasons, she wanted him as the father of her children. But was that love? Was being afraid to be alone good enough?

Her heart twisted. Maybe she didn't feel the same heat and passion for him as she did for Rafe, but that was no excuse for causing grief and pain to those who cared most about her. This wasn't a movie or a romantic novel. This was real life. She suddenly knew exactly what her mother would have to say on the subject of adultery. In Katherine Mornay's opinion, too many people used love to excuse otherwise inexcusable behaviour, confusing it with self-gratification. Wasn't that exactly

235

what *she* was doing, putting her own feelings for Rafe before what she owed Patrick, James, Elizabeth and Henry?

She wished she could lie to Patrick, tell him what he wanted to hear, but she knew nothing less than the truth would satisfy him, and right now, the truth would mean the end of their marriage. 'I don't want to leave you,' she said at last.

Patrick nodded and climbed into bed. She got in beside him and lay staring into the darkness long after he'd fallen asleep, praying that their marriage was strong enough to last until whatever it was she felt for Rafe had burned itself out, and she could tell him she loved him again and know she meant it.

'Stevie, are you absolutely *sure*?'

Stevie glanced distractedly at the mute television in front of her. It looked a lot better on that trendy black wooden stand Julia had bought from IKEA than balanced precariously on top of her unused step aerobic, the way it had been during the four years of her reign here. In fact, the whole flat looked completely different since she'd moved out. The heaps of dog-eared old *Cosmos* and half-empty bottles of red nail varnish had vanished, along with the poster of Linford Christie and a four-foot-high orange motorway cone complete with flashing amber light that she'd acquired one exuberant New Year's Eve. She'd spent the next six months hiding in the bathroom every time the doorbell rang unexpectedly. The glossy potted plants were new, and so was the cream and peach rug on the floor and the smart grey CD rack in the corner. If it wasn't for the list of 99 things to do with a cucumber still Sellotaped to the fridge door, she might have wondered if she and Julia really were the soul sisters she'd always thought.

'Stevie, stop watching the bloody box,' Julia complained. 'The race isn't due to start for half an hour, I'll tell you when he comes on.'

Stevie dragged her eyes away from the screen. God, who'd have thought *she'd* end up a racing groupie? Four months ago, she wouldn't have known the difference between a Grand Prix and a Grand Master. Now here she was in her ex-sitting room, barely able to recognise the carpet – had it always been that colour, or was she just seeing it without its usual patina of Chinese takeaway and spilt Coke? – and desperate not to miss a moment of the action at Silverstone.

Julia nodded at the television. 'Have you told him yet?'

'No, of course I haven't,' Stevie said. 'I don't want to tell him unless I have to. Why d'you think we're doing this first?'

'Well, how late are you?'

'I don't know exactly,' Stevie admitted. 'I'm always forgetting to write it down. All I know is it's been ages since I had a period, my tits are huge and I just have to hear the theme music to *Chariots of Fire* and I burst into tears.'

'Sounds like you've been pregnant for years.'

'This isn't funny, Jules.'

'Sorry, sorry.' Julia opened a packet of chocolate digestives and chucked her one. 'I don't understand how you let yourself in for this. Haven't you been using something when you –?'

'Yes, of course I have, I'm not a complete idiot,' Stevie said, scattering crumbs. 'I used my diaphragm. Maybe the damn thing's gone off.'

'Rubber doesn't go off, Stevie. It perishes.'

'It bloody well will after this, I can tell you.'

Julia's eyes narrowed. 'You *sure* you didn't just forget to use it?'

'Yes, I'm sure,' Stevie said. 'It took me long enough to get the sodding thing in –'

'Are you telling me you only did it *once*?' Julia said incredulously.

Stevie grimaced. 'It hasn't been from want of trying, I can tell you. The trouble is, Rafe's father is Catholic, he's got this thing about Rafe settling down with a nice Italian girl. If he finds out about us, he might chuck Rafe out of the team.' She helped herself to another biscuit. 'It wouldn't be so bad if Rafe

237

didn't live at the end of the bloody drive. It's impossible to get it together without someone finding out. I tell you, Jules, it's nearly killing me. I wasn't cut out to be celibate. I just keep telling myself that as soon as the Grand Prix season's over, we can come clean. If Rafe does well, he can always switch to another team if his father *does* freak out.'

'He may have to,' Julia said. She opened her leather brief-case and fished out her Filofax. 'Before we do the test, I think we should work out exactly how late you are. You know what you're like, if it's only a week or so it could just be the prawns or something. Anyway, if you're not very overdue, these kits don't always work.'

'Do you mind, I'm not a library book. And it's not the prawns, I'm pregnant, I know I am.'

Julia ignored her. 'When, *exactly*, was your last period?'

'As if you need to ask. It was fairly memorable, if you recall.'

'Dates, Stevie. We need some dates.'

'I don't know when the dinner party was, I told you. I think it must've been some time in May –'

Julia stopped turning pages. '*May*? Stevie, it's the seven-teenth of July now.'

'I know,' Stevie said miserably.

'Well, when in May was the dinner party? Please tell me the thirty-first.'

'It was about two weeks before the Monte Carlo Grand Prix, I remember that –' She broke off as she saw Julia's face. 'What? *What*?'

'Monte Carlo was when you bonked Rafe, wasn't it? That means if you're right, you had your last period two weeks before you had him. Are you sure the dinner party wasn't *after* Monaco?'

'Give me a chance to think.' She chewed her nail. 'The dinner party was on the same day Jamie sat on Saddam and squashed him – no, you idiot, don't look at me like that,

Saddam was Jamie's gerbil. Mr Arcor buried him in this empty Quality Street box he'd given Mrs Arcor for their wedding anniversary the day before –'

'She ate all the chocolates in a day?'

'Well, Jamie and Lily had most of them – look, Jules, does it really matter? Their wedding anniversary was the fifteenth of May, I remember that because Mrs Arcor kept going on about it being the Ides of March only it was May. After two years doing *Julius Caesar* for GCSE, that's not the kind of remark you forget.'

'It would've been a lot easier if you just wrote things down in your diary,' Julia muttered. 'So the dinner party was on the sixteenth of May.'

Stevie peered over her shoulder. 'Yes, the Tuesday. I remember being pissed off Annabel was having one so early in the week when I was still getting over my hangover from Sunday.'

'It doesn't look good,' Julia admitted, counting. 'You're – three, four – nearly five weeks late. And you didn't exactly use the safe period, Stevie. You had sex two weeks after your period, that's a prime egg-sperm-baby time.'

'I thought the safe period was only for Catholics.'

'If I were you, I'd start praying.'

'Oh, Jules. What am I going to do?'

Julia closed her Filofax. 'The first thing we need to do is find out for certain if you are pregnant. Then we can decide exactly how you're going to mutilate Rafe.'

'It's not his fault,' Stevie said loyally. 'Well, it is, of course, but he didn't mean to –'

'Never mind that now. Where've you put the kit?'

Stevie nodded towards a bulging Boots polythene bag she'd brought with her. 'In there.'

'Bloody hell. Have you taken out shares in *Clearblue* or something? How many did you buy?'

'They're not all pregnancy kits, idiot. I was trying not to

look obvious, so I bought some condoms to fox the assistant.'
She took the box from Julia and headed towards the bathroom.
'I need a drink if I'm going to do this, Jules. Double vodka,
neat.'

'You can't. The baby.'

'Oh, Jesus. If I am pregnant, I won't last nine months drunk,
never mind sober.'

She shut herself in the bathroom and perched on the Day-
Glo orange loo seat as she studied the slightly quizzical
expression of the woman on the front of the box. Silly bitch
looked more like she'd missed a train than a period. What they
ought to have was someone staring at the camera with blank-
eyed terror. At least it would make you feel you weren't alone.

She unwrapped the cellophane and prised open the card-
board box. It looked more like an IRA bomb kit than a
pregnancy test. She studied the array of test tubes, plastic
paddles and clear plastic containers. If she was stupid enough
to have got herself pregnant, how on earth did they expect her
to have the wit to figure out this lot?

She poked around in the box until she found the little
booklet of instructions. Oh, God, diagrams. She'd had enough
trouble coming to grips with Lil-lets. It had been two years
before she'd realised you didn't have to stand with one foot in
the air on an invisible step to get them in. She turned the paper
over and decided to follow the instructions without the aid of
pictures.

Julia knocked on the bathroom door. 'Have you done it yet,
Stevie?'

Stevie opened the door. 'Can you time five minutes and then
have a look, Jules? I'm too scared.'

'Oh, thanks. You get all the fun, I get all the worry.'

Stevie curled up on the sofa as Julia went to pour the tea. On
the silent screen in front of her, the Silverstone Grand Prix
finally got under way. She felt her stomach lurch as Rafe's
purple car whizzed past. What the hell was she going to do if

she *was* pregnant? There was no way she was ready for a baby – working as a nanny was possibly the most effective contraceptive in existence, apart from Bronwyn Halford's childbirth video. Being paid to look after someone else's little sod was one thing, but having your own was something else. You couldn't hand it back at weekends, for a start. There was so much she didn't want to give up – her lap, for one. And she had none of the romantic illusions that got most women through nine months of piles and indigestion and ballooning tits. She knew exactly what it was like to get up at three in the morning to be puked over. As far as babies were concerned, twenty-four hours of excruciatingly agonising labour was the *good* news.

And what about Rafe? She picked up another chocolate digestive – if she was going to swell to a size twenty, 120 calories wasn't going to make much difference. What the hell would Rafe say? He was always telling her he loved her, he brought her back beautiful presents whenever he was away: a pair of gold maple leaf earrings from Canada, a pale blue and silver silk Hermès scarf from Paris. But their relationship was hardly on solid ground. They'd had one night of mind-blowing sex in Monaco, a few clandestine meetings at The Gilt Edge – Sharon and George Cobbit had really thrown themselves into the whole thing, acting as lookouts and warning them in cocktail code if any of the Terroni team were lurking nearby: a Brandy Alexander meant Patrick was coming, Bloody Mary was Annabel, and Nigel Purvis was a Between the Sheets. They'd managed a few sneaky snogs in the kitchen when no one was looking, but it had been impossible to get up to anything more – the minute they got going, Annabel would materialise behind them as if there was some sort of homing device attached to Rafe.

She munched another biscuit. Oh, God, it would be so unfair if she'd got pregnant after just one bonk with Rafe. He'd be bound to run a mile – she couldn't really blame him, she'd been pushing her luck to get this far. She might have known it

241

would all go Horribly Wrong. Men like Rafe Dussi just didn't happen to her.

'Your five minutes are up, Stevie.'

Stevie clutched the sofa cushions. 'Don't you think we should leave it a bit longer –'

'No, you have to get the paddle out now or it won't work. Do you want me to look?'

'No, no, I'm not a complete wimp.' She stood up and headed towards the bathroom, then froze on the threshold. 'Oh, Jules. Will you come and hold my hand?'

She perched on the edge of the bath and closed her eyes as Julia picked up the paddle. 'What is it? What is it?'

'Remind me which way round you should read the result.'

Stevie opened her eyes and grabbed the instruction booklet. 'Dark pink: go directly to Mothercare. Do not pass Go, Do not collect £200. Light pink: you got away with it this time, have a huge fucking drink and don't do it again.' She jiggled on the side of the bath. 'For Christ's sake, Jules, put me out of my misery, I'm getting hysterical.'

'Well, it *is* pink –'

'Oh, you're no use, give it here.' She grabbed the paddle and stared at it. 'Oh. *Oh, Jules.*'

Stevie wandered dazedly into the kitchen the next morning, just managing to avoid Mrs Arcor as she backed away from the Aga holding a frying pan brimming with bacon, sausages, mushrooms and tomatoes. She still couldn't believe the result. The one test you couldn't cheat on.

'Your young man's here,' Mrs Arcor said, digging her in the ribs and nodding towards the kitchen door.

Stevie blushed. So much for secrecy. 'Mrs Arcor, he isn't –'

'Go on, love. Aren't you going to let him in?'

Stevie gave up and opened the back door, womanfully suppressing the urge to rip Rafe's clothes off as she breathed the scent of him in. It must be her hormones. 'What're you doing here this early?' she whispered. 'It's not even eight o'clock.'

'I couldn't wait to see you,' Rafe murmured, his hand skilfully brushing her T-shirted nipple as he slipped past her into the kitchen. 'Mrs Arcor invited me to a celebration breakfast,' he said, more loudly. 'How could I resist a chance to enjoy her cooking?'

'Get on with you, you smooth devil,' Mrs Arcor chided, her cheeks pinking.

Rafe manoeuvred himself behind the housekeeper so that she couldn't see his face, and blew Stevie a kiss. 'Did you see the race yesterday?'

Stevie refrained from saying that she'd spent the first dozen laps in the loo contemplating the imminent prospect of motherhood. 'Of course I did, I watched it with Julia at the flat. It was so exciting, I really thought you were going to win when Damon Hill and Michael Schumacher crashed and knocked each other out. You were in the lead for ages after that.'

'I would have won if it wasn't for Cusack's bloody pit-stop strategy,' Rafe said, grabbing a piece of crisp bacon from the frying pan and dodging as Mrs Arcor swatted him away. 'He still insists we stop twice to refuel. I lost a place to Johnny Herbert when I had to go back into the pits on lap 39, and it was impossible to get past him again.'

'You did brilliantly, though. You came second. You even beat Patrick.'

Rafe shrugged. 'He is still ahead in the championship.'

'Yes, but only by one point,' Stevie pointed out. 'After he came third, he's got thirty points, and you've got twenty-nine. There are nine races left, and Schumacher and Hill have only got forty-six and thirty-five points. Everyone else is miles behind you, so you could easily still win –'

He laughed. 'My loyal Stevie. You probably know more about it than the FIA themselves. Have you been up all night working it out?'

'She probably watched the breakfast news, the same as the

rest of us.' Annabel's crisp tones announced her imminent entrance. Stevie noticed that she was wearing yet another new outfit, this time a short, strappy white Versace dress just like one Princess Diana had been wearing last week. Three thousand pounds' worth, according to the *Daily Mail*. 'Stephanie, as Henry is still sleeping, would you mind chasing James and Elizabeth down for breakfast? Patrick has already gone down to the track with Martin, so I'm afraid he can't mind them. They're going to be late for Summer Camp if they don't hurry.'

'But I'm just dishing up breakfast,' Mrs Arcor said, glaring at Annabel. 'It won't be the same if it's cold.'

Stevie glanced at Annabel's face. 'It's OK, Mrs Arcor, I'll be really quick,' she said hastily. 'Two minutes, I promise.'

'I'll put yours on top of the Aga then, keep it warm,' Mrs Arcor said. 'Rafe Dussi, if you don't keep your hands out of my bacon, there'll be trouble. I'm just doing your plate.'

'Mrs Arcor, I think I love you,' Rafe grinned.

'Cupboard love,' Mrs Arcor said as she placed a heaped plate in front of him. 'This should keep you quiet for a while. Give me a call when the kiddies are down, I've got to get on.'

Annabel sighed as the housekeeper bustled out to the scullery. 'Oh, *really*, Mrs Arcor, not the ironing again . . .'

'You look very beautiful this morning,' Rafe said, pulling his plate towards him and casually spearing a burnt sausage. 'A new dress?'

'Thank you, yes. Mrs Arcor –'

'Going somewhere special?'

'I'm meeting Lillian Purvis for brunch after I've dropped the twins at Summer Camp.' Annabel's voice was cool. 'I'm sorry, Rafe, I really don't have time to stand and chat –'

'I knew it,' Mrs Arcor interrupted suddenly, coming back into the kitchen and opening the fridge. 'No eggs. I told Mr Arcor we was getting low.' She pulled off her apron. 'I won't be a mo, Mrs Alexander, I'll just nip out to the hen run and pick up half a dozen. They'll be nice and fresh, anyway, Jamie loves them like that.'

Annabel started to deadhead a vase of flowers on the windowsill as Mrs Arcor left, deliberately putting the kitchen table between herself and Rafe as he stood up and moved towards her.

'Annabel, please, talk to me. Stevie could be back at any minute –'

'How nice for you.'

'Don't be like that. Jealousy doesn't suit you.'

She whirled towards him. 'I am *not* jealous!'

'I am,' Rafe murmured, closing in on her. 'I am jealous every minute of every day you are with your husband and not with me. I'm jealous of the fact that he's the one you turn to at night and wake up with every morning.' He pushed her hair away from her neck to kiss it, his hand gently trailing down her backbone as he pulled her against him. 'How do you think it has been for me, unable even to telephone you in case he is listening? I want so much more than these stolen moments, Annabel, I love you –'

She tried to push him away. 'Stop it, Rafe!'

'You didn't want me to stop in Monte Carlo –'

'You humiliated me in Monte Carlo!'

'I did not humiliate you. I told you, I was protecting you. I couldn't take the risk that Patrick would find out about us.' He stroked her cheek. 'I wouldn't do anything to hurt you, you know that.'

'This can't happen, Rafe,' Annabel whispered. 'Monte Carlo was a mistake, I should never have agreed to meet you.'

'You don't mean that –'

'I think perhaps she does.'

Annabel gasped and spun round. Charles Cusack stood in the kitchen doorway, his cold blue gaze levelled on Rafe. 'How long have you been there?' she asked fearfully.

'Long enough.'

Rafe stepped forward, pushing her behind him as if to protect her from physical harm. 'It wasn't her fault, it was mine –'

'Oh, I don't doubt that.'

'It's not what you think –'

'Shut up, Dussi.' Cusack turned to Annabel. 'I don't want to know the sordid details. I just want your word of honour that whatever it was is now over.'

'You have no right to ask me –'

'Damn you, Annabel, I have *every* right!' Cusack snapped. 'Patrick is my oldest friend. I won't stand by and see him cuckolded by this slimy piece of shit just to spare your finer feelings.'

Rafe flushed. 'We go outside, Cusack, just you and me. Then I hear you say this again –'

'Rafe, don't.' Annabel pushed past him and spoke directly to Cusack. 'I have never slept with Rafe, nor do I intend to,' she said coldly. 'Is that good enough for you?'

'I have your word?'

'Yes.'

Cusack nodded stiffly. 'I need Rafe to come down to the track. Patrick and Martin are already waiting –'

'Jamie and Lily are just coming, Mrs Alexander, they'd managed to squeeze out most of the toothpaste and Jamie was trying to get it back in the tube –' Stevie skidded to a halt as she took in the tableau by the Aga. 'Is anything wrong?'

'Not at all. Everything is fine,' Rafe said calmly. 'Lord Cusack was just leaving.'

Cusack turned on his heel, his mouth set. Stevie watched his departing back in bewilderment. 'Have I missed something?'

She didn't miss the swift glance Rafe shot Annabel, suddenly remembering what Oliver had said that day at the pub. Maybe Cusack and Annabel *were* having an affair, maybe Rafe had said something –

Her thoughts were pierced by a single, terrifying scream from the hallway. She spun towards the kitchen door as Lily stumbled through it, her tiny face white, tears running down her cheeks.

Stevie ran and knelt beside her. 'Lily, what is it? What's happened?'

Lily stared blankly at them.

'Lily,' Stevie said urgently, suppressing the urge to shake the information out of the child. 'Are you hurt?'

The little girl shook her head slightly, blinking rapidly as if she was staring at a bright light.

'Is it Jamie? Lily? *Tell me!*'

For the first time, something seemed to register. Lily pointed towards the hall. 'Jamie cut his hand,' she whispered, so quietly Stevie had to strain to hear her. 'Is he going to die?'

'Of course he isn't, sweetheart.' She scooped the child up and turned to Annabel. The other woman seemed frozen. Stevie felt a surge of irritation. One of her children was hurt, the other was in shock, and Annabel just bloody stood there. She pushed Lily into Mrs Arcor's arms as the housekeeper came in through the back porch, crushing half a dozen fresh eggs against the startled woman's chest. 'Look after her. There's been an accident,' she said quickly. 'See if you can get Dr Knighton on the phone.'

Mrs Arcor nodded in confusion, ignoring the egg yolk dripping on to her feet as Stevie raced into the hall. Her heart pounded with fear as she shouted Jamie's name. She suppressed the urge to run screaming from room to room; in this huge house, the little boy could be anywhere. She had to think, she had to find him. She stopped uncertainly by the front door, barely noticing Annabel and Rafe as they followed her into the hall. She had to hurry, she had to *find* him –

Suddenly she heard a muffled sob. 'The drawing room!'

She ran towards the sound. As she pushed open the heavy double doors, she saw Jamie sitting with his back towards her near the fireplace, his fair head bowed, his hands clutched against his chest. The hooks which had held his great-grandfather's sword above the mantelpiece were empty, the Hanoverian occasional table Jamie had used to reach it upturned beside him. The sword itself lay at his feet, a tiny speckle of blood near its hilt. As Stevie ran towards the child, Annabel moved automatically to right the table.

'Jamie?' Stevie tried not to let her shock show on her face as she knelt and saw the blood covering his chest and arms. 'Jamie, have you hurt yourself?'

The little boy nodded, his mouth wobbling as he bravely fought back tears.

There was so much blood it was impossible to know where he was injured. She didn't dare move him until she knew. 'Can you show me, Jamie?'

'My hand,' Jamie whispered. 'I cut my hand on the sword.'

He held his hands a few inches away from his chest to show her. Both of them were bright red and slippery with blood. She still couldn't see the actual wound. She tried to clamp down on her panic. He hadn't stabbed himself through the stomach or heart, she should have time to get him to a hospital if it was only his hands –

'Oh, Jesus,' Rafe muttered suddenly, pointing towards the fireplace. 'His finger. He's cut off his little finger.'

Annabel screamed as she saw the tiny white oblong lying in the stone grate, neatly severed just below the second knuckle. 'Oh, God. Oh, God. Oh, God.'

'Shut her up, Rafe,' Stevie said, trying not to feel sick. 'Don't let her panic Jamie.' She ignored them as Rafe put his arm round Annabel and pulled her away. 'Jamie, you're going to have to be very, very brave,' she said calmly. 'I need to take you to the hospital, but first I don't want you to bleed any more.' As she was talking, she was pulling off her T-shirt and ripping one of the sleeves away to form a makeshift tourniquet. 'I'm just going to wrap this round your hand, Jamie, you don't have to be frightened.'

'It hurts,' Jamie whispered.

248

'I know it does, sweetheart, that's why I'm going to take you to hospital so the doctors can make it better.' As soon as she'd fastened the tourniquet tight enough to stop the bleeding, she picked Jamie up and cradled him against her. His face was so pale against the scarlet splashed across his chest.

Jamie struggled feebly in her arms. 'I want my mummy. *I want my mummy.*'

Stevie glanced desperately at Annabel. For Christ's sake, what was *wrong* with her? This was her child, her baby, and the woman was just *standing* there. 'Bring his finger, Rafe. We need to pack it in ice and take it to the hospital with us. The surgeons may be able to sew it on again.'

'We don't have any ice,' Annabel said. Her voice sounded strangely matter of fact.

'Frozen peas, then, anything. Just be quick.'

The two of them just looked at her. Stevie fought back a scream. 'Rafe, please. You have to hurry if we're going to save his finger.'

Jamie whimpered. 'I want my mummy,' he said again.

Annabel backed away. 'I – I can't,' she gasped. 'Stevie, I just *can't.*'

'It's OK, darling, I've got you,' Stevie soothed. Inwardly, her panic was rising. Rafe and Annabel were worse than useless, and she had to get Jamie to hospital, she couldn't wait for the doctor. But she couldn't drive and hold him. 'Rafe, for God's sake, *his finger.*'

'I'll deal with it,' Cusack said suddenly behind her.

Stevie didn't have time to wonder why he was back. 'Do you have your car?'

Cusack nodded.

'I need you to drive us to hospital.'

'Fine. Annabel, you travel with Lillian Purvis,' Cusack said curtly, picking up Jamie's severed finger and swiftly wrapping it in a white cotton handkerchief. 'I don't want you coming with us and panicking the boy. Go down to Mrs Arcor's cottage and phone from there. She's got Lily. The child could do with a bit of reassurance from her mother.'

Annabel nodded stupidly. Stevie could hardly believe this was the same calm, controlled woman who organised sit-down dinners for sixty without turning a hair. She looked like a bewildered child.

'I need something cold for this,' Cusack said.

'Peas in freezer,' Stevie gasped, staggering under Jamie's weight.

Cusack opened the drawing-room door for her and she moved as swiftly as she dared towards the kitchen. She nodded towards the fridge and Cusack grabbed two packets of frozen peas, sandwiching the severed finger between them. Stevie knew the handkerchief should prevent the cold packets sticking to the finger and ripping the flesh away. She stumbled after Cusack as he headed towards his Range Rover, which was parked in the courtyard outside, the engine already running. It was only when she felt the warm summer breeze stroke her skin that she realised she was still half-naked. As if it mattered. She climbed into the back seat with Jamie in her arms, trying to quell her fear as she saw how pale and still he was.

'Which hospital?' Cusack barked.

Stevie thought quickly. There were three hospitals near Edenfield, all roughly the same distance away, but she wasn't sure if they all had casualty departments. 'The Queen Victoria in East Grinstead,' she said, making up her mind. They were famous for exactly the type of pioneering microsurgery Jamie needed now. 'If you hurry we should be able to make it in fifteen minutes.'

Cusack picked up his carphone and dialled a code which put him through to the operator as he sped down the drive. 'I need the number for the Queen Victoria Hospital,' he snapped. As soon as he had the information, he broke the connection and dialled the hospital.

Stevie tried to make Jamie more comfortable as Cusack

250

swiftly explained the situation to the Casualty staff. The little boy was still moaning for his mother, his forehead pale and clammy. Stevie could feel the warmth of his blood seeping through the makeshift bandage. She leaned forward. 'Please hurry. He's lost a lot of blood.'

Cusack nodded. Stevie felt thankful he was driving. She might not like him, but she instinctively trusted him. He'd taken control, coolly and authoritatively, and she knew that Jamie stood a better chance in his hands than in those of either Rafe or Annabel.

Jamie stirred in her arms. 'Hang on, sweetheart,' she murmured as Cusack pushed the Range Rover up to sixty. 'It'll be all right, I promise.'

Oh, God, let it be true.

Fourteen

Jamie was almost unconscious by the time they arrived at the hospital. Still wearing only her bloodstained bra and jeans, Stevie half-fell out of the Range Rover as it screeched to a halt outside Casualty, clinging to Jamie and refusing to hand him over to the team of doctors and nurses alerted by Cusack's telephone call, until Cusack himself prised the child from her arms with surprising gentleness. Jamie was put on a trolley and wheeled to theatre for his pre-med, Stevie holding his undamaged little hand tightly in hers as she trotted beside it. Cusack ran ahead with Jamie's severed finger, still wrapped in his handkerchief and clamped between the two packets of frozen peas.

Jamie screamed as the nurse gave him his injection. 'Mummy! Mummy! I want my mummy!'

'Mummy's right here,' the nurse soothed. 'Look, see, there she is –'

'That's not my mummy!' Jamie cried. 'I want my mummy! *I want my mummy!*'

'I'm not his mother. I'm his nanny,' Stevie explained.

The nurse frowned. 'I'm going to need the child's mother to sign the consent form,' she said. 'Is she here yet?'

Stevie shook her head. 'She's on her way –'

'I'm afraid we can't proceed until one of the child's parents signs the form. I'll need to speak to the doctor. Can you wait here, please?'

She disappeared down the corridor. Stevie turned as Cusack came back, smiling wearily. 'They said his finger's not too badly damaged,' Cusack said. 'The peas preserved it perfectly. He was very lucky in some ways: the sword cut straight through the finger, very clean wound. Apparently there was almost no incidental damage to the nerves or tissue. He's got a good chance of the finger taking if they operate straight away –'

'I want my mummy,' Jamie repeated drowsily, his voice thickened by the pre-med. 'I want to go home.'

'Have you seen Annabel?' Stevie said urgently.

'She still isn't here.'

'Oh, God, they won't operate without her. They won't let me sign the consent form – they know I'm not his mother. The doctor said the longer we delay, the less chance there is of his finger being all right when they sew it back on again –'

Cusack cut her off as the doctor came back towards them. 'Give the form to me, I'll sign it.'

'And you are?' the doctor said.

'I'm his father.'

Stevie watched in disbelief as Cusack signed Patrick's name and the doctor hurried to tell the theatre staff to proceed. 'You can't do that!'

'Why on earth not? Do you think Patrick would object?'

'No, but –'

'Paperwork, rules,' Cusack said dismissively. 'You have to know when to break them or there's no point having them in the first place.'

Stevie couldn't help but admire his cavalier attitude, even while she bristled at his arrogance. She'd never imagined she'd have anything in common with Cusack, but his contempt for pointless rules and bureaucracy was something she understood. She and Damien had clashed with them often enough – she still didn't see the point of one-way streets.

Jamie was wheeled into theatre, still moaning softly for his mother. Stevie started to pace frantically up and down the corridor as they waited for news, unable to sit still. Cusack watched her for a few moments, then took off his Barbour and handed it to her.

'If you must do that, I suggest you wear something a little less *décolleté*,' he observed drily. 'Unless, of course, this is the way you prefer to dress.'

Blushing, she pulled the coat on, reminded suddenly of the night in Monaco when Rafe had given her his leather jacket. Cusack's Barbour smelled of dogs and leaf mould and the wax he used to keep it waterproof and supple. It was a strangely masculine and reassuring mixture.

Neither she nor Cusack felt much need to talk, too wrapped up in their own thoughts and fears for Jamie, but Stevie was unexpectedly glad of his presence. He made her feel uncomfortable and awkward, but she knew that whatever happened next, he'd be able to deal with it. His cool, authoritative confidence was very different from Oliver or Rafe's youthful bravado. When Cusack had pushed the Range Rover to its limit on the way to the hospital, she'd felt unquestionably safe. Driving with Rafe still terrified her. He seemed to be constantly challenging himself, flirting with danger, testing his control. Cusack's control was absolute.

'I'm going to get a coffee,' Cusack said after they'd been waiting an hour. 'Would you like one?'

Stevie shook her head. 'Cusack, do you – do you think he's going to be all right?'

'He's with the best there is,' Cusack said quietly.

'But he's only five years old. It'll be so terrible if he loses his finger – think of the scars, the way the other children will tease him. He'll be marked for life.'

'He's a boy, Stevie, it won't be so bad for him. And he'll adapt. Somehow, you always do.'

Stevie watched as he limped down the corridor for his coffee, the strain of their frantic drive clearly taking its toll on

254

his damaged leg. She tried and failed to picture what his stump and artificial foot must look like, wondering if he was remembering that day when he'd been rushed to a Monaco hospital for hours of similar surgery that had ultimately ended in failure. If he was, he gave no sign. His pale, chiselled features when he returned – without the coffee – were as unreadable as ever.

It was nearly two hours before Annabel and Lillian Purvis finally arrived. Annabel ignored Stevie and Cusack completely and rushed over to the Casualty doctor, sobbing and clutching his lapel as she demanded to know what they'd done to her baby.

Stevie dragged Lillian aside. 'What on earth took you so long?' she hissed. 'Cusack had to sign the consent form, pretend he was Patrick. Poor Jamie was screaming for her.'

'You have no idea,' Lillian said. 'Annabel just refused to leave Lily – delayed shock, I suppose. She wouldn't put her down, crying all over her. It was all I could do to get her here at all.'

Stevie glared at Annabel with fury. Of course she was upset, but histrionics in front of Lily would only unsettle the terrified child even more. She'd probably have nightmares for weeks as it was. Jamie was much tougher. Even though he'd been the one who'd had the accident, she knew he'd bounce back even before the scars had healed.

She turned as Laurie Knighton hurried through the door and went over to meet him.

'Stevie, I've only just heard what happened – Mrs Arcor left a message at my surgery, but I was out on a house call, suspected meningitis,' he said. 'Had the child admitted to Crawley Hospital in the end, but I think it's only a bad case of flu. Better safe than sorry.'

'It's sweet of you to come at all,' Stevie said.

Laurie shrugged. 'Nothing much I can do apart from translate the medical jargon, but I just wanted to be here – Lillian! I didn't realise you were here too.'

'I drove Annabel over –'

'Oh, Laurie, oh, God, this is too awful!' Annabel cried, unceremoniously dumping the Casualty doctor and falling on Laurie's shoulder, weeping and clinging to him like a child. 'I can't bear it, my poor baby –'

Stevie watched her dramatics with mingled pity and exasperation. She'd completely gone to pieces; she was like a different woman. What was the point in being able to dress perfectly and organise charity balls for three hundred people if you fell apart the minute there was a real crisis? Annabel had been mollycoddled for too long, that was the trouble. Her idea of a disaster was probably finding out the caterers had used margarine instead of butter.

Ten minutes after Laurie arrived, Patrick himself ran through the door, his usually tanned face as white as Cusack's.

'I came as soon as I could,' he said anxiously. 'I was at the track, I've only just heard. Is he OK?'

Annabel refused to let go of Laurie's arm. 'Patrick, you've no idea what I've been through!' she cried. 'It's been so awful, I don't know how I've coped!'

Badly, Stevie thought grimly. She saw Cusack take Patrick into a corner to explain exactly what had happened and breathed a sigh of relief. Thank God someone around here knew what they were doing.

The surgeon finally appeared in mid-afternoon. Jamie had been in the operating theatre for more than three hours as the tiny nerves and blood vessels of his severed finger had been painstakingly reconnected to his hand.

Despite her anxiety, Stevie couldn't help a small smile as Cusack, Patrick, Annabel, Laurie, Lillian and herself gathered around the surgeon. He must think half the village had come with Jamie.

'Well, I can't give you any guarantees,' the surgeon said, giving up the attempt to work out who was who. 'But I think we've got a good chance. Provided the reconnected nerves and blood vessels knit together properly, Jamie should regain one hundred per cent feeling and movement in the finger, although it's going to feel numb for a while.'

'Oh, thank God,' Lillian breathed.

Stevie silently echoed her prayer. She was relieved, but somehow not surprised. The moment Cusack had signed the consent form, she'd been certain Jamie would be OK. With Cusack decreeing success, the Fates wouldn't dare do otherwise.

Four weeks later, Stevie tried not to stare at Jamie's lightly bandaged hand as he gave her the huge painted birthday card he'd made for her, not wanting to make him feel self-conscious. The doctors had finally removed the heavy bandage they'd put on his hand after the accident; through the thin gauze now covering it, she could see the narrow black line and neat row of stitches at the base of his little finger where the plastic surgeon had sewn it back on.

He'd stayed in hospital for a week, his injured hand elevated above his shoulder and out of reach of the other so that he couldn't scratch it. His recovery had been swift. Despite the surgeon's optimistic forecast, even he had been astounded when Jamie had walked into Out-Patients last week, stuck his thumbs in his ears, and rudely wiggled his fingers at them on either side of his head. All eight of them.

She took the card and pulled Jamie on to the garden swing beside her, rocking gently and enjoying the feeling of the warm morning sunshine as it played across her skin. Lily was inside, baking jam tarts with Mrs Arcor; the baby was sleeping in his pram beside her, protected from the sun by the cool green shade of the oaks bordering the back lawn. It was only nine o'clock in the morning, but already the day was unrolling hot and dry. She jumped as water from the lawn sprinkler spattered across her bare feet. Edenfield Manor had its own well, exempting it from the traditional August hosepipe ban.

The lawns sloping gently away from the house towards Cusack's woods were green and verdant. She could feel the soft blades between her bare toes every time she rocked the swing.

She opened the card and smiled as she saw the picture Jamie had painted inside. She pointed to a red stick figure with a huge grin, topped by a wild streak of yellow and brown striped hair. 'Is that me?'

Jamie giggled.

She indicated a black figure with two bright blue dots on an otherwise blank face. 'And who's that?'

'Guess.'

No smile. And those eyes. Had to be – 'Lord Cusack?'

'Yes!' Jamie leaned across her lap to point. 'I did him a crown, see, there, not a big one 'cause he's not a king, only a Lord. And that's his dog, look. He's called Canulf. He looks scary but he's very frengly really.'

'I didn't know you'd seen his dog, Jamie,' Stevie said, surprised. 'When was that?'

'Oh, in the woods, when he made us go away 'cause of the trap,' Jamie said offhandedly. 'He gave me a picture of Canulf when he visited me in hop-sital and I copied it. Canulf had a brother, but he died.'

Stevie vaguely recalled the Irish wolfhound lurking behind Cusack the day he'd turned them off his land. She didn't know Cusack had visited Jamie in hospital. The idea took her by surprise. Somehow it didn't quite tally with her image of him. 'What happened to Canulf's brother, Jamie?'

'He fell in a drink and broke his leg, so he had to shoot him.'

'He fell in a *what*?'

A shadow fell across her lap. She looked up and saw Cusack standing by the edge of the lawn a few feet away, the Irish wolfhound at his heels.

'I think he means a gin,' Cusack explained, smiling slightly. 'Ganute, my other hound, got caught in a gin-trap left by poachers last autumn. He was in a lot of pain. I had no choice but to shoot him.'

'I *told* you it was a drink,' Jamie said triumphantly.

Cusack stood awkwardly by the edge of the lawn, staring at the ground, as if uncertain whether to stay or go. Despite the fact that it was mid-August he was still wearing that bloody Barbour over a faded denim shirt and rumpled jeans. He completely confused Stevie. She'd thought she'd got him taped ages ago: a tight-arsed rich bastard, too wrapped up in his own misery to give a toss about anyone else. But when it had mattered, he'd really come through – not just in getting Jamie to the hospital, she'd have expected that from someone as cool and efficient as he was, but in bothering to visit the little boy afterwards, taking the time to talk to him about Canulf and Ganute. Suddenly she didn't know if he was friend or foe.

He glanced up suddenly, his blue eyes so clear she found it hard to look at them. She dropped her gaze as Jamie scrambled off the garden swing beside her and ran over to him.

The little boy stopped and smiled up at Cusack, suddenly too shy to speak. Cusack dropped on to one knee next to him, his inky black hair flopping forward and obscuring his face. 'How's the hand?'

'Much better. Look.' Jamie waved his hand, his confidence returning. 'They sticked it on really well. It hasn't fallen off. I drew Stevie a birthday card, do you want to see?'

'It's your birthday?' Cusack said.

Stevie felt absurdly embarrassed. 'Yes.'

'She's twenty-five,' Jamie put in helpfully.

'I see. I didn't know.'

'There's no reason why you should.'

Jamie took a shy step towards the dog, then paused and looked over his shoulder. 'Can I stroke him?'

'Of course. He won't bite,' Cusack said quietly, seeing the look of concern flash across Stevie's face. 'He's very even-tempered.'

259

Jamie stroked the huge Irish wolfhound, unselfconsciously using his damaged left hand.

'He's done very well,' Cusack said.

'Yes.' She hesitated. 'I never really thanked you for helping me that day.'

He shrugged. 'I was there.'

'If it hadn't been for you –'

'I didn't have much choice,' Cusack said. 'Annabel was having hysterics, and you'd have got nowhere with Rafe. Someone had to do something.'

'Rafe was looking after Annabel,' Stevie said, her antagonism instantly resurfacing. 'He couldn't be everywhere at once. If you'd given him a chance, instead of criticising all the time –'

Cusack eyed her. 'Not you as well,' he drawled. 'He's got to you too, has he?'

'If you mean he's told me the truth, then yes, he's got to me!' Stevie cried, her hackles up. '*He's* the one who should hate *you*, not the other way round! I don't know how you've even got the balls to work with him, after what you did!'

'And what might that be?' Cusack asked in an icy voice.

'You know exactly what! Trying to ruin his reputation, spreading all those lies about him, blaming him for what happened to you –'

'Ah.'

'*Well*? It's true, isn't it?' Stevie pressed.

'I blamed him, yes.'

'You *admit* it?'

'I blamed him because it was his fault. Your *lover* –' Stevie flinched as he hurled the word at her – 'tried to overtake Patrick's car on one of the most lethal bends on the Grand Prix circuit. He got it wrong. He clipped Patrick's car, which ricocheted into mine. We crashed. We were both lucky to survive. If you consider being made a cripple lucky.'

'What happened was terrible, I know that, but even if what

260

you say is true, he made a mistake. You didn't have to try to ruin his life –'

'It wasn't a mistake.'

'What *that* supposed to mean?'

'I suggest you ask him, since you clearly don't believe a word I say.'

Cusack's face was cold and shuttered, his blue eyes like ice. Stevie faced him, cheeks pink with indignation, stomach churning.

'Stop arguing!' Jamie slipped his hand into Cusack's, as if calling time out. Stevie abruptly felt her anger dissipate. Cusack had few scruples about being rude to those he disliked or despised, nor did he trouble to hide his scorn for people who failed to match up to his exacting standards. He was caustic and cynical; but she had never known him to lie. Honour mattered to him – he was probably the type of man who'd die to defend his name even if it meant leaving his family in penury. Instinctively she knew he'd consider vengeful tittle-tattle beneath him. And yet there was exactly what Rafe had accused him of.

She watched him turn and limp across the lawn with Jamie, Canulf at their heels. Rafe wouldn't have lied to her, so what he'd said about Cusack *must* be true. He knew Cusack far better than she did, after all. She'd got him wrong all the way down the line so far.

She picked up Jamie's birthday card and bent to release the brake on the baby's pram. It was her birthday, she wasn't going to let Cusack's foul temper spoil it. Patrick had given her the day off after breakfast; he and Annabel were taking all three children to the beach. She and Rafe were free to spend the whole day together for the first time since Monaco.

So why did she feel so flat, as if some of the sparkle had already been taken from the day?

By the time Rafe arrived to collect her an hour later, Stevie had managed to push Charles Cusack out of her mind. From her bedroom she heard Rafe's car crunch on the gravel as he drove round to the courtyard and parked. She knelt up on her bed, watching through the window as he climbed out of his silver Porsche and strolled towards the back door. God, he was handsome. He was only wearing a pair of faded blue Levis and a white T-shirt, but somehow they looked exotic and glamorous on him in a way they never did on an Englishman. Maybe it was the dark shades and gleaming brown leather boots. The Italians just seemed to wear their clothes differently: they fitted perfectly, for a start, and were always immaculate, no stray threads or missing buttons. This morning Cusack had looked like he'd slept in his jeans; they'd been covered in dog hair and spattered with mud. Rafe looked like a film star.

She checked her reflection quickly in the mirror. Rafe had suggested she show him around Oxford; he'd decided he wanted to try punting – God knew why – so she'd dug out a tapering, ankle-length honey skirt she'd borrowed from Julia last week and teamed it with a long cream overshirt in the same silky material. Chic and romantic but not OTT. The outfit skimmed her plentiful curves without clinging to any unsightly bulges, and she'd worn a smooth silk body underneath so that there were no tell-tale bra or knicker lines. She decided not to risk heels – she'd only puncture the boat or something – and pulled a pair of safe beige deck-shoes on to her bare feet. The net result was surprisingly cool and elegant.

Even her hair looked better now the bleached bits had finally gone. She'd had the last remnants cut out two days ago, leaving her with a reasonably glossy chestnut bob that just brushed her shoulders. The rich colour made her face look slimmer somehow, and brought out blues and greens in her eyes that she'd never known were there. She'd been so impressed she'd even stopped plucking her eyebrows as a mark of respect.

She hurriedly applied some peach-coloured lipstick and left

her room, running happily down the stairs. Rafe was already ensconced in the kitchen, munching one of Lily and Mrs Arcor's slightly burnt jam tarts as the housekeeper renewed her assaults on the ironing board out in the scullery.

'*Bella*!' Rafe exclaimed. 'You look beautiful!'

She blushed. 'You'd say that whatever I looked like.'

'No, today you look –' he pantomimed an hourglass in the air – 'like a woman. A beautiful, confident, sexy woman.'

'Well, it's thanks to you,' Stevie said, embarrassed.

Rafe pulled her into his arms. 'Happy birthday.'

Stevie felt her whole body tingle as he kissed her, his lips sweet like wine. Bugger punting, she just wanted to drag him upstairs.

Rafe reluctantly broke the kiss and stepped back, his eyes sliding over her body. 'The skirt is beautiful, but I hope you can drive in it.'

'Drive?'

He held out the keys to his Porsche.

Stevie grinned delightedly. 'Really?'

'Why not? I think it must be my turn to be terrified.'

'Charming. Well, you asked for it.' She grabbed the keys and ran out into the courtyard, climbed into the driver's seat and leaned across to open the passenger door for him.

'I can't even reach the pedals,' she complained. 'How do I move the seat forward?'

'Let me do it.' He reached between her legs and released a lever. 'It's OK?'

Stevie giggled and turned the key in the ignition. As she eased the car nervously out of the courtyard and into the drive, she could feel the power throbbing beneath the bonnet even moving at less than fifteen miles an hour. She turned into Edenfield Lane, barely needing to tweak the power steering. If she'd been driving Damien, she'd have had to haul on his steering wheel like a Russian tug-of-war team.

She'd been to Oxford dozens of times when Oliver was up

263

at Corpus, so she knew the way. She headed for the M23, growing slowly more confident as she found all the buttons and switches and discovered that one of the beauties of a powerful car was its readiness to forgive mistakes. She could ride the clutch, forget to change up, slam on the brakes at the last minute, and whereas Damien would have taken umbrage and stalled, the Porsche simply indulged her like a besotted sugar-daddy. By the time they hit the M25, she was daring enough to do a sneaky bit of overtaking whenever the snarled traffic loosened up enough for her to get out of first. She savoured the envious glances cast at her by the female drivers of economic little hatchbacks as she shot past them. Not only was she driving a brand new N-reg Porsche, but she was blatantly defying the First Fuckability Law of car ownership. No wonder the Fiat drivers looked pissed off. Sheer clitoris envy.

When they finally reached the M40 Stevie really put her foot down, streaming along the half-empty road, her eyes shining with exhilaration.

She was still pink-cheeked and tingling as they drove through Cowley and into the city itself. She turned into a small side road just before Magdalen Bridge and stopped the car in the middle of the road near a free parking space. 'Not a hope,' she said firmly.

'Thank God. After the way you drive, I was not looking forward to seeing how you park,' Rafe said. 'I prefer to keep my car the shape it is now.'

'Any more remarks like that and *you* won't be.'

She climbed out of the car, pulling the damp fabric of her shirt away from her back as she straightened up. God, she was hot. And not just because of the blazing sunshine. She watched as Rafe slid over into the driving seat and deftly manoeuvred the Porsche into the parking space. A sudden rash of faces appeared at the window of a nearby college as he got out and reached into the back for a crisp beige linen jacket. See him

264

and weep, she thought smugly. If you want one like this, you'll have to go out and find your own.

'So. Where should we go first?'

Stevie tried to concentrate on the matter in hand. 'Have you ever been to Oxford?'

'No.'

'The first time I came up to see Oliver, he took me up to the top of St Mary's Tower. You can see the whole university from there, it's a beautiful view.'

He smiled into her eyes. 'I already have that.'

They strolled lazily over Magdalen Bridge. Shouts and shrieks of laughter echoed below them as people tried to punt their way beneath the wide bridge without running aground in the shadowy darkness. A group of enterprising students were making good use of their summer vacation by charging Japanese tourists £10 a time to take pictures of them punting elegantly down the river in turn-of-the-century blazers and straw boaters. Others posed thoughtfully on the bridge in mortarboards and black subfusc with heaps of battered library books in their arms, despite the fact it was at least two months since Finals had finished.

As they made their way down the High Street, Rafe put his arm around her shoulders. Stevie relished his closeness. God, she wanted to fuck him, he was so bloody *gorgeous*. When she was with him she couldn't think of anything else.

They turned down a narrow cobbled street and headed towards the church tower. Stevie stood in its shadowed entrance and watched Rafe as he went to buy a couple of tickets, her gaze lingering on his tight-jeaned buttocks. She could be struck down for what she was thinking on holy ground. But it *had* been three months since Monaco, and this was the first time they'd even walked down a street together, never mind anything else.

It was ridiculous. Here she was going out with the sexiest man on the planet, and she was getting less action than the

Pope at the Kiss of Peace. She hadn't had a moment alone with Rafe in weeks – she hadn't even had a chance to tell him about the pregnancy test and had almost started to wonder if their whole relationship was just a figment of her fevered imagination. Admittedly, Rafe had been away for a week in Germany for the Hockenheim Grand Prix. His mood hadn't been improved when he'd only finished seventh, particularly as Patrick had come second and was now seven points ahead of his team-mate in the World Championship, in second place behind Michael Schumacher. Rafe had practically lived at the track since then.

But work wasn't the main problem. It was having to keep their relationship secret that caused the trouble. She'd reluctantly accepted that nights of wild passion were going to be few and far between until the championship was over and they could go public. Unless Annabel and Patrick were away, there was no way she and Rafe could spend the night together. She'd persuaded herself she'd survive on their secret meetings at The Gilt Edge and furtive kisses when Rafe came up to the Manor. But since the weekend of Jamie's accident, Rafe had abruptly stopped coming to the house unless he had to see Patrick, meaning that covert snogs – and anything else – behind the bookcases were out. Stevie rather missed them. She'd quite liked the added element of risk. It was clear sexual frustration was turning her into some sort of pervert.

But there was *definitely* something funny going on. Rafe was avoiding Annabel, she was certain of it. Something had happened that day in the kitchen with Cusack. She found it hard to believe that Cusack and Annabel were having an affair – it just didn't seem his style. Much as she wanted to believe ill of the rude bastard, it simply didn't gel. But why was she wasting her time thinking about Cusack when she had the whole day to enjoy with Rafe? God knew why he'd come up to the house this morning anyway. He was just a pain in the arse.

She forgot Cusack as Rafe came back with the tickets and

manoeuvred her into a corner, pushing her gently against the honeyed wall of the church until she felt the cold stone dig into her back. Her nipples stiffened as he eased his knee between hers so that his thigh was pressing hard against her. He kissed her, his tongue probing her mouth. Her nagging doubts withered. Rafe wanted her as much as she wanted him. There wasn't any problem. He was just being careful that no one found out about them until after the championship.

'Are you going to show me this tower or not?' Rafe murmured in her ear.

'I'll show you mine if you show me yours.'

He laughed. 'Later, *cara*, I promise.'

Two hours later, she leaned back against a heap of red plastic-covered cushions as Rafe steered an ancient wooden punt along the Cherwell, trying to maintain his Italian cool as the heavy metal pole repeatedly got stuck in the mud at the bottom of the river and nearly pulled him in after it. He was balanced on the flat deck at the rear of the punt, Stevie sitting in the boat facing him, her legs stretched out in front of her. A heap of discreet stiff-paper-and-logo shopping bags were piled against her feet, Rafe's extravagant birthday presents to her. They were definitely a cut above her usual polythene jobs from Top Shop and Hennes.

Rafe had swiftly dismissed all that Cornmarket and the Westgate Shopping Centre had had to offer. With an instinct honed by years of shopping in Rome, he'd dragged her down a chic cobbled street and immediately found the most expensive boutique in Oxford, a tiny shop whose window display was limited to one exquisite, unpriced beaded silver dress.

'We can't go in there,' Stevie had gasped.

'Why not?'

'Well – for a start it'll be full of horrible size eight salesgirls who'll follow me round like I'm going to shoplift something.'

'No, it won't.'

267

'It will, you don't know these places,' Stevie said darkly. 'They'll throw you pitying glances and write their phone numbers on the back of your receipt when they think I'm not looking.'

'Anything else?'

'Yes, it's too expensive. Look, you need to ring the doorbell even to be allowed in –'

'I think I can manage that.' He'd pressed the bell. 'Are you coming in, or do I have to bring the dresses out?'

She'd gone in. The salesgirls' supercilious little smiles had been wiped off their cheekboned little faces when Rafe had selected the most sensational dress in the shop, a voluptuous sheath of Ferrari-red silk that encased her from neck to toe in sensuous, expensive, mouthwatering luxury. It made her look like a film star. She didn't even dare count the noughts on the cheque Rafe had written. She'd never *seen* anything so stunning, much less owned it.

'Let us hope we can find some shoes to match,' Rafe said as they left.

'Shoes?'

'I find it helps. Socks just don't quite do it for me –'

After the beautiful four-inch scarlet heels – 'Fuck-me shoes', Rafe had called them – they had bought in quick succession a La Perla silk basque, half a dozen pairs of cream stockings from Fogal, an exotic pair of elbow-length red silk gloves, and a magnificent swirling black velvet cape lined with watered cream silk that reached all the way to her ankles. Stevie tried to stop him then, protesting that she'd never have anywhere to wear it. Rafe had calmly watched the salesgirl wrap the cape in layers of filmy tissue, then handed Stevie a white envelope.

'What's this?' Stevie asked.

'Open it and see.'

When she opened it, a Club Class ticket to Rome fell into her lap. 'I don't understand –'

'I want you to meet me in Italy next month, after the Grand Prix at Monza,' Rafe had said softly. 'I want you to see my home, where I grew up. Roma is the most beautiful city on earth. I want to be the one to show it to you.'

'But I can't – what about my work – supposing someone finds out about us?'

'You are permitted a holiday each year, yes? Well, who is to know where you go when you are not working?'

Her eyes sparkled. 'You mean meet you in Rome without telling anyone?'

'*Precisamente*. I will have a car meet you from the airport at Fiumicino to take you to my villa. After that –' he stroked her cheek gently, his eyes full of promise – 'after that, it's just us.'

Just us. She trailed her fingers in the cool water of the Cherwell as his words echoed round her head, wondering if she'd ever been this happy in her life. Rafe was so exciting, so overwhelming, with his kisses and presents and air tickets. She felt as if she were being swept along on a delicious tide with nothing to think of beyond the pleasure of the moment. Impulsively she decided not to say anything about the pregnancy test. Why spoil everything now, when it had been negative anyway?

She giggled as he ducked suddenly to avoid an overhanging bough and rammed the bank.

'You're supposed to push with the pole, then as the punt moves forward, you sort of lift the pole and use it like a rudder at the back,' she called helpfully.

'Easier said than done,' Rafe complained. 'Every time I stick it in, it wants to stay there.'

'I told you not to stand on the end,' Stevie said. 'That's the Cambridge way. At Oxford, you stand *inside* the punt. You're less likely to fall in for a start.'

'I look stupid like that.'

'You'll look a lot more stupid if you fall in.'

A punt full of students glided past them, the pole man deftly steering clear of the trees and another becalmed punt of American tourists further down the river. He smiled and called something to his companions, who laughed and waved mockingly to Rafe as he struggled to push off from the bank.

'*Cazzo*,' Rafe muttered.

'Everyone has a few problems at the beginning,' Stevie reassured him.

She tried not to laugh as Rafe finally managed to push the punt free and it spun in a wide, lazy arc towards the opposite bank. He jabbed the pole into the water to fend off and swore again as the punt drifted out towards the centre of the river. The pole stuck in the mud and Rafe clung on to it, half of his body suddenly suspended over the water as the punt shot forward without him. Stevie grabbed a branch and pulled the punt back towards the bank. Rafe's linen jacket was crumpled and wet, his leather boots soaked from the water dripping off the pole.

'There's something wrong with this punt. It won't go straight, we should go back and change it.'

'There's nothing wrong with it,' Stevie giggled. 'We can't go back yet, this is the easy bit. It's much harder going back, you're punting against the current.'

'*Va fangule*! This is impossible!'

'It's lucky you live in Rome, not Venice,' Stevie said.

'If you think it's so funny, you do it.'

'I thought you liked pole position?'

Rafe glared. There was a definite culture gap here, Stevie decided. The one vital item required when one went punting – apart from a pole and a bottle of champagne – was a sense of humour. The Italians were genetically unable to laugh at themselves, which was why they didn't like jokes about it being easier to make soldiers out of a piece of toast than an Italian. No Englishman would ever go punting and expect either his dignity or his clothing to remain intact. If he didn't fall in at least twice and depart with his brogues still at the bottom of the river, the expedition would be deemed a failure.

Rafe plucked at the front of his jacket as they drifted back towards the bank. 'This is an Armani. Look at it. This fucking water is filthy, these marks will never come out.'

'Look, let me have a go,' Stevie said.

'You won't do any better. I told you, there's something wrong with it,' Rafe scowled.

'Let me try. I can't do any worse.'

Rafe shrugged and handed her the pole. Stevie stood up and carefully swapped places with him, standing inside the punt the Oxford way. She pushed off from the bank and swiftly brought the pole up, hand over hand, using the end of it as a rudder to steer her into the centre of the river the way Oliver had taught her. Rafe watched as she expertly punted past a fork in the river, barely scattering a drop of water on her clothes. 'You've done this before,' he accused.

'I told you I had. Oliver used to take me punting every summer, he was brilliant at it. Lawyers always are, they've got nothing else to do.'

'I have better things to do with my life,' Rafe said crossly.

Stevie manoeuvred the punt into an inlet, leaped ashore and tied the mooring rope at the front of the punt around a tree, tugging to check the knot was secure. She laid the pole carefully along the inside of the punt and climbed back on board. Easing her way on to the cushions, she slid between Rafe's legs. 'Such as?'

'I don't think I should tell you.'

Stevie slowly started to undo her buttons. 'So don't. Show me.'

Fifteen

It was almost midnight before Mace walked into the packed warehouse. He glanced around and saw Jake standing in his usual place by the fire exit, his stringy blond dreadlocks flopping across his face as he closed a deal with a couple of teenagers. The kid looked up and smiled nervously. Mace nodded without smiling back. No wonder Jake was nervous. His turnover had been way down since the new kid had started three months ago. It made Mace wonder how much Jake had been using instead of selling.

He eased his way through the crowd of gyrating teenagers and let himself into the private room at the back of the warehouse. It smelt of sweat and stale sex. Briefly he remembered the dark girl – Portia – he and Jake had shared here a few months ago. He'd had her a couple of times on his own after that, but then she'd stopped coming to the raves – he guessed she'd found someone else. Pity, she'd been a good fuck, one of the best. Took after her mother, by all accounts.

He opened the small fridge in the corner of the room and took out a half-empty bottle of champagne. The little tart he'd had here yesterday hadn't needed much persuasion, there was still plenty of champagne left. He poured himself a glass, took a swig and grimaced. Flat. He finished the glass anyway.

He pulled a new bottle from the fridge and settled against the heap of cushions in the centre of the room, the bottle clamped between his thighs as he worked the foil free. No shy teenagers to loosen up tonight, but who cared. The amount of money he was turning over, he could afford to bathe in the stuff. The rent he paid for the warehouse was minimal; he earned it back in an hour's dealing. The Angel Dust was selling well, really beginning to take off over here. There'd been a couple of scare stories in the shit tabloids, emotive crap about 'Evil thugs peddling the drug from hell' and young mothers in America frying their babies in boiling oil, but the ravers didn't seem to care. Shit, frying your kids was probably the latest craze in the States anyway. All he knew was the users who'd tried it kept coming back for more, and they didn't seem to care how much it cost. Limited supply kept the price high. Angel Dust was still pretty new here, not much of it around yet. He had no idea if it did what everyone claimed, he'd never tried it. He stuck to dope and a couple of Es now and then. You needed to keep a clear head in his line of work.

A small breath escaped from the bottle as he eased the champagne cork free. No froth all over the place, he only did that when he wanted to impress the girls. One of the first things his father had taught him was to turn the bottle, not the cork. That way it didn't bubble up, nothing was wasted.

He poured himself a glass and tasted it. Much better. Satisfied, he flipped open the Thomas the Tank Engine lunchbox he used when he was carrying – easier to chuck it away and deny any responsibility if he got searched – and studied the contents. Angel Dust, of course, but still mostly Es. Jake hadn't got the wit to talk the kids into trying anything stronger. He always played up the effects it had, went on about fuck fantasies and blowing your mind. It scared the kids off. OK, maybe one or two users might freak when they took it, but that could happen with paracetamol, for God's sake. Chance in a million. He wouldn't be selling the stuff if he thought it was dangerous. He wasn't some kind of cold-blooded pusher like the South Americans. He was only in this for the laughs, anyway. Show a few kids a good time, teach them a bit about the fun grown-ups had, make a little pocket money in the meantime. After all, it wasn't as if he really needed the cash. It was the risk he was after, that's what gave him his high. Same as always.

He snapped the lunchbox shut. He was going to dump Jake, the kid's mind was blown. Too much too often. You needed to pace yourself – never have too much of a good thing. He knew all about that, he'd learned the hard way. Never again. He'd have to find a way of persuading his new recruit to push the Dust. If that didn't work, he'd dump it on him anyway, call it something else. So far, the kid had only sold Es and dope, refusing to touch anything heavier. A pusher with morals. You learned something new every day.

This kid was a bit different from the others, though, a cut above. Mace guessed he had to be desperate for the money, or he'd never have got involved. Either that or he was just looking for a way to kick over the traces, same as Mace himself. Bit of rebellion, his way of saying *Fuck You* to the rest of the world. At least Mace didn't have to worry about this one seeing past the baseball cap and shades and filthy Stüssy sweatshirt, and realising who he was. The kid already knew, but he was hardly about to let on. He was in it up to his neck himself. Double jeopardy. You keep quiet about me, I'll keep quiet about you.

There was a gentle knock at the door. Mace kicked the lunchbox under some cushions. 'Who is it?'

'It's me.'

He relaxed and stood up. Perfect timing. He was going to be out of town for a few days, it would've been a pain if the kid had no-showed now. He opened the door.

The kid looked relieved. 'Mace.'

Mace smiled. 'Hello, Oliver.'

Nigel Purvis threw open the door to the bedroom he shared

with his wife and stood back to let Portia enter. She sauntered in and surveyed the room with its huge double bed – wide enough so that he and Lillian never actually had to touch each other during the night – scattered with frilly little Laura Ashley cushions in the same shitty pattern as the duvet. Half the house was decked out in the stuff, curtains and wallpaper and fucking lampshades. The bedroom was the worst of the lot; here Lillian had really gone to town – matching pelmets and chair covers and God knew what else. He hated this shit; he preferred bold blocks of colour and geometric patterns, she knew that. Probably why the stupid cow had done it. He smiled nastily. It was the only thing in the bedroom she *did* control.

His cock stirred as he watched Portia bounce on the edge of the bed. He'd always wanted to do it right here with her, in the marital bed. Right on top of the fucking Laura Ashley.

He watched her for a moment, then walked over to her, taking her hand and putting it on his erection. 'Look what you've done to me, you little slut.'

'Hey, big man.' She glanced towards the door. 'Are you sure she won't come back?'

'I told you, she had to take Will shopping, he starts at Bristol next month. Political frigging history. Makes me wonder what I paid his fucking school fees for.'

'Where?'

'Where what?'

'Where's she taking him shopping?'

'Christ, I don't know,' Nigel said impatiently, kicking off his shoes and throwing himself into a chair by the window. 'Silly bitch has probably gone to Crawley, she said something about meeting Annabel there for lunch. Time she gets back, I'll be gone.'

'What do you mean, you'll be gone? Where are you going?'

'What is this, twenty questions? I'm going to Milan, it's the Italian Grand Prix tomorrow, remember?'

'You don't go to all of them,' Portia said sulkily. 'Why should you go to this one?'

'Because this is an important one. I've got a lot of money wrapped up in Rafe and Patrick. I want to keep an eye on my investment.' And the competition, just in case, Nigel thought silently. If Rafe or Patrick didn't deliver, Quisling Mild would just find someone who did.

'Who's winning now?'

'Fucking Schumacher. The bastard's unstoppable.'

'So what's the point in going to Italy, then?'

'The *point*, Portia, is that everyone knows Schumacher is going to win,' Nigel said. 'He's on sixty-seven points already, and there are still six races to go. He's so far out in front it almost doesn't count.' He moved to sit on the bed next to Portia, sliding his hand slowly up her thigh. 'The big question now is who will lead the rest of the field. *That's* why I'm going to Italy.'

'Who do you think it'll be?'

'If I knew that, I'd be down at William Hill making myself a fortune,' Nigel said. 'Damon Hill and Patrick are just a point apart at the moment – Damon's got forty-nine to Patrick's forty-eight. Could be either of them. Patrick had better hope it's him.'

'Why, will you get rid of him if it isn't?'

His hand eased over the top of her thigh-high black socks. 'I don't think that's something you need to know, is it?'

Portia knew he wanted her to ask, really. He loved showing off how much power and control he had over these superstar racing drivers, it gave him a bigger hard-on than when she flashed her tits. She didn't give a flying fuck about racing, but it got him going, so she played the game. It was always worth it in the end.

'You will, won't you?'

'Let's just say I'm not a charity. Patrick Alexander's one of the oldest drivers on the circuit. If he can't hack it –'

She wriggled away, teasing him. 'But if he beats Rafe, surely *he's* the one you should ditch?'

'Not necessarily. Rafe's fourth at the moment, eighteen points behind Patrick. He's unlikely to catch Hill or Alexander now, but he's doing pretty well for his first GP championship. He's young, he's good-looking, he's got no skeletons in his cupboard. He's a lot more attractive to the sponsors than a thirtysomething family man.' His hand resumed its journey across her thigh. 'If Rafe keeps this up, he'll be worth moving to the number one slot even if Patrick ends up ahead of him.'

'You bastard,' Portia breathed.

'You love it.'

'I love it.'

Nigel pushed her back on to the bed, catching his breath as her short silver satin skirt flipped upwards. Jesus, no panties, the hot little bitch! He wrestled with the belt of his trousers, trying to loosen the buckle.

Portia lay back watching him, her dark hair spread across the floral duvet. He was almost there, time to go in for the kill. 'She didn't go to Crawley with Will,' she said suddenly.

Nigel froze. 'What did you say?'

'Lillian didn't go to Crawley. I saw her going in to see Dad in the surgery when I left this morning.'

He relaxed. 'Jesus, Portia, don't do that to me. I thought you were going to say she was coming back here. She was probably stopping for some pills or something, then going on to Crawley afterwards.'

'Will wasn't with her.'

'Look, Portia, give it a rest. I didn't bring you here to talk about the fucking Grand Prix or my wife.'

'So what *did* you bring me here for?'

'You're about to find out.'

Portia knelt up on the bed as Nigel shucked off his trousers, her small fingers nimbly undoing the buttons of his shirt. Lillian Purvis had definitely not been going shopping with

Will. She knew that for certain because she'd met Will sloping off to Lingfield for the races this morning and he'd said nothing about going to Crawley with his mother. Clearly Lillian was lying to Nigel. Portia smiled as she eased Nigel's shirt over his shoulders. More power to her. If she was doing what Portia *thought* she was doing, it was no less than Nigel deserved.

She ran her small hands across Nigel's chest. He wasn't bad for an old guy, firm in all the right places. She looked down. Oh, yes, *definitely* firm in all the right places.

Nigel pushed her grey skinny-rib up, sucking in his breath as he saw the filmy black bra covering her perky little breasts. She didn't need it, but she liked giving him surprises. Like wearing no panties. Kept him guessing, kept him keen. She didn't want to lose him just yet. He was one of the most dangerous lays she'd ever had, and it was nice to be appreciated. She glanced at the Rolex he'd given her last month; her slut mother thought it was some fake she'd picked up in London. *Very* nice to be appreciated.

Nigel's cock pressed against the inside of her thigh as he ran his tongue over her breasts, their chocolate nipples poking out beneath the delicate fabric. His hand dived between her legs, prising them open.

'You're soaking wet, you little bitch,' Nigel breathed. 'You're fucking desperate.'

His fingers found what they were looking for and Portia groaned as he began to stroke her. Nigel eased back from her body slightly, smirking with satisfaction as she squirmed beneath his touch. His cock leaped against her thigh in time with her movements.

'Ohh, yes,' she murmured hungrily. 'Ohh, yes, don't stop, baby, don't stop.'

Her hands clawed his back, scoring his skin. Nigel made no move to stop her. Lillian wasn't going to notice, she never came near him long enough to see. He didn't give a fuck if she did, anyway. She wasn't going anywhere.

278

He pushed Portia's bra up over her breasts without bothering to undo it, his cock pulsing as he licked her nipples. She was wriggling frantically against his hand now, her soft silky pussy hair stroking his palm as she moved. Now he knew why it was called a pussy, that's exactly what it felt like. He felt the moisture flood out of her, her face flushed and her tits standing to attention as she neared her climax.

He pulled his hand away suddenly. 'Not yet, Portia.'

'Please –'

'I said, not yet.'

He knelt up over her, his cock inches away from her mouth. Portia obediently opened it and took him in, her tongue whirling around and around like she was licking ice-cream. He rubbed his knee against her cunt; not much, just enough to keep her on the boil while she brought him off.

'Ohhh, yes,' Portia mumbled.

He shoved himself deeper into her throat. 'Hasn't anyone ever taught you not to talk with your mouth full?'

He could see their reflection in the dressing-table mirror. She was lying up against the pillows, her grey jumper and bra pushed up almost to her throat, her silver skirt tangled about her waist, that beautiful wet dark pussy glistening against the white of her thighs, those long legs in their schoolgirl stockings spread wide for him. Her tits jiggled as she moved, sucking on him, his knee forcing her thighs wider as he balanced on his forearms on either side of her head. Jesus, she turned him on. He felt himself coming and pulled out of her mouth, not to spare her but to keep himself going longer. He rubbed his wet cock between her breasts, teasing those little button nipples with his fingers as she hooked her legs round his back, pulling him into her.

'I thought you were going to come,' she complained.

'It's hardly polite to come in a lady's mouth without asking.'

He jammed his fingers inside her. Christ, she was tight and

wet and ready for him. He pushed himself up on his arms, watching her eyes dilate with anticipation. Fuck the condom, he wasn't pissing around with that shit now. He thrust into her, groaning as she tilted her hips to pull him in deeper. He'd slept with a lot of whores in his time, but he'd never had a bitch hotter than this one.

'You bastard, you were supposed to use something,' Portia panted as he moved inside her.

He laughed. 'Since when did you eat chocolate with the wrapper on?'

'Since I learned about the birds and the bees, big man.'

'Look, I'll pull out, don't worry.'

'Yeah, and the cheque's in the post.'

'Trust me.'

'I never trust a man who says trust me.'

'Right now, you haven't got a lot of choice.' He cupped his hands round her buttocks and rolled over on to his back, pulling her with him. Portia knelt up over his crotch, one hand fingering her clit as the other played with one of her nipples, her head thrown back so that her dark hair poured across her shoulders. He could feel the scratchy wool of her black stockings against his thighs, see his cock disappearing into that soft little pussy as she rode him. He wanted to shoot his stuff right up into her now: just watching her firm little tits bounce and jiggle was enough to send him off. He held back with an effort, knowing the longer he waited, the better it would be. In the mirror he could just see her buttocks split to take him, her legs splayed on either side of his waist. Fucking jailbait.

Portia groaned and fell forwards on to his chest, her nipples rubbing against him as she squirmed. 'I'm going to come, *I'm going to come!*'

He could feel her cunt clenching around his cock as she started to spasm, her whole body shuddering against him. It was too much for him, he couldn't hold out any longer. He bucked upwards, his hands digging into her arse as he pulled her cheeks apart, driving even deeper into her as he came.

Portia flopped to one side of him, her arms and legs splayed out on the Laura Ashley like a starfish. For a long moment she said nothing, then suddenly she sat up.

'You stupid bastard, you promised you'd pull out.'

Nigel grinned at the ceiling. 'Didn't anyone ever tell you never to trust a man who says trust me?'

Lillian Purvis quietly tiptoed back down the stairs, unobserved by the couple writhing on the bed. So it was Portia Knighton. That complicated things. She'd known Nigel had been messing about with someone for the last couple of months, of course, she always knew; but she'd never guessed it was Portia. Nigel really should have known better. The silly child was younger than Will, for heaven's sake.

In the kitchen she put the kettle on, her hands perfectly steady. She hadn't expected Nigel to bring the girl back here today, assuming he'd take her to one of the airport hotels near Gatwick as he usually did – she'd seen the credit card slips – but in the end it didn't really matter. She'd have to wash the Laura Ashley, of course, but that was hardly the end of the world. If she was honest, she was a just a bit surprised Nigel had been so careless. He hadn't even bothered to shut the bedroom door. She'd seen them as she'd taken the clean washing upstairs to the airing cupboard. Suppose Will had walked in on them? He was rather sweet on Portia himself, he'd be terribly hurt if he found out.

She spooned some Lapsang Souchong into her cup and added some boiling water. She'd counted on Nigel being out this morning so that she could go through her things. By the time he left for Italy this afternoon, Will would be home, and she didn't want her son to see her and guess what she was going to do. He'd find out soon enough, of course, but she wanted to wait until he'd left for Bristol, started a new life of his own. It was only another month, she could wait that long.

After all, she'd waited nearly twenty years.

She propped her worn copy of Keats against the biscuit tin and sipped her tea. Poor Portia, it wasn't her fault. Oh, she didn't think Nigel had seduced her, or anything – young Portia was no innocent, Lillian knew that well enough – but the child had hardly had a good example from her mother. Rosie had led Laurie Knighton a dog's life for years, and the whole village knew it. What Portia needed was a nice young man who'd cherish her but wouldn't stand for any of her nonsense. Such a shame she hadn't gone for Will instead of Nigel. If the number of girls chasing her son and ringing him at all hours of the day and night was anything to go by, Will was probably the better bet in bed as well.

She smiled. It was amazing what the love of a good man could do. She felt ten years younger already. She had no doubt Nigel would be terribly shocked when he discovered what she'd been up to; he'd written her off sexually years ago. They all had. It was a bit of a shame she wouldn't be here to see their faces when they found out.

She set her tea down and put on her reading glasses. Nigel would get over it, he'd have plenty of help. Not Portia, of course, she'd have to see to that, but there'd soon be somebody else. He'd be a bit annoyed about the maintenance, perhaps, but it wasn't as if she hadn't earned it. She'd been at his beck and call for years. As for Will, once he got over his surprise, he'd probably be delighted. He'd been telling her to leave Nigel since he'd been old enough to talk.

She smiled as she opened her book and started to read the familiar lines. '*Season of mists and mellow fruitfulness, Close bosom friend of the maturing sun . . .*'

Who said the sap didn't rise in the autumn?

Stevie pulled her pink chiffon scarf closer round her head and edged near the BA desk, feeling like an Arab terrorist. Rafe had made her promise to keep the trip to Rome secret, so she'd turned the collar of her pink and cream felt jacket up at the neck and put on a pair of huge dark sunglasses just in case she met anyone she knew. She glanced furtively around the concourse. A young couple were standing by a news-stand staring at her and whispering excitedly to each other. Maybe the sunglasses were making it worse. After all, she *was* indoors in the middle of an airport concourse, and it was raining outside anyway. They probably thought she was a film star or something trying to travel incognito. She took the glasses off and the young couple glared at her as if she'd disappointed them on purpose.

'Ticket, please.'

She jumped guiltily as the check-in girl held out her hand. Shoving the sunglasses into her pocket, she rummaged around in the trendy Moschino tote bag Julia had lent her. Oh, shit, don't say she'd forgotten it, please God, don't let it still be sitting in the shoebox at the bottom of her wardrobe where she'd hidden it, I'll do anything, I'll go to church, I'll give money to the poor, I'll watch *Songs of Praise*, only – oh, thank you, God, thank you. She pulled the ticket out and waved it triumphantly. 'Got it!'

The check-in girl drummed her scarlet talons on the desk. Stevie handed the ticket over, nervously glancing behind her like some sort of spy. She'd told everyone – except Julia – that she was spending her week off in London with some friends. She'd had to tell Jules the truth, of course; the two of them had been in urgent wardrobe consultation for the last month. What *did* you pack for a romantic three-day tryst in Rome? Stevie had been all in favour of just taking her underwear, but Jules had tactfully suggested that it might seem a little bit forward. Eventually they'd settled on the silk shirt and skirt she'd worn when they'd gone punting, some new 501s, a couple of white T-shirts and a pair of honey-coloured suede boots for sight-seeing round Roman ruins – Rafe had told her once that only tourists wore trainers for anything other than jogging and tennis – and the slinky Ferrari-red sheath Rafe had given her. The rest of her bulging suitcase was filled with all the dresses, jackets, trousers, shoes, T-shirts, leggings, jumpers, skirts, shirts and shorts she'd thrown in at the last minute just in case.

The check-in girl was staring suspiciously at her ticket. 'This is Club Class.'

'Yes, I know.'

The girl nodded towards a counter a few metres away, in front of which lay a red carpet protected by barriers and black silk ropes. Most of the luggage being gently lifted on to the conveyor belt by the airport handlers was Louis Vuitton. '*That's* Club Class check-in.'

'I'm sorry. I didn't realise. Can't I check in here?'

The girl ignored her and studied the ticket again. Stevie wondered if she was going to hold it up to the light or bite it to check if it was a forgery.

'You *are* Stephanie Colvin?'

'Yes, of course I am.' Cheeky cow, just because she wasn't wearing fucking Chanel and dripping with diamonds. 'Look, is there some sort of problem?'

'No, I don't think so,' the girl said reluctantly. 'Passport?'

Stevie gave it to her and watched as the girl punched details into her computer with about as much enthusiasm as if she was poking her scarlet-tipped fingers into a heap of shit. She wondered if they sent check-in girls on special courses to learn how to insult their customers as efficiently as possible. She wouldn't have thought they'd have time, what with perfecting the art of sending your luggage on a two-week tour via Frankfurt and Moscow when you'd gone to Crete, and learning how to apply orange foundation to a minimum depth of three inches, stopping abruptly at the jawline.

'Luggage?'

Stevie heaved her suitcase on to the conveyor belt.

'D'youpackityourself?' the girl chanted.

You must be kidding, Stevie thought. It had taken the

284

combined weight of Julia, Mrs Arcor, two doorstops and Jamie and Lily to get the lid closed, but she *had* been the one who'd orchestrated the whole enterprise. 'Yes,' she said.

'Anybatteriesoranythingelectrical?'

'Hair-dryer count?' Stevie queried.

The girl looked blank. Stevie eyed the bleached frill back-combed around her face like an albino turkey's bum. No wonder the girl looked confused. It'd take a fucking hurricane to shift all that hairspray, not a hair-dryer.

'Acceptedanygiftsfromanyone –'

'No –'

'– orleftyourluggageunattendedatanytime?'

Stevie shook her head, wishing the girl would hurry up. She was busting for the loo, it was all that coffee she'd drunk to calm her nerves.

The girl stuck a hideous green label on the handle of the suitcase – it'd take hours to get the sticky off – and pressed a button. The conveyor belt jerked forward and spilled Stevie's case on to the moving belt behind it, where it was immediately buffeted by two heavy Samsonite suitcases before disappearing out of sight.

'Aisle or window?'

This was a tricky one. She wanted to see Rome from the window when they landed, but Oprah Winfrey had said last week that the safest place to be in the event of a crash was in the aisle so that you didn't burn to death stuck behind some woman wider than she was tall. 'Middle?' she compromised.

'Not in Club,' the girl said tartly. 'Aisle or window only.'

Bugger it, live dangerously. 'Window, then.'

The girl returned her ticket and passport to her and handed her a boarding card. 'Gate 38, boarding at 2.30. Next.'

Stevie shoved them all back in her tote bag and headed towards Departures. Snooty bloody cow. If she'd been any more insulting they could've promoted her to stewardess. She

285

already had the prerequisite go-faster stripes of blusher and pearlised pink eyeshadow down to a T.

She glanced at her watch. Twenty-five to two, perfect. What she needed now was a stiff drink to get over all the drama. A couple of gin and tonics and she'd be –

She froze, paralysed with shock, as she heard a strangely familiar voice speak behind her. Oh, God, not now, she prayed. You've got me this far, don't go and screw it up now.

She ducked into W.H. Smith's and took refuge behind the bestsellers. Maybe she'd got it wrong, it wasn't him. Gingerly she stuck her head over John Grisham to check. *Fuck.* Humphrey Prince was merrily bowling down the concourse towards Departures, a straw panama on his head, arm in arm with his wife who was wearing a long pink jacket and floppy rust-coloured velvet hat. Definitely in happy travel mode.

Stevie groaned. As Rafe and Patrick's sponsorship agent, Humphrey must be going to Italy too. Rafe had won the Italian Grand Prix yesterday with Patrick a close second; there were probably all sorts of deals to be done. She might be able to hide from Humphrey while they were in the airport, but once they got on board the plane there was nothing much she could do. He'd be bound to recognise her if he saw her, they'd met several times when he'd come up to the house for team meetings. He'd have no idea this trip was supposed to be secret; he might say something in all innocence to Annabel or Patrick and she'd be landed right in it. But she daren't risk asking him to keep it quiet either, he was the most appalling gossip. He wouldn't be able to resist telling someone if he thought he knew a juicy secret no one else did.

Well, she couldn't hide in here all day. She'd just have to keep her head down and cross her fingers he didn't spot her. She pulled the scarf low over her forehead and shoved the dark glasses back on again. Better an imitation soap star than a direct hit from Humphrey.

She edged out of W.H. Smith's and joined the queue into

Departures, hanging back just in case Humphrey turned round. From behind she could tell that Susan Prince had lost a lot of weight since she'd last seen her at the dinner party in May. It suited her, made her look several inches taller. And that pink jacket was gorgeous, really different from the buttoned-up Crimplene stuff she usually wore. It nipped in at the waist and then flared halfway down her thigh, like a dandy's frock-coat. What with that and those velvety black leggings –

The woman half-turned to listen to something Humphrey was saying and Stevie nearly walked into a pillar. It wasn't Susan Prince he was canoodling with at all. Nor was it another woman. It was *Peter Appleby*!

Stevie flashed her passport at the official by the gate and trailed the loving couple into the Departure Lounge. Well, bloody hell, Humphrey was knocking off Annabel and Patrick's *gardener*! Everyone knew about Peter – it was hardly a secret given his penchant for pink silk suits and heavy black kohl – but she'd never heard a whisper that Humphrey was knocking on the other side of the door. Mind you, with a wife like Susan you could hardly blame him.

Stevie watched them sit down, their arms entwined. This was obviously the *In* week for illicit trysts as far as Edenfield Manor was concerned. At least *she* was safe now. Peter had told everyone he was off to Paris for the fashion shows and Humphrey was supposed to be working, so they were no more going to own up to a bit of nooky in Rome than she was. She walked past their table and winked, grinning as she saw their horrified faces. They'd work out they were safe soon enough, same as she had. In the meantime, a bit of abject terror wouldn't do either of them any harm.

Sixty minutes later, she pressed the recline button in the arm of her chair and leaned back, a glass of champagne in her hand, as the plane levelled out above the clouds. It was glorious sunshine up here, and the pilot had promised blue skies all the way south to Rome. It was wonderful just to get away from the September drizzle. This trip couldn't have come at a better time. Jamie and Lily were just back to school and Annabel had been happy to grant Stevie a few days' holiday. But despite the welcome peace and quiet, she couldn't help feeling flat without them.

A stewardess passed through Club Class with a tray of hot white towels, flashing come-hither smiles at all the men and glaring at all the women. Stevie took the warm flannel and smoothed it across the back of her neck, deliberately making the snooty stewardess wait, then handed it back and closed her eyes. Champagne, hot towels, leg room. It was a bit different from cheap charters to Majorca. It was hard not to be seduced by the luxury of the life Rafe offered – not that that was the reason she was with him. She'd have loved him if he'd been a garage mechanic. But it did make a rather pleasant change to be bought gorgeous dresses, taken to casinos and whisked all over the world at the drop of a hat, there was no doubt about that. It more than made up for the tiny twinges of doubt that surfaced now and then.

She sipped her champagne thoughtfully. It wasn't that anything was wrong, of course, she was crazy about him, but still, just every so often . . .

Maybe it was all just too good to be true, that's why she was looking for problems when there really weren't any. Men like Rafe just didn't happen to people like her. Any woman would have fallen for him – he could have had anyone he wanted. And yet he'd chosen her. No wonder she kept doubting their relationship, it was a sort of umbrella-and-rain thing: if you took one, it never rained. If she expected it all to go Horribly Wrong, maybe it wouldn't happen.

It was hard to feel secure when she couldn't even be acknowledged as his girlfriend in public. The day in Oxford last month had been wonderful – particularly the hour when the punt had been moored to the riverbank – but the four weeks since then had gone back to normal. No Sex, Please, I'm Italian. She understood the logic behind Rafe's fear of discovery if his father really was such a strict Catholic – she imagined Emmanuele Terroni would be a dangerous man to cross – but it was still difficult to live this half-life of snatched phone calls and whispered assignations. It was worse than having an affair with a married man. Even Prick Whittington had managed a regular Friday afternoon bonk. Surely Rafe could have fitted in *one* afternoon or evening with her in four weeks if he really wanted to? She'd had more fulfilling relationships with pen-pals.

It was Charles Cusack's obvious dislike of Rafe, that's what was really getting to her. Ever since Jamie's accident, it had been gnawing away at her peace of mind. Both men couldn't be telling the truth. She didn't want to believe Rafe could be lying about something so important, yet at the same time she *knew* Cusack couldn't be.

Since her birthday last month, Cusack had come over half a dozen times to take James fishing or walking in the woods with his dog. Whatever constraints he might feel around adults seemed to disappear when he was with the little boy. Stevie had come upon them in the woods only last Sunday, lying on their stomachs in the reeds by the small river that ran through Cusack's land, apparently tickling fish. Cusack had been whispering instructions to Jamie, who'd tried to comply as quietly as possible, only to shriek with laughter every time a fish brushed against his fingers. Eventually Cusack had started laughing too, the pair of them giggling and splashing until every fish in the river must have been driven away. Stevie had left without letting them know she'd seen them, unable to stop herself grinning inanely.

She felt a brief flicker of surprise at herself. The grudging chance she'd given Cusack had somehow flowered into genuine respect for him over the past few weeks, despite their *contretemps* in the garden on her birthday. She wished he didn't know about her relationship with Rafe. She didn't know how he'd found out – a shrewd guess, perhaps, or maybe her heated defence of Rafe had given it away – but she would never forget the contempt in his eyes when he'd spoken of her 'lover'. She hated having to keep it all secret. It made it seem sordid and squalid, somehow, as if she should be ashamed – as if Cusack's contempt was justified. Of course, she knew it wasn't. But still.

She levered her chair into the upright position and smiled sweetly as the snotty stewardess placed a linen tablecloth and real metal cutlery – none of that plastic rubbish – on her tray table. Rafe was flying her club class to Rome, they'd be together for three glorious days and – she shivered with delicious anticipation – nights. Even if it was the last time they were together until after the final Grand Prix in November, at least she'd have this to keep her going.

She asked the stewardess to refill her champagne glass. If this was it for two months, she might as well make the most of it.

She fell in love with Santa Maria the moment Rafe's driver swung the black Mercedes into the drive. The villa was beautiful: huge, but somehow welcoming as it opened up before them, the atmosphere more that of a country retreat than the *Gran Casa* after which the village nearby was apparently named. It was perched on top of a small round hill, reached by a rutted drive lined with uneven rows of cypress pines that had clearly been planted over decades, new saplings put down every time an old tree was lost to wind or time. Unkempt lawns withered by the dry summer rolled away from the front of the house; behind it Stevie caught a glimpse of an ancient swimming pool set with tiny pale blue and aquamarine tiles, its stale water green and murky. Next to the pool were two tennis courts, one clay, one asphalt, their nets sagging. To the right of the villa was a rose parterre, its cracked pavements covered with layers of velvet petals turning brown in the sun. To the left of the house, less than twenty metres away, was an old church. We could get married here, Stevie thought.

She threw herself into Rafe's arms as he came out of the villa to welcome her. 'Oh, God, I've missed you!'

'And I you. Do you like the villa?'

'Oh yes, of course,' Stevie said, slightly surprised that it should be his first question.

'Let me show you round, Leonora will put your bags away.'

Stevie smiled rather uncertainly at the tiny old woman standing in the shadows. Leonora didn't smile back.

'Stevie –?'

'Sorry, I'm just coming.'

Rafe led the way into the villa and Stevie followed, noticing but not commenting on the mildew on the wooden shutters, the mouse droppings and broken sink tiles in the kitchen, the curtains left closed for so long she doubted the faded silk ties would be able to open. The whole place had an atmosphere of benevolent neglect, like a rich dowager left alone to live out her final years in private.

'This place has only ever been a summer house, of course,' Rafe said as they reached the hall. 'It used to be tenanted and kept open all year round, but the family only actually used it in July and August. After my mother left for America twenty years ago, my father shut it altogether and returned to the family's main home in Tuscany. Only Leonora's here now.'

If this was their summer cottage in the country, Stevie couldn't imagine how big the house in Tuscany must be. She saw that the villa was built in the shape of a U and seemed to have three floors. At the centre of the U, beyond the entrance lobby, the vast hall rose for two floors, its ceiling so high Stevie had to crane her neck to see the carved wooden beams covered with flaking gilt. A small dais was built into one end of the hall like a stage, dusty books lining its three walls, a grand piano dwarfed into insignificance in one corner.

As they progressed through the villa Stevie saw that the other rooms were all in the same state of decaying elegance: sagging cushions edged with gold braid, silk-covered walls marred by rusty water-stains, priceless-looking oil paintings in chipped, grimy gilt frames. Stevie quite liked the fact that the villa was crumbling to pieces: in its original state, she couldn't help thinking it would have been a bit forbidding. She didn't say anything to Rafe. She had the feeling he would take any criticism rather personally.

They climbed the narrow uncarpeted stone stairs to the third floor and she trailed Rafe down endless corridors as he strode past dozens of closed bedroom doors towards their own. She slowed down as they passed a door somewhere near the centre of the east wing, the corridor window opposite looking out over the rose garden. For some reason the door piqued her curiosity and she made to open it. But Rafe turned and placed his hand over hers, pulling the door shut again just as she glimpsed a brass bed amid a sea of white lace and satin, a walnut dresser in the far corner covered with pots and bottles and silver-backed brushes.

'Whose room is that?' she asked curiously.

Rafe paused, then locked the door and pocketed the key without looking at her. 'My mother's,' he said shortly. 'We don't go in there.'

By the time Rafe had finished showing her around the house and grounds, Stevie was tired and it was almost dusk. They ate Leonora's delicious spaghetti carbonara and salad and then tumbled into bed in Rafe's vast, echoey bedroom, where they stayed for most of the next morning. Tuesday passed in a lazy, hedonistic haze: eating, making love, drinking, making love, sleeping and making love. It felt like a dream. Stevie was so happy, sated with Rafe; she could hardly think beyond the next kiss.

Wednesday was Leonora's half-day. Stevie awoke to the

already-hot Italian sun streaming through the shutters, filled with energy, determined not to let their time together just drift along any longer. At lunchtime, she decided to cook Rafe an omelette, and spent twenty minutes surveying the ancient cooker in the kitchen, unable even to turn it on, before admitting defeat and sending Rafe into the village for some bread and salami. There was no point in asking him if he knew how to work the cooker; he'd already made it clear that in Italy the kitchen was a foreign country to men. She couldn't imagine Oliver getting away with that kind of attitude, but in this old-fashioned backwater somehow it didn't seem out of place. Thank God Julia wasn't here to see her.

She started to make a salad instead, alone for the first time since she'd arrived. She'd been dying to ask Rafe about his mother's room, it seemed so spooky, leaving it untouched like that for twenty years, but Rafe hadn't mentioned her again, and she didn't like to ask. In fact, he'd talked very little about his family or his childhood. She'd hoped three days with him here, in his own home, would allow him to relax and open up to her of his own accord, but so far he'd revealed nothing. He'd been warm and loving and charming, of course, but she couldn't help feeling as though she hardly knew anything about him at all.

That night, she tentatively suggested going into Rome to see more of the ruins for which she'd been so sartorially prepared. Rafe just smiled and started to unbutton his shirt.

'Why would I want to go anywhere, *cara*?' he murmured as his mouth descended on her breast. 'I have everything I want right here.'

Thursday, her last full day here, was a repeat of the previous two: restful, tranquil, undemanding. They hadn't left Santa Maria together during the entire three days. She hadn't even bothered to unpack. Bloody Julia, she *should* have just brought her knickers. It was idyllic, she knew she should have been in seventh heaven; and yet somehow she felt restless and ill at ease. She and Rafe were together, but it seemed almost coincidental, as if their paths had just happened to cross. He was happy to be with her, she didn't doubt that; he was attentive and considerate, the perfect lover. But it was as if they were two leaves who'd fallen into the same river, floating in the sunshine wherever the current took them, no joint purpose linking them together. The moment the current changed, they would drift apart.

That night, Rafe asked her to put on the red dress he'd bought her in Oxford. Excitedly she hooked up her basque and smoothed on her stockings over sunburnt legs before pouring herself into the sheath of red silk, wondering where he was going to take her. But when she came downstairs, Rafe told her to close her eyes and then took her hand. Puzzled, she followed him for a couple of minutes and then at his command she opened her eyes and found herself in the dining room, the table set with the best linen and silver, crystal goblets glittering under the candlelight.

Leonora then proceeded to serve them a delicious meal which was completely wasted on Stevie. For some reason she felt suddenly confused, insecure and upset. This was what she'd always wanted; and yet suddenly, it all seemed wrong.

She'd dreamed of being alone like this with Rafe, for six months now: sharing his home and his bed, waking up next to him every morning, being a part of his life – his real life, behind the glamorous image everyone else saw. But none of this seemed real. *He* didn't seem real. It was all *too* perfect – the romantic, extravagant gestures, the sweet words, the golden idyll of this villa. She'd wanted Rafe to take her to his home, but she knew nothing more about him now than she had a week ago. She'd never done anything *ordinary* with him in the whole time they'd been together. It had all been a beautiful illusion: Monaco, Oxford, and now Rome. It had been lovely to be spoilt like this, but it wasn't enough. She wanted a real relationship with a real man, not some kind of dream life, however wonderful.

On the Friday that she was due to leave, she stood on the terrace behind Rafe's villa, the sun dazzling her eyes as she gazed out over the bone-dry countryside. In the distance she could see grapes browning on the vines. Whatever her misgivings about Rafe, she had loved her stay here. She would be sorry to leave.

She glanced up as Leonora walked out on to the terrace, her lined face expressionless as she delivered her message. 'Renato is here to take you back to the airport, *signorina*.'

'Already?' Stevie glanced at her watch. 'God, it's three o'clock. I hadn't realised.' She stood and waved to Rafe, who was chatting to the estate manager in the distance. He nodded and waved back.

'I need to go and pack –'

'I have already done it for you, *signorina*. Your case is in the hall. I will tell Rafe to put it in the car.'

Anyone would think the old woman was glad to get rid of her.

In the distance there was a faint clang.

'If you will excuse me, *signorina*.'

'Where has Leonora gone?' Rafe asked as he climbed the steps to the terrace.

'I think she went to answer the door to Renato.'

'Good, I need to talk to him.' Rafe kissed her. 'I want him to collect some screws and fuses from the *ferramenta*. This place is falling apart. I won't be long, *cara*.'

Stevie stood up, re-tucking her white T-shirt into her 501s, and with a quick glance round to make sure she hadn't left anything on the terrace, wandered into the villa through the hall, enjoying its sudden coolness. She'd miss this glorious weather. Rome in September was perfect: warm and sunny but lacking its summer stickiness. It was probably pissing it down now in London.

There was no sign of Renato or Rafe in the entrance hall. The front door was wide open, so she wandered out on to the steps, then paused as she saw the two cars parked in the wide gravel courtyard that fronted the villa. One was Renato's black Mercedes – he was loading her suitcase into the boot – but she had no idea whose the gleaming BMW was. Rafe hadn't told her he was expecting anyone. He was leaning in through the car window, deep in discussion with its owner.

Stevie ducked back into the doorway, uncertain as to what she should do. She watched curiously as the driver's door of the BMW opened and a beautiful pair of women's legs in fine-denier black stockings and black-and-tan court shoes slid out. Her view of the woman's face was blocked by Rafe.

Rafe spoke to the woman in rapid Italian and she answered him swiftly in the same language, pushing him away from her, her back towards Stevie. Lustrous dark hair cascaded down her shoulders, stopping a couple of inches above a childishly slender waist. Its owner looked the height of Italian chic in a boxy jacket and short skirt in some nubbly cream wool edged with black braid. She was tiny, perhaps five foot two or three, and Stevie immediately felt huge and clumsy in comparison.

'Cinzia, *cara*,' Rafe was saying. '*Per favore* –'

'*Basta! Io non* –' She saw his gaze flicker over towards the front door and broke off suddenly, whirling round. Stevie stepped back into the shadows, but it was too late. The woman had seen her. She spun back to Rafe and slapped him a stinging blow across the cheek. '*Cazzo!*'

Stevie flew down the steps. 'What on earth is going on?'

'Stevie, please,' he said wearily. 'Just go back inside, I'll be with you in a minute. I'll explain everything then.'

Despite herself, Stevie stood her ground. 'Not until I know what's going on.'

'Aren't you going to introduce us, Raphael?' the woman said, speaking English for the first time.

Rafe was silent.

'Then I see I shall have to do it myself.' The beautiful Italian turned to Stevie. 'My name is Cinzia Capone Terroni. I am Rafe's wife.'

Sixteen

'This is getting to be a bit of a habit, Stevie,' Julia said as Stevie downed her third glass of Frascati. 'First Prick Whittington, and now Rafe.'

'It's so humiliating!' Stevie wailed. 'It's bad enough being cheated on, but when the other woman's his own *wife* –'

'Didn't you have *any* idea?'

'No, of course not. The bastard didn't give anything away.' She held her glass out for a refill. 'I never even dreamed he was married. God, I feel such a fool. All that shit about not wanting his father to find out. It was his fucking wife he was scared of!'

'Do Patrick and Annabel know he's married?'

'I doubt it, they've never mentioned it. I don't think anyone knows. He's kept it fucking quiet. Bad for his image, I suppose. Apparently he got married last year to the daughter of one of his father's friends. Cinzia Capone, can't get much more Italian than that.' Stevie reached under the sofa for the emergency supply of chocolate digestives she'd left there last time and brushed off the fluff. 'The bastard had been having a story with her for six years.'

'A *what*?'

'A story – it's what the Italians call a serious relationship. I can see why: stories are all they ever tell.'

Julia curled her long legs up under her. 'I can't believe no one said anything in Italy. I mean, he took you back to his *home* –'

'You'd have to see the set-up there, Jules. He's the Lord of the Manor. Leonora worships the ground he walks on – only son and all that. She'd let him set up a brothel there if that's what he wanted.'

'Even so –'

Stevie dipped a chocolate biscuit in her Frascati. 'It's a culture thing; they're all stuck in the bloody Middle Ages. Italian men are spoilt brats. Their mothers do everything from the minute they're born, and their wives take over when they get married. They're allowed to do whatever they want.' She sucked her soggy biscuit. 'How many Italian men do you think it takes to change a light bulb?'

'I give up.'

'Just one to hold it while the world revolves round them.'

Julia laughed. 'I take it your love affair with the romantic Latin temperament is over?'

'Bloody right it is,' Stevie said. 'They all cheat – Renato was actually boasting that he's had the same mistress for twelve years. Every time she nags him about getting married, he buys her a new pair of earrings. She has no idea he's already got a wife and four kids stashed at home.' She sighed. 'No one thinks it's a big deal as long as they don't get caught. The women stay at home making pasta and having babies and the men go out picking up English nannies.'

'Rafe's wife seemed to think it was a big deal.'

'Yeah, well, she's the equivalent of a radical feminist in Italy,' Stevie said.

'What on earth did you do when she said who she was?'

'I wish I'd had the guts to wallop the other side of his face,' Stevie said. 'I just got in the car with Renato and came home. What else could I do? I bawled my eyes out for the entire journey – I must've looked a terrible sight because even the cow of a stewardess I had on the way over was giving me tissues and telling me all men are bastards by the time I got to Heathrow.' She reached for the wine bottle. 'I came straight over here when I got back, but you were away again.'

'If I'd known you were having a crisis I'd have raided Oddbins and stayed in,' Julia said.

'Where were you, anyway?'

'In Brighton for a conference. I only got back last night.'

'*Another* one? Are you having an affair with the manager or something?'

'I wish,' Julia sighed. 'He's only got eyes for the guy in Compulsory Purchasing. That stewardess was right about one thing. All men are bastards, even the gay ones.'

'I wouldn't say all of them. Just the ones worth having.'

'You're right, I take it back. The nice ones can't get it up, the sexy ones can't put it down.'

'It's my own fault, I should've known Rafe was trouble,' Stevie said dismally, chasing crumbs round the bottom of her glass with her finger. 'I really liked him, Jules. He was so bloody gorgeous. I knew he was a bit of a loverboy, but I couldn't resist the temptation of being seduced by such a professional. I just couldn't *help* myself.'

'Maybe men would like monogamy more if it sounded less like monotony,' Julia pondered.

'And he kept saying he loved me. Men who love you never say that, it's one of the first laws of physics.'

'Physics?'

'Well, *Cosmo*. That's as scientific as I get.'

Julia reclaimed the Frascati in time to stop Stevie finishing the bottle. 'Have you ever noticed,' she mused, 'that when you're out driving with a man and he stops and asks for directions, it's always your fault for not listening when you get lost?'

'You can never tell a man anything in public,' Stevie said. 'If you're suitably humble you can get away with it in private, but in public, he has to *know*.'

Julia nodded sagely. 'They like phones with lots of buttons, too. It makes them feel important.'

'They always have better stereos than women. Like flight decks, all flashing lights and gravity equalisers.'

'I think you mean graphic.'

'No, that's their language if you muddle up their CDs when they've just got them into alphabetical order.'

'Where do they put the compilation albums, that's what I want to know,' Julia said. 'I mean, how do they decide which letter to file them under?'

'Rafe had a DAT system in his Porsche.' Stevie stared mournfully into her empty glass. 'Bastard.'

'I bet his wife gave him hell after you left,' Julia said.

'I hope she cut his balls off and fried them for breakfast,' Stevie said. 'All that shit about his mother's room. It was *hers*, that's why he wouldn't let me go in there. She'd come back to the villa to collect a ballgown she'd left there, that's how come she caught him. Renato said Rafe had taken her to a masked Lovers' Ball the weekend before he saw me, the shit!'

'It probably had to be masked, otherwise half the women in Rome would have lynched him. I shouldn't think you're the first he's cheated with.'

'Prick Whittington always told me I was the only affair he'd ever had.'

'Men who are having an affair and say they've never done it before have *always* done it before.'

'Why is it I always pick the bastards, Jules?' Stevie was on the edge of tears. 'I thought Rafe was different, but he was the worst of the lot. At least Paul told me he was married.'

Julia picked up the empty wine bottle. 'I'm going to make some tea before we start on the Liebfraumilch. The Portuguese Grand Prix is on in ten minutes. We need to be able to focus so we can throw cushions at the television screen.'

Stevie glowered at the mute television as Julia headed into the kitchen. It was like a re-run of the day they'd done the pregnancy test, only this time she was *really* depressed. The last ten days had been miserable. Without Julia to talk to, she'd had to keep her broken heart to herself. Everyone had asked her how her holiday in London had been and commented on what extraordinarily good weather she must have had to get so brown since it had poured all week in Sussex. Meanwhile, all she'd wanted to do was crawl into a corner and lick her wounds in peace.

She'd really loved Rafe. She'd thought he was finally *It*. OK, she'd known he was a bit out of her league, but he'd always acted as if he was as crazy about her as she was about him. He'd come on to her. She remembered the way he'd comforted her in the rose garden after she'd screwed up Patrick's interview with INN, how he'd walked out of the hotel in Monte Carlo with his arm round her in front of everyone. He'd told her he loved her, he'd said all the right words, done all the right things. How could she *not* have fallen for him? He was gorgeous, and he'd known exactly which buttons to press. The Casino, the mind-blowing sex, the transatlantic phone calls, the Club Class air tickets. He'd made her feel like the luckiest woman in the world. She'd been so bowled over by the glamour and romance of it all, she hadn't questioned a word he'd said. All the secrecy, the excuses for not being able to see her more often – she'd swallowed the lot.

It was her own bloody fault for being so gullible. She should have known better. Her mother had always said if a man didn't call you, it wasn't because his phone had been cut off or he'd lost your number, it was because he didn't want to call. If Rafe had wanted to see her, even if all the shit about his father had been true, he'd have found a way.

The warning signs had been there from the beginning, if she'd only bothered to look. The obsession with keeping their relationship secret; the extra days away even after Patrick had returned from a race abroad; the insistence that he always call her from his hotels, never the other way round. All those times he must have been with his wife – or some other woman.

She grabbed for another tissue as the tears started free-falling again. How *could* he have done this to her? He'd said he loved her, he'd talked about their future together as if it had really meant something to him. Why? It couldn't just have been the sex, they hadn't exactly done it often. Had it all been a game to him, to see how long it would take him to get her into bed? Or – her cheeks burned with humiliation – had it just been a pity fuck, because he felt sorry for her? Oh, God, how could she have been so *stupid*?

She blew her nose. She loved him more than anything else in the world, she'd never get over it. The bastard.

But had she really been in love or just infatuated? She felt a flicker of uncertainty. She'd never really stopped to think beyond the sex. Maybe that's why he'd rationed it: to keep her desperate. If she was truly honest, when she'd been away from Rafe's seductive influence, doubts *had* begun to surface. A part of her had known something was wrong ever since Jamie's accident – as a hero in times of crisis, Rafe Dussi made a bloody good dustbin. But he'd played her like a virtuoso: every time she'd really begun to wonder about him, he'd swept her off her feet all over again. God, what an idiot.

She felt an abrupt flare of anger. Who the hell did he think he *was*, playing with her feelings like that? He might have thought a little of him was better than nothing, but he could have asked her if she felt the same way. She suddenly realised it wasn't so much her heart that was hurt as her pride. She wasn't upset: she was *furious*. Of course she hadn't loved him, you couldn't love someone you didn't even know. Her brain had just been completely addled by rampant sex hormones.

It was ironic. She'd fallen for Rafe the first time she'd seen him, believed every word he said, whereas from the moment she'd met Cusack outside Sainsbury's the day he'd nicked her parking space, she'd hated him. And yet it had been Cusack who'd turned out to be the decent guy, and Rafe who was the cheating, lying, bastard son-of-a-bitch.

She balled the soggy tissue in her hand. OK, Cusack had been an arrogant sod sometimes, but thanks to Rafe she'd never really given him a chance.

Julia came back into the sitting room and handed her a cup of tea.

'*Shit*, that's hot.' Stevie put the mug on the floor. 'Can't I have wine? It's safer.'

'*It* may be. *You're* not.'

Stevie sniffled. 'I don't think you're being very sympathetic, Jules.'

'That's because you're better off without him.'

'Julia, you do realise you're in danger of turning into a bitter old spinster?' Stevie said. 'Kids will start giving each other dares to ring your doorbell.'

'Could be worse. I could end up someone's wife.'

'I don't think that's likely.'

Julia raised her teacup. 'Here's to celibacy.'

'Are you *mad* – oh, God, there he is!' Stevie leaped up, just missing her full cup of tea which was still on the floor, and pointed to the silent television screen where Rafe's car was moving into view on the grid. 'I can't bear to watch!'

'You'll survive,' Julia said briskly. She groaned as she saw a sudden glint in Stevie's eye. 'No, no, I didn't say that, I didn't say that –'

'*First I was afraid, I was petrified* –'

There was no stopping her now. She jumped up on to Julia's new IKEA coffee table, holding her wine glass in front of her like a microphone.

Julia buried her head in her hands.

On the television behind Stevie, Rafe's purple car swerved to avoid a crash ahead of him and silently skidded across the screen and off the track, coming to a gentle stop on the grass near the crash barriers. Rescue services raced over to the car as Rafe climbed out of it and yanked off his helmet, then threw it furiously on to the ground.

'*I will survive –*'

'But it's the first time I'll have seen him since Rome,' Stevie wailed into the phone. 'What am I going to *do*?'

'You'll be fine,' Julia said reassuringly down the phone.

'*I will survive –*'

'Don't you *dare*. I had enough of that last Sunday. You were completely off your head by the time you left. I don't know how you even found your way back to Edenfield Manor.'

'Well if you don't know, I bloody well can't remember,' Stevie said. 'My mind is a complete blank.'

'Nice to know some things don't change.'

Stevie glanced frantically up and down the hall. 'Look, Jules, what am I going to do? He'll be here in twenty minutes, I can't stand the tension.'

'He's not coming to see you, he's just coming for the Terroni team meeting. Everyone else will be there, you won't even have to talk to him.'

'I will. Annabel wants me to serve the bloody coffee, she doesn't trust Mrs Arcor to do it right.'

'Asking him if he wants milk or sugar is hardly *talking* to him, Stevie.'

'I don't know why bloody Nigel Purvis couldn't have it at his house as usual,' Stevie complained. 'He rang up this morning and said it'd have to be here instead. I just don't want to see Rafe, it's too soon.'

'It's the third of October, Stevie. It's nearly three weeks since you got home. You've got to see him some time.'

'But I feel such an idiot –'

Julia's voice was indignant. 'If anyone should feel an idiot, it's *him*. He was the one who got caught with his trousers down, not you. Just remember, you're the one with the goods on him, not the other way round. Patrick and Annabel still don't even know he's married.'

305

'I suppose so – oh, God, that's the door. Look, Jules, I've got to go. I'll ring you and tell you what happened later.'

She put down the telephone and darted up the stairs, hiding on the half-landing as Annabel emerged from the drawing room to open the front door. Martin Romaine strolled into the hall, his baby-blond curls gleaming in the weak autumn sunshine.

'You look beautiful, as always, Annabel,' he drawled.

'No Rosie?' Annabel said tartly.

'No Rafe?' Martin countered.

Annabel flushed as she closed the door. How the hell did he know? – Monte Carlo, of course. She'd told him she was meeting a girlfriend. The story as far as everyone else was concerned had been that Rafe had arranged a surprise reunion with Patrick. It would hardly take a genius to put two and two together.

Martin let her off the hook. 'Anyway, Rosie is history.'

'*She* doesn't seem to think so.'

'Rosie's grasp of reality is somewhat limited,' Martin said. 'It's what makes her books so popular. Why, are you jealous?'

'Don't be ridiculous.' Annabel turned her back on him as the doorbell rang again. 'Patrick and Charles are in the drawing room. Why don't you go through?'

As she re-opened the front door, Nigel Purvis nodded briefly without saying anything and pushed past her towards the drawing room. Annabel stared after him in surprise. Nigel looked *terrible*. His dirty-blond hair was limp and greasy, his eyes bloodshot. He hadn't even bothered to shave this morning and his baggy grey suit looked as if he'd slept in it. What on earth was wrong with him?

Swift on Nigel's heels, Humphrey Prince bounced perkily over the doorstep.

'Morning, Annabel. Isn't it a lovely day?'

'Lovely,' Annabel echoed, her confusion growing as Humphrey almost skipped down the corridor.

'*Ciao*, Annabel.'

She jumped as Rafe came up behind her. Without even looking round, she started walking towards the drawing room.
'You're the last to arrive, everyone else is already here. I'm
sure they'll want to get on –'

'Annabel, *cara*, can't we talk?'

She slowed but didn't stop. 'What about?'

'About us –'

'There *is* no us, Rafe,' Annabel said briskly. 'Now, if you'll
excuse me, I need to go and find Stephanie, she's supposed to
be making us coffee.'

As Rafe disappeared into the drawing room Annabel was
surprised to find that her heartbeat was barely above normal.
She still found Rafe unbelievably sexy, of course, but she was
suddenly able to rationalise it. Time had helped. She would
have slept with Rafe in Monaco given the chance and her
marriage would have been over. But the moment had passed.
She couldn't help her physical reaction to Rafe, but she knew
she would never act on it now. The madness that had engulfed
her then had gone.

She caught Patrick's eye as she pulled the double doors to
and smiled. He smiled back, his eyes full of a warmth she
hadn't seen there for many months. She felt a sudden lightness
in her chest, as if one of the iron bands gripping her heart had
shattered. They *would* come through this. It wouldn't be like it
was before; it would be better.

Stevie wondered what Annabel was smiling about as she
came back down the corridor. She hadn't been able to see Rafe
from her position in hiding on the stairs, but she'd heard the
murmur of his voice in the hall. She'd have to see him soon.
Just the thought made her stomach feel as if she'd been
bungee-jumping.

Annabel spotted her as she sneaked back down the stairs.
'There you are, Stephanie. Coffee in ten minutes, please.'

Stevie nodded as Annabel spun on her heel. Bloody woman,

bloody coffee, bloody Rafe. She glowered as she headed towards the kitchen.

Fifteen minutes later, she smoothed her hair, licked her dry lips and picked up the silver tray with its coffee pot and seven cups and saucers. Shit, she hoped she didn't drop it on the way through, it'd be just her luck. She reached the door to the drawing room safely and braced herself. She wouldn't have to talk to him, she'd be fine. Julia was right: *he* was the one who should be embarrassed.

She took a deep breath and bumped open the door with her hip. Without looking round, she placed the tray on the Hanoverian side-table that had played such a major part in Jamie's various escapades. Her limited circle of vision showed her Rafe's black leather boots and black Levis less than four feet away. Her hands shook as she laid out the crockery. She'd do Patrick first, work her way up slowly.

She poured him a cup – black, no sugar – and handed it to him, then turned to Cusack. 'Sugar and milk?'

'Neither, thank you.'

She handed him his cup. 'Mr Purvis?'

'As it comes,' Nigel snapped.

What the hell was that supposed to mean? Well, stuff him, he could have the milky sweet one she'd done for Annabel and like it.

'Mr Prince?'

Humphrey bounded out of his seat. 'No worries, I'll do mine. Wonderful coffee, Annabel. Brazilian, is it? You can almost smell the beans –'

'What's wrong with you, Humphrey?' Nigel asked nastily. 'You've been acting like a cast member from *Neighbours* all day. Susan let you off the leash or something?'

'I'd rather you didn't talk to me like that,' Humphrey said, his voice shaking slightly. 'I am not a member of your staff, I'm an independent negotiating agent. I am a *person*, you know. I won't be treated like a doormat any more.'

'Does Susan know about this?' Nigel sneered.

'I've left Susan,' Humphrey said.

Nigel's jaw dropped. 'You've done *what*?'

Humphrey raised himself up to his full five-feet six and straightened his narrow shoulders. 'Actually, everyone, I've got a bit of an announcement to make.' His cheeks flushed even pinker. 'I left Susan last weekend. I – I've moved in with Peter Appleby. We're going to be living together from now on.'

'You're what?' Annabel gasped.

'*Living* together?' Patrick said. 'As in –'

'Yes.' Humphrey started to enjoy the effect he was making. He winked at Stevie. 'We're hoping to have a little party at our house next Saturday to celebrate. We'd really be pleased if you could all come.'

There was a stunned silence. Stevie shot a quick glance at Rafe. He was shifting uncomfortably in his chair and leaning back as if to put as much distance between himself and Humphrey as possible.

'Congratulations,' Cusack said calmly. 'I'd be happy to come.'

Nigel stared at him. Clearly it was In to be Out amongst the upper classes. He must remember to stop calling them shirt-lifters in front of Lord Cusack. 'Oh, yes, of course, love to come,' he echoed quickly. 'If I can fit it in, of course – terribly busy these days – you know –'

'Do you think we could get on with the meeting now?' Cusack asked mildly.

Stevie poured Martin and Annabel's coffees as Humphrey sat down, glowing with achievement. There was only Rafe left to serve. Her heart thudded as she forced herself to look up at him. 'Coffee, Rafe?'

'Mmm?' He glanced distractedly in her direction. 'Yes, black, one sugar please.'

He could at least look a *bit* embarrassed, Stevie thought

furiously. He'd barely even noticed she was there, the miserable bastard. She deliberately put seven sugar lumps in his coffee and stirred it thoroughly before placing it on the table next to him. She hoped he choked on it.

'OK, just a quick recap,' Cusack was saying. 'The two races since our last meeting: Portugal, bit of a mixed bag, with Rafe being knocked out on the fourth lap, but Patrick more than made up for it with an excellent win at Estoril. The European Grand Prix last Sunday was an improvement. Patrick nearly caught Schumacher on the penultimate lap –'

'Couldn't quite get past him,' Patrick said regretfully. 'Not safely, anyway.'

'Second was a good result. Rafe also did very well coming third,' Cusack said. 'The current points situation puts Schumacher on eighty-one, just eleven points ahead of Patrick, well within reach. Hill's third, Rafe's in fourth with forty-four. Too far behind to win now, but it still gives us an excellent shot at the Constructors' Championship.'

'Um, Lor – um, Cusack, how many races are left?' Humphrey asked.

'Three,' Stevie said automatically.

Cusack smiled slightly. 'Thank you, Stevie. Would you like to take the rest of this meeting, or shall I?'

Stevie blushed scarlet. 'Sorry. You.'

'Fine. The races Stevie was talking about –' his mouth twitched suspiciously – 'are the Pacific on the twenty-second of this month, Japan the week after, and finally Australia on the twelfth of November.'

'Ooh, everything to play for,' Humphrey said, beaming round the room.

Rafe scowled as he picked up his coffee. 'Schumacher's not going to be easy to catch. Patrick will have to beat him in two out of the remaining three races, and even then – *stronza*!' He suddenly leaped up, sending his cup flying across Cusack's lap. 'What the hell did you put in it?'

'Just sugar, like you asked –' Stevie said guiltily.

'I meant one *spoonful*, not one *cup*!' Rafe shouted.

Cusack stood up, furiously rubbing at his stained jeans. 'That coffee's fucking hot! Did you have to chuck it all round the room? Look, I need a cloth. Would somebody mind?'

'Stephanie –' Annabel said.

'Yes, of course, sorry, please, come with me,' Stevie gabbled. 'I'm really, really sorry, Rafe, I didn't mean it.'

Rafe waved his hand dismissively. 'Yeah, sure.'

Pig, Stevie thought crossly. He looked like a sulky little schoolboy slumped in his chair like that. She saw the corner of Annabel's mouth curve unexpectedly. Clearly she was thinking the same thing. And there was Stevie assuming Annabel really liked Rafe!

A hundred tiny pieces suddenly slotted into place as past events flashed through Stevie's mind. Things were blindingly clear. Of course! It wasn't Annabel and Cusack who'd been having the affair, it was Annabel and *Rafe*!

In a daze, Stevie barely noticed Cusack as he followed her down the hall. *Annabel and Rafe*. Why hadn't she seen it before? It all made sense. Those little looks between them, the way Rafe refused to let her come to the lodge house – he could hardly have been scared his wife would find out about them when she'd been in Italy. It had to be someone closer – much closer – to home. No wonder Annabel seemed to have had ESP whenever Stevie and Rafe had been engaged in a secret clinch. She'd been protecting her own interests. And that was why she'd been sitting in the hotel bar in Monte Carlo dressed up like a dog's dinner: she'd been meeting *Rafe*. Cusack must have caught on at some stage and said something, that's why there'd been that atmosphere between the three of them that day in the kitchen.

What a complete and utter bastard. Not only had he been having an affair with *her* without telling her he was already married, he'd been carrying on with Annabel as well. Patrick was his team-mate; he was supposed to be his *friend*. But Stevie knew, with a sixth sense, that this was Rafe's sick way of getting his own back on Patrick for outranking and outclassing him on the Grand Prix circuit. He just couldn't stop competing.

Still pondering on this blinding revelation Stevie groped under the sink in the empty kitchen for a cloth. She found a clean one and turned on the tap, waiting until the water ran warm. Then she noticed Charles, standing and waiting impatiently behind her.

'I'm really very sorry,' she said.

Cusack folded the cloth and bent slightly to rub the coffee stain on his jeans. 'It was an accident.'

Stevie stared at the top of his head. God, his hair was black, almost blue in this light, long and soft and incredibly silky –

She caught herself sharply. Was she completely mad? Now she was fantasising about *Cusack*. She'd have to start taking more water with it.

'I think they're beyond redemption at the moment,' Cusack said. 'I'll just have to chuck them in the wash later. They've seen a lot worse.'

His blue eyes seemed to look straight through her. This was crazy, she didn't even *like* him. She needed to go and lie down or something before things got out of hand –

'Stevie?'

'Yes? Oh, oh, sorry.' She took the cloth and turned to rinse it out under the tap. There was the strangest tightening in the pit of her stomach. She wished Cusack would go away. He was making her nervous; her hands were literally shaking.

'Stevie?' Cusack said again. 'Look, I know it's none of my business –' he paused. 'I just wanted to say I'm – I'm sorry about Rafe. I know you were very – fond of him. Anyway. Look, I'd better be getting back. Finish the meeting.'

Stevie nodded stupidly and watched him limp out of the kitchen. He'd always hated Rafe, and she hadn't exactly been his Number One fan either. She had no idea what had prompted him to say what he'd just said, but she knew he meant it. Cusack lacked Rafe's easy charm, but there had been more sincerity in his few awkward words than in all the sweet nothings Rafe had ever whispered to her.

She took a deep breath. 'Um, Cusack –'

He put his head back round the door.

Her words tumbled out in a rush. 'I'm sorry too. For not believing you about Rafe before. You tried to warn me what he was like, and I didn't listen to you. You were right, I was wrong. I should never have trusted him.'

'He can be very convincing.'

'Yes.' She paused. 'Can you – can you tell me what really happened? Why you said the accident wasn't a mistake, I mean. I – I'd like to know. I promise I won't say anything to anyone. It's just that he lied to me. I want to know the truth.'

'I told you the truth before. Rafe tried to overtake Patrick's car just before the tunnel entrance. He got it wrong, clipped Patrick's car, and it ricocheted into mine –'

'You said it wasn't an accident.'

For a long moment Charles said nothing, then: 'Rafe didn't crash on purpose, so in that sense it was an accident,' he said finally. 'But it could have been avoided. The reason he misjudged the bend – the reason he thought he could handle it in the first place – was because he was taking drugs. He was in no fit state to drive. He was as much to blame as a drunk-driver who mows down a child on a zebra crossing.'

'*Drugs*? What sort of drugs?'

'Cocaine.'

Stevie struggled to take it in. 'But how do you know?'

'He had a bad habit. Everyone knew about it. He was still flying when he came off the track after the accident. His father hushed it up, but rumours were rife. Why do you think no one wanted to take him on afterwards?'

Stevie flushed.

'Ah.' Cusack smiled tightly. 'He told you that it was

because of me, didn't he? That I spread all the lies that made sure he was effectively black-balled.' He shook his head. 'I didn't want to destroy his career, in some childish tit-for-tat. I'd already lost mine; one ruined life was enough. Despite what you may think, I tried to stop Rafe driving again because I knew he was dangerous: to himself, and to other drivers on the circuit.'

'But the inquiry cleared him –'

'The inquiry cleared him because they had no evidence that allowed them to do otherwise,' Cusack said. 'They didn't test him immediately after the accident – I wasn't there to suggest it, I was still being put back together on the operating table. By the time anyone caught up with him, it was too late to prove anything.'

Stevie thought of Santa Maria, the power it had represented. Emmanuele Terroni could easily have extended his protection to his son, hushed up something like this. Five years later, Rafe changed his name, was given a place on his father's team, and no one was any the wiser. No wonder Cusack was so bitter.

'Couldn't you have told someone?'

Cusack shrugged. 'He was cleared. There was nothing more I could do.'

'And Emmanuele Terroni let him join the team, *knowing* what he'd done –'

'Rafe says he's clean now. Maybe he is.'

'How can you bear to work with him?' Stevie asked.

'Racing is a disease. Once it takes hold, it's very difficult to shake free of, Stevie. My career was cut short just as it was about to take off. I never had a chance to grow out of it – if anyone ever does. I wanted to get back on to the circuit, even if I couldn't race myself. Terroni was the only person who offered me the chance.' Charles smiled ruefully. 'He owed me one.'

Stevie stared at him as he leaned against the Aga, his hands thrust deep into the pockets of his coffee-stained jeans. He no longer seemed cold and forbidding. He seemed uncertain and strangely bereft.

'What did you do before you joined Terroni?' she asked. 'After your accident, I mean.'

'Felt sorry for myself, mostly.'

They shared a brief smile.

'I didn't mean it when I said that,' Stevie blushed. 'I just lost my temper. I'm sorry.'

'No, you were right. I *did* feel sorry for myself. I spent five years after the accident making my life and everyone else's miserable. It took my father's death to make me see how much I still had left to lose. I was trying to get a life –' he smiled – 'by joining Terroni, but it's been different from what I expected. I thought it would solve everything. All it's really done is make me realise how much my life has moved on since the accident. I'm not sure I even want to be involved in racing any more.'

'Will you quit?'

'If I can find something else to fill my life, perhaps. I don't want to cut myself adrift for nothing. I've wasted too much time already.'

Stevie wondered how she'd ever thought him cruel and unfeeling. He could be arrogant sometimes, and caustic, but perhaps that was just his way of deflecting the pity he so hated. He was a typical aristocratic Englishman, brought up to believe that feelings were something you didn't talk about. It didn't mean he didn't have any. But when it mattered, he was always there. While others talked, he acted.

Her mother had a favourite phrase, a relic from her own childhood nanny. *Fine words never buttered no parsnips.* Particularly fine Italian words.

She suddenly wished desperately that Cusack hadn't known about her and Rafe. She didn't want to be allied with the superficial, dishonest world he represented. It was ironic: now that she finally appreciated Cusack's worth and wanted his respect, she'd obviously lost it for ever.

*

Nigel Purvis unlocked the front door and stood for a moment in the hall, listening as if he'd somehow expected things to change. The house was silent, the air cold and still as if the place had been deserted for years. He could hardly believe it was only twenty-four hours since she'd gone.

He kicked the door shut behind him and walked into the living room, yanking his tie loose and throwing his crumpled jacket over the back of the sofa. He'd sat up half the night waiting for her to come home, knocking back Scotch and feeling more and more sorry for himself. He'd finally fallen asleep where he sat, still fully dressed. He'd woken this morning cold and stiff, his head pounding from the alcohol and staggered upstairs to their bedroom. Lillian must have returned while he was asleep and gone straight to bed without waking him –

The neat floral counterpane lay smooth and undisturbed. When he'd yanked open the wardrobe, a row of empty metal hangers gleamed mockingly at him.

He'd laughed at her when she'd told him she was leaving last night. He'd turned his back on her and calmly poured himself a tumbler of Scotch from the bar in the corner of the living room as she'd picked up her two suitcases and headed into the hall.

'You'll be back,' he'd sneered. 'You haven't got a hope of surviving out there on your own. Where d'you think you're going to go?'

Lillian had put down her suitcases and turned to face him, her face pale but unexpectedly determined. 'I've slaved for you for twenty years, Nigel Purvis. I've put up with your women, your foul temper, the vicious way you've treated me and Will, because I'd made my vows and I was determined to keep them, even if you didn't. But I've had enough. No one deserves to be treated the way you've treated me.'

Nigel leaned forward so that his face was inches from hers. 'Look at you. You look like shit. Fat and past it. Let me tell you, fucking you was never an enjoyable experience. D'you really think I'd have done it if I hadn't had to? It was like screwing a corpse.'

'Not everyone thinks so.'

She hadn't even seen the blow coming. She'd held her cheek, shock temporarily rooting her to the ground.

'You *bitch*!' Nigel had snarled. 'You'll come crawling back, you wait and see! You won't last five minutes on your own! No one else is going to want you, you're psychotic!' He'd been almost incoherent with rage. 'You're fucking crazy, you should see a doctor –'

'Funny you should say that,' Lillian's voice was shaky. 'That's exactly what I'm going to do.'

She'd opened the front door. A car was parked on the other side of the road, its engine idling. As Lillian emerged, Laurie Knighton climbed out and stood waiting for her.

'*Him*?' Nigel snorted. 'That fucking lily-livered cuckold of a doctor?'

Lillian ignored him and walked towards the car.

'You'll be back!' Nigel had screamed. 'You bitch, you'll be back by tomorrow morning!'

But she hadn't been. Not when he'd called Annabel at ten and told her the Terroni team meeting would have to be at Edenfield Manor; not when he'd stumbled out of the house at midday to attend it, still in his crumpled clothes from the night before; not when he'd returned home afterwards at 2.30 this afternoon.

He poured himself a glass of Scotch and threw himself into a chair. Who needed her, anyway? Let her go. He'd refuse her a divorce, for a start. They'd soon see how keen Knighton was after five years of waiting. He'd tie her up in so much legal red tape she wouldn't be able to shit without getting a court order.

Maybe he should join forces with Rosie Knighton. He smiled nastily. She was away at the moment – supposedly on some book tour, yeah, *right* – but the shit would hit the fucking fan when she got back and found out the Doctor had done a runner.

He finished his Scotch and idly rotated the crystal tumbler in his hand. Oh, this was lovely. He was screwing Knighton's daughter and all the time Knighton was screwing his wife. Talk about keeping it in the family. Shame Rosie hadn't had Will, complete the circle. Or knowing her, maybe she had.

The front door slammed suddenly. Nigel half-started out of his chair, then sank back, smiling. So she was back. Well, well, well. That hadn't taken long. So much for love's young dream. But if she thought she could just waltz in here like nothing had happened, she had another think coming. Oh, he'd let her come back – eventually – but she'd have to pay for it first. He was almost looking forward to it.

'Hello, Dad.'

He stared. 'Will! I thought you were at Bristol –' he broke off as he saw Portia follow Will into the living room. 'What the hell is *she* doing here?'

Portia smiled. It wasn't friendly. 'Surprised to see me?'

Nigel looked from one to the other.

'Mum gone has she? I can't think why she stuck it so long. If I'd been her, I'd have walked a long time ago.'

'She'll be back,' Nigel said.

'I don't think so,' Portia said. 'She and Dad seemed pretty happy to me when I saw them yesterday evening. Off to Dorset, I think. Romantic weekend.'

'They've got no money, no house, no nothing,' Nigel spat. 'Lillian won't see a penny from me. And by the time I'm through, your precious father can say goodbye to his fucking career, too. Let's see how long they last then.'

'You wouldn't do that,' Portia said.

'Wouldn't I?'

'It wasn't a question,' Portia said. 'I'm telling you.'

Nigel stood up and slowly put his empty glass down. 'And who the hell do you think you are to be telling me anything?'

Portia glanced at Will. He nodded briefly and took her hand, his grip reassuring and surprisingly firm. Thank God she'd turned to him when she'd found out. Somehow she'd known he'd support her, even in this. He'd always been in love with her, ever since school. She'd been a complete fool not to have gone to him before.

She met Nigel's stare without flinching. 'I'm going to be the mother of your child,' she said calmly. 'And if you don't want the *News of the World* to know about it, I suggest you let me tell you whatever the fuck I want.'

Seventeen

Oliver flicked through the rack of CDs in front of him. Had Julia got *Automatic for the People* or not? She liked R.E.M., but he didn't think she had this one. No, it was definitely *Out of Time* she'd got, she'd been playing it at the weekend – full blast, so Stevie must've been with her. His sister only used two volume settings: off, and ear-splitting. At least she wasn't sitting at home pining for that Italian bastard. He was amazed how quickly she seemed to have recovered, given that she'd been ready to throw herself off a cliff when she'd got back from Rome six weeks ago. She'd lost a bit of weight, and she'd looked a bit pale when he'd last seen her, but obviously discovering your lover was a lying, cheating, married son-of-a-bitch went some way towards putting you off him fairly permanently.

He picked up the CD and headed for the till, bathed in a smug glow. He'd actually remembered Julia's birthday four days before the event. Usually it took three rousing choruses of 'Happy Birthday' vibrating through the floorboards to remind him. Mind you, he'd probably have forgotten this year too if her birthday hadn't happened to be November the twelfth, the same day as the Australian Grand Prix. There were going to be some hangovers around on the thirteenth, that's for sure.

It had been an amazing season. After sixteen Grand Prix, the World Championship title hung on the very last race in

Adelaide. Schumacher had won the Pacific Grand Prix three weeks ago, putting him fifteen points ahead of Patrick Alexander with only two races to go. Everyone had thought the German had had it in the bag then: the advertising sponsors had been eagerly lining up, the rival teams finessing their bids to poach him from Benetton for next year's season. But then the Japanese Grand Prix a week later had thrown the championship wide open again: having led for most of the race in Suzuka, Schumacher had suddenly had to retire on the penultimate lap when faulty electrics had sidelined his Benetton, handing Patrick the ten-point victory he'd so desperately needed. The German was now five points ahead of him; he only needed second place in Australia to secure the title. But as Japan had proved, nothing was certain in Formula One. Patrick was closer now to winning his first World Championship than he had ever been. And the whole country was on his side, willing him to win the title his father had so briefly held before his life had been cut short on an icy Sussex bend nearly thirty-three years ago.

Oliver absently tapped the plastic CD in the palm of his hand as the queue for the till inched forward. If *he* was Terroni's team manager, he'd be putting some heavy pressure on Rafe to mark the German and stop him coming second at all costs. But Rafe would probably need some pretty sweet persuasion, knowing how competitive these drivers could be. It all depended on how much of a team Terroni were. From what Stevie had told him, there was no love lost between Rafe and Cusack.

The middle-aged woman in front of him opened her large beige Queen Mother handbag and started to count out gift tokens. Absolutely typical – this kind of thing always happened to him. He only had to walk into a bank for an old age pensioner to materialise out of thin air with a sweet jar filled with one and two-pence pieces with which he wanted to pay his electricity bill.

The spotty youth behind the till picked up the two video cases the woman had put on the counter and disappeared into the stock room behind him to find the relevant videos. *Poldark* and *The Love Boat*. No wonder she didn't want to pay real money for them.

'Next.'

Oliver jumped. Pimple-face was holding out one eczema-stricken hand for his CD, his mouth hanging open as he waited for Oliver to comply. He removed the security lock from the CD as Oliver pulled out his one remaining valid credit card. He watched the boy swipe it through his machine and prayed it wouldn't spit the card back out. His flexible friend was going to need to be a contortionist to get him through the next couple of months. Even with his cut from the deals Mace put his way, he was having trouble keeping all his financial balls in the air. Peter was fed-up with being done over to pay Paul. The bank had refused to extend his overdraft, and were now charging him seven quid for every ten he went over his limit. Barclaycard and Amex had declared him *persona non grata* and demanded the return of his cards, and the garage had threatened to repossess his car if he didn't pay their last bill. Some barrister he was going to make, bankrupt before he started.

He had been so obsessed with passing his Bar finals in the summer that he'd managed to block out the financial problems he'd face once they were over. He'd been one of the lucky forty-odd per cent of pass students who'd actually got a year-long pupillage at one of the London Inns of Court. That meant he had to spend six months doing unpaid grunt work in Chambers, another six months earning a pittance handling a few minuscule cases, and then had a one in three chance of being taken on at the end of it. Less than two months into his pupillage, the bank was already writing letters baying for his blood and Oliver was ducking down behind his desk every time the doorbell went in case it was the bailiffs.

'Can you sign here, please?'

He blinked. God, he was really losing it today, he felt really ropey. He'd phoned in sick this morning, thinking perhaps a day away from Chancery actions and corporate law might clear his head, but he still wasn't firing on all cylinders. Couldn't be the dope, he hadn't touched a thing since June. You needed to keep a clean head in this business. Maybe he was just going down with something. He felt out of it. As if there were a thick glass wall between him and the rest of the world.

A wave of dizziness swept over him and he gripped the edge of the counter in alarm. Jesus, he was going to have to take it easy for a bit. He took a deep breath as the faintness eased. Forget the rave tonight, there was no way he was up to it. He'd still got half the stash Mace had given him last week, anyway. He'd told himself he'd been too busy to sell it, but the truth was that he was losing his nerve. Every deal he did shortened the odds on getting busted. Sooner or later, everyone got caught. And Mace was a dangerous man to be around, he was too high-profile. So far the kids at the raves had been too spaced out to get a fix on him, but someone was going to recognise him soon, even with the shades and baseball cap. If Mace was caught, Oliver knew the publicity fallout would be impossible to avoid. Oliver had had enough anyway. Mace still kept trying to push that bloody Angel Dust on him, and there was no way Oliver would be responsible for selling that kind of stuff to kids. Es and grass were one thing – though he was even beginning to get jumpy over Ecstasy. The bastards were mixing it with too many dodgy ingredients these days, some of the kids were having bad reactions. But Angel Dust was on a par with coke and crack, a Class A killer drug. He didn't want any part of it: the risks *or* the guilt.

He suddenly realised he was standing outside the shop in the Mall. He didn't remember getting here; he didn't even re-member *paying* for the CD. Great, all he needed now was a shoplifting charge, particularly with the stuff burning a hole in his jeans pocket. He opened the plastic carrier bag he found himself holding and saw with relief the till receipt nestling in the bottom against the CD. Talk about absent-minded. What the fuck was *wrong* with him?

He forced the panic down and started to walk along the Mall, eyeing the glittering Christmas lights shaped like angels and hot-air balloons suspended from the ceiling. The second week in November and Santa's Grotto was already open. He could live without the festive season. His bank balance looked bad enough as it was. Julia'd better be pleased with this bloody CD, he was beginning to regret ever coming into town. Must be flu or something. Jesus, he hoped it wasn't meningitis. What a waste of his genius that would be.

He'd wanted to get Julia something for her birthday, though. Julia had always seemed so controlled, little Miss Estate Agent. But since Stevie had moved out, the two of them had had a few good nights together, sharing the odd confidence, keeping each other company, often waking up slumped on his sofa the next morning. Nothing heavy – they were just friends, he hadn't even thought about kissing her – but still. She'd like the CD, anyway.

He stopped suddenly. He felt sick. His thoughts seemed tangled, he couldn't make his mind work properly. A faint rushing filled his head until it swelled to a roar of static. The Mall began to swirl around him: shops and people and dresses and lights and concerned faces and marble pillars and muddy shoes and filthy floors –

And darkness.

Annabel poured boiling water on to the coffee grounds, then placed the steel coffee pot back on the Aga's hot plate.

'Are you still dieting, Rosie, or do you want cream and sugar?' she asked over her shoulder.

Rosie shoved her hennaed hair out of her eyes with the flat of both palms, the way Lily did when she'd been crying and she wanted to make sure you knew.

'Rosie?'

'Oh, what does it matter?'

Annabel sighed inwardly. The martyr role Rosie had adopted ever since Laurie had left her five weeks ago was beginning to wear a little thin. She reached into the cupboard above the Aga and pulled out a small biscuit tin in the shape of a thatched cottage. 'Digestive or Hobnob?'

Rosie pushed the tin petulantly across the kitchen table. 'I don't want anything.'

'Come on, Rosie,' Annabel coaxed. 'Hobnobs are your favourites. If you don't eat them, Mrs Arcor will.'

'I don't care. I don't care about anything any more,' Rosie said in a self-pitying voice. 'What does anything matter, now my husband's run off with that *slut*?'

'Lillian's hardly a slut –'

Rosie closed her eyes and turned her head away as if she'd been slapped. 'Don't! Don't mention that woman's name in my hearing! I can't bear it! Oh, how *could* he, Annie? How could he leave me for that – that *troll*! And she's older than I am!'

That's stretching it a bit, Annabel thought. Rosie had to be at least forty-eight, though she'd refused to admit to anything over thirty-nine for years. Lillian was probably no more than forty-two or forty-three, though living with Nigel was enough to put ten years on anyone.

'Tell me, Annie, what's she got that I haven't? Am I so repulsive he has to run away with some middle-aged blue-rinse tramp with tits sagging halfway to her knees and stretch marks on her spare tyres?'

'*Really*, Rosie –'

Rosie was smoothing her hands across her red lycra stomach and bottom as she studied her reflection in the window. 'Actually, I think I'm doing all right. Everything's where it should be. My boobs are still pointing skywards. I'm a size ten, for God's sake. I just don't understand it, Annie. Why did he do it?'

Maybe he *wanted* someone who looked middle-aged, Annabel thought. Maybe he was fed up with the face-lifts and tummy-tucks and liposuction and colonic irrigations, maybe he preferred to be with someone who didn't cram herself into PVC minidresses and high-heeled black stilettos every time she went to Sainsbury's. Or maybe he just wanted someone who'd stay faithful to him for five minutes.

'Annie?'

'I really don't know why you're putting yourself through all this,' Annabel said. 'What about Martin?'

'What *about* Martin?' Rosie said sullenly. 'The bastard won't even return my calls. I haven't seen him for two months. Sharon fucking Cobbit took great delight in telling me she'd heard he was going out with some eighteen-year-old stick insect he met at a nightclub in Paris.'

Annabel sighed. 'You can't really blame Laurie for getting fed up, Rosie. You never loved him, you were unfaithful to him all the time.'

'That's different.'

'Why?'

'I was discreet!' Rosie cried. 'I never left him for any of them! I didn't make him a complete laughing stock by running off with some two-faced husband-stealing trollop! They were on the front page of the *Brighton Evening Argus*! Have you any idea how *humiliating* that was?'

Annabel gave up. All Rosie cared about was the embarrassment of being cast in the unfamiliar role of the rejected, deserted wife instead of that of the glamorous *femme fatale* she liked to play. It was her pride that was hurt, not her heart. She didn't actually give a damn about losing Laurie.

She picked up the hissing coffee pot and poured two steaming mugs, wondering yet again why she bothered with Rosie. The woman was selfish, unprincipled and completely shameless; most of the time Annabel didn't even really like her. But she had to admit she got a kind of vicarious thrill from following Rosie's tangled love life. It was like watching a friend go scrumping next door from the safety of your own garden. Rosie was living the life she didn't dare and – apart from a few wild, forgotten moments – certainly didn't want.

'The thing that really infuriates me is Nigel just rolling over like this,' Rosie was saying. 'I thought he'd at least make some kind of stand. I mean, his wife has made *him* look a fool, too. I never figured him for such a wimp.'

'All bullies are wimps when you stand up to them,' Annabel said. 'Nigel's no different.'

'Well, I bloody well am,' Rosie spat. 'If Doctor fucking Knighton thinks he's going to run away with his cheap little whore and I'm going to pay for it, he's got another think coming. He won't have a bloody penny after I'm through with him, I'm taking him to the fucking cleaners.'

Annabel wished she wouldn't swear so much. Last time she'd been over, Jamie had announced in front of Patrick that he didn't want any more sodding Ribena and she'd spent an hour calming them both down after the battle that had ensued.

'But he's entitled to a share in the house, Rosie – '

Rosie gave a twisted smile. 'Well, we can't sell that now, can we? Not with Portia up the spout. Silly little bitch has got to live somewhere. I suppose in that sense she's done me a favour –'

'Portia's *pregnant*?'

'Didn't I tell you?'

Annabel was shocked. 'No, you didn't –'

'Well, you might as well know, she won't be able to keep it secret for much longer,' Rosie said. 'Yes, darling Portia's with child. Two months gone, apparently. It's due in June. How nice, a summer baby.'

'But who's the father?'

'Oh, you'll love this, Annie. Pass the biscuits, will you, I

327

think I will have one after all.' Rosie crammed a Hobnob into her mouth. 'Little bit of poetic justice, this. It seems the Knightons and the Purvises are just made for each other.'

'Not *Nigel*?'

'Try again,' Rosie said.

'*Will* is the father?'

'So it would seem. He's got deplorable taste, young William. I always rather liked him myself. He's been keen on Portia since they were at school, though God knows what he sees in the undernourished little trollop.' She shrugged.

'Is she going to keep the baby?'

'So it would appear. Chivalrous Will is standing by her – or rather, Nigel is, chequebook-wise, until Will's finished university. Terribly decent of him, given that his wife has just run off with the child's grandpa. Perhaps I should get together with Nigel. At least it would keep it in the family.'

Rosie and Nigel seemed made for each other, Annabel thought. Aloud she said, 'Nigel's OK about this?'

'Oh, jolly old Nigel's OK about everything,' Rosie said bitterly. 'He's even selling his fucking house so that he can give his soon-to-be ex-wife her fair share.'

Annabel was as surprised as Rosie was. 'Are you sure?'

'Well, the poor dears have to have somewhere to live, seeing as Big Bad Rosie won't let them flog her home from under her. Daddy Warbucks himself is seeing to it. That and a nice fat maintenance cheque every month should keep the Doctor and his lady in hearts and flowers for a while.'

'Poor Portia. Even with the money, it'll be terribly hard for her with Will away. She's only – what? Sixteen?'

'Seventeen last month. And never mind the *Poor Portia* bit, if she's old enough to fuck, she's old enough to live with the consequences. The silly tart got herself into this. I told her to have an abortion, but she's suddenly developed moral scruples, says she can't murder her baby. Well, she asked for it. Three months of sleepless nights and she'll be *begging* me to murder the little brat.'

Annabel felt a pang of pity. Portia had hardly been over-whelmed with good role models. It was a shame she couldn't live with Laurie and Lillian, but they probably needed some time alone first. All this unhappiness, just because people let their genitals rule their brains. She'd come so close to doing the same herself. Thank God she'd seen the danger in time, managed to back away.

She cursed as the coffee pot once more bubbled over on the Aga with a hiss of steam. 'Damn, I forgot to turn it off. What a mess.'

'Oh, let Mrs Arcor clear it up,' Rosie said. 'Where is she, by the way?'

'Thursday's her day off. I can't leave this, it'll be disgusting by tomorrow morning.' She lifted the coffee pot away from the hotplate and carefully sponged it clean. 'At least it means the ironing board gets a rest. She's gone into Crawley with Peter and Humphrey to help them choose wallpaper or something for their cottage.'

Rosie grinned. 'And how are the loving couple? Still besotted?'

'Sickeningly. Susan's a bit miffed about it all, but I think she's getting over it. She's thrown herself into raising money for Chechen refugees; seems to be rather good at it, actually.'

'I always thought she'd make a great Joan of Arc,' Rosie mused. 'That fervent Puritanical streak. I can't help feeling a bit sorry for the Chechens, though.'

Annabel held up her hand. 'Hang on, I think that's the tele-phone. I'd better get it before it wakes the baby, I won't be a minute.'

Rosie pulled the tin of Hobnobs towards her as Annabel disappeared. Might as well make the most of it while her hostess wasn't looking. She quickly crunched her way through two, guiltily stuffing a third in her mouth as Annabel came back into the kitchen.

'It was for Stevie,' Annabel said. 'I've never known a girl get so many telephone calls. She must double BT's profits on her own.'

'Boffrem?' Rosie mumbled, scattering crumbs.

'What?'

Rosie swallowed. 'I said, was it a boyfriend?'

'No, it was a girl – Julia, I think she said her name was. You know, I don't think any of her boyfriends have telephoned the house since she's been here, actually – at least, not that I know of. Who knows what she gets up to when we're out. The telephone bill hasn't trebled, so I suppose I should be thankful for small mercies.'

'You're lucky. Most nannies are bloody man-mad. Sneaking boyfriends up the fire escape, chucking condoms down the loo, the lot.'

'You're just jealous.'

The door to the kitchen flew open and Stevie rushed in, tears streaming down her pale face.

'Stephanie, dear, whatever's the matter?' Annabel cried.

'Something terrible's happened!' Stevie sobbed. 'It's Oliver, my brother –'

'Is he ill?'

'Yes – no – I don't know, there's been an accident, I've got to get to him. I'm sorry it's such short notice, Mrs Alexander –'

'No, no, don't worry,' Annabel said. 'Of course you must go to him. Would you like to borrow the car or shall I call a taxi?'

'The car, please, if that's all right.'

'The Metro's in the garage being serviced. Will you be all right with my Range Rover? It's terribly easy to drive.' And she is insured, she thought.

'Are you sure you don't mind?'

'Of course not. You *will* be all right to drive, won't you? We don't want you having an accident as well.'

'I'm fine, I promise.'

330

She took the keys from Annabel and suppressed the urge to run, forcing herself to walk calmly out of the kitchen and around to the courtyard as she tried to quell her panic. Annabel was right, it wouldn't do Oliver any good for her to have an accident as well. She pulled open the door of the converted stable where Annabel's Range Rover was parked. Thank God this thing was an automatic, the last thing she needed was to have to battle with some clapped-out gearbox.

She kicked the broken brick they used as a doorstop into place, as a shadow fell across her.

'I'm sorry, Cusack, I can't stop,' she said frantically as she saw who it was. 'I have to go, I have to see my brother –'

'My God, what's the matter?'

'I must go. Please, can you move your car, it's in my way?'
π

'No, I'm sorry, no, nothing,' she babbled. 'It's my brother, Oliver. He's had an accident. I've got to get to the police station –'

'The police station? Don't you mean the hospital?'

Stevie burst into fresh tears, unable to speak. Cusack said nothing, waiting in silence until she eventually brought her sobs under control and was able to talk. 'They've taken him to the police station. I don't know why. He collapsed at the shopping mall in Crawley yesterday and they took him to hospital and no one told us, and then this morning they took him to the police station, and I think they've arrested him, and I've got to go to him –'

Cusack put his hands on her shoulders. 'Stevie, calm down. This isn't going to help Oliver at all, you're in no fit state to go anywhere. Now, tell me what happened, from the beginning.'

'But I must go *now* –'

'If they've taken him from the hospital to the police station, he can't be in any immediate danger,' Cusack said reasonably. 'If you want to help him, we have to stay calm. Now, Stevie, from the beginning.'

Stevie took a deep breath and tried to force her thoughts into some sort of order. 'Julia rang me just now. She said Oliver had called her from the police station, he's in some sort of trouble. He wanted her to telephone some friend of his, a lawyer. He didn't want me or our parents to know, but she thought I should –'

'Wait a moment. Oliver collapsed in Crawley, yes, and then they took him to hospital, is that right?'

Stevie nodded. 'They kept him in overnight. I don't know why he collapsed, Julia said Oliver wouldn't tell her – oh, God, you don't think he's got a brain tumour or something, do you? I couldn't bear it if anything happened to Oliver, he's so good and clever –'

'Stevie, let's stick to what we know,' Cusack said. 'After the hospital, the police came back and arrested him? Do you know why?'

'One of the nurses found this packet of pills in his jeans. She got suspicious and called the police.' Stevie rubbed her eyes as the tears started again. 'Julia says they think he's a *pusher*! Oliver wouldn't do that, I *know* he wouldn't! He's training to be a lawyer, he knows this would ruin his career!'

Cusack let go of her.

'I want you to tell me the truth. Does your brother use drugs?'

Stevie flushed. 'Grass, maybe, a couple of times when he was a student, but nothing serious. He's *not* a pusher! He's not like that! And the pills the nurse found were something else, anyway, some American drug, PVC or something –'

'Yes, that's it. But Oliver wouldn't sell it, I know he wouldn't,' Stevie repeated stubbornly. 'Not something that *kills* people!'

'How does he say it got in his pocket?'

'I don't know. He must've been a bit woozy still, because Julia said when he asked her he just kept saying: *that bastard mace, that bastard mace,* over and over –'

332

'He said Mace?' Charles's voice was razor sharp.

'Yes. I don't understand. What does he mean, *mace*? I thought that was some kind of spray –?'

'Stevie, you need to get over to him as soon as you can,' Cusack said. 'Don't let him say anything – well, he knows that, he's a lawyer. But it's important, make sure he understands. Not even if they promise to drop the more serious charges if he admits to the rest.'

Stevie nodded, confused.

'I'm sorry, I've wasted enough of your time,' Cusack said abruptly. 'I'll move my car and get out of your way. I hope you manage to sort things out.'

Stevie watched him in a daze as he returned to his car, his black hair inky against his pale cheeks. Oh, God, why had she told him about the drugs? Julia had made her swear to keep it secret, she hadn't even phoned her parents to let them know. No wonder Cusack was getting the hell out. She'd half-hoped he'd offer to come with her to the police station. *He'd* have made them see how wrong they were to accuse Oliver. But she couldn't really blame him for not wanting to get involved in something like this, not after everything Rafe had put him through. He must really despise her. He'd probably never speak to her again. It was so ironic: six months ago, she'd have been only too pleased. Now, she felt as if she'd never known such misery . . .

Suddenly, she realised. Oh, my God. *She was in love with him.*

She was in love with him, that's why she felt this terrible, aching emptiness as she watched his car disappear down the drive. That's why she hadn't been able to eat or sleep for weeks. The tension, the nerves, the acute self-consciousness when he was around – it wasn't because she hated him, but because she *loved* him! His thin, arrogant face, his awkward limp and shy, challenging stare: she loved it all. Had done so ever since that day in the rose garden, only she'd been too blind – and too besotted with Rafe – to see it. But what she'd felt for Rafe hadn't been love, it had been a crazy infatuation, a freak wave breaking over the sea wall and just as quickly seeping away. This – *this* was like the ocean, seemingly endless, impossible to ignore. How could she not have seen it before? How could she not have *realised*?

She stumbled into Annabel's Range Rover, filled with despair. Whatever she felt for Cusack now was irrelevant. He must utterly loathe her. She'd been rude to him from the day they'd met, she'd had an affair with the man who'd ruined his life, she'd argued with and offended him at every opportunity. Each time the ice between them had started to thaw, she'd plunged them straight back in the deep freeze again with some fresh insult. And now this had happened. God knows what he must think of her. He would never respect, much less love, her now.

She forced him out of her mind. She had to concentrate on Oliver. He needed her. She had the rest of her life to grieve for Cusack.

She walked into the police station forty minutes later and immediately felt guilty. Every red traffic light she'd ever jumped flashed before her eyes. The young blond PC behind the reception counter probably knew about that overdue library book on Australian sheep farming hidden under her bed at Julia's just by looking at her. She'd taken it out when she'd been doing her GCSE geography project at school, and then completely forgotten about it. No wonder she'd failed. By the time she'd discovered the book stuffed into her gym-bag four years later, she hadn't been able to afford to take it back because of the fines. She still felt guilty about depriving the country of its heritage.

'Can I help you, Miss?'

Stevie jumped as the young PC interrupted her hysterical thoughts. 'Oh, yes. I'm here to see my book – I mean, my *brother*.'

'Is he a prisoner?'

Stevie immediately had visions of Oliver in handcuffs wearing pyjamas with arrows all over them. 'I think so. He was brought here this morning. From the hospital.'

'Name?'

'Oliver Colvin. Um, seven, ten, seventy-two.'

The young PC looked confused. 'Sorry, Miss?'

'His date of birth,' Stevie explained. 'The seventh of October 1972. I thought you might need it.'

'Ah. No, it's all right, Miss.' He thumbed through the book on his desk. 'Colvin, Oliver. Yes, he was signed in at 9.20 this morning.'

'Can I see him?'

'If you'd like to take a seat over there, Miss. I'll just check.'

Stevie glanced behind her as the young PC disappeared. Two of the three torn black PVC seats on the other side of the square reception room were occupied by an incredibly fat man somewhere in his late fifties, his bald head and gold stud earrings gleaming under the flickering neon light overhead. His sweat-stained T-shirt stretched inefficiently across a vast belly, two hairy inches of pasty white flesh ballooning over the top of his filthy jeans. Stevie decided she'd stand.

The PC returned and nodded at her. 'You can see him in one of the interview rooms, Miss. Got any bags?'

Stevie shook her head.

'He's got a bit of a bump on his forehead, that's from his fall,' the PC said, pressing a buzzer beneath his desk to unlock the door connecting the reception area to the rest of the police station. 'Looks much worse than it is, though. The hospital checked him out thoroughly before they released him, and we've had our doctor give him the once-over this morning, just to be on the safe side.'

'Do you know what's happened?' Stevie said anxiously.

'Sorry, Miss.'

She pushed open the door and followed the PC down the

corridor. Like most of Crawley, the police station had been built in the Sixties and possessed the same grey, utilitarian gracelessness that characterised much of the town. Poor Oliver, he must be feeling so miserable. Just walking into this place was enough to drive you to drink.

The PC showed her into an interview room sparsely furnished with a black vinyl table and four grey plastic chairs. A waste-paper bin filled with cigarette ends and scrunched plastic cups stood in the corner. 'Can't give you too long, I'm afraid, Miss. Fifteen minutes, tops.' He pulled a face as she glanced round the room. 'Not quite the Ritz, is it, Miss?'

She smiled. 'Not exactly.'

'You should try living with it all day. Fancy a cup of tea?'

She nodded, and the PC withdrew from the room, closing the door behind him. Moments later it opened again and Oliver appeared, acutely shamefaced as he met her gaze. An older man Stevie guessed to be CID nodded curtly at her and glanced at his watch. 'Fifteen minutes, Colvin.'

Oliver smiled shakily. 'I might've known you'd turn up.'

Stevie rushed over to hug him. 'Oh, Oliver! Your poor head!'

He hugged her back for a long moment, then gently disentangled himself and gingerly eased his long frame into one of the chairs by the table. 'Hell of a party, huh?'

'What on earth happened?'

'It's a long story.'

'It must be.' Stevie sat down opposite him. 'Why didn't you call me yesterday from the hospital? Julia was worried sick about you, she didn't know whether to tell me or not because you'd sworn her to secrecy.'

'Was she really worried?'

'Yes, she was. Thank God she had the sense to let me know −' Stevie broke off. 'Oliver, why didn't you call me yourself?'

'Didn't want to worry you,' Oliver mumbled, embarrassed.

'You nob-end.'

He gave her a lopsided grin. 'That just about sums it up.'

The door opened and the young PC entered with two plastic cups of tea on a small wooden tray. 'Thought your brother would like some too, Miss. I put milk in it, helps to disguise the taste, but I thought I'd leave the sugar up to you. I'd go for it, you need all the help you can get with this stuff.'

Stevie waited until he'd left again. 'Oliver, what happened?' she asked. 'Why did you have to go to hospital?'

Oliver was silent.

'Was it drugs?' Stevie pressed. 'Did you pass out or OD or something?'

'No, it wasn't,' Oliver said angrily. 'I haven't touched anything for months, I swear. The police know that, they did a blood test, I was completely clean.'

'Then *what*?'

He hesitated. 'I sort of – sort of had a fit,' he said finally.

'A fit? What, like an *epileptic* fit?'

He nodded.

Stevie remembered a boy in her class having a fit one afternoon in the middle of PE. He'd just fallen on the ground and rolled around, shaking all over the place with his tongue hanging out. 'But you're normal! You're not epileptic! How could you have just had a fit like that?'

'You can be normal *and* epileptic,' Oliver said roughly. 'They're not mutually exclusive. Being epileptic doesn't make me a freak or a trainspotter.'

'I'm sorry, I didn't mean –'

'Look, I'm not mental, or anything. The doctors say it sometimes happens, particularly with young men my age. It's like a nose-bleed or something. The brain just seizes up and you have a fit, then it's over, OK? It's no big deal.'

'Will you – could you have another one?'

He shrugged. 'They don't know. They're going to do some sort of brain scan to check that's what it was, but they're pretty sure. They'll give me some pills and then I'll just have to wait and see if I have any more. It means I've lost my driving licence, of course. I'll have to go two years without a fit to get it back.'

'Oh, *Oliver*.'

'It's not the end of the world,' Oliver said, forcing a smile. 'I thought I was going to die when I came to. I'm glad it was just a fit and nothing worse.'

'How long did it last?'

'Not long. A few minutes. But I felt pretty out of it afterwards. I just wanted to sleep.'

'Didn't you have any idea what was coming?' Stevie asked.

'I felt a bit weird all day, but I never thought anything like this would happen,' Oliver said. 'My brain kept sort of blacking out like a faulty video – I was buying this CD, and then the next moment I was outside with no idea what happened in between. The doctor said it's called *petit mal*, it often happens just before you have a fit, like a warning.'

'Why did they keep you in overnight if it was just a fit?'

Oliver touched his bruise again. 'Just being careful. They thought I might have got concussion from bashing my head on the marble floor of the Mall, I was really woozy when I came to. I slept straight through for eighteen hours. When I woke up, the police were there.'

Stevie stared into her plastic cup. 'Oliver, were those drugs yours?' she said quietly.

'It's not that simple to explain –'

'Of course it is!' Stevie cried. 'Either they were or they weren't!'

Oliver ran his hand through his dirty-blond curls and sighed. 'Look, I've been selling a few things for a friend – nothing heavy, Stevie, don't look at me like that. Just grass and some Es, I *swear*.'

'Are you mad? You're a fucking lawyer, Oliver, this could ruin your career!'

'I needed the money,' Oliver said urgently. 'Stevie, you've no idea –'

338

'You could've come to me – or Mum or Dad, they'd have given it to you if they'd known! You didn't have to sell drugs! What on earth possessed you?'

'I don't know. It was stupid, I know that, but I was desperate. And Mace can be very persuasive.'

'Mace is a *person*?'

'He could be loosely defined as such.' He smiled tightly. 'He's my supplier.'

'But Julia said it wasn't grass they found in your pockets. It was TCP or something –'

'PCP. Angel Dust. I never sold that, Stevie, I swear to God. That bastard kept trying to get me to push it, but I wouldn't touch it. He must have slipped it in with my normal stash without telling me.'

'Have you told the police this?'

Oliver shook his head.

'Why not? You've got to tell them, Oliver, make them catch this man –'

'Stevie, if I tell them about him, it means admitting that I sold stuff for him. Even if it was just Es and dope, it's still enough to get me a drugs conviction. That means my career is over before it starts.'

'But if you don't, they'll charge you with selling this terrible drug anyway!'

'They've got to prove it first –'

'Oliver, you had it in your jeans. The packet's probably got your fingerprints all over it, hasn't it?'

He nodded miserably, his bravado deflating like a punctured balloon. She could see the panic in his eyes. He suddenly looked three years old again, not twenty-three.

'What am I going to do, Stevie?' he said, his voice shaky. 'I've really fucked everything up now. I can't believe I've been so stupid. My whole life, everything, down the drain. All those years of exams, all that work, everything gone. What am I going to tell Mum and Dad? Stevie, what am I going to *do*?'

She remembered Cusack's warning that Oliver should admit nothing, even to reduce the charges. But Cusack hadn't known that there was hard evidence against her brother. Oliver couldn't hope to get out of it. His only chance was that if he led them to a bigger fish, they'd be more lenient towards him. It wasn't much to hold on to, but it was something.

'You've got to tell them who Mace is,' Stevie said.

'I can't do that, Stevie.'

'Why not? Are you scared of him?'

Oliver stared at the floor. 'It's not that. There just wouldn't be any point. No one would believe me. I've no proof, nothing.'

'Oliver, who is this Mace?'

He hesitated.

Stevie narrowed her eyes. 'I know him, don't I? That's why you won't say. Who is it, Oliver? You have to tell me!'

'It won't do any good, Stevie. You can't prove anything –'

'*Who is it*?'

Oliver exhaled slowly. 'It's Rafe, Stevie. Rafe Dussi. That's who Mace is.'

Eighteen

The familiar fear twisted Patrick's gut. His back was clammy inside the flame-proof body suit, tension cramping his thighs as he completed the parade lap that preceded the start of the Australian Grand Prix. This was the most important race of his life. Everything depended on it. He couldn't afford to make even one mistake.

Immediately ahead of him was Michael Schumacher. The German had taken pole position for the final race of the season with a magnificent qualifying time no one had been able to match. He had never been on better form. It was going to be almost impossible to beat him today; and yet Patrick had to do it. The World Championship was within his grasp. He would never get another chance like this. He was already thirty-five years old. The young bloods were baying at his heels, waiting for him to show just one sign of weakness. If he failed now, he'd be finished in Formula One for ever.

Sweat gathered in the creases of his eyelids and he blinked it away. Emmanuele Terroni would not renew his contract if he lost this race; his career would be over. He could probably find the backing to go into Indy car racing if he wanted to, but the problem was that he wouldn't win. However you dressed it up, whatever gloss you put on it, if he lost today he would have failed. And you didn't win races by thinking of yourself as a failure. He'd last a season in Indy car, perhaps two. Then it would all be over.

He wanted this race, he wanted it with a deep-seated animal greed that overrode every other instinct, even his fear. He wanted the title that his father had once held, to equal the great James Alexander and finally be able to feel proud of himself. He had devoted his life to it. He couldn't fail now.

His gaze flickered across the track as they neared the starting grid. Rafe was in second place, next to Schumacher. He was the only person who could hold the German off, push him into third. After sixteen races, it had all come down to a simple mathematical equation: even Jamie could have worked it out. Schumacher was five points ahead of him. Victory was worth ten points, second place six. Even if Patrick won now, if Schumacher came second he'd take the championship by one point. One point. A lifetime of striving defeated by just one point.

Patrick knew Rafe would never help him, no matter how much pressure Cusack put on him. He had too much to prove himself. He couldn't win the championship now, he was forty points behind, but he could still beat Patrick. Right now that was all the Italian wanted.

Patrick knew where Rafe was coming from. He'd seen the hero worship battling with bitter, competitive envy in the boy's eyes and understood it. To Rafe, it must seem as if Patrick had everything: a successful career, a past without skeletons, a beautiful, poised wife and three happy, healthy children. Patrick knew at first hand what it was like to grow up the son of a man who had already achieved all the goals you valued, to compete with the person you loved most in the world until you almost hated them. Competition became a way of life; you needed to win everything just to prove you could. If Rafe's rivalry had been confined to the Grand Prix circuit, Patrick could have forgiven it; admired it, even. Teamship only went so far. But Rafe had extended the competition, switched the arena from the race track to the bedroom. He'd gone after Annabel, and Patrick couldn't forgive that.

342

He felt a surge of red-hot anger as the cars lined up on the grid. It had nearly killed him, standing back and watching as his wife fell for another man; but he hadn't done anything, had pretended he didn't know, realising that Annabel was teetering on the brink and that one false move might propel her into Rafe's arms. He'd simply waited and prayed that her infatuation would run its course before their marriage was damaged beyond repair.

He'd known about the affair from the very beginning: that April evening when he'd walked into the kitchen and Rafe and Annabel had sprung guiltily apart. He'd seen the way they'd looked at each other at the dinner party a month later, the studied casualness of their conversation as they'd chatted. He'd seen the shock and disappointment in his wife's face when he'd met her at the hotel in Monte Carlo; the bitter jealousy when Rafe had left with Stevie. He'd listened to her telephone calls with her lover, hating her treachery, hating himself for spying on her; but hating Rafe more. He'd watched their marriage gradually fall to pieces, his heart breaking inside him. He'd wanted to run the fucking bastard off the road every time he drove on to the grid, but he hadn't. He'd waited. And eventually, he'd started to win.

He knew the precise moment Annabel had come back to him. There had been no dramatic rapprochement, no plea for forgiveness. It had been a stupid thing, really, the kind of incident only two people who had been married for ten years would understand. They had been going to a dinner party one evening, about a month after Jamie's accident. He had been sitting on the edge of their bed, buttoning his shirt. Annabel had suddenly appeared in the doorway, a small box in her hand. His cufflinks. He'd known how much she hated going into the dusty priest's hole where the safe was housed, how scared she was of it. He'd understood what she'd been saying when she'd handed them to him.

The green flag went down to signal all the cars were in place

343

on the grid, and a red light glowed at the head of the field. Patrick's fear evaporated. He couldn't do anything about Rafe or Schumacher or anyone else. He could only drive the best race of his life and hope it was enough to win.

Rafe waited for the light to change down from red to green. His body was taut, coiled, adrenalin racing through him. This was the moment he loved best, this tight, rippling anticipation. It was a better high than any drug he'd ever tried. If he'd been able to race every day, even every week, it might have been enough to hold in check the boredom brought about by a life-time of being given every material thing he'd ever wanted. But there were only sixteen or seventeen Grand Prix a year. He'd had to find other ways to get his kicks; not the coke, he'd given that up after the Monaco crash which had shocked even him out of his careless playboy negligence. Racing had taught him that the thrill of living on the edge, taking risks, was better than any chemical.

Mace had evolved almost by accident. A friend he'd known from his coke days had asked him to do him a favour, just one, for old times' sake. The friend had needed someone to carry some stuff from Sicily to London; nothing much, he swore, but his usual courier had dropped out and he'd had a contract to meet. Rafe had felt like a challenge; he'd let his friend pack the drugs at the bottom of his suitcase – he hadn't touched it him-self, just in case: fingerprints were difficult to argue your way out of – and had calmly walked through customs at Heathrow with two kilos of heroin on his trolley. The high it had given him had been incredible. It hadn't been Formula One, but it had been close. After that, the dealing seemed to follow natu-rally. His father would've killed him if he'd found out. Another risk; another thrill.

The green light glowed and he saw Schumacher streak ahead out of the corner of his eye, even as he shot forward himself. He knew Patrick was behind him, determined to win.

344

He tucked himself tightly behind the German. Not as determined as he was.

It had hurt to lose Annabel. His pride had been wounded. He'd so nearly had her; he'd been playing her on a line for months, leaving her dangling then reeling her in. It had made it so much more of a challenge, that she'd been so settled and content, had so strongly resisted the threat to her neatly ordered life. But in the end she'd given in and agreed to sleep with him that night in Monte Carlo. He'd arranged for Patrick to be with him at the hotel and then left with Stevie so that she'd know just how much she wanted him, be fully aware of the extent of her submission. He'd been certain she'd come back to him even more desperate than before.

But it seemed he'd misjudged her. Something had changed after that night. He'd given her time to think, to weigh up the consequences. A mistake. The *puttana* had decided against him. She'd still wanted him, he'd seen it in her eyes, but she'd gone back to Patrick. He'd known for certain that he'd lost when she'd laughed at him after he'd spilt coffee all over himself and Cusack at the Terroni team meeting.

If he'd won Annabel, he might have been tempted to let Patrick have this race. But not now. Whether he'd known it or not, Patrick had defeated him once; it had been very *brutta figura* – bad loss of face. He wasn't going to let it happen again.

Stevie curled up on the sofa at Julia's flat, a cool can of Coca-Cola open in her hand, another – not open – pressed against the flat of her forehead. She had the most appalling hangover, too much red wine last night. Well, not quite last night, more like earlier this evening, but anyway. She rolled the can across her throbbing temples. So much for drowning her sorrows. Next time she'd just get them in a stranglehold and murder them quietly one by one. She was never going anywhere near that bloody tapas bar again, and if anyone ever said the word Chianti in her hearing . . .

Julia stumbled into the darkened living room, her nut-brown hair tumbled in becoming dishevelment across her slender shoulders.

'Stevie, it's four in the morning! I can't believe you've got me up at four in the morning to watch a blank television screen.'

'It's not a blank screen. It's Teletext.'

'Blank enough.'

'Look, did I ask them to hold the last Grand Prix in Australia?' Stevie said, fiddling with the remote control. 'It's two in the afternoon there. This is the only way I can find out what's happening.'

'Can't you just wait until tomorrow?'

'No, I want to watch it live.'

'What do you mean, watch it live?' Julia complained. 'Even the BBC don't think it's worth showing in the middle of the night. You're watching a fourteen-inch screen with lots of little white letters on it. It's hardly getting the smell of petrol in your hair, is it?'

'Actually, if you can smell petrol when you're racing, Jules, you're in trouble. It means the whole show is about to go up –'

'I should be so lucky,' Julia said grumpily.

Stevie leaped off the sofa. 'Oh, God, look, it's started!'

'What? Where? Who's winning?'

'I thought you didn't want to know?'

'Look, you've got me up, haven't you? The least you can do is tell me who's winning.'

'Schumacher's first, that fucking miserable son-of-a-bitch ratfink bastard's second –'

'Excuse me, that's my name for him,' Julia said.

'Have you taken out a patent on it?'

'No. I just might need it for your next boyfriend, that's all.'

'If there ever is a next one,' Stevie said dismally, sitting back down. 'At my rate of conquest, you could be in for a long wait.'

Julia said, 'Where's Patrick?'

'Still in third.'

Stevie resumed her Cola-can massage. The two of them sat side by side on the sofa and stared in silence at the blue screen. After a moment, Julia closed her eyes, stretched out her legs and crossed her ankles on the coffee table, neatly arranging the folds of her Victorian white-cotton-and-lace nightdress over her calves. Stevie pulled her purple Joe Bloggs T-shirt down over her bottom, wishing she'd remembered her Dumbo slippers. Her feet were bloody freezing.

'Who's winning now?' Julia asked.

'You asked me that a minute ago.'

'Well, I still don't see why you want to watch it, anyway,' Julia said, opening her eyes again. 'I could understand if there was a man involved, but Patrick's hardly your type and now that you've finished with that –'

'– ratfink bastard drug-dealing son of a bitch –'

'Thank you. Now that you've finished with him, what do you want to watch this for?'

Stevie blushed guiltily.

'Stephanie Colvin, you tart!' Julia screamed, sitting up. 'There *is* a man involved, isn't there? Who? Who?'

'No one. There isn't anyone.'

'You don't get up at four in the morning out of loyal devotion to your employers. I should've known. Who is it? Oh, God, it's not *Patrick*, is it –'

'Of course it isn't Patrick!'

'Ah! So it *is* someone?' Julia said triumphantly.

'No, it isn't. I just want to watch the last race, I've seen all the others – oh, shit, look, Rafe's overtaken Schumacher, he's in the lead! The bastard!'

'Where?'

Stevie scrambled on to the floor and pointed to the row of text on the screen. 'I hope his wheels really fall off this time.'

'Why stop there?' Julia muttered.

'I can't believe I ever liked him, Jules,' Stevie wailed. 'I just can't believe how stupid I was, to be taken in by him. He lied to me about everything – being married, the car crash in Monaco, the whole lot. And now that business with Oliver. If I hadn't introduced them –'

'It's not your fault,' Julia said. 'If Oliver wanted to do something so stupid, he'd have found a way, whether he met Rafe or not.'

'You don't know Rafe. He's so charming, and he can be bloody convincing.'

'What's happening with Oliver?' Julia asked. 'I haven't seen him since he got bail.'

'He was only released on Friday night,' Stevie said. 'He was lucky he wasn't remanded in custody – it's only because he's got a good job and hasn't got a record that he got bail. But he's got to appear in court again on the twenty-seventh. No-one knows anything about it, you mustn't say anything. Not even Mum and Dad know.'

'But I still don't understand what happened. What was wrong with him? Why did they take him to hospital in the first place?'

'Oh, it's a bit complicated,' Stevie said evasively. 'Ask Oliver, he'll explain.'

'Well, whatever happened, he was bloody unlucky, to get caught like that –'

'He was bloody *stupid*, Jules. He should never have got involved in the first place. If they'd charged him with possession it would be bad enough, it could still ruin his career – but they've done him for intent to supply a Class A drug. Even though it's his first offence, he'll probably get sent to prison. Oh, Jules, I can't bear to think about it.'

Julia blanched. 'Prison! I didn't realise, I thought they'd just tell him off or something. Oh, poor Oliver! Isn't there anything we can do?'

Stevie sighed. 'His lawyer's trying, but he *was* carrying

those drugs, Jules, even if he didn't know what they were, and anyway, who's going to believe that? He can't deny the drugs were his, the packet had his fingerprints all over it. I tried to persuade him to do a deal over Mace, but he just wouldn't, he refused even to mention his name. He said he'd rather take his chances in court because if he does a deal and admits to anything now, even possession, his career's over. He says the jury's his only chance. But he's never going to get off, Jules, whatever he thinks, there's just too much evidence against him!'

'Can't *you* tell them about Mace?'

'There wouldn't be any point,' Stevie said wearily. 'Oliver's right, no one would believe him. Rafe's no fool, he'll have covered his tracks, and it'd be bound to get out that Oliver had accused him, sooner or later. The publicity would wipe out Oliver's chances of saving his career, even if he was found innocent in the end.' Her voice wobbled. 'I can't believe Rafe could have done this to him. Oliver was his friend. I should've listened to Charles Cusack.'

Julia stared at her in surprise. 'I thought you hated his guts?'

Stevie flushed. 'Well, I didn't like him that much to begin with, but that was before I knew him,' she said. 'He's not that bad, really. Quite nice, in fact. He's been really sweet with Jamie, and I'm sure his bad temper is partly because of his leg, it really was a terrible thing that happened to him, Jules, and it was all Rafe's fault –'

'Well, you've changed your tune.'

'I just think you shouldn't judge everyone before you know them properly, that's all. Cusack's had a really hard time of it, and no one really understands him.'

'You *fancy* him, don't you? I don't believe it! After all the terrible things you said about him –'

Stevie groaned. 'Don't remind me.'

'So you *do* like him?'

'Yes, I like him. I'm nuts about him, if you must know, for all the good it's done me.'

'Has he – does he – are you two –?'

'Not even as far as zero.' Stevie drained her open can of Coke and pulled the tab on the second. 'He doesn't know I exist. Actually, I think he hates me. I can't say I blame him, really, after all I've done.'

'I bet he doesn't. I bet he nurses a secret passion for you, really.'

'I really think I might be falling in love with him, Jules,' Stevie said. 'I've never had it like this before. It's not like it was with Rafe, I just wanted to rip his clothes off all the time. With – with Charles, I just – oh, God, I just want to be near him, I don't care if he hates me, I'd even wax his Barbour or feed his dogs if it meant I could be with him.'

'It'd never work. He's a complete stuffed shirt, you said so yourself.'

'Well, I didn't mean it. He's not arrogant – well, he is, but that's just the way he was brought up. Once you get to know him he's really sweet and funny and kind and –'

'Oh, Lord. You've really got it bad.'

'I know. It's hopeless. I wish I could go back to being crazy about Rafe, it never hurt as much as this does –'

Julia leaped up and wrested the remote control away from her. 'Stevie, quick, move, move, let me see the screen! I think something happened!'

Nigel rubbed the sweat out of his eyes and shifted his position at the side of the Adelaide track so that his hand casually slipped further towards the right breast of the girl around whom his arm was draped. She didn't seem to notice. He inched his hand lower as Patrick shot past Schumacher and into second place behind Rafe. God, she had amazing tits. Big, beautiful, luscious and browned by the Australian sun with – yes, lean forward, darling, perfect – huge chocolate nipples playing peek-a-boo with the top of her bright green sundress. He'd picked her up in the hospitality tent; just one of the many perks of the job. At least he didn't have to worry about Lillian finding out now – not that he'd worried that much before. He leaned forward for a better view, wondering if it was an all-over tan. Her arse was probably the same glorious honey colour, he could just picture it spread before him as he shoved his dick into her, doggy-style –

'Well, do you?'

'Huh?'

The girl pouted. 'I said, Nigel, do you think your Patrick's going to win?'

Nigel wished she wouldn't talk so much. Women should put out and shut up. But with a pair of tits like hers, he was prepared to forgive her. 'Yeah, maybe,' he said, contemplating such an outcome with some surprise. If Patrick *did* win the championship, he was going to have to start being very nice to him indeed. And with Schumacher currently in third, the possibility was starting to look a good deal less remote.

'I always liked Rafe,' the bimbo said. 'Daddy knows his father, we used to play together when we went on holiday to Sicily in the summer.' Her smile grew fond. 'He knew all the right buttons to press, even then.'

Nigel's hand slipped inside the girl's dress and caressed one firm breast, then squeezed a nipple. Shit, she was hot, even if she was a bit older than he usually liked them. Over twenty, easily. 'Who's Rafe's father then?' he asked without much interest. 'Anyone I should know?'

'Emmanuele Terroni, of course,' the girl said, surprised he didn't know. 'Rafe took his mother's name after that terrible accident a few years ago. Oh, dear. You look a bit – well, purple. Did I say something I shouldn't have done?'

'No, no. Forget it.'

Nigel's mind raced furiously. There *had* been a son involved in motor racing, now he thought about it. Disappeared from view about five or six years ago. Raphael Terroni, that was it! It was all coming back now. Something to do with a drugs scandal, hushed up pretty quickly. No wonder Emmanuele Terroni had been so keen to sign the kid on to his team. Rafe Dussi was his own son! Oh, Jesus, he could just imagine the bad PR for Quisling Mild if it came out that he'd unwittingly hired the boss's cokehead son! He was the marketing exec who'd arranged it all; it would be his head on the block. He couldn't afford to lose his job now, particularly with that juicy share option coming up at the end of the year. He needed the money to pay Lillian off and keep Portia quiet.

He watched as the two purple Quisling/Terroni cars swept past again, Rafe still holding Patrick off. This must never come out. If anyone ever knew he'd taken on Raphael Terroni without realising who he was, he'd be a laughing stock; never mind the fallout from the bloody drugs scandal.

He tried to calm himself by counting to ten and groping the bimbo's arse under her dress. Rafe wasn't going to tell anyone who he really was. He couldn't, not while Terroni were his employers; everyone would say he'd only got on the team through nepotism. It'd be different if he were elsewhere. There'd be no reason for him to keep quiet if someone like Benetton or Ferrari hired him, he'd have proved he could make the grade on his own merits.

God, how he hated that bastard. He'd spent the whole season thinking of ways to get rid of him, and now he just had to pray he'd stay.

Rafe could feel Patrick bearing down on him, almost sense the rage and frustration emanating from him as he tried to find a way past. He wondered how far he could deliberately obstruct Patrick without contravening some arcane FIA regulation. Why the fuck did they bother with all these rules? This wasn't a game of gentlemen's tennis, for God's sake. There was no room for weakness in Formula One. You played to win, or you didn't play at all.

They were just over halfway through the race. He was going

to have to go in to refuel on the next lap. He wished they could carry enough fuel and just race without having to piss about in the pits. More fucking FIA rules. It'd give Schumacher and Patrick the chance to get past him; it wouldn't be easy to get the lead back. He'd have to wait until they went into the pits themselves.

He saw the pit lane ahead of him and swerved into it, reducing his speed so that he wouldn't break the speed limit and incur a time penalty. He could see Cusack's tall figure hovering in the background, his dark glare a reminder of the deal they'd struck.

The pit mechanics refuelled his car and changed his tyres in less than ten seconds. Cusack could forget his deal. He didn't need him. If he won this race, his name would be on everyone's lips as the man who had thwarted Patrick Alexander's chances. Very *bella figura*. It wouldn't win him any popularity medals, but as long as his past didn't come out, it might get him a contract with another team – no nepotism involved – Benetton or McClaren, maybe. He felt fleetingly sorry for Patrick, but that was life.

As of now, all bets were off.

'You could at least sing me "Happy Birthday",' Julia grumbled.

'Oh, God, sorry, Jules,' Stevie said, glued to the screen. 'I'll sing it tomorrow, promise.'

'It *is* tomorrow.'

'I can't bear this, I feel sick,' Stevie said.

Julia struggled upright from her prone position on the floor. 'Is it nearly finished?'

'Yes. About another ten laps.'

Julia disappeared into the kitchen to make a cup of tea. She'd had more peace when Stevie was actually living here – at least she'd been able to rely on Stevie's hangovers keeping her in bed until after midday every weekend. Now she was up at the bloody crack of dawn, coming round here to watch Grand Prix races and bemoaning her becalmed love life. Prick Whittington and Rafe had been bad enough, but at least they'd been out-and-out bastards, she'd known they'd screw it up sooner or later and Stevie would see the light. This Cusack sounded dangerously interesting, and he was certainly gorgeous enough to get Stevie well and truly hooked. It was a shame Stevie was so blind to the benefits of a celibate life. Julia was actually beginning to enjoy it herself. There was a lot to be said for giving up sex. No cystitis, for a start, and she didn't have to shave her legs every three days. She wouldn't be able to have this nice friendship with Oliver if sex was an issue, either. She'd be too busy trying to work out if he'd let her watch *Pride and Prejudice* instead of *The World at War*.

She poured her tea and wandered back into the living room where Stevie was perched on the edge of the coffee table inches away from the television screen, her face bathed in blue light.

Julia quietly put down her tea and opened a bottle of sherry. Somehow she had the feeling this was going to be a long day.

Two laps to go. Rafe gripped the wheel and swung into the next bend. Schumacher and Patrick were still ahead of him. He could have got past the German several times, but why give Patrick the satisfaction?

It was a shame, really, he actually liked Patrick. If he hadn't been married to that *puttana*, maybe things could have been different.

He should never have gone near her, he should have stuck with Stevie. Sweet, funny Stevie, with her soft eyes and crazy smiles. He'd never meant to hurt her. He hadn't realised she'd take him so seriously. He'd thought they could just have a good time, enjoy themselves for a while. She'd seemed so unlucky, such a disaster, he'd just wanted to make her smile. The power to do that had been a potent aphrodisiac. It wasn't as if he'd wanted to cause anyone pain. He'd never meant her to find out about Cinzia, certainly not the way she had. Poor Stevie. He'd genuinely liked her.

He felt an unfamiliar flash of remorse. He hadn't meant to hurt Oliver, either, he'd just thought if he kept quiet about the Angel Dust he'd mixed in with the Es he'd given Oliver to sell, the kids who bought it would have a far better time than they'd ever imagined, and Oliver's finer feelings would be left unchallenged and unhurt. As it was, he'd come close to destroying Oliver's life, and had given Stevie yet more pain. Maybe Cusack was right. Maybe it was time he took some responsibility for the damage he'd caused.

What the hell. Cusack's deal was still on the table. He had nothing to lose.

Patrick saw the chequered flag ahead of him, knew he was about to win the Australian Grand Prix, his third and final win of the season. Instead of exhilaration, he felt only a deep, heavy despair as he whizzed across the finishing line. Against all the odds, he'd held the German off for the entire race, he'd driven the best Grand Prix of his life; but it still hadn't been enough. Schumacher had been behind all the way. He'd come second, got the six points he'd needed, and Patrick had lost the championship.

He climbed out of his cockpit and yanked off his helmet, misery and defeat slowing his movements as Charles raced across the sticky tarmac towards him, his limp barely noticeable.

'You did it! Fucking hell, Jesus Christ, you did it!'

Patrick smiled wearily. 'Almost.'

'What the fuck are you talking about?' Cusack cried, gripping his shoulders. 'You won! You silly bugger, you *won*!'

'It wasn't enough though, was it?' Patrick said. 'Maybe if I'd won a few more races, earlier on in the season, had the cockpit I needed right from the beginning –'

Cusack let go of him. 'Patrick, you stupid sod, I'm not talking about the bloody Grand Prix. I'm talking about the World fucking Championship!'

'*What?*'

A slew of journalists and film crews were streaming across the tarmac towards them, already howling questions. Patrick stared at them in bewilderment.

'Schumacher came third!' Cusack yelled above the din. 'I don't know how he did it, but Rafe got past him. On the final fucking lap. His car must have wings, he found a gap I would never have seen. He got past him, Patrick. He fucking well got past him. We won. *We won!*'

Patrick gazed across the track as Rafe climbed out of his cockpit and pulled his helmet free. Abruptly he pushed his way through the throng of journalists crowding around him and made his way towards Rafe. The two men stared at each other for a long moment, then Patrick held out his hand.

'Thank you,' he said.

Rafe smiled and shook it. 'You deserved to win.'

They both knew he wasn't just talking about the race.

'Would you mind doing that again, Patrick?' one of the journalists shouted. 'Just turn this way a bit, too much sun from that angle –'

Rafe held up his hands to stop them as a battery of flashes went off. 'I'm sorry, I have to go. An important phone call.'

The journalist grinned. 'Must be a woman.'

There was a roar of laughter from his colleagues as they surged back towards Patrick, still shouting questions. Rafe watched them for a moment, then pulled off his gloves and headed towards the pits. Tammy Baynard, their race manager, always had an international mobile phone floating around somewhere. He reached the Terroni trailer and ducked inside. It was deserted. Everyone was already in the Paddock getting half-cut on free champagne at Nigel's expense.

He found Tammy's phone lying on the dashboard of the

trailer and switched it on, tapping in the code for international directory enquiries. A brash Australian voice asked him which number he wanted.

'A UK number, please,' Rafe said.

'Which town, caller?'

'Crawley.'

'What number did you want?'

Rafe hesitated. Once he'd made this call, there'd be no going back. He'd be an exile from the part of England he'd made his home for the last year. He'd probably be able to build himself a window long enough to go back to the Gate House and pack – two or three days, perhaps – but after that, his life at Edenfield would be over.

He shrugged. So, he'd have to live in Rome. That was hardly a hardship. He spent most of his time racing away from his home, anyway. And Cinzia would be pleased. If he was going to quit the drug dealing, maybe they should think about having a baby. He couldn't think of anything riskier: he might end up with a son exactly like himself.

'Hello, caller?'

Rafe asked for the number he wanted.

Stevie and Julia were halfway through their second bottle of Pomagne by the time the BBC condescended to screen the race on Sunday afternoon. They watched it properly this time, cheering and shouting abuse – Julia physically had to restrain Stevie when she started marching round the flat singing 'Heil Patrick!' to annoy Michael Schumacher – as they finished off the Pomagne and hit the Tia Maria. Stevie hated Tia Maria, but it was either that or Julia's mother's cooking sherry. Once the race was over, of course, they had to celebrate Julia's birthday. This necessitated a raid on Oliver's empty flat – God knew where he was, he'd gone to ground since he'd been released on bail on Friday night – with the help of his own keys, which he had foolishly entrusted to his sister. They scrumped four cans of lager, an almost-full bottle of gin and some very flat lemon-ade, retreating to Julia's flat with their booty to watch the high-lights of the race on the evening news. It was only after they'd finished everything and were weighing up the pros and cons of mixing the white spirit from Julia's fondue set with some time-expired Ice Magic chocolate sauce that Stevie admitted defeat and passed out.

She was still off her head when Julia poured her into a taxi and sent her home in the wee small hours of Monday morning. By the time she started to sober up and her hangover set in some time on Monday afternoon, Patrick and Annabel arrived from the airport with the children in tow, looking more in love than Stevie had ever seen them, and the celebrations started all over again.

On Tuesday morning, Stevie hauled herself from the bed, her head thumping, her stomach churning and her mouth feel-ing like the floor of the tapas bar after an enthusiastic hen-night, to hear shouting and laughter beneath her bedroom window. Peering out, she saw Annabel and Patrick loading children and suitcases into a taxi as journalists once more thronged around them, yelling questions. Stevie staggered into her bathroom, wincing at the bright November sunshine streaming through the window. Thank God Patrick and Annabel had decided to take refuge from the press by dis-appearing to Ireland for a week's holiday. It was going to take her that long to recover.

It was no wonder the journalists were going crazy, Stevie thought, scooping up her squirt of toothpaste from where it had fallen into the sink and shoving it back on her toothbrush. This story had everything: romance, glamour, excitement and lash-ings of tragedy. The orphaned son who'd finally won the title his tragic father had held thirty-three years before, coached to victory by the equally tragic Charles Cusack, whose career had also been (tragically) cut short.

She climbed into the bath, sat down and turned the shower

on, resting her aching head against the cool tiles as the water ran over her. The misery welling up inside her had nothing to do with her hangover and everything to do with the tragic Charles Cusack. She hadn't even seen him last night; apparently he'd returned from Australia with Patrick and the team, but then left the airport with Rafe. Oh, God, why did she have to go and fall in love with *him* of all people? Her chances with Rafe had been slender, but with Cusack it was even more impossibly, ludicrously, painfully hopeless.

She washed her hair – how come she'd never noticed shampoo was so heavy before? – got out of the bath and dressed, wincing as she pulled her new scarlet M&S chenille sweater over her head. It was a gorgeous colour, it really brought out the coppery tints in her hair. Shame her face was this bilious shade of green, it made her look like an upside-down traffic light.

She yanked on some silvery-black leggings and a pair of thin grey deck shoes and made her way gingerly downstairs. Mrs Arcor was over at Peter and Humphrey's again ironing their new curtains, so the kitchen was deserted. She made herself a cup of tea, resisting the impulse to lace it with vodka and postpone the inevitable onset of sobriety, and opened the back door, heading discreetly round to the journalistic mêlée at the front so that she could earwig. She was just in time to hear one forward-thinking specimen ask Patrick if he believed he had a good chance of winning next year's championship as well.

'Not really,' Patrick said.

'Why not?' the journalist asked.

'Because I won't be taking part.'

There was a buzz of surprise from the journalists. Several who'd got bored and started making their way down the drive for a quick one at The Gilt Edge before lunch made an about-turn and came back.

'Why not?'

'Are you retiring?'

'Where are you going?'

Patrick held up his hands to stem the flood of questions. 'I'm retiring as a Formula One driver, yes – but I'll be taking over as team manager for Terroni after Christmas.'

There was another surprised murmur.

'Does that mean Lord Cusack – Charlie Lytton – is quitting?' a journalist asked.

'Why?'

'I'm afraid you'll have to talk to him about that.' Patrick moved round to the side of the taxi just in time to stop Jamie's stealthy escape as Annabel finished fastening the baby into his car seat.

'Why have you decided to retire now, at the peak of your career?'

'I just feel now is a good time to go,' Patrick said. 'I've done everything I wanted to do, I'm thirty-five – it's time to spend a bit more time with my family.'

The journalists laughed. Spending more time with one's family was usually political shorthand for retiring in high dudgeon before the ship sank.

'And –' Patrick smiled, squeezed Annabel's hand, 'I'm going to need even more time now that my family's expanding yet again. Not to mention my wife.'

There was a renewed flash of cameras. Annabel blushed prettily and crossed her arm self-consciously across her stomach. From her vantage point sitting on the low wall of the rose garden, Stevie stared at the happy couple, then buried her head in her hands. It was all very well for the tabloids, they loved a schmaltzy ending. They weren't the ones who had to deal with the shitty nappies and endless broken nights. She'd only just got Harry sleeping through; he wouldn't even be at nursery school when the new baby arrived in – she did some quick maths: if Annabel was, say, three months pregnant, that meant a May or June baby – shit, Harry'd only be fourteen months old. She'd never cope, she'd be a nervous wreck, her social life – what was left of it – would be about as exciting as an old episode of *Tomorrow's World*.

'Will you be appointing Rafe Dussi as Terroni's senior driver?' one of the journalists called.

Patrick shrugged. 'I haven't had a chance to talk to Rafe yet. I'll be dealing with all these things very soon, but now I'm going on holiday. If you'll excuse me, I hope you all have a very happy week and I'll see you when I get back.'

Stevie watched as Patrick and Annabel squashed themselves into the overcrowded taxi and sped off down the drive. The journalists took a few last pictures, then ambled off for their postponed rendezvous at The Gilt Edge. Stevie was about to go in search of Mrs Arcor when she heard the phone ringing. Damn, probably some news editor trying to catch up with his elusive correspondent.

She ran into the hall and grabbed the phone. 'Yes?'

'Stevie?'

'Oliver! Is everything OK? You haven't had another –'

'No, no, everything's fine,' Oliver shouted, his voice bubbling with excitement. 'Stevie, they've dropped the charges! The police have dropped all the charges against me!'

'What?'

'They rang just now, they said they'd be watching me, but I was lucky, they were dropping everything! Oh, Stevie, I can't believe it!'

Stevie sank down on to the bottom step of the staircase. 'But why? I don't understand –'

'They said something about receiving further information which suggested I'd been caught up in the middle of something much bigger than I was – rude bastards, make me sound like a complete prat – but Jesus, I don't care! No charges, no record, nothing, Stevie! I'm in the clear!'

'Oh, Oliver! That's wonderful!'

'It's like waking from a nightmare. I swear, Stevie, I won't even touch paracetamol from now on.'

Stevie forgot all about her hangover. 'Oliver, come over, let's go out and celebrate, everyone here's gone away –'

'Um, I can't right now.'

'Why?'

'Um –'

Stevie heard muffled giggles in the background. 'Have you got someone with you?'

'Yes, sort of.'

'Well, bring her along. Is she nice?'

'I think you'll like her.'

There was laughter in his voice. 'Oliver, is there something you're not telling me?'

'Well –'

'There's no point trying to hide it, I'll ring Jules, she'll fill me in,' Stevie warned.

More helpless giggles down the receiver.

'I don't see what's so funny –' she paused as the penny slowly started to head south. 'I don't believe it! It's *Jules* you're with, isn't it?'

'It just sort of happened, Stevie, I still can't believe it myself,' Oliver said, his voice a mixture of happiness and bewilderment. 'After I got bail I spent the whole weekend in Brighton getting pissed, then yesterday I came back home because I'd run out of money and I bumped into Jules in the hall, and we got chatting, we were just messing about and – well – and one thing sort of led to another –'

'What number?'

'What do you mean?'

'Just ask Julia what number.'

She heard him repeat her question. 'She says eleven, Stevie. What on earth does she mean?'

'I'll let her explain.' Stevie put down the phone. Julia and Oliver. About bloody time too, she didn't know why she hadn't seen it before. They were perfect for each other, they'd been arguing like an old married couple for years.

She wandered back outside, relief suddenly making her feel drunk again and making her impervious to the November chill. Thank God, thank God, Oliver was going to be OK. They'd dropped all the charges. His career was safe; no one would ever have to know. She sat down on the wall of the rose garden again, smiling stupidly as she watched the bare branches of the oak trees by the lawn bending in the wind. He was going to be OK. *He was going to be OK.*

She picked up a tiny matchbox Lamborghini Jamie had left in the drive, fiddling absently with its wheels as she mulled over what Oliver had just said. The police had received further information. She frowned, suddenly puzzled. What sort of 'further information'? From whom? And when?

'*Ciao*, Stevie.'

She jumped at Rafe's voice behind her. 'God, did you have to creep up on me like that? I nearly fell into the rose bushes.'

'Sorry, *cara*. I just wanted to say goodbye.'

'Why? Where are you going?'

'Back to Rome.' He glanced at his watch. 'In about an hour or so. I won't be coming back.'

Stevie felt a spurt of fury. This bastard had lied to her, cheated on her, made Cusack hate her, all but ruined her brother's life; and now he was calmly swanning off back to Rome without a word of apology, getting away with everything. She dropped Jamie's car and leaped off the wall, her cheeks burning with anger. How dare he –

Further information.

The words cut across her anger, stopping her short. There was only one person who could have provided the information that had got Oliver off the hook. Mace.

'What did you say to the police?' she asked abruptly.

'I'm sorry, *cara*. I don't understand.'

'Yes, you do. You told them something, I know you did. That's why they dropped the charges against Oliver, isn't it?'

Rafe shrugged. 'Maybe the police just realised he was only a small fish in the pond –'

'Or maybe someone gave them the names of some bigger fish,' Stevie said shrewdly.

Rafe smiled. 'Perhaps, if someone offered a great deal of information – a great many names – in return for dropping a few minor charges based entirely on circumstantial evidence against a man who has no criminal record – maybe the police would decide it was in the best interests of justice to do so. Maybe if someone whetted their appetite, gave them a few details to check out to prove his information was reliable – maybe they would release this small fish to obtain the rest of the information they required.'

'You told them about Mace's drug ring, didn't you?' Stevie breathed. 'You gave them everyone they wanted – except Mace, of course. He'll vanish, won't he? There'll be no trace he ever existed.'

'Mace?' Rafe looked suitably perplexed. 'Who is Mace?'

'Your ex-friends will lynch you if they ever catch up with you,' Stevie said. 'Why'd you do it?'

Rafe stroked her cheek. 'I always cared about you, *cara*. I promise you.'

For a moment, she almost believed him. He was so plausible, so convincing. She really didn't think he had deliberately set out to hurt her – beneath the charm and good looks, he was just a spoilt child, acting without thinking, indulging himself. A spoilt, dangerous child. She couldn't really hate him – he had done the right thing in the end; even now, she was softening towards him – but he would never beguile her again. His power over her had gone.

'Bollocks,' she said rudely. 'You didn't do it for me. What was it, a sudden attack of conscience? You've really screwed things up for yourself, you know that, don't you? You won't be able to train with the rest of the team here in England, you'll have to leave Terroni. You could've been their Number One driver –'

'I don't need Terroni any more.'

'What do you mean?'

'I will be racing for myself. My own team. Quisling Mild will be backing two teams: Terroni and Dussi International.'

'I don't understand,' she said, confused. 'Quisling are backing *both* of you?'

'It seems Nigel has as much to lose from my past being revealed as I do,' Rafe said. 'When it was made clear to him that a lack of support for Dussi International might mean that all sorts of things came out that he might prefer hidden, he was quick to reconcile himself to the idea.'

Stevie frowned suspiciously. This was all just a bit too convenient. Rafe Dussi, mega-bastard, suddenly decides to help Patrick win the championship and get Oliver off the hook, putting himself in some jeopardy to do so; and at the same time he just happens to find some mystery backer who can pull enough strings to get him the sponsorship he needs to start his own team and force Nigel to support him?

'Who is he?' she asked.

'Who is who?'

'You know who I mean.'

Rafe casually leaned against the garden wall. 'You know, Stevie. It is surprising where you find your friends.'

The penny finally hit bottom.

For a long moment she stared at him open-mouthed, then suddenly she whirled round. She ignored Rafe as he called her name and swerved across the lawn, her feet squelching in the mud as she reached the silver birch woods and kept on running. A stitch started in her side as she flew up the overgrown path, her heart thumping. It was *Cusack* who'd arranged everything. He'd done a deal with Rafe. That day when she'd heard about Oliver being arrested and confided in Cusack, she'd mentioned the name Mace, unaware what or who it signified – but Cusack had understood. He must have known who Mace was – he'd probably made it his business to find out everything about Rafe Dussi – and had raced to work out a deal that would persuade Rafe to clear Oliver. No one else could have had the contacts, pulled the strings, to give Rafe what he wanted. Attack of conscience, my foot. Rafe didn't know the meaning of the word. He'd agreed a deal to help himself.

Stevie hated to think what that must have cost Cusack: to go for help to the man he hated most in the world, the man who'd ruined his career. She had to thank him, she had to stop him thinking she didn't care about him even if he never spoke to her again.

Her lungs felt as if they were going to burst as she reached the top of the hill where Cusack had once saved her and the twins from the gin-trap. She paused, catching her breath, trying to decide which of the two tracks in front of her led to Cusack's property. She'd never been there before, but she knew Jamie had, on one of their fishing expeditions.

The left path leading around the hill looked better trodden. She veered towards it, trying not to think about what she was going to say to Cusack when she found him. He'd probably think she'd gone completely mad. Well, she didn't care. She'd make him listen; she had to. She couldn't bear him to think she didn't appreciate what he'd done.

She didn't even notice the tree-root snaking across the path until she fell over it. One minute she was upright, the next she was sprawled across the forest floor, her left forearm aching unbearably where she'd instinctively used it to break her fall. She eased herself into a sitting position, wincing at the pain throbbing at the base of her skull. She must have landed really awkwardly, it's lucky she hadn't broken her neck –

'Stevie?'

Oh God, why did she have to be making a fool of herself in front of him yet again?

Charles Cusack materialised from the trees in front of her and held out his hand to help her up. 'Are you OK?'

'Yes, yes, I'm fine,' Stevie said crossly. 'What are you

doing here?'

'I was out with Canulf, I saw you running through the woods. Is anything wrong at home –?'

His normally pale cheeks were ruddy, his chest heaving slightly. Stevie realised he must have run all the way down the hill to catch up with her. He must have thought she was a trespasser.

'No, no, everything's fine, they've all gone to Ireland, thank God. It's been crazy, the last two days.' She hesitated, then grabbed her courage with both hands and dived in. 'Cusack, I wanted to say something, I hope you don't mind, but I just can't sit back and keep quiet, not when I know how difficult it must have been for you –'

'How difficult *what* must have been for me? What are you talking about?'

'Rafe told me everything,' Stevie said quickly. 'About what you did for him, I mean, helping him set up his own team and everything – well, he didn't come right out and say it was you, but I guessed –'

'I just spoke to a few people, that was all,' Cusack said, clearly embarrassed.

'Yes, but Nigel would never have agreed to sponsor two teams if you hadn't made him, would he? And it can't just have been him, Rafe must need other backers and someone to provide the car and engine – well, Terroni won't be doing that, will they, so someone must be –' she paused, collecting herself. 'I can't believe you did all this, just to make Rafe tell the police the truth. I wanted to say thank you. I know it's not enough, but, well. Oliver will be terribly grateful –'

'I didn't do it for him, Stevie,' Cusack said quietly. 'I did it for you.'

Stevie stared at him, too stunned to say anything. Cusack's blue eyes were suddenly hazy with uncertainty. 'Stevie, I know we haven't always got on – well, that's an under-statement, you hated me, I know that. You once told me you

367

wouldn't marry me if I was the last man on earth.' He smiled painfully. 'I need to know if that's still the way you feel.'

'No, of course it isn't,' Stevie gasped. 'I don't hate you – I never hated you, I was being stupid, childish, I didn't mean it, it was a terrible thing to say –'

'I think I deserved it that particular day,' Cusack said.

'No, no, you didn't.'

'I did. You might have hated me for the wrong reasons, but I didn't exactly behave well towards you. In fact, I behaved dreadfully.'

'I was awful, too,' Stevie admitted. 'Some of the things I said: I felt guilty the moment the words were out of my mouth, I wanted to say sorry even then but –'

'But I didn't make it easy.' Cusack sounded rueful. 'I'll never forget the expression in your eyes when you told me to get a life. And I knew you were right.'

'Oh, God, don't remind me,' Stevie groaned.

'It was my own fault. I seem to recall saying something about looking into the eyes of the woman who's saved me from myself and realising the debt I owe her, isn't that right?'

'I – I can't remember –'

'Tactful of you,' Cusack smiled. 'But the joke was on me, wasn't it?'

'What do you mean?' Stevie whispered.

'Because everything I mocked that day has happened.' Cusack took a step towards her, still not touching her, his weight on his good foot as he gazed earnestly into her eyes. 'Oh, Stevie. I know that I can't be your favourite person in the world, I know how you feel about Rafe, but I need you to know how much you mean to me, even if you can never think of me the same way –'

'I don't care about Rafe!' Stevie burst out. 'It was just a crush, I was crazy to think I felt anything for him.'

'Do you mean that?' Cusack asked.

'Of course I do!'

'I – I know I'm not saying this very well, but this sort of thing isn't something I find very easy,' he said. 'I have never met anyone like you, Stevie. So energetic, so full of passion. From that first day in the rose garden –'

'Sainsbury's,' Stevie said. 'In the car park. You pinched my parking space and threatened to run over Damien if I didn't move it.'

'Damien?'

'My car.'

'Ah, of course.' Cusack laughed awkwardly. 'You're not making this easy, Stevie, are you? All right, I apologise to Damien, too. And that day in the woods, I should have taken the time to explain why I was shouting at you. Is there anything else I've missed?'

Stevie giggled.

'You are so beautiful when you laugh,' Cusack said. 'I think it was your mouth I fell in love with first. I just wanted to kiss it, I couldn't think of anything else. It made me so angry, that you could do that to me without even thinking about it, my feelings frightened me. I tried to hide from them, but –'

'Say that again.'

'What, it made me so angry –'

'No, the other bit. The bit about you fell in love with my mouth first.'

'I fell in love with your mouth first, and then the rest of you just followed naturally. You're so easy to love, Stevie.'

'You're not. It took me ages.'

'I know I'm not. I can't expect you to feel –' he paused. 'What did you say?'

'I said it took me ages to fall in love with you. Or at least to know I had.'

They stared at each other for a long moment, neither of them saying anything, drinking each other in. Stevie could hear the faint murmur of the brook in the background, Canulf snuffling through the sodden leaves at their feet, his breath fast and heavy. Cusack took her cold hands in his, chafing them between his own, his expression serious but his blue eyes infinitely soft.

'This won't be easy, Stevie, for either of us,' he said quietly. 'Your friends will think I'm cold and arrogant, they'll wonder what you see in me.'

'And yours will think I'm common and stupid, not good enough for you.'

'My sisters may be difficult –'

'– Annabel will freak –'

'– God knows what my mother will say –'

'– God knows what *my* mother will say.'

They smiled.

'It hasn't exactly been easy this far, has it?' Stevie said.

'Not exactly.'

'Are you – are you sure this is what you want?'

'Oh, Stevie. What will it take to convince you that I love you, have loved you since the day I saw you, will love you until the day I die?'

'Perhaps you could start by telling me that a bit more often.'

'How much more?'

She grinned. 'Once every ten minutes should do it, until I get used to the idea. Say, the next twenty years. And after that, probably once every five, so I know you haven't gone off me –'

He pulled her towards him, enveloping her in the smell of dogs and leaf mould and the wax he used to keep his Barbour supple. It was the most erotic scent she'd ever encountered. Her heart started to beat faster as he slowly bent his head towards hers.

'Cusack, I love you,' she whispered.

He paused. 'Stevie?'

'Mmm?'

'Do you think you could call me Charles?'